STAND UP AND DIE

THE JACKALS

STAND UP AND DIE

WILLIAM W. JOHNSTONE
WITH J. A. JOHNSTONE

THORNDIKE PRESS
A part of Gale, a Cengage Company

Thorndike Press® Large Print Western.
The text of this Large Print edition is unabridged.
Other aspects of the book may vary from the original edition.
Set in 16 pt. Plantin.

LIBRARY OF CONGRESS CIP DATA ON FILE.
CATALOGUING IN PUBLICATION FOR THIS BOOK
IS AVAILABLE FROM THE LIBRARY OF CONGRESS.

ISBN-13: 978-1-4328-8560-1 (hardcover alk. paper)

Published in 2021 by arrangement with Pinnacle Books, an imprint of Kensington Publishing Corp.

Printed in Mexico
Print Number: 01   Print Year: 2021

STAND UP AND DIE

PROLOGUE

About a week or two after Matt McCulloch had settled into the dugout he called home on what once had been a sprawling horse ranch in that rough land known as West Texas, he remembered the dream that had happened before all this death, misery, and hardships had begun.

The old Comanche warrior appeared in the middle of a dust devil that spun as furiously as a tornado. When the wind died, dozens of wild mustangs parted, snorting fire from nostrils and hooves looking like something in a Renaissance Era painting of old Lucifer himself. An old Comanche, face scarred, braids of dark hair wrapped in otter skins that dripped with blood, emerged from thick clouds of dust and walked through the gate of the corral. He walked through the damned wood. Didn't bother opening the gate. The old man walked straight to the dugout where Matt stood, curious but not frightened.

"You will travel far." The warrior spoke in Comanche, but McCulloch understood as though the warrior spoke with a thick Texas drawl.

"How far?"

"Farther than you have ever gone in all your life. Farther than you will ever go."

"Where will I travel?" McCulloch asked the apparition.

"To a place far away."

"How far?"

"Into the hell that you in this country call the Territory of Arizona."

"Where?" McCulloch asked again. He had little patience for men or spirits who spoke in riddles.

"It is a place known as the Dead River."

McCulloch shook his head. He remembered understanding the Comanche . . . but didn't know how he could have. Hell, the Indian could have been speaking Russian, for all he knew. He could have been a lousy white actor playing a damned redskin in some stupid play at the opera house in El Paso for all that Matt McCulloch could tell. He remembered every detail. He could describe the designs on the shield slipped

8

over the Indian's left arm, the quillwork on his beaded leather war shirt . . . the number of rawhide strips wrapped around the otter skins that held his long braids together.

Even the number, length, and colors of the scalps secured by rawhide on the sleeves of his medicine shirt.

He remembered the old warrior telling him he would travel farther than he would ever go "until the time comes when you must travel to your own Happy Hunting Ground."

Some drunks in saloons might have silently chuckled at a vision or a dream or a damned big windy using such a ridiculous cliché, but none doubted that it was exactly what he had heard — he was Matt McCulloch. He had been branded a jackal, along with bounty hunter Jed Breen and former army sergeant Sean Keegan who had taken the mystical, violent journey with him. His word was as good as any marker an honest gambler put up in Purgatory City. If any honest man ever set foot in the roughshod Texas town.

McCulloch remembered everything, including his last question: "And what awaits me at this place in the Territory of Arizona?" he had asked.

No matter how many times he told the

story, or where he told the story, or how drunk or sober his listeners were by that time, he always paused. He wasn't an actor, but it came naturally, and the mustangers, soldiers, or Texas Rangers always fell silent. So quiet, one could hear a centipede crossing the sand over the crackling of the fire, or hear the breathing of the audience outside the barbershop, or hear the bartender cleaning a beer stein in some Purgatory City saloon with a damp bar towel. It always remained the same. The listeners would always hang on to every word.

When McCulloch had finished, he would sip his beer, whiskey, coffee, or the water from a canteen. Although he knew the ending always led to a gasp from the collected breaths of his listeners, he returned his thoughts to the nightmare.

"What awaits you at the Dead River," said the mystical warrior, "Is what awaits you. What awaits all men at some point on this long, winding road of life."

"At the Dead River . . . you will find . . . death."

CHAPTER ONE

A woman might say "This has to be the prettiest spot in Texas" about the Davis Mountains in West Texas. A man, on the other hand, could respond "What's so damned pretty about Apaches hiding behind slabs of volcanic rock over your head and keeping you pinned down below with fire from a rifle they took off a dead cowboy whose horse give out at the wrong time? Or moving from canyon to canyon trying to find that herd of wild mustangs you've been chasing forever? Or getting baked by the sun because you're five thousand to maybe eight thousand feet higher than you ought to be in Texas, then, five minutes later, freezing your butt off and getting peppered by sleet?"

As he crouched by the campfire along Limpia Creek, sipping his last cup of coffee before starting his day, Matt McCulloch smiled. It was a pleasant memory, that

11

conversation he recalled having with his wife shortly after they had married. She thought they should settle here, grab some land. There was good water — though you might have to dig pretty deep to find it — enough grass to feed cattle and horses, an army post for protection, and a thriving, friendly town, with churches, a good restaurant or two, and a schoolhouse so that their children, when they got around to having children, could get a good education. But McCulloch had figured he could get more land for his money farther west and south, so they had moved on with a farm wagon, a milk cow, the two horses pulling the wagon, the horse McCulloch rode, and the two broodmares tethered behind the Studebaker that carried all their belongings.

Yeah, McCulloch thought as he stood and stretched. All their belongings. They'd had a lot of extra room in the back of that wagon to collect the dust as they traveled on, eventually settling near the town of Purgatory City . . . which wasn't so pretty unless you found dust storms and brutality pleasant to the eyes . . . where churches met whenever a lay preacher felt the call . . . where the schoolhouse someone built quickly became a brothel . . . and where the best food to be found was the dish of peanuts served free to patrons at the Perdition Saloon.

He tossed the last mouthful of the coffee onto the fire and moved to the black horse he had already saddled, stuffing the cup into one of the saddlebags. Found the well-used pot and dumped the last of the coffee, hearing the sizzle, letting the smoke bathe his face and maybe blind him to any bad memories, make him stop thinking about that dangerous question *What if?*

Would his wife and family still be alive had he settled here instead of over there? Would his daughter not have been kidnapped, never to be found again? Taken by the Apaches that had raided his ranch while he was off protecting the great state of Texas as one of the state's Rangers?

Besides, even Purgatory City wasn't as lawless as it had once been, especially now that a certain contemptible newspaper was out of business and its editor-publisher-owner dead and butchered. Even the Perdition Saloon had been shuttered. After a couple of fires and a slew of murders, the owner had been called to rededicate his life after learning that he had come down with a virulent case of an indelicate disease and inoperable cancer on top of that. The Perdition Saloon was now — McCulloch had to

13

laugh — a schoolhouse. The city still boasted five other saloons, and all did thriving business when the soldiers and cowboys got paid, although Texas Rangers and some dedicated lawmen generally kept a lid on things.

He kicked rocks and dirt over the fire, spread out the charred timbers, and stuffed the pot into the other saddlebag.

McCulloch was getting his life back together, had even begun to rebuild that old ranch of his. Not much, not yet anyway. Three corrals, a lean-to, and a one-room home dug into what passed for a hill. It was enough for him.

The corrals were empty, but horses were what had brought Matt McCulloch to the Davis Mountains. Wild mustangs roamed all over these mountains, and he had decided it was a good time to get back into the horse-trading business. Find a good herd of mustangs, capture those mares, colts, fillies, and the boss of the whole shebang. Break a few, keep a few, and sell a bunch. It was a start, a new beginning. All he had to do was find a good herd worth the bruises and cuts, and maybe broken bones, he would get trying to break them.

Folks called the Davis Mountains a "sky island," and McCulloch knew his late wife would have considered that pure poetry. The sea was just sprawling desert, flat and dusty, that stretched on forever in all directions. But nearby greenery and black rocks, rugged ridges and rolling hills rose out of nowhere, creating an island of woodlands — juniper, piñon, pines, and aspen. Limpia Creek cut through it, and canyons crisscrossed here and there like a maze.

He had a square mile to cover, six hundred and forty acres, but he could rule out much of the high country, those ridges lined by quaking aspen trees. So far, all McCulloch had seen were wild hogs, a few white-tailed deer, one antelope, and about a dozen hummingbirds. But he had also seen the droppings of horses — and the scat of a black bear.

He stepped into the stirrup, threw his leg over the saddle, and moved south to find the grasslands tucked in between slopes where a herd of mustangs would be grazing. Keeping one eye on the land and one eye scanning for any Indian, outlaw, snake, or some other sort of danger, he noticed that the black bear must have had the same idea. Well, an old mare or a young foal would make a tasty meal for a bear.

McCulloch stopped long enough to pull the Winchester from the scabbard.

15

When he came upon the next pile of excrement the bear had left, he swung out of the saddle, and broke open the dung with his fingers, rubbing them together. He smiled, picturing the looks on the faces of his wife and daughter had they been around to witness it. He could hear both of them screaming to go wash his hands in lye soap. Quickly, he shut off those thoughts, not wanting to ruin such a beautiful morning with a burst of uncontrollable rage at God, his life, his decisions, and this tough country where he had tried to make a life.

All right. The scat was about a day or so old. A mile later, when the bear had started up the mountain, McCulloch did not follow. But he did keep an eye overhead.

Eventually, he forgot about the bear, for something else commanded his attention — tracks left by unshod horses. And not of a war party of Comanches, Kiowas, or Apaches. He dismounted for a closer look. No, some of the tracks belonged to youngsters, the colts that eventually might challenge the big stallion leader. It was a big herd, too, and McCulloch thought how he would handle such a large bunch. He'd have to trap them at a water hole or in a canyon. Do some breaking there. Then drive all he could all the way to his spread to start the

16

real work. The bone-jarring, backbreaking work.

He was about to mount his black horse when something caught his eye. He moved a few yards away and sank his knees, protected by the leather chaps he wore, into the dirt. One of the horses he was following wore iron shoes. The rear hooves had been shod. Maybe a mare had wandered into the herd from some ranch or farm. Perhaps it had lost the iron shoes on its front feet. But some men in these parts were known to put shoes on only the rear feet of their mounts, so McCulloch might have competition for the herd.

Texas, he reminded himself, was a free country.

The other thought that crossed his mind, however, was that whoever was trailing this herd — if that indeed were the case — might not like competition. Especially if the horse had been stolen by an Indian.

His own horse had four iron shoes. Traveling across the volcanic rock and stones that lined the trail he had to follow would produce far too much noise. He leaned the Winchester against a rock and fished out leather pads from a saddlebag. These he wrapped around the black's feet, and the heavy hide would muffle the noise of his horse's footfalls. Carbine back in hand, McCulloch mounted the horse, and rode through the canyon.

When he came into the opening, he didn't see the horse herd, but he found the black bear.

It lay dead at the base of a rocky incline to the east.

McCulloch reined in, dismounted, and wrapped the reins around the trunk of a dead alligator juniper. The blood from the dead bear made his horse skittish, and the last thing McCulloch wanted was to be left afoot in this country. He stepped a few feet away from the horse and squatted, studying the country all around him, including the dead bear. No birds sang, no squirrels chattered, and the wind blew the scent of death and blood across the tall grass. Fifteen minutes later, he moved closer to the bear, seeing the drying blood soaking the ground.

The bear hadn't been dead very long, McCulloch thought after he reached his left hand over and felt the thick fur around the animal's neck. His fingers ran across the stab wounds. Knife? Lance? Certainly not the claws from another animal. Wetting his lips, McCulloch again looked across the canyon, up and down, and listened, but the only sound detected came from the stamping of the black's hooves and the wind moaning through the rocks and small trees.

He moved to the bear's head and saw the flattened grass and the blood trail that led into the rocks. Whoever had killed the bear had been wounded and dragged itself — no, *himself* — into the hills. A busted Spencer carbine lay in the grass, and McCulloch saw the holes in the bear's throat. Two shots that had done enough damage, caused enough bleeding, to end the bear's life, but not before that bear had put a big hurt on the . . . Indian.

Most likely, McCulloch figured, seeing the beads scattered about the scene of the tussle and the studs that had been nailed into the broken Spencer's stock. He spotted one eagle feather that had been caught against a jagged bit of rock.

"Now what?" he whispered.

The Indian likely crawled into the rocks. Maybe to die. McCulloch didn't see the Indian pony, but when a bear comes charging at you, horses run like hell. If that horse with two rear iron shoes hadn't been part of the mustang herd, it might have joined up already. Even wild horses and trained horses knew the value of teaming up in numbers in that part of the United States.

He looked up at the rocks, and again at

the trail of blood and trampled grass. The wind cooled him. Despite the morning chill, he had started to sweat. He had lived too long to risk his hide going after a wounded Indian. Besides, the bear and maybe the Indian had made finding that herd of mustangs a whole lot harder.

McCulloch rose, moved to the side of the rocky wall and slid around the bear. Stepping back a few feet, he looked up the mountain and listened again. Still nothing but the wind. Not completely satisfied but in a hurry to get after those mustangs, he decided to make for his horse. He didn't think the Indian would have another long gun. Maybe a short pistol, but probably nothing more than a knife. Odds were McCulloch could make it to the black, mount up, and ride away without any trouble. Better odds were that the Indian had bled out and would soon be feeding javelinas and coyotes.

Three steps later, McCulloch leaped back, more from instinct and that hearing he prided himself on. Even then he almost bought it. The knife blade sliced through his shirt, through flannel and the heavy underwear. The Winchester dropped from McCulloch's hands and into the dirt as he

staggered away. Blood trickled.
The Indian came at him again.

CHAPTER TWO

Sean Keegan had been drummed out of the
United States Cavalry after saving the lives
of a bunch of new recruits but having to
shoot dead a stupid officer who was inclined
to get everyone under his command killed.
Keegan had learned to accept the fact that
he no longer wore the stripes of a sergeant,
no longer had a job to whip greenhorns into
shape and teach green officers the facts of
surviving in this miserable country of
Apaches, Comanches, rattlesnakes, card-
sharpers, bandits, hornswogglers, and vari-
ous ruffians.

He often missed that old life he had led,
but every now and then he came across the
opportunity to relive some of that old glory.

The morning proved to be one of those
times.

Purgatory City had become civilized,
damned close to even gentrified, with mar-
shals, sheriffs, Texas Rangers, city councils,

school boards, churches, and a new newspaper that wasn't the rag that old one had been. The editor kept preaching — along with the Catholics, Baptists, Methodists, Presbyterians, Hebrews, and Lutherans — about the need for more schools, better roads, a bridge or two, and higher taxes on the dens of iniquity that allowed gambling, dancing, ardent spirits, and, egads, in some cases . . . prostitution. But there was one place a man could go and feel like Purgatory City remained a frontier town.

The Rio Lobo Saloon, although no river named Lobo flowed anywhere in the great state of Texas, and certainly not one in the vicinity of Purgatory City. The saloon had been open seven years and had not closed its doors once. Twenty-four hours a day, seven days a week — no matter how much the Baptists raised holy hell — serving liquor that would either put hair on a man's chest or burn off the hair he had on his chest. Potent, by-gawd, forty-rod whiskey that would make Taos Lightning seem like potable water. Even that fire that had swept across the bar two and a half years back had not shut down the Rio Lobo, and Sean Keegan had done his best, starting the fire and the fistfight that landed him in jail for thirty days and got him busted, briefly, back down

23

to mere trooper.

Keegan had arrived the previous afternoon, ate the sandwiches the bartender set out for free to patrons paying for their drinks, did a couple of dances with the prettiest chirpies, put a good-sized dent in the keg of porter, arm-wrestled the blacksmith Wiśniewski, and lost, that was fine. Nobody had bested the Polish behemoth in four hundred and eighty-three tries, but it took the smithy seven minutes before he damned near broke Keegan's wrist and forearm.

Finally Keegan found a seat in a friendly poker game at about two-thirty that morning, and set down with a bottle of Irish and seventeen dollars and fifteen cents.

When the game broke up while the Catholic church bells were ringing eight times, and folks were opening their shops on Front Street, Keegan tossed the empty bottle toward the trash bin, missed, and smiled at the sound of breaking glass and the curses of Clark, the barkeep.

"It's been a fine game," Keegan said, grinning at the dealer, and sliding him a double eagle. "But I suppose all good things must come to an end."

"Thank Queen Victoria for that," said the weasel in the bowler hat.

The railroad hand with the ruddy face

leaned back in his chair and waited for Sean Keegan to react.

"The hell did you say?" Keegan asked, though he wasn't sure if he was looking at the right pipsqueak, since for the moment he saw two, and both of them were fuzzy.

"I said thank Queen Victoria that you're leaving. You took me for better than two hundred dollars."

"Queen" — Keegan closed his eyes tightly — "Victoria?"

"Yes."

When his eyes opened, Keegan saw only one runt of a weasel.

"She's your queen."

"The bloody hell she is. She's the queen of England. I'm Irish," said Keegan.

"She's the queen of England and Ireland, and, if I remember correctly, Empress of India."

"She's a piece of dung like every other English pig, sow, and hog."

The runt rose and brought up his fists. "You shall not insult Queen Victoria in front of me, you drunken, Irish pig."

What confused Keegan was that he didn't detect one bit of an English accent rolling off the weasel's tongue, and while he was trying to figure out why a drummer in a bowler hat who didn't sound like a Brit

25

would bring up Queen Victoria in West Texas, the little weasel punched Keegan and split both of his lips.

He had been leaning back in his chair, trying to clear his head, and wound up on the floor, tasting blood and seeing the punched-tin ceiling of the saloon spin around like a dying centipede.

Chair legs scraped as the bartender said, "Oh, hell."

Keegan rolled over and came to his knees, just as the weasel brought his right boot up. The boot, Keegan later recalled, appeared to be a Wellington, which didn't make the runt an Englishman but hurt like hell, and sent Keegan rolling toward the nearest table.

"I'll teach you to libel Queen Victoria and servants of Her Majesty."

The Wellingtons crunched peanut shells and a few stray poker chips as the weasel rushed to give Keegan another solid kicking, but Keegan came up with one of the chairs from the nearest poker table, and the chair became little more than kindling after he slammed it into the charging, puny devil.

"Keegan!" the bartender roared.

Out of the corner of his eye, Keegan saw the bartender lifting a bung starter and removing his apron.

Keegan figured that would give him

enough time to pick up the bleeding, muttering, sobbing fellow and throw him through the window, which he did. As the glass rained across the boardwalk, hitching rail, Front Street, and the now quiet weasel, Keegan turned to meet the morning-shift barkeep and saw something else.

The railroad worker was helping himself to some of Keegan's winnings.

"You damned sneak thief." To his surprise, he realized he still held the broken chair leg in his right hand. The railroad thug swore, tried to stuff some more coins and cash into his trousers pocket, then grabbed the pipsqueak's chair and came after Keegan.

"You men stop this!" the bartender yelled. "You'll wreck this place!"

Like that had never happened before, Keegan thought with a smile and a few fond memories about previous times when he had tried to shut down the Rio Lobo Saloon. He'd never been able to manage it, but he had done his best, bless his Irish heart.

The railroad man was used to swinging sixteen-pound sledgehammers, and lacked the savvy needed for surviving saloon brawls. He brought the entire chair over his head, likely intending to slam it hard over Keegan's head, but as he swung that chair back toward Keegan, the old army sergeant jammed the broken chair leg in the man's solid gut.

Not the broken, jagged end. This wasn't one of those kinds of fights. That would have likely proved to be a mortal wound, and the way Keegan had it figured, this fight was on the friendly side. He was surprised, though, at how hard that man's belly was. The big man grunted and his eyes bulged, but the chair kept right on coming, and the next thing Keegan knew he was rolling on the floor again, bleeding from his scalp and nose, and his shoulders and back hurt like blazes.

But he came up quickly, saw the railroad man shaking his head to regain his faculties, saw the barkeep slipping on a pair of brass knuckle-dusters, and saw the house dealer, still at the table, rolling a cigarette and counting his chips.

Keegan grunted, spit out blood — but no teeth — and lowered his shoulder as he charged. He caught the railroad man in the side, just above the hip, and drove him all the way to the wall. The impact caused both men to grunt, two pictures to fall to the floor, and the bartender to curse and scream that he would kill the both of them if they didn't stop right this minute.

The railroad man's head faced the wall. He had lost his railroad cap, but had a fine head of red hair. Hell, maybe he was Irish, too, but it didn't matter. Keegan latched on to the hair, jerked it hard, and then slammed the man's forehead against the wall of pine planks. Another painting hit the floor. Keegan pulled back the man's head and let it feel pine again. The pine had to be expensive to get all the way from wherever you could find pine trees to the middle of nowhere that was Purgatory City.

He pulled the head back and was going to see if he could punch a hole in the wall and give the Rio Lobo Saloon a new door, but the railroad worker's eyes had rolled back into the head, so Keegan let the man drop to the floor.

Besides, the bartender was bringing back his arm to lay Keegan out with those hard brass knuckles. Keegan ducked, felt the man's right sail over his head, and heard the crunch as the barkeep's fist slammed into the wall where there was no painting — actually a cut-out from some old calendar that had been stuck into the frame — to soften the blow.

The barkeep screamed in pain and grasped his right hand with his left. Tears poured like he was some little baby, and

Keegan figured those broken fingers must hurt like hell. They'd likely swell up, too, so that fool would have the dickens of a time getting those knuckle-dusters off. Hell, the doc might have to amputate his hand.

That wasn't Keegan's concern. He grabbed the man's shoulder, spun him around, slammed a right into the stomach, a knee into the groin, jerked him up, pushed him against the wall, and let him have a left, right, right, left, and finally grabbed his shoulders with both hands and hurtled him across the room. He caught the closest table, slid over it, knocked down and busted a chair, and lay spread-eagled on the floor.

After sucking his knuckles, Keegan went back to the railroad man and pulled out most of the money the thief had tried to steal. He did leave a few coins, chips, and greenbacks to help pay for the man's doctor bill, and for damages, and a tip for a hell of a fun fight.

He then went back to the poker table where the dealer raised his coffee cup while sucking on his cigarette, and smiled.

"Nice fight, Keegan," the dealer said.

Keegan knocked him out of his chair. The man rolled over, his cigarette gone, his coffee spilt, and lifted himself up partly, leaning against a cold stove.

"What the hell was that for?" the dealer demanded.

Keegan gestured toward the unconscious railroad worker. "For not stopping him from lifting my winnings." He stepped back to the table, and began getting the rest of his money, but kept his eye on the dealer.

The batwing doors at the front of the Rio Lobo rattled, and Keegan recognized a familiar voice.

"Sean, let's take a walk to the calaboose, old friend."

Keegan laughed, shoved the winnings into his pocket, tossed a greenback at the dealer, and dumped some more money on the felt top of the table. "For damages," he told the dealer, nodded good-bye, and walked to the old man waiting with the handcuffs.

"Sergeant major," Keegan told the old horse soldier from Fort Spalding.

"It's deputy marshal these days," Titus Bedwell said. "Retired from the army a few months back."

"Buy you a drink, Titus?"

"After you've served your time, Sean."

Keegan shook his head at the handcuffs. "You don't need those, Sergeant major."

"That's good to know. Let's take a walk." Bedwell pushed open one of the doors and nodded at the dealer standing in the back of the saloon. "I'll let you know, George, if and when you need to testify. And when Millican comes around, have him get with Clark and figure out the damages. But don't cheat Keegan after what he has paid you already."

Bedwell and Keegan walked down the street, Keegan admiring the stares from men and women alike, and laughing as others cleared off the boardwalk to let them pass. When they reached the city jail, Bedwell opened the door, and Keegan walked in and made his way toward his cell.

"Not that one, Sean," Bedwell said.

Keegan stood at the iron door, grabbed the bars, and stared inside.

"Get out of my face," the dark figure on the bunk said bitterly.

Keegan turned, and Bedwell grabbed a set of keys. "That's Tom Benteen, Sean. We're hanging him tomorrow."

Whirling, Keegan tried to get a good look at the man in the bunk. Tom Benteen. The Benteen brothers and their old uncle, Zach Lovely, and cousin Tom — who had taken the Benteen name after getting sick and tired of folks making jokes about being Tom Lovely or Lovely Tom — had been rampaging across Texas for four years, robbing banks, trains, killing two sheriff's deputies, a judge, a jailer, four bank tellers, two railroad conductors, and one lawyer from San Angelo . . . but no one cared much about the lawyer.

"How'd you catch him?" Keegan asked.

"Jed Breen brought him in."

"Alive?" Keegan laughed and spit out blood. "Jed's getting soft in his old age." He turned around and shook his head. "I must have missed the trial."

"Didn't last long," Bedwell said.

Keegan looked back at Tom Benteen. "Hey, Tom, what're your cousins Bob and Hank gonna do without you?"

The front door opened and a deep voice said, "Yeah, Tom. What exactly am I gonna do without you?" The metallic cocking of a revolver punctuated the end of that sentence.

Chapter Three

Whoever named Deep Flood, Texas, had a sense of humor Jed Breen appreciated. He was willing to bet that the wells dug in this town reached two hundred feet, the nearest ground water had to be twenty miles away, and the last time this one-road town had experienced a flood occurred when a gent named Noah had built himself an ark. But it was a town, with a pretty decent café, a livery, a saloon, a barber shop, and a hotel with a soft mattress — plus it was on the way to Purgatory City. The hotel, café, livery, and saloon were what Jed Breen needed for the time being. He had boarded his horse for the rest of the day; he had gotten a bath, shave, and a haircut from the barber; had asked the waitress at the café if she could bring a steak, pot of coffee, potatoes, and that last slice of cake to his room; had treated himself to two whiskeys at the saloon; and was heading to that hotel.

A good meal, a soft bed and . . .

Deep Flood had a bank, too, Breen noticed for the first time, but not much of one. From the size of the town, he didn't know how a banker could make any money, unless he charged outrageous interest, but it was indeed a bank. That's what the sign said that was bending with the wind. Breen tugged down the brim of his hat and leaned against the wooden column in front of the general store — Deep Flood had one of those, too, but it was closed for some reason, likely the lack of business.

What interested Jed Breen was the fellow swinging out of the saddle of a dun horse in front of the bank. He looked at Breen, who snapped his finger, and turned toward the door to the store. It didn't open, of course, but he pulled the handle a couple of times, then cursed loudly, and stepped back and stared at the window, as though those lace-up Creedmoor shoes were exactly what his wife needed. Breen didn't have a wife, but he rubbed his freshly shaved chin and focused on the reflection in the window.

The man with the dun horse studied Breen's back several seconds and then moved to his saddlebags. He pulled out a couple of sacks — wheat, grain, something like that — but one of them wouldn't hold much meal. Holes had been cut out near the bottom. The man also unbuttoned his coat, looked at Breen again, and finally moved to the door of the bank.

Breen turned, began whistling, and bounded down the boardwalk, crossed the dusty alley, climbed up the next boardwalk, whistling even louder, and pushed open the door to the hotel, letting the door slam, and stopped long enough to tell the hotel clerk, "There's a gal from the diner bringing me some food upstairs. Don't worry. She's just dropping off my supper and then going back to work. I know a classy place like this would frown upon overnight visitors of the friendlier sex." He made it to the stairs and said as he took the steps three in a bound. "Don't mind the shooting you'll likely hear in a few minutes from upstairs. If the girl makes it inside, tell her to take cover behind the stove there, and try not to spill my coffee. And if I were you, buster, I'd drop down behind that counter right now and stay there until the ruckus is over."

By the time he finished, he was at the top of the stairs, racing down the hallway, and kicking open the door to his room. He didn't have time to wait for that bumbling clerk to find his key. He slid to his knees and quickly pulled the leather scabbard from under the bed, slipped out the .45-70 Sharps rifle — the one with the brass telescopic sight — and thumbed out four heavy cartridges from the holder on the scabbard. By the time Breen reached the window, the Sharps was loaded, and the other shells laid perfectly on the floor. He looked out the window, amazed at his luck.

He'd stopped in Deep Flood because he didn't want to bake in the sun any more, and it happened to be on the way to Purgatory City. On a whim, he'd decided he did not want to eat in the town's café, and the waitress who doubled as cook decided that she could manage to bring him some supper to his hotel room as he had offered to add fifteen percent to the regular price for his order. He would tip her, of course.

And, bless the saints, he'd been walking back to his room, minding his own business, when Hans Kruger decided to show up to rob the First Bank of Deep Flood.

Well, it might not be Hans. It could be the bank robbing fiend's twin brother, Otto. A man — even a judge, coroner, or county sheriff — would be hard-pressed to identify one from the other. Not that it truly mattered. Both Hans and Otto were posted for five-hundred dollars each, dead or alive, in Texas and three territories. Breen didn't think the constable at Deep Flood would mind which Kruger it was.

One little matter concerned Breen as he adjusted his rear sight. He had seen only one of the Kruger boys. Granted, warrants had been issued for a Kruger here, a Kruger there, another Kruger for some crime — one burglary, one horse theft, one murder. Sometimes they did not work together, and often split up. A robbery of a bank in a town of this size could possibly be handled by one man, but Breen had trouble recalling any banks that had been robbed in Texas, Arizona, New Mexico, or Colorado in which only one of the Krugers had been seen — and charged. Not that he was an expert on the Krugers. A horse theft or two, and the time Hans Kruger — or was it Otto? — had gotten upset at losing at a faro layout in Laredo and had robbed the entire gambling parlor of a little more than nine hundred dollars and put a bullet through the faro dealer's elbow were the types of documented crimes attributed to just Hans or Otto, not both.

Breen peered down the streets, checking for a horse or a man paying too much attention to the bank. No one was on the street that he could see. He didn't have much of a view for the street below him. He studied the rooftops, such as they were, and found no one.

Well, he couldn't wait anymore. Breen carefully slid the window up about halfway and then moved back, taking the Sharps with him. He lifted the heavy weapon and aimed at the front door to the bank, making sure that the barrel did not poke out of the window. If someone saw that — especially if the bank robber's pard saw it (if the robber had a pard) looking out for his well-being — then things might get a bit ticklish, and Breen would have no reward to cash in.

Breen's plan was simple. When the robber stepped out for his horse, Breen would blow a fist-sized hole through his middle. Hell, bank robbery was a crime no matter if it were being committed by Hans Kruger, Otto Kruger, or some out-of-work cowboy who made the mistake of robbing his first bank and looking too much like one of those Huns. If Hans, or Otto, saw Otto, or Hans, lying in the dirt, most likely the surviving Kruger brother would ride over to assist his dead or dying brother, and even more likely to ride over to get the sack filled with the bank's money. By that point, Breen would have reloaded the Sharps and after taking quick, deadly, careful aim, he would see the button on the last Kruger brother's shirt and shoot that bank robber dead, too.

Simple enough. Breen relaxed, controlled his breathing, made himself as comfortable as possible, and stared through the telescopic sight at the bank's front door.

A church bell in Deep Flood, Texas began ringing five long, drawn out, drowning out, drones that echoed. Finally, the last of the ear-splitting noise ended. Breen sighed. Five o'clock. The bank would be closing. The robber had timed his job perfectly, knowing few people would be inside at this time of day. Well, Deep Flood didn't have more than a few people living and working in town anyway.

The door to his room — the one he had kicked open and broken the lock — pushed open.

Breen did not look back, but he cursed the bit of poor timing. He should have ordered his steak well done, and his potatoes peeled before being boiled, and a fresh pot of coffee, and maybe even a slice of cake that hadn't been on the counter, uncovered and attracting flies most of the day.

"Sweetheart," he said without looking back, "If you would be so kind as to just leave the food on the dresser and leave, I'll be with you shortly. And then, please, just wait out in the hallway. Things are apt to get a little hot in here. Don't worry. I'm a lawman, sweetheart. Your bank's about to be robbed."

He wasn't a lawman exactly. He just helped lawmen out. By bringing in outlaws, for which he was generally paid a pretty decent reward. Folks called him a bounty hunter, and though that was a fairly correct description, Breen liked to think of himself as a . . . professional.

He smiled at what one of the newspapers had called him. *A jackal.* Well, yeah, you could argue that point, but the newspaper had also called a former Texas Ranger named Matt McCulloch and a hard-drinking Irish cavalry sergeant, Sean Keegan, jackals, too.

Breen hadn't seen Keegan or McCulloch in months. When he got to Purgatory City with his five hundred bucks for Hans or Otto Kruger, he'd buy them a beer or whiskey.

The hairs on his neck started tingling, and he let his eye rise from the telescopic sight even before he heard the revolver behind him being cocked, and the German-accented guttural voice say, "Ja. I know it be robbed. Too bad ya not live to see us spend all dat money."

Well, Breen thought as he eased down the

hammer on the big rifle and slowly brought the rifle up and leaned it against the wall beside the window. Nobody told him to raise his hands, but he figured that was the general idea. By the time he turned around on his knees, his hands were high, and he saw the big man with blond hair and a Remington revolver aimed at his chest.

"Kruger." At first he thought Hans, or Otto, must have hurried away from the bank, climbed to the second floor — the church bells drowning out the noise of his spurs on the stairs — and figured to dispatch Breen before robbing the bank. But no, that wouldn't make any sense. The bank would be closed by the time that happened. Suddenly, he remembered the Kruger that went into the bank wore striped britches. This Hun's pants were checked.

"I am Otto," the German said with an even-toothed grin. "And ya be dead ven da shooting starts."

"Maybe there won't be any shooting." Breen smiled.

"Ha. Alvays dere be shooting ven Hans rob bank." Otto Kruger walked to the foot of the bed, never lowering the revolver.

Every plan that passed through Breen's brain never slowed down. Every idea he thought of that might not leave him dead

42

was stupid, hopeless, and would have him deader than dirt.

Then a lovely woman stepped into the room, carrying a tray that brought with it the aroma of fried steak, boiled potatoes, hot coffee, and chocolate cake.

CHAPTER FOUR

As captain of the wagon train that had left Dead Trout, Arkansas, the Reverend Sergeant Major Homer Primrose III called every man, woman, and child he was leading to the promised land to kneel in the camp's circle. He was captain of the train, but preferred his rank of sergeant major, which he had earned through hard campaigning with the Thirteenth Arkansas Infantry for the late Confederacy.

All twenty-six people knelt, bowed their heads, and took hands as the Reverend began to pray.

"Dear Lord," he said, "please guide us safely through the evil, sinful town that blocks our path to the glory that awaits us in Rapture Valley, Territory of Arizona. God, spare our children from the sights of debauchery, lewdness, smut, immorality, and from the offensiveness and drunkenness. Spare them, Lord, spare all of us, from the wretched, the gamblers, the confidence men and, Lord have mercy, the confidence women. And the fornicators — especially the fornicators, prostitutes, the soiled doves, the bawdy women, the strumpets, concubines, the harlots, the ladies of the evening, the courtesans, the lost lambs. Oh those poor lost souls. Lord have mercy on them — those scarlet women, those Jezebels, shameless hussies, the dance hall girls. Oh, God, if you could just strike down all those dancers with a thunderous bolt of lighting — and the floozies and the tramps and the trollops. And God, please spare us from the nymphomaniacs, if thus be Thy Will!"

He went on for deliverance from the evils of the gamblers and the confidence men (again), and the cutthroats and murderers and any Jayhawkers that might have drifted down from Kansas into the Panhandle of Texas, and any Yankee-loving son of a cur dog that dared slight the great Confederate States of America and, in especial, the state most noble to that glorious of now lost cause, Arkansas.

"Lord, you know after years of Yankee rule and the curse of Reconstruction, there was nothing left for us, your poor servants in Dead Trout, but you showed us the glory that awaits us if we make it to Rapture Valley," he prayed on, sweating. "And if by your grace we survive this Sodom of Texas, the Gomorrah of our travels, if we can live to see New Mexico Territory and aren't bushwhacked, raped, pillaged and tortured to death — all for your glory — by Mexicans or Apaches, and maybe Mormons if any of them live in the territory, and get us to . . . ."

By that point, raven-haired Annie Homes' neck hurt from such an eternally long bow, and her knees hurt from the prickly pear cactus on the flat expanse of Texas. She lifted her head and looked beyond their camp at the trail that led to Five Scalps, Texas. She breathed a little easier seeing that Winfield Baker had stopped praying, too, as had Betsy Stanton. Betsy, harlot that she was, began rolling a cigarette.

"You better hope the sergeant major doesn't see you," Annie whispered.

Betsy licked the paper and stuck the cigarette into her mouth.

"Got a match?" she asked Winfield, who tried to stifle his laugh. After winking at Annie, Betsy unbuttoned the top button on her blouse and dropped the unlit cigarette between her ample bosoms. "I'll smoke it later, I reckon." She giggled.

Winfield Baker's eyes bulged.

That didn't make Annie happy, but she

held her temper and tongue and made herself look down the road at the dust sweeping across the first buildings on the outskirts of Five Scalps. Maybe, she prayed, that was the Lord hearing the long prayer of the reverend and sending his vengeance to destroy the evil that awaited them just a mile down the trail.

"Amen," the preacher said.

Annie, Winfield, and Betsy quickly dropped their heads, answered, "Amen," and then raised their heads and looked up at the heavens. They thanked the Lord again, helped each other off the cactus, thorns, and ants, and slapped at the dust and bits of gravel. Cactus spines stuck in their clothes and flesh.

"Reverend Sergeant Major Homer?" Annie heard her father Walter ask. "Flat as this country is, wouldn't it make sense to just ride around Five Scalps, and not go through it?"

"Yeah," said Horace Greeley, whose name often was the butt of many a joke. The Horace Greeley from Dead Trout, Arkansas, only touched a newspaper when he took one to the privy since he could neither read nor write. But this Horace Greeley was going West — just like that other Horace Greeley had invited and urged Americans to do.

47

"Well," the preacher said in a blast of fire and brimstone, "you may flee if such is your will. Ride around a test that God himself has put before us. Nay, say I. Nay, will I. As a sergeant major in the Thirteenth Arkansas Infantry, I, the Reverend Sergeant Major Homer Primrose the Third, will see what is God's will."

He had already preached too much fear into the hearts of his fellow Arkansas travelers. Twenty-one of them elected to ride around Five Scalps, so Annie climbed into the back of the covered wagon, settled on the blanket and sack of flour between the chifforobe and her mother's pie safe, and felt the oxen start walking. As the wagon lurched, Annie bumped her head against the wagon and cursed — but not loud enough for her parents or the pious sergeant major to hear. She bounced this way and that, although she really could not tell the difference between the path they had been following and the plains they crossed to go around the nefarious town.

Eventually, the wagons stopped, and she heard her mother and father climb down from the driver's box. Annie pulled herself out from between the two pieces of furniture and rubbed her upper left arm where she felt certain she would see a bruise by tomorrow. She crawled through the tangle of blankets, clothes, and sacks, and peered through the rear oval opening in the canvas covering the wagon. Other members of the train — men, women, girls about Annie's age, boys a few years older, and the little kids, were gathering and looking back east at the town of Five Scalps.

"Huh," Winfield Baker was telling Jimmy Donovan when Annie came up beside him. "From all the stories we heard, I figured that Five Scalps would be a great deal larger."

"It sure ain't like the picture of that wicked city of Gomorrah that we got in our Bible," Jimmy said, leaning forward and grinning. "Howdy, Annie."

She returned the greeting and took a step closer to Five Scalps, Texas, so she could always say she got closer to that evil place than any of the other members of the Primrose Train.

"I don't see the captain," said one of the men off to Annie's left.

"Or the others," an old lady murmured.

"My God," said Aunt Rachel, the oldest woman on the wagon train, who, as far as Annie knew, wasn't related to anyone in Dead Trout, but everybody called her *Aunt.* "Maybe they've been taken in by those evil villains."

"Either that or the prairie swallowed 'em up," someone else said.

A few of the men huddled together to determine their next course of action.

Annie inched her way about another foot closer, though Five Scalps still had to be a quarter mile, from where they had stopped.

"Huh," she said, holding her scarf when a gust of wind blew.

The town might have five scalps somewhere, but it didn't have five buildings, even if you included the privy.

A good-sized adobe structure, two stories with a high wall enclosing the flat roof, and gun ports on all sides. Too small for a fort, certainly not a jail, but from the number of horses at the hitching rail, it had to be the center of town. In fact, it was the town's center. To its left and across the trail stood a smaller building, but it wasn't anything more than a sod hut. To the big adobe's right and on the same side of the trail stood another soddie, but a mite larger than the one on the left-hand side of the trail. Three buildings. Four if you included the privy. Five if you wanted to count the corral.

Annie pointed. "Isn't that the Reverend Primrose's wagon?"

It was hard to tell. The wind had picked

50

up again and was blowing dust.

Her father tensed. "By the terrors, those dirty dogs must have bushwhacked the Reverend. And Thad, Jim, Hawg, and Muldoon."

Another man said, "Isn't that our captain wandering to that hovel across the street?"

Added Hawg's cousin, "With that gal hanging on his arm?"

For about the time it took the man who looked a lot like the Reverend Sergeant Major Homer Primrose III cross the dusty street, no one in the Primrose Train spoke. The wind blew dust as the man managed to keep his hat on with one hand, his other hand holding on to the scantily clad damsel in distress. A moment later, the reverend — or someone who looked a lot like the reverend — and the girl were inside the soddie.

"Maybe that's the church," said Mrs. Primrose, whose husband had insisted that she travel with Aunt Rachel around Five Scalps. Mrs. Primrose said it again and nodded in affirmation. "Yes, that is the church."

"What are we to do?" Aunt Rachel asked, then spit out juice from her snuff.

"Wait for the baptism," Hawg's cousin said.

Winfield Baker could not stifle his snigger, which caused him to get a quick scold-

51

ing from his mother, father, and grand-mother.

Annie's father pulled his hat down tighter and turned around. "Let's just see to our teams and our families. We'll wait here. Stay close to your families, and I'm sure the captain will rejoin us later when he has . . ." His voice trailed off as he sighed.

Annie followed her parents back to the wagon.

She liked the way her father prayed. He sounded sincere, never so pompous as the Reverend Primrose. Her father prayed like he meant it. He didn't ramble like the wagon train boss, but got to the point and wrapped it up. When he thanked God, he sounded sincere.

Annie's family had corn pone, salt pork, leftover beans, and hot tea for their supper. They rolled out their bedrolls and sat on them, watching that big ball of orange slowly sink in the west like it had found quicksand in the distance and was being pulled underneath. The skies turned red, orange, purple and yellow, and finally the tip of the sun bid good-bye for the night.

"We never saw anything like that in Arkansas," Walter said. "Did we, Mother?" Annie's father often called his wife Mother.

"Too many trees." Harriet shook her head. "Never thought I'd miss those trees till we got out here. When's the last time we saw a tree?"

He laughed. "We'll see them in Rapture Valley, Mother." He winked at Annie. "The hillsides are filled with trees, piñon, and juniper, even pines farther up the hills. But the valley is wonderful and lush with grass. Paradise for sure. I'll build my two girls a home in the hills, and the rest of the valley I'll cover with my cattle."

He had been talking about this for years.

The Reverend Primrose said the residents of Dead Trout had been driven out by carpetbaggers and Yankee scalawags, but Walter had been dreaming of leaving the Arkansas hills since even before the War Between the States. When that flyer showed up from the Concord mail stage, and someone posted it on the wall at the general store, he had seen it. He had been the first to suggest that a few families set out for the new country. Get away from the poverty and mosquitoes of the hills. Do what Horace Greeley — the newspaper man — said. Go West.

If anyone asked Annie, the men of the wagon train should have elected her father as the head of the train, but the reverend had been a good soldier, at least if you listened to what he said. He had even once set out for California, spent three years there before returning to Arkansas. He knew the trails even though the one he had taken to California and back had been much farther north.

"Do you trust the reverend?" Annie heard herself ask.

"Child," her mother, Harriet, scolded, "He's a man of the cloth."

Annie's eyes shot toward Five Scalps and the soddie across from the big trading post or whatever it was. She wondered if her first thought, *Sergeant Major Primrose likely is not wearing any sort of cloth right now,* would be declared a sin come Judgment Day.

Her father smiled with the patience of a father. "He has been to California."

"We're not going to California," she pointed out.

"But he knows the trails, or at least, how to handle a wagon train on the trail." Walter reached over and patted her arm. "You see how he taught us to circle our wagons at camp, and he guided us across the Red River into Texas. Now here we are, deep in Comanche and Kiowa territory, and we have not been attacked yet."

"And he preaches a good sermon." Har-

54

riet had always been one to admire some brimstone and vinegar.

"We have traveled six hundred miles, Daughter. Perhaps farther, and that means we are almost halfway to our new home. I would not disservice our train's duly elected captain by complaining or making disparaging comments as to his wisdom or leadership abilities. We are all in good health and have run into no trouble to speak of." He looked over at Five Scalps and shook his head with a smile, sipped the last of his tea, and turned back toward Annie.

"The Reverend Sergeant Major is a man, Annie, and men are —"

"Idiots," her mother said.

They all laughed.

"Well, I am not idiot enough to argue with your mother, Annie, so I will agree with her. When the Reverend Primrose returns with the others we shall continue on to our destination. Perhaps we are delayed by the evils that men do, but let the boys be boys. There is not much left for them until we reach Arizona Territory. Do not frown too much at this delay. It is, I feel, needed."

Her father's face told Annie that he wasn't speaking entirely truthfully. He was just trying to make things seem better than they were. That was her father's way.

"You didn't want to go with them?" her mother asked and chuckled at her good humor.

"I might have, Mother," he said with a smile, and rose to collect the dishes. Most men would leave washing dishes to the women, but Walter liked to do things, liked to stay busy. He wasn't one to waste time playing cards or drinking intoxicating spirits when he could be accomplishing something, like going to Arizona Territory to start a new life, or going around a place like Five Scalps to avoid unnecessary delay, or even washing the supper dishes.

She helped him because she loved her father. Her mother came to help, too.

This is the way a family should be, Annie thought.

When she prayed that night before going to sleep, she thanked God for that greatest of gifts.

CHAPTER FIVE

Matt McCulloch leaped away from the slashing knife again with yet another curse, and the momentum carried the Indian back toward the rocks. That gave McCulloch enough time to look at his belly. A scratch. He had cut himself worse shaving, although he had never been drunk enough to cut his stomach shaving. Hell, he wasn't Sean Keegan. McCulloch rarely got drunk. But getting into fights? Well, that seemed to occupy a lot of his time — as a horse trader and as a Texas Ranger back in the day.

The Apache turned, but stood with his back against the rocky wall. His right hand still held the blade of the deer-handled knife, a mean looking weapon. The blade had probably been taken from an old horse soldier's saber, cut down to something a kid could use quite handily.

McCulloch figured that this Indian was a kid, no more than sixteen years old, though guessing an Indian's age often could be as risky as guessing a woman's.

A few facts became obvious. The boy was Comanche, not Apache. Remembering his late wife, his dead sons, and his missing daughter, had his opponent been Apache, McCulloch would have drawn his Colt and blown the kid's head off. It wasn't that McCulloch had any love for the Comanche — they could be as fearsome, as ruthless, and as hard to kill as any Apache — but this one was just a kid. And he was wounded.

His left arm hung broken, raked with the claws from that bear he had managed to kill. He was sweating hard. The boy panted like he had just run all the way from the Rio Grande and needed time to catch his breath. McCulloch could wait in a Mexican standoff and hope the boy would finally pass out.

Those eyes were like obsidian, staring briefly at McCulloch, then at the Winchester lying in the dirt between them, then back at McCulloch, and then at the belted Colt holstered on the white man's right hip. Never did the Indian's eyes focus on one particular spot for too long. His eyes moved like most Indians moved — like the wind.

As the boy's breathing slowed to some sort of normalcy, McCulloch figured he had little time before that deadly blade came slashing. He wasn't too worried. If things got desperate, all he had to do was draw the revolver and punch a hole through the kid's middle. But he tried something different.

He spoke a short warning in Comanche. "No. Me friend."

That being his entire Comanche vocabulary, "Let me help," came out in English. He could turn to sign language easy enough, but the blackness in that boy's eyes told him that he needed to keep both of his hands free. He pressed them down a little like he was training a puppy to stay down. Stay down, don't jump.

Don't rip out my intestines with that damned pig-sticker you have.

The black eyes of the Comanche brave hardened, moved again from McCulloch to the rifle to McCulloch to the holstered revolver, and finally the Indian lunged. He had lost a lot more blood than McCulloch figured. Although the kid's first move was sudden and with lethal intensity, by the time he stepped over McCulloch's Winchester, he was practically falling. The knife passed easily as McCulloch moved to his right, and the Indian boy staggered over. Falling headfirst, the knife plunged into the grasslands. He moved his left arm in an attempt to push himself up and screamed from pure agony. It looked like a bad break. The boy tried with his right hand, but collapsed, shuddered, and lay still.

For a moment, McCulloch thought the boy was dead, but after gathering his Winchester and laying it behind him — out of the young warrior's reach — McCulloch gently rolled the boy over. He looked at the knife, buried almost to the hilt, but left it untouched. It was out of the kid's reach, at least from his right hand. His left arm remained useless and the boy would have to reach over his body to grab the deer-horn handle. If he ever woke up, that is.

Kneeling over the unconscious brave, McCulloch studied the kid. No moccasins, no shield. Just that knife and a heavy woolen breechcloth covering the rest of his nakedness. His hair hung loose and long, but not in braids wrapped in otter skins or tied with ribbons, and there was no headband, not even a single feather of honor. McCulloch lifted the broken arm gently and laid it across the boy's dehydrated stomach. Now that his own heart wasn't racing and his only instincts were about staying alive, he thought the boy looked like he was half-starved. McCulloch untied his bandana and wrapped it over the boy's deeply scratched

60

forearm. He tightened it just enough to stop the bleeding for the time being. Cleaning it would have to wait. Most likely, his best bet would be to walk till he fetched his horse, then return and care for the kid.

Or he could just let the boy die. Hell, the kid was a Comanche. If the tables had been turned, McCulloch had a pretty good idea that he'd already be dead and scalped. He looked at the knife. That was no Indian knife, nothing a brave or boy would have traded with some Comanchero. The blade was, to McCulloch's horror, fairly rusted over. Quickly, the old Ranger turned his attention to his own wound, but saw that the blood had already congealed and wasn't deep at all. He had just been cut slightly. But that rusty blade made him stand up long enough to pull the flask out of his hip pocket, and poor rye whiskey over the wound, just enough to cleanse it some. He knelt beside the unconscious Indian and did the same over his scratches. The kid jerked, moaned, screamed, and spoke in short bursts of the Comanche tongue, before shuddering and sinking into an even deeper sleep.

McCulloch looked at the knife again, understanding at last that the boy had likely found the blade, somehow managed to break it apart, and fashion it into a knife, using the antler from a dead deer. The starving teenager had been alone, trying to survive.

"Vision quest," McCulloch said aloud, looking at the kid.

It certainly made sense. A Comanche boy, maybe thirteen to sixteen years old, before he could become a warrior, would have to leave his village on his own in search of his vision, to learn what was his power, and earn the name he would carry into manhood. McCulloch was no expert on Comanches, but he had been in Texas long enough to know a lot about them. It paid to know your enemy, and the Comanches hated all Texans. But he did know that when a Comanche boy went off on his vision quest, he wore only his breechcloth, and carried his pipe and a buffalo robe. The robe and the pipe, he figured, had to be around somewhere.

"If you live," McCulloch said, "I think I'd name you *Bear Killer.*" To his surprise, he realized he was smiling down at the kid.

All right, he told himself. *Get on your feet and start walking. Let's get that horse and get back here and figure out what to do with this buck before you go traipsing through these mountains looking for a herd of wild mustangs.*

62

A horse whinnied, and McCulloch looked up to see his black coming toward him. He let his right hand fall onto the butt of the Colt.

It was his horse, all right. He knew that whinny, and he knew the color and the saddle, but the horse carried a stranger. Three other men rode with him, two on paints, one on a dapple gray. One had an eagle feather flapping from his black hat. Another wore a Mexican sugarloaf sombrero with bandoliers crisscrossing his chest and a Spencer repeater braced against his thigh. The third was dressed in buckskins. The fellow riding McCulloch's horse carried a Winchester across his pommel, had red hair down to his shoulders, and scalp locks secured to his vest like medals.

They reined in about twenty-five feet from McCulloch, keeping about ten yards between them. Spread out.

Smart, McCulloch figured.

The Indian boy's eyes shot open, and he seemed alert, like he knew there were four strangers with them.

"Be quiet," McCulloch whispered in Spanish, hoping the boy understood that. "Don't move." He would have said, "Play dead," but he couldn't figure that out in Spanish.

He waved with his left hand and painted on a welcoming smile that wouldn't fool an imbecile. "Thanks for bringing back my horse." His head tilted to the man on his far left, the one on his horse.

"Your horse?" asked the man in buckskins, mounted on the dapple. He laughed. "Bert found this horse lopin' across the valley like it didn't belong to nobody. And seein' his come up lame and we had to shoot 'em, he figured it was a gift from God."

"You shot a lame horse?" McCulloch figured this man to be the group's leader.

"Well, not really. That's just a figure of speech. Amigo yonder slit his throat. Didn't want to risk firin' a shot. But had we knowed there was a horse lover around us, we woulda brung him directly to you."

Amigo, McCulloch guessed, would be the Mexican with the Spencer, riding one of the paints.

Bert said, "You got any proof that this horse is yourn?"

McCulloch said, "You'll find my brand on his left hip. You'll find my name and my brand burned on the underside of that saddle. You'll find a book with my name in it in the saddlebags."

"You got a book with your own name in it?" The leader laughed again. "That makes you famous."

McCulloch chuckled and nodded. "Hell, boys, I bet that book's got your names in it, too. It's the List of Fugitives from Justice. They hand those out every year to Texas Rangers."

The smiles vanished. The faces tensed. Two hands inched slightly closer to holstered revolvers, but not close enough to make McCulloch lose his cool and make the first move. The one holding the Winchester wet his lips. The man with the Spencer straightened in his saddle.

"You a Ranger?" asked the man on the dapple gray.

"Open that saddlebag," McCulloch said calmly, "and you might find a *cinco* pesos star." That was the Mexican coin most Rangers used to carve out their badges. Some were quite crude, but they all meant one thing. *Frontier Battalion.*

His Mama would have been pleased. He had not told a lie. He said they *might* find a badge in there. Hell, they might not. To put it bluntly, they wouldn't. And that List of Fugitives from Justice was two years old. McCulloch brought it along to rip out pages when he couldn't find anything dry enough for kindling to light his evening or morning campfire.

"Well," the leader said, "I guess that proves beyond any reasonable doubt that that horse is yourn, all right. But this is a hell of a place to be left afoot. Since we was kind enough to bring you your hoss back, how 'bout you offer us a reward?"

"Now, wait a minute, Linton," Bert said.

Without taking his eyes off McCulloch, Linton said to Bert, "Shut up. You was the fool who didn't realize your hoss had tossed a shoe." He smiled, even took his right hand away from his holstered revolver and waved. "Trade. The Texas way."

"What do you have in mind?" McCulloch asked.

The man's head tilted directly at McCulloch. "That red devil you got there. Looks half dead already."

McCulloch answered with a lethal stare.

"Mister," Linton said dryly, "I got three men with me. And I ain't no slouch with a handgun."

"You got three *scalp hunters* with you," McCulloch said, spitting out the words like a disgusting curse.

"It's a livin'. We been trailin' him for nigh on four days."

McCulloch laughed. "If it takes you four days to find a puny little boy on a vision quest, I'm surprised you even caught my horse."

The Indian boy's eyes widened and focused on something behind McCulloch.

He saw relaxation settle over the four strangers and knew he had been stupid. There were five men — not four — and the fifth was behind him. McCulloch saw the boy lunge over, reaching for the knife. Saw the redhead with the Winchester and the Mexican with the Spencer bring up their long guns.

Some extra sense told McCulloch not to worry about the man behind him. Looking for him would put his back to the four horsemen. Besides, he already knew where they were.

The Colt leaped into his right hand, and he fanned back the trigger and shot the long-haired redhead off his black horse. McCulloch moved just as the Spencer barked. From his new position, he took careful aim while the big Mexican was cocking the rifle on his stutter stepping horse. McCulloch touched the trigger and dived before the smoke cleared.

The Indian boy fell as the knife he had ripped out of the ground sailed. McCulloch rolled over in the grass, glanced behind him, and saw a man in leather pants and a white beard trying to pull the rusted knife blade from his belly. His hands kept slipping off the bloody deer-horn handle already coated with crimson blood. Then the man's eyes glazed over and he fell to his side. The Indian boy didn't move. McCulloch did. He fired the next three shots as fast as he could, while crawling toward the Winchester. A bullet punched a hole in the dirt to his left, but he grabbed the lever, pulled the rifle to him, and fired from the prone position.

By then, Linton was hightailing it as fast as he could, and the guy with the eagle feather in his hat was trying to control his paint while helping the redhead onto the back of his saddle. Although McCulloch could have shot him out of the saddle, he drew aim on Linton, whose dapple was raising dust like there was no tomorrow. If McCulloch hadn't rushed his shot, there wouldn't have been a tomorrow or even another hour for Linton. He could have chanced another shot, or he easily could have shot Bert in the back as he was carried off to lift scalps another day.

Backshooting bushwackers was all right, he figured, for some people. But even a jackal might not be willing to do some things.

CHAPTER SIX

Hank Benteen held a short barreled Colt revolver, the front sight filed down for a faster draw, and grinned. "Looks like you two deputies are —"

"He ain't no deputy," Titus Bedwell said. "I'm arrestin' him for bustin' up one of our saloons."

"He don't look like he got busted up much," Hank said.

Sean Keegan chuckled. "I appreciate the compliment, Hank. I did all right, if I have to say so myself."

"You mean to tell me the law here just left one deputy to guard my cousin?" Hank Benteen looked insulted.

"County's dirt cheap," Bedwell told him. "The Purgatory City Council is even tighter with a coin. That's why we got only one jail for the city and the county."

"Will you get me out of here, Hank?" Tom Benteen pleaded.

Hank Benteen waved the pistol. "You heard Tom. Open the cell, Pops, and we'll swap out prisoners. Maybe you can hang the big mick instead of Tom. I mean, you don't want to disappoint the crowd that'll be coming in here directly, expecting to see a man swing."

Bedwell looked at the pistol on his hip, and Keegan stopped grinning, hoping his friend wouldn't be so foolish. Hell, that would likely get them both killed, and all Keegan wanted right now was a place to sleep off a rip-roaring good drunk. He could care less what happened to Lovely Tom Benteen or the rest of those killers.

"Pops," Hank Benteen said. "I ain't got all day." He raised the revolver.

With a sigh, Bedwell started to unbuckle his gun rig, but Hank's head shook. "No time for that. Tom'll take that hogleg when you let him out. Get moving, old man. Now."

Bedwell nodded and passed Keegan on the way to the cell. For half of half of a second, Keegan considered the odds of him managing to jerk the pistol out of Bedwell's holster and plaster Hank Benteen's blood over the wanted posted by the door. The odds convinced Keegan to just stand here with that stupid grin on his face and his

70

hands raised high, reminding him of just how bad he needed a bath, too.

Besides, Bob Benteen, Uncle Zach, and anyone riding with the Benteens would likely be outside, spread out so not to get too much notice.

"What time's the hanging?" Keegan asked.

"Two this afternoon," Bedwell answered.

"That late? Why not dawn?"

"Big to-do." Bedwell had the big key and jammed it into the lock. "Wanted to give folks plenty of time to get here. Everybody in this part of Texas wanted to see Lovely Tom swing."

"Watch your mouth, you dumb piece of horse dung." Tom Benteen spit.

The door opened, the iron bars moved in front of Keegan. Keeping the keys in his hand, Bedwell stepped back and raised his arms. Lovely Tom Benteen came out, jamming on his hat, then jerking the hogleg from Bedwell's holster.

"*Vámanos,* cousin," Hank Benteen said. "Folks are startin' their day."

"I'm comin', Hank." Tom grinned evilly, thumbed back the hammer of Bedwell's Schofield, slammed the barrel into the old horse soldier's gut and — as Keegan yelled, "Nooooo!" — pulled the trigger.

The impact of the bullet sent the old-timer flying back to the town marshal's desk, scattering papers, pencils, and an empty jar over the floor. Bedwell sat on the edge of the desk for a moment, trying to beat out the flames on his vest started by the closeness of the revolver. Then he gave up, stiffened, and sank onto the floor, blood spilling and sizzling against the burning cloth. The old man shuddered, gasped, and fell to his side in front of the desk.

"You stupid chucklehead!" Hank roared. "The idea was to get you out of here quietly!"

"I don't take no insults, cousin," Tom said, and started to turn around.

All of this had happened in mere seconds, almost too fast for Sean Keegan, drunk as he was, to comprehend. But suddenly, he did not feel one ounce of all the rotgut liquor he had been drinking throughout the night and into the dawn. He became sober, alert, and intent.

"Come on!" Hank Benteen turned and moved toward the open door. Outside, horses whickered, hooves stomped, and men cursed. Another pistol sounded from outside.

"I'm coming," Lovely Tom said, "But first I got to give this Irish pimp what he's got comin', too."

The cold-blooded killer was turning, but Keegan was already moving, gripping the iron bars and shoving the door with all his might. The connection of iron against bone and flesh sounded almost as loud as the deafening pistol shot that had left the room in a cloud of acrid, white smoke. Down went Lovely Tom with a thud, and the big Schofield slid across the room. Keegan caught just a glimpse of the killer's bloody face, the broken nose, and the dazed eyes.

He wouldn't comprehend all of that until later, when he had the chance to recall everything with clarity — when he wasn't so busy trying to keep from getting killed.

Keegan slid past the iron-barred door and dived for Bedwell's .45. He heard a curse from the doorway, then his ears were ringing and his cheek stinging as Hank Benteen snapped a shot from the doorway, the bullet hitting a bucket and sending slivers of oak into Keegan's face. The next bullet ricocheted off the stone wall. By that time, Keegan had slid to the corner, pulled his legs up, and quickly fired a shot at the real Benteen.

Benteen fired again, kicking up dust from the stone, and Keegan cocked the revolver. He glanced at Lovely Tom, who had rolled over and pushed himself onto hands and knees, shaking his head, trying to regain his faculties. If he lifted a leg, he'd look just like the pathetic, mangy cur dog he was. It took every ounce of self-control for Keegan not to put a bullet in the outlaw's head. Titus Bedwell had served in this man's army for forty years. They didn't make a soldier any better. For him to be cut down, unarmed, for no damned good reason — Keegan slid down about a foot, then fired another shot at the doorway.

"Tom!" Hank barked. "Get out now or get hung!"

Horses thundered outside. Bullets started bouncing all over Purgatory City. Slowly, Keegan pushed himself up and peered around the corner. The door remained open, but outside about all he could see was dust. The Benteen gang was heading straight for the border, it appeared, and since Lovely Tom was a Lovely, not really a Benteen, the brothers had decided to "Vámanos." Uncle Zach might shed a tear or two over his son, but the old man had better sons — the two who hadn't taken the owlhoot trail. Not ignorant sons like that cold-hearted devil.

Boots sounded on the floor, and Keegan turned his head to see that Tom Lovely had righted himself and began making for the open door. The Schofield in Keegan's hand was already cocked, and he shifted his aim and was ready to blow a hole in the man's back. He would have, too, but Lovely Tom slipped on the blood that had poured out of Titus Bedwell's body. His feet shot out in front of him, and he landed hard, his head slamming against the floor. He groaned and rolled over.

The only noise came from outside. Slowly the ringing left Keegan's ears, and he stepped toward the dead hero and the lousy, groaning killer. Church bells — the town's warning alarms — sang out across the city, and shouts, curses, but no more gunfire, echoed across the street. After lowering the Schofield, Keegan walked slowly to the two men, one dead, one about to be. He felt the urge to put a bullet between Lovely Tom's glazed eyes, but a figure appeared in the doorway, then disappeared immediately.

"Hell's bells, boys!" the voice outside called out. "There's a man in there with a gun!"

"It's me, ye blithering idiot!" Sean Keegan said, and yelled out his name. That caused a bit of silence. He figured the people in town now wondered if Keegan — the blight of the city, the county, and most of West Texas — had joined up with the Benteen brothers.

75

"They've killed poor Titus Bedwell, boys. Shot him down in cold blood. But the one who murdered my friend is gonna live to face the hangman."

He waited. Then blew up with a stream of profanity that ended with "Get your yellow asses in here, boys, and I mean now."

A head appeared. Then another. Finally two men slowly came into the marshal's office and jail, keeping their hands far, far away from their holstered revolvers. Another man showed up, wet his lips, and leaned his rifle against the doorjamb. The first fellow had the decency to remove his hat and bow his head as he looked down at the late Titus Bedwell.

"Where's the marshal?" Keegan asked.

"I don't rightly know," said another newcomer standing in the doorway.

"Probably hiding under his bed," came a comment from someone outside.

"They kilt Titus," said the second man to have entered the building.

"This, me boys," Keegan said, "is what you bloody well get when you don't hang a vermin like Tom Lovely at dawn. When you want to wait to give more folks a chance to see his neck pop and his britches get soiled."

"Well . . ." someone said.

Another person outside cursed.

76

The church bells faded into mere echoes, and a moment later, the echoes even stopped. Nothing but silence, except for Lovely Tom's groans.

"My goodness," said a woman's voice somewhere on the street. "They went and shot down poor Mr. Kligerman as he was coming to do his job."

"Who the hell is Mr. Kligerman?" Keegan asked.

The man in the doorway raised his head. "The hangman."

"Our luck," said someone else outside. "Now we can't hang Tom Benteen."

"The bloody hell." Keegan tossed the Schofield onto the marshal's desk, marched over to Lovely Tom, and jerked him to his feet. The killer's eyes fluttered then closed from the fist Keegan planted into his temple. The unconscious man flopped over Keegan's shoulder, and the big Irishman marched him outside.

"We shan't be waiting till the crowds arrive this bloody afternoon, and we won't let this piece of filth wait till the county can find another hangman." Keegan stepped into the street, looked around, saw the gallows behind the courthouse, and made a beeline. "C'mon, boys, ladies, kids . . . you, too, Reverend. The hanging of Tom Lovely

77

— like hell if I'll call him a Benteen — starts right now."

"You can't do that!" A white-haired woman gasped.

"I suspect that the death warrant says this man dies today. It's today, and he's going to die today. It might not be two this afternoon in Purgatory City when he swings, but it'll be two o'clock somewhere."

The crowd parted like the Red Sea, and Keegan moved like the old soldier he was, a body over his shoulder and fierce determination in his eyes. He rounded the corner and looked for the gate to the courthouse's backyard.

Purgatory City had become civilized at some point, and no longer let every man, woman, and child, come to see the hangings. These had become private affairs, with invitations extended and tickets sold, and carpenters paid to not only build a gallows but to put up a high fence to keep gawkers from watching a man, or woman, swing.

He stopped long enough to kick the gate off its hinges, turned back, and yelled, "Come on, you yellow-livered trash. Lovely Tom murdered a good man in cold blood, without a care or concern or a moment of guilt, and he's gonna pay for that. Not for whatever crime got him sentenced to die today — but die today he will. And I want everyone out on these streets to come see him swing."

He marched into the rear yard, saw the canopies and benches arranged for ladies or the weak of heart, saw a few carts for vendors. How much did the city council charge for those hawkers of peanuts and parched corn? He stopped briefly to look up.

Good. They had already set the noose.

He moved to the steps, and without breaking stride, climbed them. On the platform, he glanced to see several people actually coming into the gated enclosure. Keegan didn't actually think the people of this town would have the guts to do it, but here they came.

After stepping to the trapdoor, he gently lowered Lovely Tom to his feet. Holding him with his left hand, he slapped the man's face several times with his right. The eyes finally opened, focused, then dulled.

After another slap, a hard one, Lovely Tom moaned, "Stop hittin' me, damn you."

"Can you stand?" Keegan asked.

"Huh?"

"Can you stand on your own without me holding you up?"

"Oh." Tom's eyes rolled around. He

79

drooled a bit and eventually made his head bob.

Keegan released his grip, but remained tensed to catch him if Lovely Tom's knees folded. When they didn't, Keegan said, "Stay still," and moved behind the man, grabbed the hangman's noose, and slipped it over Lovely Tom's bleeding head.

"What the hell are —"

Keegan choked off whatever else Lovely Tom had to say by quickly and roughly tightening the noose. He pulled it as hard as he could, and when the condemned man tried to reach up with his right hand to get out of the noose, Keegan jerked Lovely Tom's arm out of the shoulder socket.

Screaming in pain, the killer reached over with his left hand and grabbed his useless right arm.

That should hold him long enough, Keegan figured, and he moved to the lever. He saw men, women, and a couple of kids. Blacks, whites, and Mexicans. Fat, skinny, and average sized. A preacher with his Bible, head bowed. A fellow with bare feet and just his longhandles on with a hat and a gunbelt around his waist. Even some of the boys he had tangled with in the saloon. More people shoved their way through the gate, but Keegan wasn't going to wait on anyone else.

"Do you have any last words, Tom Lovely?" Keegan called out.

The murmur in the crowd stopped instantly. More people shoved their way into the enclosure.

"What?" Tom Lovely turned his head and saw Keegan's hands on the lever. His eyes widened. "Wait!" he called out. "No. You . . . *Don't!*"

Not the best last words a man ever said, but that was all for Lovely Tom. The lever yanked, the trapdoor opened, and Tom Lovely dropped into eternity.

CHAPTER SEVEN

When the waitress from the Deep Flood café entered his room, Jed Breen frowned. He realized when the shooting started, he wouldn't be the only person dead. Otto Kruger would kill the redhead, too.

Kruger was savvy enough, experienced enough, and most certainly deadly enough, to stand back and find the perfect position where he could keep an eye on Breen and the handsome woman. His eyes seemed independent of one another; one looked at Breen, while the other focused on the girl. The Remington remained level at Breen's chest.

"Fräulein," Otto said. "Ya put food here on bed and step back. Run, yell, try anyting and ya die. I vill kill ya. And him, too. *Ruhe."* He motioned with his left hand toward the bed.

The tray shook in the redhead's hands.

"Be quiet!" Otto shouted. "If people hear

ya, I vill kill ya now." He pointed the gun at her, and her Adam's apple bobbed twice, but she somehow managed to stop shaking, and placed the tray on the end of the bed.

A shot rang out outside, and the girl jumped back, almost turning over the coffeepot. Instinctively, she reached for it.

Otto turned back, kept the gun aimed at Breen, and laughed as a second gunshot echoed outside.

"Hans do good vork, ja?" He laughed again and drew careful aim at Jed Breen.

The wide smile on Breen's face stopped the German.

"Vat make laugh?" Otto Kruger frowned. "Ya vant to die vith a smile on yer lips."

Breen's head shook, and he laughed out loud as yet another gunshot came from the bank.

"No. It's just so damned funny." He pointed at the waitress from Deep Flood's only eating joint.

Quickly Otto Kruger jerked his head toward the redhead, and that sent Breen diving for the Sharps. About to turn back and put a bullet into the bounty hunter's head, the German instead raised both hands to protect his face and screamed. He screamed before the redheaded waitress tossed the scalding hot coffee into his face.

Behind him, Breen heard the German shrieking in agony, writhing on the floor, and the redhead cursing him. The coffeepot clattered on the floor. The waitress kicked Otto Kruger — where it counted.

Breen jerked back the heavy hammer of the Sharps, leaped to his feet, and swung it at the window. The barrel smashed the glass for he had no time to try to slide the barrel and its fancy brass telescope through the crack. He saw the horse, but only the tail, heard another gunshot, and then Hans Kruger was galloping out of Breen's sight.

"Damn," Breen barked, and broke more glass from the window as he pulled the Sharps back inside.

Otto, his face an ugly mess of red, white, purple (and brown coffee), rolled back and forth, gasping in pain from damage to his face, neck, and groin. The redhead didn't look happy either, and she kicked the man in the shin.

"No . . ." Otto Kruger found enough strength to push himself up. "Hussy!" He spit at the redhead.

Breen brought the stock of the heavy Sharps onto the top of the outlaw's head. Otto Kruger groaned, yelped, and slumped into the coffee that was slowly disappearing into the cracks on the floor.

Outside and downstairs and even on the second floor hallway of the hotel, people began shouting and asking questions.

Breen nodded at the woman.

"You all right?"

She didn't answer. She pointed at Otto Kruger. "Who is that wicked, little weasel?"

"Otto Kruger. Bank robber, ma'am. Now out of commission." Breen lowered the rifle and grinned. "There's a five-hundred-dollar reward on him. I think it would be fair for us to split it."

He expected her to argue, but she just stopped and blinked, and looked down at him, then back at Breen.

Her lips trembled. "What?"

"The bank robber is a killer, ma'am. That was his brother down below, robbing the bank here in Deep Flood."

"Who are you?" she managed to ask.

"Breen, ma'am." He reached up as if to tip the hat that was hanging on the horn of a longhorn steer on the wall. "Jed Breen. I'm sort of what they call . . . a . . . man hunter. Part-time . . . um . . . peace officer."

"Bounty hunter." Her eyes turned rigid.

"Yeah. That's another way of putting it. Five hundred dollars." He pointed his chin at the unconscious outlaw. "For him. Two hundred and fifty suit you, ma'am?"

"Keep your blood money," she said. Then she spit on the floor, kicked the unconscious Hun in the ankle, and hurried out the door. As she disappeared, Breen heard the echoes of her heels on the stairs, then the front door slam.

Eventually, another face appeared in the door. The man looked first at the door Breen had busted open, then at the coffeepot, eventually finding the broken window. He looked at length at the ugly face of the ugly bank robber, and then, finally, at Jed Breen.

"What the hell has been going on here?" the hotel clerk said.

"Fetch the town law." Breen lowered the Sharps onto the bed and moved to the plate of steak and potatoes. But he lost his appetite. Seeing all the coffee and such over his meal, he figured it had been contaminated with Otto Kruger's snot, hairs, and sweat.

Inside what passed for a lawman's office, the constable of Deep Flood, Texas, rolled out the reward poster close to the still-unconscious face of the notorious man-killer and robber. "This is Otto Kruger."

Breen nodded and poured himself a cup of coffee since his supper was turning out to be the constable's coffee. "Yeah. Once those scars are all set, there shouldn't be any trouble in telling him apart from his brother, Hans." The coffee tasted like lukewarm water flavored by two or three coffee beans.

"And you are . . . ?"

"Jed Breen."

"The jackal?"

"I've been called worse."

The constable rose and rolled up the wanted poster. "Well, sir, what is it you want from me?"

Breen made himself drink what some idiot might call coffee and tossed the empty tin mug onto the counter. "Well, sir, I'd like for you to identify this man, then go over to the bank, and bring me back my five hundred dollars. Just like that reward poster says. The great state of Texas and the territories of Arizona, New Mexico, and Colorado will pay you and the bank back. That's what it says on that dodger, doesn't it?"

"Bank's closed," the constable said.

"No, it's not. They're busy trying to figure out how much money Hans Kruger got away with."

"If it was the Kruger brothers, they likely cleaned out everything," the constable said, choking out the words.

"No. I saw Hans Kruger drop a sack in the dirt while he was trying to get his horse to giddyap."

The constable frowned, looked at Otto Kruger, and shook his head. "And then what?"

"Then you lock this low-down dog up, and the Texas Rangers will ride over in a day or so and haul his sorry ass off to wherever they want to hang him."

The constable straightened, smiling as he shook his head. "Well, we can't do that, Mr. Breen." He made a lazy gesture toward the backdoor. "Jail only has room for one prisoner, and that'd be Orrin, our local drunk. Besides, you don't want to keep a villain like Otto Kruger." He looked down at the man's ugly, swollen face, and shook his head before looking again into Breen's cold eyes. "There's no lock on the door, Mr. Breen. This is Deep Flood. It ain't Purgatory City."

"Son of a gun," Breen said, which wasn't what he wanted to say. He moved to the constable's desk and sat on the top, glancing at the wanted posters, then at the door that led to the backyard where he might find a one-room jail that currently housed a drunk named Orrin behind a door that didn't lock.

"You'll need to haul him off to Purgatory City," the constable said. "They have a good jail."

"I know," Breen said. "I just delivered it a customer a week or so ago." He looked up at the lawman. "Tom Benteen."

The constable straightened in appreciation. "Well, that's fine, just fine. You got one of the Benteen boys and now you got one of the Krugers." He looked at the unconscious German. "If it is Hans Kruger."

"It's not Hans Kruger," Breen told him. "It's Otto Kruger."

"Yes, sir. If you say so, Mr. Breen."

"Well, hell." Breen slid off the desk and walked to the line of posters. His head shook. "That means I have to rent a horse to carry this sorry heap all the way to the county seat."

"Jarvis won't rent you no horse to go that far," the constable said. "In a town like Purgatory City, that horse would be likely to get up and stole."

Breen stared hard at the idiot with a badge and kept talking. "And if I'm splitting the reward with that redhead from your eating house . . ."

"But you said she said she don't want no reward," the constable said.

"I know what she said. And I know what's

right. Even a jackal knows what's right some of the times. She'll get two hundred and fifty dollars . . . once I get my five hundred." He smiled at the young idiot and tried another attack. "You know, if she were to get her reward now, before I left, all that money would stay in your good town. You might see the economy grow. All you have to do is —"

"You need to take that prisoner to Purgatory City, Mr. Breen. Get your reward there."

"Hell." Breen turned back to the wall and stared at the wanted posters. Suddenly, he smiled. "How much do you think it would cost me to buy a wagon and a team of mules?"

Breen strode easily into the one place a body could eat in Deep Flood, looked around, and asked the man holding the pitcher of water, "Where's the redhead?"

"You mean . . . Constance?"

Breen smiled. "If that's what she's calling herself."

"She went home. Had a rough day, you —"

"Where's home?"

The man hesitated, but Breen looked out the window and shook his head. "Never mind," he said, and walked outside.

He found the redhead at the Wells Fargo office, though why a town like Deep Flood had a Wells Fargo office was beyond him, and she turned, holding the ticket in her hand.

The clerk looked up and said, "May I help you, sir?"

"No, thanks." Breen walked over and plucked the ticket from the redhead's hand. He looked at it and shook his head. "El Paso." He stared at her. "You know, two hundred and fifty dollars could help you out in Mexico, which I figured is where you'd be going as soon as you got off the El Paso stage. You should have accepted my generosity, Charlotte."

"My name," she said, "Is Constance."

"Is this man bothering you, Miss Pettigrew?"

"No," Breen answered. "I'm not." He withdrew the wanted poster from his back pocket, unfolded it, and held it up for her inspection. "Miss Charlotte Platte." He laughed, shook his head, and showed the Wells Fargo agent the dodger.

"If you took your supper at the place here in town, you might want to see a doctor," Breen said. "I feel lucky I didn't eat."

He stepped back and motioned to the

door. "Come along, Charlotte Platte. The law wants you in Precious Metal, Arizona Territory, for poisoning fifteen miners, but killing only eight of them. Five thousand dollars, but that reward will go all to me. I'm still splitting the reward with you for Otto Kruger, though. You can use it for your lawyer or your coffin. Come along, darling. I have a wagon with two mules waiting for us at the constable's office. I know it's getting late, but I'd like to get you and Otto in a jail as quickly as I can. It's supposed to be a full moon, clear skies, and we can be in Purgatory City before daybreak."

He stepped aside and motioned to the door. "After you, Miss Platte. Or would you rather be called by that other handle they've put on you . . . Poison Platte?"

CHAPTER EIGHT

McCulloch looked at the Indian boy, unconscious, and at the dead scalp hunter whose job was to shoot McCulloch in the back. He probably would have succeeded had the Comanche kid not sprung into action. McCulloch's black danced approximately thirty feet from him, but didn't seem inclined to run anymore, and the Mexican's horse had loped after the other scalp hunters. He wouldn't be able to catch it. The Mexican looked dead, probably was.

McCulloch still had to figure out what to do with the Indian boy. The dead men he'd leave for the vultures and other varmints. But he figured, most likely, this old white-bearded scalp hunter had a horse, probably had hobbled it somewhere behind him.

To let the blood flow a little, McCulloch first loosened the tourniquet he had fashioned around the boy's arm. After retying the bandana, he rose, walked past the

Mexican — indeed, the man was dead, likely burning in hell at that very moment — and eased his way to his skittish horse. Once he had the reins, he cut a wide loop around the dead and the blood, and hobbled his mount in a spot with plenty of grass and no dead bear, dead bandit, scents from the other now-gone scalp hunters and horses, and one badly injured Comanche boy.

The black lifted its head and whinnied. Almost instantly, a answer came from up the hill.

After a quick glance at the kid, still out of this world for the time being, McCulloch figured his best plan was to find that dead man's horse before his colleagues went after it — if they had such an intention. He found a deer trail and followed it up the hill before the trail slipped through some rocks a man of McCulloch's size would find a tight squeeze. He took a firm grip on a juniper branch and pulled himself up the steep slope, sending gravel and larger stones rolling down. and inching his way till he made it to the other side of a rock. He rested for a moment, then climbed up the slope. Often, he had to crawl his way on all fours. That told McCulloch there had to be an easier path down than the one he was taking up.

Fifteen minutes later, he found the horse

tied to a dead piñon on the other side of the slope. McCulloch admired the view and the horse, a blood bay with an army McClellan saddle. A sash hung around the horse's neck, and from it hung a few scalps the dead man must have found too important or too pretty to sell for whatever the Mexicans were paying for scalps.

He ripped that off, dug a hole with the heel of his boot, and buried those disgusting trophies.

Matt McCulloch had done a lot of things that disgusted him over his years in the wilds, but he didn't care much for scalping. In that regard, he had a bit of respect for the Apaches. They didn't scalp, either. But the Apaches had killed his family, and the Apaches had taken his daughter. Comanches had tried to kill him over the years, but he still had his topknot.

He grabbed the reins to the bay, rubbed his hand over the neck, and started studying the ground until he found the prints of the dead man the Comanche boy had killed. He followed that trail, pulling the horse behind him, and — as he had expected — it was a much easier climb down than it had been up. At least until he reached the end and saw he had a ten foot jump down. Easy for a scalp hunter. That killer had likely just grabbed hold of a juniper root, held on to it as he lowered himself, let go, and dropped silently to the soft grass below.

Getting a horse down might prove harder. McCulloch looked at the bay and decided this stallion could handle ten feet. He went back up to the horse, took the reins, and swung into the saddle. The stirrups were too short for him and McCulloch had never understood why those damned fool Yankee horse soldiers survived riding on something as backbreaking and *huevos*-pounding torture contraptions like a McClellan. The horse showed a moment of anxiety, dancing around, but McCulloch eased it down to the edge, let the blood bay measure the distance, then rode it back up as far as he could. Turning the horse around underneath the piñons, he spurred it, and the horse showed no fear, no doubt. A moment later Matt McCulloch felt the wind, the freedom, the wonders of flying, and the horse landed, jarring him, but not spilling him. Mc-Culloch laughed as he righted himself in the saddle and gave the stallion its head, letting him run by the bear and the dead Mexican and a hundred and fifty yards up the valley, before he turned the horse around and galloped back, slowing down about thirty yards from his black and trotting the rest of the way.

He swung down, tied the horse up a few feet from his black — so they could get to know one another — loosened the cinch and found the dead scalp hunter's canteen. He sniffed. Yes, it was water, not whiskey. You couldn't be sure about scalp hunters. He filled his hat with the lukewarm liquid and let the bay drink. Then he did the same for his black. Keeping the canteen, he went back to the unconscious Comanche.

And McCulloch went to work.

He jerked out the Comanche's homemade knife from the white-bearded scalp hunter and went to the bear. For a rusted blade, the knife cut well. The Indian boy had honed a sharp edge on that old saber, and McCulloch carved up some fat and a little bit of meat. A few minutes later, he had a fire going. Then came the hard part. Using his own knife, he heated the blade, then removed his blood-soaked bandana, and placed the white-hot blade on the savage cut.

Flesh sizzled. The Indian boy screamed and tried to rise, but McCulloch's knee had been placed on the boy's chest. The pain quickly sent the kid back into deep unconsciousness. McCulloch heat-sealed the other serious wounds, found a needle in his saddlebags, plucked some hairs from the tail of his black, and stitched up the smaller cuts that weren't so deep. The bear fat he placed on all the wounds, hoping that would suck out some of the infection, and he slipped a couple of small cubes of meat into the boy's mouth.

After wiping his own brow and finding his own canteen to slake his thirst, McCulloch walked to the edge of the wooded hills and began searching until he found a piece of wood that would work all right — at least until he found a doctor, one who would actually treat an Indian boy.

McCulloch stopped. "What are the chances of that?" he said aloud, and looked at the small branch he held. *None,* he answered in his mind. *A Comanche boy? Forget it.*

After tossing that pathetic substitute for a splint, McCulloch went back into the woods and finally found something that would eventually do the job. He used the Indian kid's knife to clear off the bark, and then his own to carve, cut, and whittle until he had what he needed. Satisfied, he took the branch back to the Comanche kid, measured it for length, nodded at how well he had guessed, and snapped the branch in half over his left thigh. After that, he shaved off

98

the sharp edges with his knife and pounded down the ends against a lava rock. Finished with that part of the job, McCulloch stripped buckskin from white-bearded man's leather britches, soaked the strips in the last of the water from the scalp hunter's canteen, and returned to the still unconscious boy.

You break horses for a living, you know a few things about broken bones.

McCulloch steeled himself, hoped the boy was too out of it to feel what he was about to do, and tried to set the broken arm. It took a while, and the boy screamed after the first jerk, then shuddered, wet himself, and groaned. Rubbing his hand over the thin, bony, copper-skinned arm, McCulloch felt satisfied. He used a silk bandana he had found in the saddlebags of the blood bay, wrapped it over the arm, then placed the first of his whittled-down branches onto the upper arm and secured it with the strips from the dead man's pants. The next branch went lower, also secured with buckskin leggings.

The boy looked like hell. No, McCulloch figured, he looked damned ridiculous. But by the Grace of God and if the kid's *puha* — his Comanche power — was with him, he might live. McCulloch laughed. When a

Comanche boy went out on his vision quest, he came back with a new name. So Mc-Culloch decided it was time to give this kid a new name, too. Instead of *Bear Killer,* from how on he would be called *Wooden Arm.*

Suddenly, McCulloch felt hungry. He returned to the bear, cut off some more meat, grabbed his skillet from the saddlebag, and fixed himself some grub. After eating, he dragged the dead men to the edge of the hills, searched them, and lifted from their pockets anything he might need. Then he hauled some dead branches and left those covering the bodies. Another bear, or wolves, or coyotes would eventually find them, but McCulloch wasn't going to waste his energy trying to dig a grave for two pieces of dirt who would not have even bothered covering him with branches had they won that fight.

Finally, McCulloch went back to what was passing for his camp. He threw some more wood — which would not send too much smoke into the sky — onto the fire, leaned back in the grass, adjusted his hat over his eyes, and slept.

He sat up with the Colt in his hand and saw the boy. The Indian boy had rolled over and gasped at the arm splinted in two places

— forearm and upper arm — with tree branches.

The kid saw McCulloch, who holstered his gun and slid the plate of bear meat and fried fat over to the kid, along with his canteen.

The boy stared.

"I am called Matt," he said, making the sign for everything but *Matt.* He signed *Eat.*

Eventually, the boy sat up and used his good hand, fingering bits of bear meat and fat into his mouth. He chewed, but rarely blinked, and his eyes never left McCulloch.

Night came. McCulloch built up the fire, found the bedroll on the blood bay, and spread that over the boy, who still stared. They supped on bear meat and McCulloch's coffee, and slept, though only after McCulloch used some of the Mexican scalp hunter's whiskey as painkiller for Wooden Arm.

The next morning, as the boy watched in silence and with cold black eyes, McCulloch checked the arm, nodded at his skills as a sawbones, and brought Wooden Arm coffee doctored with a shot of whiskey, and more bear meat. After what passed for breakfast, McCulloch busied himself the rest of the morning by rubbing down the horses, keeping a lookout for any riders — especially

101

scalp hunters — and nodding at Wooden Arm every now and then.

It was after noon before the kid spoke.

Not that McCulloch understood more than a handful of Comanche words, but he stopped what he was doing and squatted in front of the kid.

He signed, *How are you called?*

The boy answered, but hell, McCulloch wouldn't remember that if he heard it ten thousand and ten times. He said, "I will call you Wooden Arm." Again he signed, *I am called,* then said, "Matt."

"Watt," the boy said.

"Good enough." McCulloch smiled, then checked the boy's wounds and arm.

The boy turned downright conversational.

In Comanche, "Why did you not kill me or at least count coup?"

McCulloch thought he got all of that. He answered with his hands and fingers, speaking as he signed, *You saved my life.*

The boy's head shook. *No, I protected me,* he signed.

"You were hurt," McCulloch said, and tried his best to sign, *There is no glory in counting coup or taking the scalp of someone injured.* He smiled and tried to add, *But I would have had women singing in my camp had they learned that I counted coup on a*

Comanche brave enough to fight and kill an angry black bear.

He must have done a good job there. The hardness left the boy's eyes and he smiled, then nodded, and muttered something in that rough tongue. He grinned at Matt and said, "Watt."

Matt laughed. "Wooden Arm," he said, and added with his hands, *is my friend.*

The boy straightened. He looked lost in thought, maybe confused. Comanches did not care much for white men and hated white Texas men.

McCulloch went back to work.

That night, eating more bear meat, what looked to be old juniper berries, and chased down with McCulloch's coffee and the last of the Mexican's whiskey, McCulloch was trying to figure out what to do with this kid. He couldn't keep hanging out there forever. If he took the boy to a Comanche camp, he figured the Comanches would kill any white man foolish enough to enter a Comanche camp before anyone had a chance to explain.

While he was considering his options and vaguely wondering Why didn't I just kill this Indian while I had the chance? the boy cleared his throat. McCulloch set down his coffee cup and stared over the fire as

Wooden Arm moved his hands. *Why are you in these hills?*

How he managed to sign with a busted arm splinted in two places amazed the former Texas Ranger.

McCulloch answered honestly. *I seek mustangs.*

Why?

Comanches like horses, McCulloch thought. He signed, *I like horses. They make me rich. Like Comanches.*

The boy laughed.

McCulloch drank more and ate the last of the bear meat on his plate.

The boy signed, *I can help you.*

McCulloch blinked. *Help me do what?*

I know horses, too. I am Comanche. No one knows horses better than Comanches.

McCulloch nodded with honesty. *That is true. Comanches are the best horsemen on the plains.*

I will help you.

Now, McCulloch shook his head. *No. Your arm is —*

Quickly signing, the boy did not let him finish. *A Comanche with one arm is better than ten Texans when it comes to capturing wild mustangs.*

Actually, McCulloch didn't think Wooden

Arm used the word *Texans.* It seemed more like *skunks,* but he figured *Texans* had to be the general idea.

As McCulloch tried to think of a way to respond, Wooden Arm signed, *You save my life. I must repay my debt.*

McCulloch pointed at what passed for the grave of the two dead scalp hunters. *You have repaid your debt.*

The boy shook his head. Then he smiled and said in Comanche while signing. *Then we will be like brothers. You and I will find mustangs. We will become rich. Together.*

And in English, Wooden Arm said, "Is right."

Staring harder, McCulloch wondered how much English this little Indian knew, but Wooden Arm spoke to end McCulloch's suspicion. "Is right. No mas." Then he signed, *I can speak ten words in the Kiowa tongue, but with these hands, I speak all languages. As do you.*

McCulloch brought the coffee cup up, lowered it, and looked over at the two horses. Like that was a sign. Two horses. A Comanche. A Comanche on horseback didn't need two arms to help work a herd of mustangs. A Comanche could likely find a horse herd faster than McCulloch could alone. And two men, even if one of those men was a boy, would have an easier time driving wild mustangs back to his ranch outside of Purgatory City. Yeah, it was a gamble, but something about it struck McCulloch as right.

Never being one to count those chickens — he knew that plans and dreams often broke like eggs — McCulloch couldn't help but believe that he might be able to pull off this crazy idea after all.

He nodded. "Is right," he said, and lifted his hand toward his new partner. They shook the Comanche way first, and then they shook like way of the white Texans.

Wooden Arm grinned, raised his head to the blackening sky, and howled like a coyote.

and
the Range
died, Linton said
Bullet hit him.

CHAPTER NINE

Linton had been a scalp hunter since he had first heard about how the Mexican government in towns close to the American border would pay a handsome amount of money for an Apache or Comanche scalp. In all those years, what had it gotten him — other than a lot of money that he usually spent in two or three nights? A dapple horse. A suit of buckskins. Some disease he never brought up, especially to the prostitutes he paid. Fading eyesight. A bad scar across his back. A bullet that the sawbones in Nogales hadn't been able to dig out of his left knee. And two pards, Bert and Fisher, neither one worth a lick of salt.

"What about Amigo?" Bert asked as they rode into Two Forks, a settlement where horses could be traded, whiskey could be drunk, and a man might be able to rest a spell without answering any questions.

"He's dead," Linton answered.

"You sure?" Fisher asked.

"Maybe you boys want to ride back to the Davis Mountains and see for yourselves." Linton's knee hurt for he had been riding a long damned time. His horse was as played out as his two pards.

"How about Greasy?" Fisher asked.

"Oh, he's definitely dead," Linton said. "Saw the Ranger's bullet hit him."

"Hell," Bert said. "Now that Texas star packer's gonna collect the bounty on that Comanche kid." He leaned out of the saddle and pointed, shaking his finger at Linton the way that schoolteacher did him back in Corpus Christi. "It's yer fault, Linton. You said taking that little kid's scalp would be easy pickin's."

Partners come easy, and Linton considered killing Bert but then he'd have to kill Fisher, too. He was the kind of person who would turn state's evidence to avoid getting his necked stretched.

"Did I ever tell you about the schoolmaster I had back home down south years and years ago?" Linton didn't wait for one of his two surviving pards, each of them a damned fool, to answer his question. He never waited. "I had my pa's razor, and I cut that man's finger off." He laughed at the good memory. "That sent Juliette Jameson and all the other ten kids in that school outside screaming their heads off. And then I used that razor to cut that rotten apple's throat. Boy, I'd never done that before — cut a man's throat like that, is what I mean. Could hardly believe how much blood poured out of that little slit I'd made. And before the light died in that schoolmaster's throat, I tried to use the razor to take the lowdown skunk's scalp. Didn't get much. Didn't even keep it. Just dropped it on his paddle." He nodded with pleasure. "That was the first time I tried to take a scalp. Can't call it my first scalp because, well, hell, boys, I wasn't no more than thirteen." He laughed and climbed out of the saddle beside the stone fortress that made up all there was to Two Forks, except for a few lean-tos, a lot of corrals, and two buildings that passed for barns out in that part of the frontier.

Bert and Fisher remained on their horses. Linton tilted his head to the door that led to Two Forks' sole place of business. "You boys ain't thirsty?"

Bert shook his head, pouting like Linton's brother used to do after Linton has whipped the kid's arse.

Fisher said, "Bert and me don't believe in not avenging the death of a pard."

109

"Two pards," Bert said.

Linton frowned. "You want to go back after that Ranger and that Indian. For a kid's scalp that'll bring us twenty-five pesos? That's not a hundred. That ain't my idea of good business, boys, but if you want to go, turn around and look. Look up at that ridge over yonder way. Not that way, you damned fools, back where we was comin' from."

They looked.

"What do you see?" Linton asked.

"You mean that little bit of smoke?" Fisher answered with another question.

"Exactly."

"That might be that Ranger's campfire. Might be he's takin' care of Amigo, if that greaser's still alive," Bert said.

"That's Comanche smoke, boys."

"Well," Bert said, "maybe the boy kilt the Ranger. And is roastin' him for supper. Then we can ride back to that little valley and kill the buck and get his scalp."

Linton stepped back. "Is that what you want to do, boys?"

He waited.

Fisher and Bert glanced at one another, and Bert was the first to bob his head. Fisher nodded, too.

Linton sighed and said, "Look, boys. That Ranger knows what we look like, so scalp huntin' ain't gonna be such a good way to make a livin' in this part of Texas. My plan is to ride north. They'll be lookin' for us south. Ride up to the Panhandle. Might run across some Comanche camps. Then cut across New Mexico."

He grinned. "They pay for bounties in Sonora, down south of Arizona Territory. I met me a fine girl down in Nogales years back, meanin' Nogales south of the border. In Mexico. We can collect a passel of scalps and sell them to whatever they call the mayor in those Mexican towns. And here's the real genius of my plan."

He paused, liked his idea, and said, "Do you know what you'll find in Mexico and Arizona?" Again, before they could think of an answer, which undoubtedly would be wrong, Linton told them. "Mexicans. Nothin' but Mexicans."

He laughed again. "And do you know somethin' 'bout Mexicans? I never paid that much notice before. Here we know a lot of those greasers, like Amigo, and he would have frowned upon it had he knowed it was somethin' I been thinkin' about. But now that Amigo's burnin' in Hell, I got no reservations." Linton thought they might have figured out his scheme, but their faces told him that had not happened, and would

111

not happen.

So he told them. "Mexican hair can't be told apart from Apache or Comanche hair. We kill us some greasers, scalp 'em, and make their topknots look like it come off some Apache or Comanche buck. Boys, it's a lot easier to kill a Mexican peon than it is to kill a Comanche Dog Soldier."

"Dog Soldiers," Fisher pointed out, "Is Cheyennes. Not Comanches."

Linton shook his head and asked, "Well. You boys comin' in? I'll buy the first two rounds."

Again, he had to wait for the two imbeciles to look at each other. They shook their heads, frowned, and told him, "Sorry," at the same time.

Bert continued. "I don't think I could kill no Mexican who ain't done me no wrong."

"And," Fisher said, "to be honest with you, I'm sort of sick to my stomach about what all we been doin'. I guess seeing Amigo and Greasy cut down in the prime of life, just make me see the light."

Linton nodded. "Well, boys, if that's your play, that's your play." He gestured, though, again at the smoke rising from the hills. "But you better take a good long look at that before you ride back to check on two dead men."

They turned in their saddles and stared at the smoke.

Linton shot them both out of the saddles. Their horses bolted, but only for about twenty yards, so worn out they were. Three men came out the door, but Linton grinned at them and said, "They pulled on me, boys. Thought they could take my scalp and pass it off down below the Rio Grande as a Comanche buck's. Never could stomach a scalp hunter. You boys help me bury them varmints, and I'll let you keep their horses. Worn out, but a little rest, a lot of water, and some hay and they'll be good as new."

He wasn't sure if Fisher or Bert really planned to go back after their now-dead-as-they-were pards, or if they might have planned to go to the law and try to collect the reward on Linton. But the main reason he shot and killed them both was that he figured it would be easier to find men who wouldn't mind being scalp hunters in New Mexico and Arizona. And well, if those two men got arrested by that hard-rock Texas Ranger who had killed Amigo, or any sheriff, marshal, or bounty hunter . . . they would likely give a complete description of Linton. Pards weren't like they used to be.

Hell, he thought, they never was a pard a man could trust.

But in Two Forks, a man minded his business. He could have a whiskey and be on his way. He'd head up north, just like he told those two corpses stiffening on the dirt. Maybe stop in Five Scalps. Then ride west.

CHAPTER TEN

"You gutless puke." Sean Keegan cursed the undertaker. "How much does the county pay you to bury a convicted murderer and owlhoot?"

Undertaker A. Percival Helton wiped his bald head and said in his irritatingly squeamish voice, "That's not the point, sir." He was a short man, pale like most undertakers were, but pudgy unlike most of the men who did business with the dead. Maybe that's because undertaking still proved to be a booming business in the remote frontier of West Texas, and a man could get fat if he ate nothing but chicken fried steaks and greasy enchiladas.

"It damned well *is* the point," Keegan said, and he pointed up at the dead man still swinging from the gallows. "He's dead, and he needs burying, and from the records I found in the county sheriff's office, you signed a contract to bury Tom Benteen, also known as Tom Lovely, alias Lovely Tom. Well, that's him up yonder, you weasel, and I don't like folks walking by and looking up at him like he was the Lord Jesus on the cross. He ain't. He's a rotten, murdering devil whose soul be burning in hell, and I want him cut down and buried. Now. With the rope still around his neck and his face planted down, so he can see exactly where he's going."

"That contract," A. Percival Helton whined, "has been invalidated. It wasn't a legal hanging."

Keegan spit on the grass. "He was to be hanged today. Sentenced legally, upheld by the governor of the Great State of Texas, and he was hanged. Just because the hangman got killed —"

"And there you have it." The high-voiced, rotten snake had found something he could sink his teeth into. "The Benteens shot the bloody hell out of Purgatory City, and I am far, far too busy preparing the dearly departed for their funerals. Citizens of our county and our glorious town. They deserve burying, and, as the only undertaker in Purgatory City since Willard Carradine coughed himself to death from consumption and Alfred Davidson decided that El Paso was more to his liking, I think my duty

116

rests with tending to the needs of those fine people." And just to cut Sean Keegan to the quick, the whining miserable excuse for a man added, "Surely, Titus Bedwell, gallant soldier and God-fearing servant to our state and our county and our country, deserves my attention much more than a pathetic killer, whoremonger, bank robber, arsonist, and horse thief like Lovely Tom Benteen. Or, sir, do you disagree?"

Keegan stared hard into the little pip-squeak's eyes, but damn it all to Dublin if the runt hadn't made a solid point. It was a dirty trick, a hit below the belt, and Keegan had the urge to pick up a rock and smash in A. Percival Helton's skull, and let the ants eat up the brains that would leak out of his head. But . . . well hell, he could not deny giving the late Titus Bedwell the attention a soldier and servant to the army and Texas deserved. Even if Titus Bedwell, had anyone bothered to have asked him, would likely have said he would have wanted to be buried by his fellow soldiers where he had fallen, wrapped in his saddle blanket and with "Taps" played over his grave. No marker. No tears. Just a few rounds at the nearest sutler's store or saloon when the boys got back from the sergeant major's last patrol.

Keegan, though, would not let Helton think he had fooled him. "You just don't want Uncle Zach Lovely or Hank or Bob Benteen to come gunning for you because they'll say you didn't bury poor Tom right. You're a gutless wonder, Helton. You still live with your ma. What kind of man are you? The Benteens and Zach Lovely aren't gonna be gunning for you, you yellow-livered coward. They'll be after my head." He pointed at the corpse. "I did that. Me. Sean Keegan. And I'd do it again."

The last couple of dozen words had been spoken to the fat coward's back. A. Percival Helton was leaving the enclosed compound behind the county courthouse.

This was the way Keegan's day had been going. The sheriff, Juan Garcia — a pretty good man, Keegan thought — had organized a posse and taken off after the men who had raided Purgatory City and left Titus Bedwell and several others, including town marshal Rafe McMillian, and the hangman, poor Mr. Kligerman, dead in the streets. All of the Texas Rangers, commanded by Captain J.J.K. Hollister, had taken off after learning that the Kruger gang had tried to rob a bank down the pike in Deep Flood.

Even the army at Fort Spalding would be

of no help. Colonel John Caxton had led out practically his entire command in search of renegade Comanches who had been hitting a few homesteads, ranches, and way stations across West Texas.

Purgatory City had suddenly become a town without any law.

That thought — and the fact that the posse Sheriff Garcia had quickly and thoughtlessly organized contained most of the hardest men in the county seat — suddenly stretched a wicked little grin across Keegan's rough, Irish face. It was the grin his mother, God rest her glorious soul, always said made her realize that "Ye have that devil's loose and cutting look about you, Sean, me son. Oh, I hope I'll have enough money to go your bail in the morn."

He looked again at the corpse stiffening under the rope and said as he walked out of the enclosed executioner's grounds, "Aye, Mother me dear, but there's no need to worry this fine Texas day. For there be no one in town who can arrest Sean Keegan."

Inside the jail, he went to the desk and found the tin stars in the third drawer he opened. He pinned on a deputy's badge and nodded with satisfaction. Seeing a Bible, he put his hand on the cover and raised the other, though for the life of him, he couldn't remember which it was supposed to be. Right hand raised, left hand on the Bible? No, the Bible be the most important thing, so your right hand should be on it, then your left hand raised. Unless you're left-handed. Which Sean Keegan wasn't.

"I do," he said and walked out without closing the door. It was his town now, and he could do as he wished.

His first stop was at the best general store where he went directly to the back of the store and found the kerosene. *Two should do the job.* He walked to the counter, set the two gallon cans on the top, and nodded at the pimply-faced teenaged clerk. "These ye'll need to be charging to the county, me boy," Keegan told him, and then pulled up his blue shirt to reveal the badge. "Official business from the sheriff's office, ye see."

"Uhhh," the kid said.

"That's a good boy. Just send the bill to Sheriff Garcia." He reached for the cans, but stopped, and pointed. "And ye might as well hand me that bag of candy. Charge it to the county, too. Oh, and I'll need a box of matches, and, yes, yes, of course, two of those cigars. Nah, nay, sonny. Those big, fat ones, with the gold band around their middles. Official business, too. And, sonny, I can't see the label, but does that hair tonic above the licorice say it has alcohol in it? Good. Bloody well good, yes, a bottle of that, and take a bit of licorice for yourself and your service to our county. I'd recommend the red one. Tastes like cherry."

He signed the receipt, so that no one could be able to tell if it had been approved by Juan Garcia or Wild Bill Hickok, gathered his plunder, stuffing the candy and matches in his trousers pocket, biting off the end of one cigar and sticking the other in his shirt pocket, and shoving the bottle of hair tonic into his rear pants pocket. He used the lamp on the counter to light his smoke, thanked the clerk one last time, and picked up his two cans of kerosene before marching to the front door.

There he stopped, and turned back around to look at the clerk.

He'd popped a healthy sized licorice strip into his mouth and began chewing. "Did you forget something, Deputy?"

"No, laddie, but have ye ever seen a Viking funeral?" He had to speak without spitting the cigar out of his mouth.

After swallowing his candy, the kid shook his little head.

"Well, it's a sight to behold, from all the drawings I've seen in magazines and such things. Step outside in ten minutes or so, son, and treat yourself to a glorious sight that hasn't been seen very often since the days of Erik the . . . Great? I doubt if one has ever been seen in these parts." Keegan nodded with finality.

Outside, he set the cans down on the edge of the water trough, pulled hard to get the cigar going good and strong, and yelled, "Ladies and gentlemen, we'll be giving the late Lovely Tom Benteen Lovely a preview of the fires of Hell in a few minutes. All are invited. And ye might want to get that newfangled fire engine out of the shed just in case the wind changes direction."

After taking another puff on the cigar, he grabbed the cans and marched off toward the courthouse.

Reaching the gallows, he set the two cans down and opened them, smelling the potency of the kerosene before remembering, like an idiot, that he had a lighted cigar between his teeth. Keegan removed the Havana with his left hand, blew out smoke, and placed the cigar on the third step. He laughed. "Bloody hell, Keegan, ye haven't even tasted a dram of Irish or porter this hole damned morn." Next he gathered brush and two armfuls of wood from the winter wood pile near the back steps of the courthouse and placed them under the feet of the starting-to-stink corpse of Tom Lovely.

Looking up at the dead man, Keegan grinned. "Lovely, me boy, if I could wait till that crap you put in your britches dried, I might not have needed those cans of kerosene, me lad. Alas." He winked, rose, and walked back to the steps, where he picked up the cigar, out by this time, and returned it to his mouth.

Then he remembered. "That's right, I haven't had a nip today."

He removed the hair tonic, cracked open the bottle on the steps' rails, and took a short pull. He spit out the first mouthful, hoping any shards of glass would come out with that, then drank greedily as he marched up the steps, soaking all the steps and the platform with the first can of kerosene. At the trapdoor, he poured the remnants of the can onto Tom Lovely's head, which hung like the head of a dove that had been shot with birdshot, then had its neck broken over the shotgun barrel to put the poor critter out of its misery.

"Titus Bedwell," he said aloud. "Remember the doves we'd shoot and then fry up for the boys at Fort Spalding? Aye, glorious days those were. Here's to you, Sergeant Major." He took another swig of tonic before shoving the bottle into his back pocket.

He dropped the can through the trapdoor, but it missed hitting Tom Lovely's corpse and clattered onto the ground near the wood pile.

Keegan looked over the fence to the center of Purgatory City's business district and saw the kid from the general store standing on the boardwalk outside the front door of the store. He wasn't saying anything, and definitely — like a good soldier — not leaving his post at the store. Other men and women began to stop and look off to where the kid was staring, which was right at the gallows and Sean Keegan.

He saluted the lad and began whistling a bawdy Irish tune as he pounded down the steps and picked up the last can of kerosene. He poured a trail of fuel from the bottom steps to under the gallows and splashed most of the liquid on the firewood, but also heaved enough onto Tom Lovely's boots, and pants, especially on the groin area.

Keegan tossed the can on the pile and walked back to the steps, where he removed the busted bottle of hair tonic and finished his drink.

Holding the bottle toward the swaying corpse, Keegan said, "Tom, you lousy dog, this is just a wee taste of what you're be feeling for all of eternity. The fires of Hell will be ten thousand times hotter than this." He threw the bottle, which smashed against the misshapen pile of firewood.

Finding the matches, he fished one out and struck it on the top of the rail. He put it to his cigar, which he pulled on until he had a wonderful glow on the tip. This match he shook out and pitched onto the gallows steps, then stepped away, found another match, and struck it against his thumbnail.

He thought, *I surely hope like bloody hell this actually works.* Smiling, he added out loud, "And Lord, if ye'd be so kind, don't let this burn down all of this blight of a city."

The match left his fingers, flickering as it fell. The *whoosh* and whirl of flame almost knocked Sean Keegan on his hindquarters. He staggered back, gasping, wondering if he had singed his hair, and feeling the warmth on his back. The gallows were already crackling.

Realizing that he wasn't on fire himself, Keagan took another hard pull on his cigar and walked to the gate. He saw that the city's volunteer fire department had managed to get the big wagon with water and hoses to the corner of the street. A few of the men in their shield-front shirts came

125

running with buckets and axes, but Keegan stopped them by raising his right hand.

"Nothing to fight yet, me boys," he said, and turned back to watch his handiwork.

My goodness, he thought, *this is not what I expected at all.*

"Oh, hell," said one of the firefighters.

Keegan laughed and tried to enjoy his cigar. "No, this is just a taste of it, like I told Tom Lovely." He looked back at the men and the gathering crowd. "Let it burn, me friends. Let it burn. Let Tom Benteen burn as his soul is already doing. Just make sure the fire doesn't spread. I'll be in my office if you need me, ladies and gents."

And polishing his badge, he moved through the crowd of gawkers as the smoke rose high and black and all so beautiful.

CHAPTER ELEVEN

From an arroyo, Breen had been watching the smoke for a good twenty minutes, letting the two horses pulling the wagon breathe, urinate, and get a little rest. Beside him, Charlotte Platte remained quiet, barely noticing the smoke, but then she hadn't said a word since he had helped her onto the seat. Otto Kruger, on the other hand, had not shut up, wailing about his face and his other injuries, vowing that he'd see Jed Breen in Hell, and that his brother would surely kill him long before he ever got Otto to Purgatory City.

But Kruger hadn't said anything for the past two hours. Not since the gag had been put into his mouth.

"Fire's contained," Breen said at last, looking at Charlotte Platte, handcuffed and with her ankles bound with pigging strings.

She remained impassive, but her face was sunburned. Her hat had blown off into the

127

back of the wagon, but Breen had yet to retrieve it. He turned to check on Kruger, lying on the hard wooden bed of the wagon. His face didn't look sunburned, but after being scalded by that hot coffee, sunburn was the least of the killer's worries.

"I don't think Indians have wiped out Purgatory City," Breen said. "Or your brother, either."

Still, he kept the big Sharps rifle cradled over his lap, and after taking a sip of water from his canteen, then offered some to his female prisoner, who neither accepted nor declined but just stared off into the wasteland of Texas. He screwed on the lid, did not offer Kruger a drink, and left the canteen between them. Finally, he had the horses moving the wagon again, but going slow — playing things safe — so not to raise much dust.

The smoke from Purgatory City wasn't the first Breen had seen since leaving Deep Flood with his prisoners. He had spotted smoke signals a ways off toward the Davis Mountains, and more coming from Comanche Springs. Purgatory City, Breen knew, had the misfortune of being built right along the Great Comanche War Trail that led from the Comanche stronghold in Indian Territory and the Texas Panhandle all the way to

Mexico. Of course, once this entire region had been part of the Comanche stronghold. And while the Comanches might not still have the numbers — thanks to smallpox — to control all of the territory, they still could be a deadly force, especially to one man traveling in a wagon with two prisoners.

Breen had already planned an emergency departure. His horse, saddled and rested, was tethered to the back of the wagon. If Comanches, or Apaches, or even Mexican bandits or too many outlaws attacked, he could mount his horse and gallop off as fast as he could, leaving the scarred Kruger brother and Charlotte "The Widowmaker" Platte for the attackers. Indians and bandits would likely see the profit in a wagon and two horses, a scalp from a defenseless man and, hell, a woman. Especially a woman. It would seem the wiser choice than chasing a man on a good horse who had a long-range rifle. Sure, it wouldn't be the noblest thing a man could do, but, hell, hadn't Jed Breen been dubbed a jackal?

Keeping the wagon in the arroyo, Breen had maybe a half mile more before he reached the sandy washout that would serve as a ramp back to the road. He had used the path before. As a bounty hunter, Jed Breen knew the advantages of keeping out of the skyline when you wanted not to be seen, and in this country, there weren't too many places where you couldn't be seen.

The smoke from town bothered him, though he couldn't quite explain why. Buildings caught fire in frontier towns all the time. A grease fire at some café. An exploding lantern in a home. A drunken prostitute falling asleep with a cigarette in her lips. Teenage boys playing with matches in a livery stable. Even arsonists with nothing better to do. Breen had survived infernos in Fort Worth . . . Leavenworth . . . Laramie . . . and Prescott, Arizona Territory. The last one made Breen grin. He had set that fire himself to flush out Wade Friday, but hadn't counted on the wind or all the rotgut whiskey Wade Friday had spilled. But he came through all right, both he and Wade Friday, and when some citizens demanded to know what had started the conflagration, Breen blamed Friday. That added another year to Friday's sentence. He probably ought to be getting out of Yuma just about now.

Two minutes later Breen thought he had only himself to blame. He had been spending too much attention on all that smoke — off across the flats again, and a sliver coming way off in the mountains, and especially down the pike where Purgatory City should be. Watching smoke instead of the fire he carried in the wagon.

Charlotte Platte moved like a wildcat. He caught her movement out of the corner of his eye, and turned, dropping the leather reins, reaching with his left hand for the Sharps on his lap, and bringing up his right to deflect the blow. Too late. For a woman who killed with poison, she moved damned fast.

The metal cuff on her left wrist caught him on the corner of his head, stunning him. Without a grip on the reins, the horses started moving faster, excited and nervous from the lurching in the wagon. Breen saw stars, heard his curse and his groan, and felt himself toppling over the wooden frame of the wagon.

He landed with a thud, rolling over to keep himself from getting his neck, back, legs, or head smashed by the rear wheel. He kept rolling, then came up, fought off the spell of dizziness, and felt blood pouring into his left eye.

"Hiya! Hiya! Move, damn your hides, move!" Charlotte Platte screamed. She slid over to the side of the seat, bent over, fetched the lines, and began whipping the team furiously. Breen saw his horse's rear hooves and tail flying like a cavalry guidon and full gallop — but only for a moment. Dust quickly blocked out the wagon, his horse, and his two prisoners.

He drew his pistol, but held his fire, not wanting to hit the horse. Brushing away the blood with his left hand, he rose, found his hat, and pulled it down hard over the left side. The hat band tightened over the cut Charlotte Platte had given him, and that might serve as a bandage. Breen holstered the revolver and picked up the Sharps as he ran after the wagon.

A moment later, he stopped and looked up above the top of the arroyo. Dust rose like smoke, higher and higher, and Breed cursed. Sure, the smoke over in the Davis Mountains and the smoke off toward Comanche Springs were too far away for whoever was sending those signals to come riding over and kill him. What party those signals were meant for worried him.

He could not consider that. He was afoot. Granted he could walk to Purgatory City in just a couple of hours, and a man afoot might even have a better chance at getting through unnoticed in this country, if he played it smart and took his time. But he had a substantial payday in that wagon, and Jed Breen prided himself on his professionalism.

Leaning forward, he took off running, keeping his head down to avoid the blinding dust and to watch out for rattlesnakes.

Boots were not meant for running. He had a pair of Apache-style moccasins for times like these, but they were on the saddlebags on his horse. He stumbled over rocks, twisting this way and that, but never losing his feet or his focus. The horses, well-rested, enjoyed the chance to run, and before long, Breen didn't have to worry about being blinded by dust. He did not slow down, though. He couldn't. That was his money driving the wagon and that was his money bouncing around in the back of the wagon.

He saw the two horses first, coming up the loamy ramp at the bend in the arroyo. Breen cursed the woman as he saw bouncing high off the bench before coming back down hard. He cursed her, driving horses that fast to get out of the arroyo, fearing she would break his horse's legs or neck or everything. Even before he had barely started the curse, he saw the back of the wagon, and Otto Kruger bounced up, too, only he came down hard on the left side. From Breen's perspective, Kruger didn't land back in the wagon. Breen caught just a glimpse of his horse, then dust covered the top of the arroyo and the road.

Breen made himself run faster. His head throbbed and bled, and Breen thought of every curse word he knew, but did not vocalize them. It was damned hard to curse and breathe and run in this part of Texas.

All right, he thought as he ran, *how far can this wicked little poisoner get? Her feet are bound. She's wearing handcuffs, and I have the key.*

He knew if she stuck to the road, she'd ride straight into Purgatory City, where there was a U.S. Army fort nearby, town lawmen, county lawmen, and Texas Rangers of the Frontier Battalion. And quite a few ornery and inquisitive citizens. Every one of them would wonder what a woman was doing in handcuffs with her legs tied at the ankles.

He also knew that his female prisoner could make up some convincing lies. She could say she had been abducted, just managed to escape. If his horse didn't pull free, or get killed, some men might find Breen's identification in the saddlebags and his grip. With his reputation, that was not going to help him in the least.

The way she was driving, Charlotte Platte might damn well wreck the wagon, kill all three horses, and herself and Otto Kruger.

That would have been most unfortunate. The reward poster for Charlotte Platte said the bounty would be paid upon delivery — alive and with proper identification — to the county sheriff in Precious Metal, Arizona Territory, for trial. They didn't want her dead. The citizens wanted the honor and privilege of hanging that murderess themselves. Oh, they would accept the body of Poison Platte — but pay only thirty-five bucks for a corpse, and that was hardly worth the effort for a man with Jed Breen's skills.

He noticed the dust fading, and over his heavy breathing, slamming heart, pounding boots, and jingling spurs — he would have stopped to remove those last two, but couldn't spare the time — he realized that he no longer heard the hooves or wheels of the wagon. The dust no longer left a trail, and Breen understood that Charlotte Platte had stopped the wagon.

And that would be the last thing she would do.

He slowed to a walk, then lowered himself and eased his way to the rise that wary travelers used to leave the arroyo before it turned west and into no man's country.

He stopped briefly, trying to recognize the sounds on the road. Waiting until his breathing was almost normal, he moved to the edge, dropped to his belly, and slithered up the dirt ramp, stopping well before he reached the top.

His hat came off, and he cringed at the pain. Felt the blood leak down over his eyebrow, eyelashes, over his eye and down his face. After laying his hat on the dirt, he busied himself untying his bandana, which he used to wipe the dirt and dust off the Sharps. Next he checked his revolver. Satisfied, he tied the bandana over the head wound. He had time to take off the spurs, which he did without making any noise. Carefully and silently, he eased himself up the ramp, lowering his head as he inched forward with the patience of an oyster and speed of an earthworm.

The noise he now understood. Otto Kruger was moaning, damned near whimpering. But someone was talking, and it wasn't Charlotte the widowmaker, alias Poison Platte.

CHAPTER TWELVE

McCulloch let Wooden Arm lead the way, admiring how the Comanche boy sat in the white man's saddle, how far he could lean to either side, studying the ground for sign. If McCulloch tried to lean that far, he would have been tasting gravel. And Wooden Arm had only one good arm to use.

The former Texas Ranger did not spend the entire morning marveling over the boy's ability on horseback. Keeping the Winchester repeater handy, he looked at the sky and saw the white smoke puffing into the cloudless blue above the mountains. That wasn't a campfire. It wasn't a forest fire. The wisps of smoke rose at intervals, and he knew it was a signal fire. White men didn't do that. Scalp hunters definitely wouldn't give away their location. So it had to be Indians. Comanches? Kiowas? Apaches?

When he and the boy stopped around

noon for jerky, stale crackers, and water, Wooden Arm signed, *I know you saw the smoke.*

I am not blind, McCulloch signed his guide.

The myth, of course, courtesy of hack writers churning out dime novels about Kit Carson, Daniel Boone, and other frontier adventurers, was that Indians conversed with smoke the way the army used Morse code. In reality, the smoke was used just to let someone know someone was around.

McCulloch made the sign of the snake, which meant Comanches.

The boy grinned and shrugged, which caused him to flinch from the pain in his busted arm.

Maybe we should rest, McCulloch signed.

Wooden Arm's head shook savagely, and he motioned with his good arm toward the area where the smoke signals had been seen. *Perhaps they are Comanche,* the boys hands and fingers said, *but they could be my enemies. I would like to find our mustangs and get out of these mountains.*

"So would I." McCulloch did not have to use his hands and fingers. Wooden Arm understood those words simply from the tone.

McCulloch tightened the cinches of both

horses, and offered to assist Wooden Arm, but the boy shook his head and practically leaped into the saddle. He said something in his own tongue and squirmed around until he managed to find something that might not have been comfortable to a teenage Comanche but was the best he was going to do. If Matt McCulloch spoke Comanche, he figured he might have blushed at the blasphemy Wooden Arm showered upon big Texas saddles.

"Well," McCulloch said as he swung into his saddle, "If it were the other way around, and I had to sit in a Comanche saddle, my backside would be raw and my huevos would be blue."

Wooden Arm stared, and McCulloch signed what he had said.

The boy cackled with delight, and kept breaking into fits of laughter for the next five minutes as they followed a deer trail up and over a gentle slope.

Holding the reins to the black in his left hand, McCulloch broke open the turd and rubbed it with his fingers, which he wiped on his chaps before looking up at Wooden Arm, still mounted. The wide grin that stretched across Wooden Arm's face was practically a reflection of McCulloch's own bright smile. He nodded at the entrance to the canyon.

Wooden Arm glanced, his head likewise bobbing, and turned back to the horse trader before dismounting easily despite the heavy splints encumbering his arms. *I will go,* he signed.

Before McCulloch answered, the boy continued. *You smell like a Texan.*

Once again, the Comanche noun for *Texan* was not overly complimentary.

I am Comanche. I smell like a horse. Your stink will scare off this herd.

"All right." McCulloch nodded toward the canyon.

The boy sprinted like a deer, ignoring the pain that must have shot up and down his busted arm.

Once the boy had disappeared, McCulloch pulled the horses to the edge of the mountain wall, so he would be hard to see if anyone was watching from the ridges above. He had not seen any more smoke, but he figured to play things safe. He hadn't survived long in this country by being careless. His left hand held the reins to Wooden Arm's horse. The right kept a firm hold on the reins to the black. The right hand also gripped the Colt revolver.

How much time passed, McCulloch

wasn't sure, for he had never been one to watch the minute hands on a clock, and he had been too busy looking for any signs of danger to get an idea of the location of the sun. But he saw Wooden Arm running lightly out of the canyon's mouth — and he had not heard a damn thing. That boy, splinted arm and all, would make a damned good warrior. McCulloch certainly wouldn't want to meet him in these mountains in a couple of years.

Without even needing to catch his breath, despite being bathed in sweat, and his mouth tight from the pain in his busted arm, Wooden Arm started up the conversation immediately. The kid was not one to beat around the bush.

There is a spring. Good water. The boy grinned widely and rubbed his stomach. He continued. *More than six herds come here for water. It is hard to read the signs for they have been coming to this spring for a long time.*

McCulloch needed Wooden Arm to repeat part of that before he got the gist of what the Comanche was saying, and the boy promised to slow down with his hand and fingers, but it was hard because he was so excited. McCulloch smiled. He had been doing this far longer than Wooden Arm had been alive, but he understood that feeling. He felt his own excitement hard to conceal.

One herd is small. Eight. Ten. Twelve horses. One is huge. Perhaps as many as sixty.

"Sixty." McCulloch whistled, before he began to shake his head. "That's too many for the two of us to handle." He did not sign that, but the disappointment in Wooden Arm's eyes told McCulloch that the boy understood.

We can set a trap, Wooden Arm signed. *For the herd that you say is right for us.*

After McCulloch nodded, they reined their horses and went to work.

Sitting in the trees that lined the canyon's mouth, Wooden Arm pointed at the Winchester cradled across McCulloch's lap. *Do you use that . . . on the stallion?* the boy's fingers and good hand asked.

McCulloch shook his head. Some mustangers would try to shoot the lead stallion of a herd, not to kill it, but to stun the horse. Then they'd capture the stallion and the others. He knew one or two men who were extremely good at that. But it was too damned risky, and more than a few greenhorns who thought they were the best sharpshooter since William Tell had killed

142

many an innocent mustang stallion. Mc-
Culloch used his hands to let the boy know
that he preferred to capture his horses the
way of the warrior. Guns were made for
hunting — and for staying alive in this
rough world.

The kid nodded solemnly.

They had led their horses up and over the
ridge, tucking them in a hollow and secur-
ing them so they would not wander off and
would be hard to steal without making a lot
of noise. As long as the wind didn't change
directions, their horses wouldn't catch the
scent of the mustangs — and vice versa —
whenever the wild herds showed.

As both boy and horse trader had expected, the first herd showed up at dusk.
The stallion, a proud blood bay, stopped a
good distance from the narrow entrance to
the canyon that led to the spring. Sniffed.
Pawed. Rode this way and that, shaking its
head. When a young colt, impatient with
thirst, tried to bolt to the canyon, the stallion charged and rammed the young black
hard, knocking it down. The horse rolled
over, came to its feet, and cowered as the
stallion reared, letting its forelegs kick the
air with a fury of violence. It was enough to
send the black colt back to rear of the herd.

Five minutes passed before the stallion

whickered, and galloped toward the entrance. The rest of the horses followed, and both the Comanche and the Texan had to turn their heads from the dust.

Once that had settled, the boy looked greedily at McCulloch, who shook his head. This was the large herd, far too many for a man and a boy with a badly broken arm to handle, even if the boy was a Comanche. Although Wooden Arm could not hide his disappointment, he slowly nodded for he understood. When the mustang stallion led its mares, colts, and fillies out of the canyon an eternity later, Wooden Arm signed to McCulloch, *I hope they did not drink all the water.*

Laughing, McCulloch picked up his canteen and tossed it to the Comanche teen.

The next herd was too small. The one after that McCulloch dismissed because the stallion, a dun, seemed too old, and the coats of the mares and younger horses did not pass the horseman's muster. Besides, one of the offspring looked to be more ass than mustang, and the horses were gaunt, easy pickings for a bear or pack of wolves. They let these drink and leave.

By then the sun was beginning to sink, and McCulloch wondered if the other herds had found another watering hole, for this one surely drew a large crowd.

Maybe there were some night herds, McCulloch began to think, and the others would not come until the moon rose — if they came at all.

Both Texan and Comanche raised their heads and stared into the thickening darkness. Both had heard the whinny of a horse. A pinto stallion appeared. It pranced around, sniffing, suspicious, and chased away two thirsty colts. Wooden Arm could not stifle his gasp of amazement. Tensing, McCulloch froze, wondering if the stallion had heard the noise, for horses had amazing hearing. Apparently not. The pinto came prancing forward, but stopped again, turned and ran back to the herd. Biting off his curse, McCulloch waited, sweated, feeling the heart slamming against his ribs and chest muscles.

Hell, Matt McCulloch even crossed his fingers.

A long time passed, then the pinto stallion whinnied, reared, and galloped off — the other horses following. Their hooves thundered past and when the last of the stragglers entered the canyon, McCulloch nodded. Quickly, he and Wooden Arm slid one juniper branch across the entrance. Then another. Another. Working furiously until they had made a gate ten feet high.

The noise, however, had alerted the pinto, for it came charging back, head low, eyes blazing, and rammed into the fence the Comanche and Texan had made. The logs quaked but did not break. The stallion went down, came up, shook its head and ran as though it planned to leap over the fence, but there was not enough room for a horse to make that jump. It slid to a stop at the last moment, then turned around, and began kicking the juniper poles with its rear hooves. Kicking, snorting, squealing. An older colt ran to help, but the pinto, furious, bit the claybank's neck. As leader of this herd, the pinto was not going to let this younger male take over. He had too much pride, too much strength, and too much power. The claybank reared, almost tried to fight, but relented, and trotted back to the water hole.

For four hours, the mustang stallion fought until it was bloodied and defeated. But the juniper posts remained, and the defeated animal snorted, turned, head down, and walked wearily back to the water hole.

It was too dark to read hand signs now, so McCulloch spoke quietly, "Let's get our horses back over here." He walked toward the path that led over the hill, and Wooden Arm understood. He followed.

An hour later, they sat in a cold camp, gnawing on jerky and drinking water from the canteens, staring at the gate they had built.

Other herds arrived with the moon's rise, but saw and smelled the humans, and galloped off toward Limpia Creek or some other water hole.

McCulloch looked at the moon, then at the gate he and Wooden Arm had managed to build, and finally at his Comanche partner. "Tomorrow, the fun begins."

He didn't need to use hand signs or speak Comanche for the boy to understand.

Wooden Arm's head nodded with a solemnity that was erased by his gleaming smile.

CHAPTER THIRTEEN

"Hahahahahahahahahahahahaha!" Wooden Arm's laughter bounced across the canyon rocks like a ricocheting bullet and went on and on that McCulloch wondered if the echoes would ever die down. When they finally did, he brushed the sand off his gloves and chaps and tried to get most of it off his beard-stubbled face.

The Comanche boy laughed again, pointing with his good hand at the horseman, whose bones, joints, and innards were starting to remind him of his age. The kid said something in that throaty tongue of his, which McCulloch figured went something along the lines of *You ride a horse damned funny.*

McCulloch watched the pinto circling around the round corral he and the boy had managed to fashion. He shook the cobwebs out of his head and told Wooden Arm, "You were a lot more fun to have around when you just talked with your hands."

But he knew this had to be done. Break that pinto stallion, and the rest of the horses would fall in line. Oh, he knew with all certainty that the colts, especially the older ones, those beginning to think they might be able to challenge the pinto for leadership of the entire herd, would require breaking. Gentling any of these mustangs would mean more bruises. He spit out blood from the cut in his bottom lip. And more blood. But it might be worth it.

Texas cowboys and ranchers were prejudiced against pintos, but this more black than white piebald was special. Solid, sturdy, with a keen mind. He could run like nothing McCulloch had ever seen. And the way that mustang stallion fought? Hell, this horse had more guts than all the defenders of the Alamo.

He had been at it since dawn, and a glance at the sky told him it wasn't yet nine in the morn, though he felt like he had aged fifteen years in those few hours, and had damned near broken his neck six or seven times. That horse had bucked him off nigh a million times. At least, that what it felt like to McCulloch. He found his lariat, shook out a loop, and on his third try, made his throw over the feisty mustang's neck. He fought like hell to get the squealing, bucking son of a gun to the center post, and saw the smoke and felt the heat as the horse pulled the rope tight across the piñon post. Once McCulloch had it tight and the devil on four legs stopped fighting, Wooden Arm was there to throw a blanket over the pinto's head.

That had a way of calming every wild mustang McCulloch had ever had to break. When an animal like this fighter couldn't see, it settled down.

"Keep it there," McCulloch told the Comanche, then tightened the cinch, checked the riggings to the stirrups and bridle, shook his head and wondered just how addled his brain must be. Nodding at the boy, he removed the lariat gently from around the horse's neck, pitched it to the ground, took hold of the reins, tried to screw his rear end all the way through the leather of the saddle, the wool of the blanket, and the hide and muscle of the pinto all the way to the horse's spine.

Another nod, and Wooden Arm used his good hand to jerk the blanket off the mustang's head.

Instantly, hellfire ignited, and McCulloch felt his backbone being smashed up and down so hard that he figured he would leave this canyon a good four inches shorter than when he had entered it.

He lasted seven jumps before he felt himself sailing into the air like one of those hot-air balloons he had seen at a fair one time in Austin during an election.

At noon, McCulloch drank some coffee but didn't think his stomach, jostled as it had been, could handle any solid food. Hell, he wasn't sure he'd even be able to keep the coffee down. One cup, that was all he wanted, and he pitched the empty tin container into Wooden Arm's lap, and walked back to the center post and the sweaty, nasty, sand-coated black and white mustang.

"You ain't gonna win this fight," he whispered into the horse's ear while checking the bridle. "You know that as well as I do. And someone's gonna catch you if I don't, but he won't be as good to you as I will. So me and you need to come to an understanding, and that means this. I'll never break you. No one could. But I can make you trust me, and I damned sure will trust you. You're that kind of hoss."

The horse threw him into the trees on that ride.

"That's one black-hearted devil," Mc-

Culloch said, spitting out juniper berries after Wooden Arm fished him out of the mess. The horse circled around, and McCulloch noticed one of the black markings in the middle of the coat of white running down the horse's neck to his underside between the front legs was shaped just like a heart. A black heart.

"Black Heart." McCulloch sighed. Then he laughed. "That's your name from now on." He laughed again, and when he looked at Wooden Arm and saw the confusion on the Comanche kid's face, McCulloch laughed even harder. So hard, he reckoned the boy figured McCulloch's mind had been jarred so much by all the rides that he was now feeble-minded, loco, a mindless wonder.

McCulloch summoned up enough endurance to make his hands and fingers move, and he told the Comanche what he had named the pinto.

Wooden Arm laughed at that, too, then they went back to that backbreaking monster of a horse.

By three that afternoon, McCulloch had worn the horse out. Oh, he wasn't gentled — not by a damned sight — but with a few more rides, a lot of hours, and maybe just a sugar cube or two, McCulloch would have that horse the way he wanted him. Hell, if Black Heart could change his colors, become either all black or all white, Matt McCulloch might keep that hard-rock, determined son of a gun for his own. Use him to breed other relentless, stubborn, strong-willed horses.

He swung out of the saddle and rubbed his hand over Black Heart's neck. "Good boy," he told the horse, but left the saddle and bridle on so the mustang would continue to get used to the feel.

He staggered over to the smokeless fire Wooden Arm had built, and the kid filled a cup with coffee, which he handed to McCulloch.

Is it good? the Comanche signed, meaning the horse, not McCulloch's coffee.

"Good enough," McCulloch answered, sipped the coffee, and turned around, nodding at the horse as it trotted through the opened gate into the other pen with the other thirty-nine horses. McCulloch lowered himself to the ground, feeling every bruise, cut, ding, and knot he had endured this day. He stretched out his legs and wondered how the devil he would be able to get his boots off. By thunder, he wouldn't even try. He drank more coffee before turning to his

Indian partner.

"We'll rest here tonight. Get an early start in the morning." Then he remembered he had to use sign language to communicate to Wooden Arm, so he translated his words with hands and fingers. *I have a place north of here,* he signed. *With luck, you and I will be able to get these horses to my ranch. Then we'll see who wants to buy them.*

Wooden Arm signed, *Not Black Heart. You must not sell him. He is too good for anyone but you.*

McCulloch's hands replied, *What about you? We are* — he paused trying to figure out how to sign the word *partners.* When he could not think of anything, he signed, *brothers.*

The kid's face brightened. *Brothers,* he signed. *Yes.* But his head shook, and he pointed back to the pinto. Facing McCulloch again, Wooden Arm managed to say with one hand, *He belongs to you. I say so. He will respect only you, my brother. And this you know is true. I have spoken.*

The conversation was over, which was fine with McCulloch. He could sleep for two days straight, but he only had tonight.

With only one good arm, the Comanche

teen was something to behold. Matt McCulloch had gone through his share of partners in his years catching and raising horses — thoroughbreds, quarter horses, mustangs. He figured Wooden Arm might be the best pard he ever had in this line of work.

Half that morning, after they got the mustangs out of the canyon and on their way to McCulloch's ranch outside Purgatory City, McCulloch spent time watching the boy in amazement. Whenever a colt or older horse, male or female, got enough courage to try to break out of the line, the boy managed to head the runaway off, and send it loping back into the string. He would raise that busted arm with the wooden splints over his head, which had to hurt like blaze, and that probably frightened the devilment out of those horses. How the kid could ride like that . . . well, a man, even a Texan, had to respect an Indian — a Comanche — for his ability on horseback and with horses.

When the herd loped along casually, without one of the animals challenging the new leaders of the bunch, the Comanche kid sang out boisterously, proudly. If the kid had been on his vision quest, maybe he had found it with Matt McCulloch's help. Yeah, the horseman thought, they were partners. In the truest sense. They had helped each other, saved each other's lives, and had a herd of great-looking animals to show for it . . . providing they could get them away from the Davis Mountains, Comanches or Apaches or Kiowas, or even scalp hunters. It was a long way to McCulloch's ranch, but the black and white pinto was leading the way behind the kid riding point and Mc-Culloch on his black, bringing up the rear.

He saw the smoke again, of course, puffs rising from the mountains. Wooden Arm must have seen the signals, too, but he paid no attention. He focused on the mustangs — the mustangs he co-owned with Matt McCulloch.

With a kid like that, McCulloch figured he had better than an even-money chance of making it out of the mountains and across the miles to Purgatory City alive.

CHAPTER FOURTEEN

From the top of the mesa, mounted on his fine pinto horse of brown and white, Broken Buffalo Horn frowned at the scene below. His Comanche friend, Lost His Thumb, lowered the binoculars he had taken off a dead bluecoat four years ago. He still wore the blue kepi, doctored with eagle feathers, ribbons, and the scalp of the white-eyed soldier who had worn the cap and carried the see-far glasses. Frowning at the older warrior, Lost His Thumb said, "Now we know why your son did not respond to our signals."

The buffalo headdress was heavy on Broken Buffalo Horn's head, but not as heavy as his heart. The shirtless Comanche nodded briefly, but did not look away from the scene below.

By his best count, a cruel Texan had captured about forty or so mustangs from the mountains, and was driving them north

157

toward the settlements in the dry country near the Pecos River to the west. Those horses would give a man like Broken Buffalo Horn more power than he already had in the camps in the Staked Plains of Comanchería. But the cruel Texan had something else, something more valuable to the holy man. He had Broken Buffalo Horn's only son.

Oh, the holy man had six other children spread among his four wives, but those were all girls. And what good was a girl to a Comanche man of medicine, a man of vision? His son had been sent out on his vision quest two weeks ago. When he had not returned to the village that had moved down south for the winter, Broken Buffalo Horn, Lost His Thumb, and Killed A Skunk had ridden out of the village, while the others — including Broken Buffalo Horn's wives, daughters, and one granddaughter — prepared to return to the Staked Plains to find shelter in the canyons that cut through the country of Comanche medicine. To a place protected from the bluecoats, the spotted death, and the more and more white travelers who dared cross what once had been territory owned and ruled and settled by only the Comanches and their allies.

"What has this white man done to your

son's left arm?" Killed A Skunk asked.

"It is a way to keep him a prisoner." Broken Buffalo Horn spoke with finality, as though he knew, when in fact he had no idea what had happened to his son, a boy who had barely seen thirteen winters. Nor did he understand why his son seemed to be helping the one white man. And what power must a white man like this one have to turn a Comanche teen's son into a tree!

A horse bolted from the trotting herd, and the boy taken prisoner by the hated Texan turned his horse quickly and with only one hand holding the reins, galloped, pivoted, twisted, and intercepted the young colt. Within moments, the boy had managed to send the horse back into the herd while the white man — the one white man — rode at the rear, keeping the mustangs moving, not even offering to help.

But these Texans were lazy men.

Killed A Skunk whistled. "Your son rides like he is part of a horse."

"With only one arm," Lost His Thumb said, his own head bobbing with admiration.

That, at least, made Broken Buffalo Horn smile briefly.

After putting the see-far glasses into the leather container behind his Comanche saddle, Lost His Thumb said, "We can ride down easily and kill this Texan. Take his horses. Return to our camp. They will sing songs about us."

"And about your son," added Killed A Skunk.

"We would have many horses," Lost His Thumb said, then quickly added, "*You* will have many horses. And we will have whatever you think is right for us to have."

"We will also have another scalp. There will be one less white man for us to kill." Killed A Skunk waited for Broken Buffalo Horn's response.

"Not yet," he said at last. If this white man had the power to turn a Comanche boy's arm into a tree branch, what other magic might he hold? Even if his power vanished, the white man, by his dress, was Texan, and Texans had killed many Comanches. It would be too easy, since the Texan had a gun and the only son of Broken Buffalo Horn had one good hand, and another arm turned into wood, for the Texan to kill Broken Buffalo Horn's son. And Broken Buffalo Horn was nearing his seventieth summer. He knew he likely would never be able to have another son. Just weakling daughters. That thought made him spit.

"No," he said, and nodded at the finality

of his decision and his wisdom. "We will follow this powerful Texan with much magic. Perhaps we will learn where he gains this power. Imagine if we could turn all of the Texans, all of the bluecoats, all of the Mexicans, and white-eyed fools who cross Comanchería into trees."

His friends nodded at the old man's wisdom.

"We would never be cold in winter with all the wood to burn," Killed A Skunk said.

"And have poles for our teepees without having to go into the hills or along the riverbanks," Lost His Thumb added.

"And," Broken Buffalo Horn said, "this man is taking the mustangs to the north and west. Let us follow him at a distance, and let him do the hard work, him and my son who appears to be doing most of the work."

"Because he is Comanche," Lost His Thumb said. "He knows how to work, unlike this lazy, though very powerful, Texan."

Broken Buffalo Horn nodded his approval although he did not care much for the interruption. He continued. "They are taking the herd of fine ponies northward. That is closer to our own camp for the spring and summer. So when we kill the Texan and free our son, take the scalp and all of those fine ponies, we will not have as far to drive them."

It was the right decision. Broken Buffalo Horn knew this.

He pointed to the dead spines of a cactus and dried weeds that would burn. "Light a fire, my friend, Lost His Thumb," the medicine man ordered. "We must let my son know we are here, that we see him. That we follow him, that we will come — or we will die — and we will rescue him from this powerful enemy. We will find a way to make his arm a Comanche arm again. One not like a piñon branch."

"Unless it is a juniper," Killed A Skunk said.

Lost His Thumb almost laughed, but the way the medicine man glared at Killed A Skunk told Lost His Thumb he should show respect and remain quiet. He gathered the tinder and wood, broke the dead cactus spine into manageable kindling, and used the iron and flint to start the flame. Killed A Skunk rode around the area on his yellow horse, never dismounting for he was a Comanche. Leaning out of the saddle, he picked up wood that would work for the signal fire.

Broken Buffalo Horn sat on the back of his horse and watched the riders and the horses stretch into a long line. Eventually, he removed his buffalo headdress, wiped the sweat off his forehead, then looked down at the dust-covered, heavy headdress with the left horn broken off. It had been broken off by the powerful bullet from one of the heavy rifles favored by the white men who killed buffalo. He'd changed his name from Brave Deer to Broken Buffalo Horn, which made him even more powerful.

Lost His Thumb earned his name after drinking too much of the white man's firewater and then playing with a white man's trap for beaver. He could have changed his name to Killed A Bluecoat, or Sees-Far-With-Bluecoat-Glasses, but he had become used to having four fingers on his left hand. He had killed that bluecoat by himself, charging when no one else would, armed with only tomahawk and knife, and the man had shot with his long gun, but missed. Lost His Thumb was upon him, and seeing his bravery and what he did to the man whose scalp he took, turned the other bluecoats into women. They fled across the creek and did not stop raising dust until they were back in their fort.

Killed A Skunk wasn't the most respected names in the village, but the skunk he had killed had been rabid, and would have wreaked death and madness and destruction on the camp had he not had the courage to rush up to the deadly, diseased, stinking animal and put a lance through its body. Younger, more accomplished warriors had not dared approach such an animal. Killed A Skunk's name might make Kiowas and Comancheros laugh, but no one laughed in front of the warrior.

Yes, Broken Buffalo Horn was a powerful man among all the Comanche villages. He had strong men of power, brave men, and good friends. Broken Buffalo Horn knew he needed such friends, such brave men, on the journey they were about to take. They would need even more strength and more power to free Broken Buffalo Horn's son from the terrible Texan.

CHAPTER FIFTEEN

Jed Breen had given up seeing out of his left eye as long as blood continued to pour over his eyebrow and eye, a slow, oozing flow that seemed as thick as maple syrup. But, hell, with a long rifle, he usually closed his left eye before taking aim and squeezing the trigger. He rose up just low enough so he might not get his brains blown all the way to Austin but high enough so that he could see what the hell was happening on the Presidio-Purgatory City pike.

"Señora," Breen heard a man's voice say, but he couldn't make out the rest of the words, though he could figure things out once he got the lay of the land.

The man on the buckskin gelding wore striped britches, a white cotton shirt, and colorful serape of orange, red, purple, white, and black stripes. Bandoliers of ammunition crisscrossed his chest. His sombrero was of the sugarloaf style with a fancy concho headband. His hair was black, greasy, stringy and hung well past his shoulders, and his mustache and goatee needed the scissors and talents of a tonsorial artist in a Kansas cattle town. His left eye was covered with a black patch. He held a big pistol, hammer cocked, at Charlotte Platte's ample bosom.

Breen could blow that bandit out of the saddle easily, but then he'd have to reload the Sharps. And two other bandits blocked the road. One of them held the reins to a fourth horse, but Breen saw no fourth man. That was troublesome. He slid down a few inches, no longer able to see the men, but listening to what the leader said, while mainly trying to hear something unnatural — the chime of a spur, the turning over of a stone, or the cocking of a weapon, the slipping of a knife from a scabbard, even a sneeze or some heavy breathing.

Surely, the bandits, undoubtedly based on the other side of the Rio Grande, had made a hard ride north looking to waylay some travelers. They'd make their haul and hightail it for the Rio Grande at Presidio. They'd never make a move on anyone without someone covering their behinds. But, Breen had to figure out, where?

The black-patched leader fired question

after question, always speaking Spanish, at Charlotte Platte, who never answered. Maybe she didn't understand the Mexican lingo. Maybe she just didn't want to say a damn thing. Perhaps she was even too busy silently praying that the man whose head she had cut open, the man who she had almost run over with the wagon he had bought in Deep Flood, and the man who had promised to split the reward for that still-moaning Kruger brother might rescue her from that old fate worse than death. Breen figured that was exactly what those four bandits had in mind for Poison Platte.

Breen's problem was that some stupid, worthless, miserable idiot kept moaning, making it harder to figure out where the fourth man might be. The guttural-throated hombre with the black patch over his left eye spit out a slew of ungentlemanly curses and barked out an order to one of the other bandits. Breen only understood a few words, but he easily filled in the blanks of what had been ordered.

"Tomás, go put a bullet in the head of that gringo before his wails drive me insane."

As Breen slid farther down the edge of the arroyo, the sweat dripping from his matted hair burned the deep cut in his forehead. His eyes began to tear from pain and the grit, dust, and heat. Clopping hooves neared, while the Mexican kept hitting the taciturn widowmaker with question after question.

Moving over a few feet to his right, Breen sucked in a deep breath, which he held for a count of ten before letting it out slowly and silently, then peered over the arroyo's rim. As he expected, the rider — a younger, thinner bandit in the white cotton outfit most Mexican peasants donned south of the border — focused on the writhing, moaning, idiot Otto Kruger, and did not even notice Breen's head in the weeds. The rider carried an old-fashioned muzzle-loading musket in his left hand. His right held the reins to a palomino. He appeared to be riding straight up to Otto Kruger, where he would likely rein in, put the barrel of the old long gun on Kruger's head, and blow the jasper's brains out.

That would bring the bandit into revolver range. The others to were too far away to hit with a short gun, and he could only take out one of them with a long gun. He would still have that tricky little problem of finding that fourth killer. His good eye moved away from the slowly approaching young bandit, and the savvy bounty hunter saw Providence was smiling down upon him one more time.

Only God knew why.

Wetting his lips, Breen wondered if the one eye he could see out of was playing a cruel joke on him. Ignoring the approaching rider, Breen focused on the two bandits by the wagon. The one with the eye patch began shouting, while the other man, potbellied with silver hair and a thick mustache the color of salt and pepper began laughing. That caused the leader to turn away from Charlotte Platte and berate the peon, who barked back with language meaning that he was not a man to be trifled with.

Breen could care less about what kind of conversation the two men were having. What amazed him was how they lined up. In a perfect line. If they didn't move, Breen reasoned one bullet, one shot, two dead men. That would definitely make the odds a little better, especially since the young fool with the long gun kept riding straight up to Otto Kruger.

Breen lowered his head slowly, looked at the Sharps, and pulled back the hammer as slowly and as quietly as he could, trying to time the cocking of the big rifle with the slow clopping of the palomino's hooves on the hard-packed road.

Knowing the trickiest part came next,

Breen rose slowly, hoping the grass and brush might conceal the long barrel of the Sharps, and that the sunlight wouldn't reflect off the brass telescopic sight. He also had to hope that the two Mexicans by the wagon had not moved since he had slid back into the hole.

He sighed with relief. They remained in perfect position.

With his head tilted and the blood still flowing over his left eye, Breen closed the eye and looked through the telescope. He wet his lips, trying to remember everything he had learned about long-distance shooting, about shooting uphill, about breathing out and remaining calm before touching the trigger. About not worrying how hard a Sharps kicked.

He couldn't see the young Mexican with the muzzle-loading rifle. He just saw the back of the serape worn by the one-eyed leader.

Breen exhaled. Waited. Stilled every nerve in his body. He touched the set trigger, and the click sounded like thunder in the desert.

The palomino stopped, and it's rider called out in Spanish, "Juan, where are you?"

Breen couldn't see that bandit, but he did spot the one-eyed monster begin to twist around in the saddle, just as Breen touched the second trigger on the Sharps.

For more years than he could count, Breen had been shooting that weapon, and every time he pulled the trigger, he felt the bones and muscles in his right shoulder lose just a little bit more tissue and feeling. The big rifle roared like a mountain howitzer. White smoke blocked out everything he had been looking at through the telescopic sight. He moved quickly to his right, pitched the heavy — and now hot — weapon onto the floor of the arroyo, and palmed the revolver.

A bullet kicked up dirt above him, spraying gravel toward Otto Kruger and the young, slim Mexican with the long, antiquated musket, telling where Juan, the fourth of the bad men, had positioned himself — somewhere behind Breen and on the west side of the arroyo — but Juan would have to wait. The young killer from Mexico had abandoned his orders to kill Otto Kruger, brought the old rifle up, and spurred the palomino into a run — heading straight for Breen.

Steadily, with patience instilled by years of surviving on the rugged Southwestern frontier, Breen cocked the hammer on his revolver and raised his arm straight at the rider, who was screaming in Spanish. An-

171

other bullet from the far side of the arroyo whined off a rock just over Breen's head, and the Mexican on the palomino pulled the trigger of his old single-shot musket. Breen heard and felt the leaden ball as it sailed just past his left ear. Breen touched the trigger and leaped down to his right.

Hitting the arroyo's wall, Breen slid down, feeling the gravel and cactus bite into his back. The palomino galloped down the sandy ramp and took off at a high lope down the arroyo, its hooves pounding as it raised dust on its way toward Deep Flood. The saddle on the palomino's back, Breen could see, was empty.

Another bullet kicked sand into Breen's left eye — or would have, if his eye had not been protected by thick, clotted blood and dirt. Breen snapped a shot, knowing that he shouldn't have, but not wanting to be shot at without defending himself. He could not risk looking above the rim, seeing who he had hit, who he had wounded, who he had killed, or, God forbid, who he had missed. Not with Juan somewhere above him with a pretty good aim.

Breen lunged up onto the loam that made the ramp, and rolled over to the other side. He landed on a bed of prickly pear, and kept rolling over till he reached the far wall of the arroyo. His pistol was cocked, the barrel pointed above. Breen sucked in a deep breath, held it, exhaled, and wondered how in the hell he was still breathing.

"Hombre," called Juan somewhere above Breen and to his left. "I have you in my gunsights, amigo." He spoke English, though with a thick Mexican accent.

Breen remained quiet, but he made himself turn around and look up and toward the road that led to Purgatory City.

Naturally, the way this day was shaping up, he couldn't see a damned thing on the road above him. He did hear Otto Kruger sobbing, saying that women never should be given the reins to a wagon, that he didn't deserve this, and that he was in mortal agony.

The Mexican named Juan snapped back. "You pathetic gringo coward. Of course you deserve this. You are a fool. An idiot."

Hearing that made Breen decide to take a chance. He called out,

"Hey, Juan."

"Sí."

The man had not changed position. Unless he moved, he wouldn't have a clear shot at Breen. On the other hand, Breen wouldn't have a clear shot at old Juan, either.

173

"Do you know who that pathetic gringo coward is?"

"Mark Twain?" asked Juan.

"Who?" Breen said.

The bandit muttered something in Spanish. A moment passed. A longer pause. Finally, "No, amigo, who is that pathetic gringo coward?"

Breen smiled. Juan had moved over closer toward him so he moved slowly, silently about twenty feet toward the south.

"His name is Otto Kruger."

Breen moved farther down the arroyo as the Mexican asked just who in hell was Otto Kruger.

"In your land, he's no one. But to the Rurales, so to speak, of us *norteamericanos,* he is worth *mucho dinero.*"

In Spanish, Juan asked, "How much is mucho dinero?" He had moved closer to Breen.

The bounty hunter took two steps back to where he had been, cited the amount posted on the wanted dodgers, and quickly added, "And the woman in the wagon . . . she's worth mucho dinero, too."

A long pause was followed by, "What did the señorita do?"

"Hell, Juan," Breen said after moving ten paces farther. "She has killed more men

174

than Otto Kruger."

"I have not seen her up close, but *la señorita* must be very pleasant to look at." Juan laughed. "Otherwise, Daniel would have killed her already." He pronounced the name Dan-yell.

"I suppose," Breen said, "that Dan-yell, Tomás, and your other pard would bring in money if they were taken to the Rurales or a town constable in Mexico."

"Perhaps," said Juan who kept moving one way or the other, trying to keep track of Breen's position.

"Well, we could become partners, amigo," Breen said. "Split the bounties for Kruger and *la patróna* on this side of the river. Take your dearly departed amigos south into Mexico and collect the rewards for them. Split the profits even — except the girl gets two hundred and fifty dollars. She did help me capture Kruger."

Juan spit out multiple curses in Spanish. "If they plan to hang her anyway," he said, "Why does she get any dinero?"

"Because deep down," Breen said as he moved in another direction, "I have a streak of honesty in me."

"*¿Es verdad?*" Juan asked.

"It's true," Breen answered.

Above, Juan laughed.

Breen grabbed a handful of small stones in his left hand, his right still holding his revolver, and took two steps forward, making as much noise as he could without being overtly obvious. "Then let's make a bargain, amigo. Fifty-fifty split. We can trust each other, is it not so?" The last sentence he called out in Spanish, kicked one stone forward, then flung the stones on the arroyo bed in front of him, while taking six long steps backward.

Juan leaped down just in front of Breen, snapped a shot into the empty arroyo, then cursed and spun around, thumbing back the hammer of his pistol while dropping to his knee.

Breen shot him plumb center in the chest and felt Juan's shot fly over his head.

The bandit crashed against the arroyo wall, let the revolver slip from his fingers, and then he rolled over and fell facedown on the dirt. Breen cocked the revolver and stepped to the Mexican in the denim trousers and colorful shirt with a purple sash around his waist. He wore no hat, but Breen figured he had taken that off before starting his ambush.

Using his right boot, Breen turned Juan over onto his back.

The Mexican's eyes fluttered, and finally

176

opened, focusing dully but steadily on Breen.

"Amigo," Juan said, laughed, and turned his head to spit out a glob of blood and pus. "You are too wily to be the partner of me."

"That's a shame, amigo," Breen said. "I've been working alone for so many years, I thought having a partner would be a good change for business."

The man coughed, shrugged, and smiled wider. *"Qué será, será."*

"I reckon so," Breen told him, and put a bullet into Juan's forehead.

Leaving his spurs, hat, and Sharps in the arroyo for the time being, Breen climbed out of the arroyo on the ramp. Otto Kruger kept moaning, but Breen walked past him without pausing. He saw the young bandit lying spread-eagled. Breen's shot had caught him dead in the throat, and ants were already marching to slake their thirsts — if ants ever got thirsty — on the river of blood surrounding the corpse who looked silently at the blue sky. The bullet had severed an artery and broken poor Tomás's neck.

When he looked at his horse, the wagon, the two other dead Mexicans and Charlotte Platte, Jed Breen broke into a hard sprint. He leaped over the body of the dead leader, lying facedown in the sand, a bloody hole staining the colorful serape and telling Breen that his shot had gone right through one of the Mexican's lungs before drilling the fourth of the bad men in his gut. It likely had taken that poor slob some time to die, but there was no mistaking that he was dead.

Breen slowed, realizing the danger had passed. Smiling, he knelt and holstered his revolver before reaching across the dead, gut-shot Mexican's corpse to take the Winchester rifle — probably the weapon the gut-shot man had been wielding — from the hands of Charlotte Platte.

She resisted Breen's first tug of the Winchester, but let go of the carbine when he yanked harder the second time.

"It's a hell of a thing, Poison Platte. It's just so damned hard to work a repeating rifle when your hands are in iron manacles."

Platte smiled and tilted her head toward the dead bandit. "If he hadn't landed on the holster of his short gun, and had the flap of that holster not been fastened, and had your shot not blown that damned killer out of the saddle and sent his Colt sailing into the cactus over yonder, you, Jed Breen, would be a dead man."

"Yes, ma'am, I suspect you're right." He touched the wound over his eye from which he couldn't see a damned thing. "But for the rest of this trip, which isn't all that far, your hands are going to be cuffed behind your back."

She spit in his face.

He punched her over her left eye.

When she woke up, he did hand her that hat she wanted to keep her pale skin from burning more. And folks said bounty hunters weren't gentlemen.

Of course, the only reason it hadn't blown out of the back of the wagon was because the stampede string got caught on a nail.

CHAPTER SIXTEEN

The last person Sean Keegan expected to see that evening in the Purgatory City marshal's office and jail was Jed Breen. From the look on the bounty hunter's face, the feeling was mutual.

The door had opened just as Keegan was opening a bottle of Irish whiskey, which he had charged to the county sheriff's office even though he knew it would look suspicious since the county sheriff, Juan Garcia, usually charged tequila to the sheriff's office. A woman with a cut on her forehead sailed through the doorway and landed on the floor. She was real pretty, Keegan thought, despite her torn shirtsleeves and mangled, wind-blown red hair. Her hat hung on a stampede string around her neck, her arms were cuffed behind her back, and her feet were bound with pigging strings and reins. A second later a man flew inside. His was the ugliest face this side of Private

Hoot Hanson's after he ran into that pack of feral hogs down in the Big Bend Country. The man tripped over the cussing woman and knocked his head against the other desk in the office, and spit out profanity.

"Shut up," a voice yelled from outside, "Or I'll stove in your heads."

The two newcomers turned mute. The third visitor then stepped inside, holding a Sharps long gun with a telescopic sight. He looked like he had just gotten the crap beaten out of him, like he hadn't slept in a month of Sundays, and his pretty white hair was about to fall out or be pulled out. But he looked a hell of a lot better than the first two folks who'd come flying into the marshal's office and jail.

Sean Keegan would have known him anywhere.

"Howdy." He held up the bottle. "I was about to have a snort or thirty. Care to join me?"

The surprise on Breen's face was replaced with the look of eternal gratitude. After leaning the Sharps against the wall, he walked straight to Keegan's desk, looked at the deputy's badge pinned to his torn shirt but made no comment, and took the proffered bottle. He drank greedily, muttered his thanks, and then returned the bottle before busying himself dragging the woman into one cell, locking the door, then hoisting the incoherent ugly-faced dude and hurtling him into the neighboring cell. That door he locked, too, as though he had experience with these kinds of things. Sean Keegan had never locked anybody up in any jail, although he had been thrown into calabooses across the frontier and even civilized America more times than he could remember.

After dusting off his hands, Breen tossed his hat onto the other desk, grabbed a chair, and dragged it to Keegan's place of honor. Keegan drank long and steadily from the bottle, wiped his mouth with his sleeve, and handed the bottle to Breen, who found a mug and let Keegan pour.

They toasted, tin cup against glass bottle, and drank a healthy swallow, chased that one with another, and sighed. Both men leaned back.

"What the hell are you doing here?" Breen asked.

With a shrug, Keegan said, "That'll be hard to explain. Over just one bottle."

Breen accepted that, and sipped more whiskey.

"Who'd you bring in?" Keegan asked.

"The woman's wanted for poisoning a

bunch of miners in Arizona Territory," Breen answered. "Precious Metal. Northern part of the territory."

"Yeah," Keegan said, "Fort Wilmont is close by. Pretty country I've been told."

"Compared to Purgatory City, Hell's pretty." Breen drank again, took in a deep breath, and after exhaling, he motioned to the other cell. "And that is Otto Kruger."

That elicited a whistle from the Irishman, who rose, crossed the room, and stared through the bars. He took a slug of Irish and steadily made his way back to his chair. After sitting down, he said, "It doesn't look like Otto Kruger."

"It doesn't look like Hans, either, and you can thank the woman for that. But it's Otto." Breen drank again, looked at the cells, then straightened. "Did they hang Tom Benteen?"

"Sort of," Keegan answered.

"What does 'sort of' mean, Keegan?"

"Well, Lovely Tom Benteen Lovely — or whatever the hell you want to call him — was hanged. We might be better off leaving it at that. It'll take too long to explain."

"Where's the marshal?" Breen asked.

"Dead."

"The Rangers?"

"The captain led them off chasing the

183

Kruger brothers."

"Sheriff Garcia?"

"He went off after the rest of the Benteen gang. They rode in and tried to free Tom. Killed Titus Bedwell and the marshal. Even the damned hangman."

Breen took the bottle from Keegan's hand and refilled his cup. After returning the Irish to the old soldier, Breen drank and hoped the liquor might clear his head. Instead, he felt a headache coming on.

"They killed the hangman?"

Keegan nodded. "Well, I don't think it was intentional. And for all I know, some citizen of Purgatory City might have done the dirty deed."

"Then who hanged Tom?"

"Me." Keegan drank greedily, burped, drank another swallow and grinned. "This is the nectar of the Gods."

"You hanged Tom?"

"Aye. Buried him, too, so to speak. I guess you didn't see the courthouse, or what's left of it." Keegan grinned. "Wind blew the wrong way. But the boys with the volunteer firefighters outfit did yeoman's work. Saved much of it, especially since the walls are stone and adobe."

Breen drank greedily, tried to shake the senses back into his head, before finally giving up. "I think you will have to start explaining."

"Agreed." Keegan nodded. "But that, Jed me boy, will take more than this one bottle. And since I don't want to blow the budget of our county, I surely hope ye'll be good enough to wander down to a fine saloon and return with a bottle. Maybe two."

"You mean to tell me, Keegan, that you're all the law there is in Purgatory City right now?" Breen should have been dead drunk by this time of night, but everything Keegan had told him made him feel cold sober.

"More or less." Keegan splashed whiskey into Breen's mug, although he put about two shot glasses worth on the floor and desk top, then took a slug himself.

"Well, I need to extradite the woman, Charlotte Platte, to Precious Metal, and I need to collect the five hundred dollars on Hans Kruger."

"Otto," Keegan corrected.

"Right. Right. Otto. Not Hans." *Good,* Breen thought, *at least I'm slightly intoxicated.* "So how do I get this done?"

"Beats the devil out of me."

"But you are a deputy?"

"Sort of. At least till Garcia gets back . . . if he gets back."

Breen thought, griped, cursed, drank some more, cursed again. The prisoners griped, cursed, but did no drinking. Finally, just to get his mind on something else, Breen took time to untie the prisoners, although he considered leaving the manacles on the woman — his head still hurt like hell. He even fed them the food that Keegan had purchased on the county's dime but could not eat all of the beans and potatoes.

He was still thinking when he walked back from the cells to the wanted posters. Seeing the one for all the Kruger outfit, he ripped off the poster for Otto Kruger.

"Well, well, well," Breen said as he walked back to the desk and showed the placard to Keegan. "This says the Krugers once robbed a bank in Precious Metal of all places. In Arizona Territory. I suppose I could take them both to Arizona. Collect the reward there."

"It is a pretty town," Keegan said. "Or so I heard."

"How do I get to Precious Metal?"

"Take a bloody stage."

Breen snorted. "The last time I took in a prisoner I rode in a wagon — the last two times, actually." He touched the knot and scab over his left eye. "Well, you were with me that time a year or so back."

186

"Aye, aye, aye, and so was Matt Mc-Culloch. And that crazy actor." He laughed. "A hell of a fight we had, Breen me pal. Hell of a fight."

"Hell of a ride, too," Breen said. "Almost our last one."

"Aye, that's the bloody truth."

They toasted and drank.

"Have you seen McCulloch?" Breen asked.

"Nay. Not in a while. Last I heard he had taken off into the Davis Mountains. Hoping to round up some mustangs. That kind of thing. Has dreams of rebuilding his life, I expect. That's McCulloch for you. Never any quit in the man. Same as you, Breen."

The bounty hunter smiled at the compliment and held up his mug. Keegan punched the tin cup with the bottle.

After clearing his throat, Breen said, "I was asking for a refill, Keegan."

The Irishman laughed, and tossed in a couple more fingers of whiskey.

"There's not much quit in you, either, old man," Breen said.

"Aye, but don't get too sentimental, darlin' Breeney boy." Keegan drank and tossed the empty bottle toward the trash, but hit the wall instead, shattering glass on the floor. "Not much work for an old army soldier forced to rip off his stripes. I've been doing odd jobs here and there, a wee bit of gambling, and finding ways to get a drink or a meal. Now I'd give me eyeteeth to do something grand, something bold, and adventurous."

The mood seemed to be turning maudlin, he began to think, but maybe that was just because the three bottles of whiskey they'd shared were empty. *What a bloody shame. Drunk with nowhere to go.*

Keegan was about to fall asleep when the door opened. The face came without any focus, and a scarecrow followed the big man. Keegan was certain it was a scarecrow. The face looked like a damned Indian, long black hair and all, and one of his arms was nothing but planks of wood or something like that.

Breen said, "Damn," and reached for his revolver.

The scarecrow stepped one way, and the big gent stepped right toward Breen and knocked the revolver out of the bounty hunter's hand.

"How much," the Texas twang drawled, "Have you two featherbrains been drinking? And where the hell is Juan Garcia?"

188

CHAPTER SEVENTEEN

Cursing but remaining determined, Matt McCulloch cooked up a second pot of coffee, making this one stronger by seasoning it with soot from the stove, a little bit of snuff he found in Sheriff Garcia's bottom drawer, and the remnants of the Irish whiskey Breen — certainly not Sean Keegan — had left in a tin coffee mug.

Wooden Arm stood in the corner, amazed at just how drunk two white men could get. Even more shocking was how these white eyes treated their women and ugly-faced men. They threw them in a dark room with rough beds and iron doors, with just one bucket for drinking water and another bucket to do their business in. He grinned at the thought of what might happen if they mixed up their buckets.

Once McCulloch had the second pot of coffee inside the bellies of Jed Breen and Sean Keegan, he opened the bottom drawer of the sheriff's desk and pulled out a bottle of tequila about three-quarters full and poured himself a morning bracer.

"The hell —" Breen had to choke back something god-awful rising in his throat. Once he had it headed back where it might exit his body through a lower orifice, he continued. "Where did you . . . find that?"

"Where Juan has been keeping it since he was first elected seven years ago," McCulloch answered. He held the glass toward Breen, who jerked away as though he had been offered arsenic.

"Tequila," Sean Keegan muttered, "is the devil's brew." He brought the coffee cup up to his lips.

Thirty minutes later, McCulloch had learned all that he was going to until someone with sense and sensibility — and not three bottles of eighty-six-proof in their bellies — could tell him. The Benteen Gang had raided Purgatory City in a failed attempt to free Tom Lovely, alias Tom Benteen, from his date with Lucifer for one final dance on the trapdoor of the gallows. Those gallows were a pile of ash and charred timbers, in the back courtyard of the county courthouse as well as the annex from nine months back. Tom Lovely was dead.

The hangman was dead. The town marshal was dead. A few other citizens were dead, but the undertaker had a free hand to make his rent and get some good folks planted since he didn't have to worry about burying Tom Lovely.

Sheriff Garcia had led a posse of about two dozen able-bodied men out in search of the Benteen Gang. Whether due to dedication or the fact that an election would be coming up next year, it wasn't known. The Texas Rangers based in Purgatory City had taken off southeast in pursuit of the Krugers.

The marshal of the town, Rafe McMillian, had caught a bullet through the body, another slug through both lungs, and a shotgun blast of double-aught buckshot in his back. The undertaker, the lousy excuse for a human being A. Percival Helton, would have a challenge making him presentable to St. Peter.

What all this boiled down to was the Rangers were searching for the Kruger brothers and the most of the troops from Fort Spalding were chasing Indians across West Texas.

McCulloch slapped Breen's face hard. "Are there any good hands left in this whole damned county?"

"I wouldn't bet my poke on it, Matt."

McCulloch made the bounty hunter drink more coffee. He looked at poor Wooden Arm and almost laughed aloud but steeled himself and signed to the Comanche *I need more time.*

Moving to the one-time army soldier, McCulloch slapped Keegan's face and said, "Keegan, here's my problem. I have forty rank mustangs that should bring me a good chunk of change if I can break them and sell them. Now . . ."

For a drunken lout, Keegan was ahead of McCulloch, "Matt, me brother, or at least a man I love like me brother . . . don't take that the wrong way, laddie, for they hanged my brother in County Cork thirty-seven years ago last Monday . . . I testified agin the bloody traitor. But where was I? Matt, do ye really think the colonel, Ol' Lard Arse Hollister, would buy mounts from ye?" He chuckled, sucked down more coffee, spit out a mouthful, swallowed the rest, and laughed.

"The army won't buy nothing from you, laddie. Not in Texas."

McCulloch sipped coffee himself, and after he had swallowed, asked, "What about New Mexico Territory? Fort Marcy? Fort Bascom? Fort whatever the hell they call it down Mesilla way?"

"What about . . ." Keegan said with a mischievous grin, "Fort Wilmont?"

"Wilmont?" McCulloch demanded.

"Arizona Territory, me lad. Beautiful country. Glorious country. The northern part of the territory. Just outside the big burg of —"

"Precious Metal," Breen slurred.

"Why Fort Wilmont?" McCulloch asked.

"Because, laddie, there are no horse breeders in that part of the territory," Keegan said. "There's nothing but miners and stagecoach jehus."

"Hell no," Breen slurred, "stagecoach, we won't go!"

Ignoring the drunken bounty hunter, McCulloch leaned closer into the stinking Irishman's face. "Wilmont?"

"Apaches!" Keegan snapped. "Bloody hell, Matt, don't ye read the papers or hear the gossips outside the striped poles of barbershops?" He burped, shot down another swallow of retched coffee, and continued. "The Apaches be raising more than their share of Cain these days, Matt, me son. And the army can't keep up with them. An Apache afoot can cover more ground than can a bluecoat like meself do on the back of an army horse."

Keegan drank again, burped a finale, and

grinned. Then he stretched his right hand out and gripped McCulloch's shoulder. "Did ye hear what I said, Matt? An army horse. Not" — he laughed — "Not, by the love of Jesus, Joseph, and Mary or whatever order ye want to put them in, not a Matt McCulloch horse."

Breen nodded. "Your reputation crosses all the way to the Colorado River, Matt. I've been to Precious Metal. Just passing through, mind you, but it looked like a damned nice town."

Standing up, without even realizing he had moved, McCulloch turned toward Wooden Arm. He signed,. *I will return as fast as my legs can carry me.*

An hour later he was back with a pot of café coffee, a pot of beans, and a bottle of castor oil.

Some hours after daybreak, and two more pots of coffee, McCulloch rolled three smokes, passing one to Jed Breen, another to Sean Keegan, and the last to Wooden Arm. He struck a match across the rough edge of Sheriff Juan Garcia's desk and lighted the smokes.

"The army at Fort Wilmont will pay forty-five dollars in minted gold for a good horse," McCulloch said, waving the telegraph reply he had received that morning. "Matt McCulloch horses, that is."

"Wilmont?" Breen held his head as though it was about to fall into a million pieces. "Isn't that . . . ?"

"Outside of Precious Metal," Keegan answered.

That's all it took to sober Jed Breen up. He grabbed the cup of coffee, swallowed about half of it, and pitched the cigarette onto the floor. Wooden Arm had the presence of mind to crush out the butt with the heel of his Comanche moccasin.

"You want us to ride with you?" Breen asked.

"My understanding is that you want to deliver a couple of parcels to the sheriff in Precious Metal," McCulloch said.

Breen grinned, sipped more coffee. "How many horses?"

"Mustangs," McCulloch corrected. "Barely broken. Some of them not even broken. Forty. At forty-five a head, you do the math."

"You do the bloody math," Keegan said. "My head's still pounding like me brothers buildin' that awful railroad north of here all those years ago."

"Not that many years, Sean," Breen corrected, but then his head slumped into his hands.

"It's eighteen hundred bucks," McCulloch said. "If we make it. The Indian and I will take fourteen hundred. You two split the difference."

"How do you figure it?" Keegan asked. "Getting there? Southern route and up?"

"No," McCulloch answered immediately. "Hans Kruger will want his brother. He'll be expecting us to go south. I figure we follow the Pecos River to Fort Bascom in New Mexico Territory, then travel straight west, following the stage route."

"That country's filled with Comanches first, then Apaches, then the bloody Navajo, and then more Apaches," Keegan said.

"Plus bandits of all colors," Breen added.

"Which," McCulloch said, "is why my pard and I are paying you two hundred dollars a piece. Providing we don't lose one damned horse."

Keegan and Breen stared at each other. Eventually both men smiled and lifted their coffee cups in the general, if unsteady, direction of Matt McCulloch. They hardly noticed Wooden Arm.

"Well," Keegan said as he turned back to stare at the horseman, "they say there is strength in numbers crossing lawless territories."

"Yeah," McCulloch said. "Numbers. One former Texas Ranger with a Winchester. A bounty hunter with nothing but profit on his mind. And a one-time soldier boy who wore the blue and hasn't spent hardly a sober day in his life."

"Don't forget him!" Keegan wailed and pointed at the teenage Comanche brave who suddenly didn't look so much like a warrior but like a frightened teenager who didn't know what the devil he had gotten himself into.

"I can add to our numbers," Jed Breen said, pointing awkwardly at the jail cells. "Kruger will fight if it means keeping his topknot. Nobody in his right mind wants to be tortured to death by Apaches." He laughed. "Even better than that, my friends, my old fellow Jackals, I've got the jim-dandiest cook you've ever seen."

CHAPTER EIGHTEEN

"There it is," Walter Homes said from the wagon seat. Harriet turned around and beckoned Annie to climb through all the debris, furniture, and foodstuffs from the back of the bouncing wagon to come see.

When she stuck her head through the opening in the canvas cover, both mother and father pointed to the southwest.

"Our first mountain," Walter said.

Annie found it in the distance, a mound of red, orange, and white against the pure blue sky.

"Papa," she said with a smile. "It's not our first mountain. The Ouachitas were practically in our backyard in Arkansas."

Her father laughed and urged the horses to continue pulling. They were climbing, which Annie found a relief after all those desolate days crossing the western plains of Texas and that abysmal Panhandle region.

"Honey," her father said. "It's our first

Western mountain."

"Papa, if someone lived in Baltimore, Maryland, or even Memphis, Tennessee, he or she would have said the Ouachitas were western mountains."

Her father chuckled, but her mother chided Annie. "Goodness gracious, child, what has gotten into you?" Harriet tilted her head toward the lone butte, and said, "You never saw anything like that in Dead Trout, Arkansas, or the Ouachitas, now did you?"

She decided to play nice and relented. "No, ma'am." Besides, it was a wonderful sight to behold, the flatness of the Panhandle making way for a rugged terrain of red rocks, red dirt, red dust, and blue skies, with short trees sprouting on the lower levels of the butte and the surrounding countryside.

"Are we still in Texas?"

"Not if I have my bearings right," Walter Homes said. "We should be in the Territory of New Mexico by now." He gestured to the north. "Fort Bascom should be somewhere in that general direction."

"Where the smoke is?" Annie asked.

Her father almost dropped the heavy leather lines to the team pulling the wagon. Jerking his head around, she lifted her arm so he could see exactly where she had detected the smoke.

Walter said nothing, but his mouth that had been turned upward over the sight of his first Western mountain, suddenly reversed course, frowned briefly, and turned into a rigid flat line.

"Looks like a series of nice fluffy white clouds," Annie's mother said.

Annie refrained from calling her mother an idiot.

"Well," Walter said, "I suppose that's smoke, all right. Maybe from Fort Bascom. It could be anything, my family, because . . ." He trailed off.

Winfield Baker was riding his mule toward them, coming from the lead wagons ahead. They saw him slow down beside the Carter wagon, then the Stanton wagon, where to Annie's jealous fit, he turned the mule around and rode alongside, likely letting that shameless hussy Betsy Stanton flirt with him, or perhaps even roll him a cigarette. Then he said something, pointed toward the smoke, turned the mule around, and finally made a rather leisurely way to the Jeffries wagon. Since that family had no girls, Winfield Baker spoke with them only a few moments, though he did point out the smoke, and then gesture toward a dry creek bed up the trail and down a ways.

At length, he rode to the Homes wagon.

"Sir," he called out. "The Reverend Sergeant Major Homer Primrose III suggested that I have a word with you, Mr. Homes."

"I see." Annie's father kept the wagon moving, but her mother was clutching the cross of German pewter than hung from her neck, her lips moving in silent prayer, and her face paling as she looked at another puff of white smoke on the far horizon.

Well, Annie had to give Winfield Baker some credit. He turned his mule around and rode alongside their wagon just as he had done with the Stantons' Studebaker — and that harlot daughter of theirs.

"That smoke over there could mean trouble, sir," Winfield said as he bounced up and down on the mule's bare back. He had only a rawhide hackamore to guide the animal, too.

"Annie just pointed it out to us, Winfield," Walter Homes said. "I'm surprised the good reverend even noticed it."

"Actually, I saw the smoke first, Mr. Homes," Winfield said. "I told the reverend."

"Well, that's a jim-dandy job, son," her father said.

"Oh, it was nothing, really."

"Well, you have keen eyes."

"Thank you, sir." Winfield stared briefly at Annie before swallowing and regaining his focus. He pointed to that spot off the trail. "Since the reverend thinks that smoke might be from Indians, he has ordered the wagons to turn off the trail at the cut — there. You can see the first wagon making its way down now."

Indeed, the Reverend Sergeant Major Homer Primrose III large wagon had made the turn and was following a narrow trail toward a rocky bed that cut deep into the country.

"How long do you think we'll have to wait?" Walter asked.

"The reverend did not say, sir."

"Is he planning on sending out a party of men to investigate this smoke?"

"I don't know, sir. I just told him about the smoke, and he saw the place down there, and he said we should circle the wagons and wait this danger out."

"Then he thinks there is danger."

"Well, I guess so. But, well, you know, sir. We're —"

"Alone?" Annie finished the sentence for him.

"Well . . ." The boy began to get flustered. "I need to —" He turned around sharply, sitting erect and looking with a deep intensity toward the smoke. "Did you hear something, Mr. Homes?"

Annie glanced briefly at her father, and tried to see where exactly Walter was looking.

"No, son, I can't —"

"There!" Walter snapped, and leaned so far he almost toppled off the mule.

Annie heard it then, a faint rolling. Echoes of . . .

"A gunshot?" her father asked. He looked off toward the smoke with keen purpose.

Another low rumble followed. And another.

"Maybe," Annie's mother said wistfully, "It's just thunder."

"Without a cloud in the sky, Mama," Annie pointed out.

"Well . . ." Harriet nodded as though she had discovered the undebatable answer. "Fort Bascom. They must be firing off their cannons."

No one looked at Annie's mother, but her father turned back and urged the mules a little closer.

"You see the trail, sir," Winfield Baker said. "Just follow the other wagons, and I'll see you in the camp." He grabbed the hackamore tighter. "I must let the other folks know, Mr. Homes." He tipped his hat at Annie's mother, then tipped his hat and blushed at Annie. Kicking his mule, he trotted off toward the Simpsons' wagon.

"He's such a nice young boy," Annie's mother said, forgetting about those darned cannons that must have been going off at Fort Bascom.

Mama sure hit the nail on the head, Annie thought. Winfield Baker was a fine young *boy*.

In the arroyo below the trail, with the wagons in a tight circle and all the animals inside, Annie Homes suddenly felt a cold dread. She had mocked her father, mocked her mother, and Betsy Stanton — but that witch deserved it. Annie had even picked on poor Winfield Baker. Yet now she wished she was surrounded by the safety and the closeness of the Ouachita Mountains and not that deadly, barren butte that looked as though it had been bathed in blood.

Actually, she'd have given anything if she could see the mountain, red as blood and pale as death or not. But she saw nothing but the blackness of the New Mexican desert. She had prayed and prayed and prayed that the moon would rise and bathe them in light, but a few minutes ago, she heard Mr. Stanton tell someone that it was the new moon. There would be no moon-light. No stars. And under orders from the Reverend Sergeant Major Homer Primrose III, there would be no campfires, no cook-fires, no pipes, cigars, or cigarettes being smoked this night. Every man in camp held a rifle. A few women held guns, too. Her father had even given Annie a folding knife, and had locked the main blade open before he slipped it onto her sweaty hand.

"Just in case, darling," he said. Then he had grinned, and tried to make a joke. "I figured you might want to pass your time this evening vittling, sweetheart."

"Do you mean whittling, Papa?"

He had laughed, before wandering into the depths of blackness.

It might have been bearable had the coyotes not started. Laughing, howling like hyenas, mocking those poor, foolish travel-ers from Dead Trout, Arkansas. For several minutes, they sang their mocking song at the wayfarers until . . . silence.

Deathly still. Nothing but blackness all around them. The wind did not blow. The coyotes did not howl. The livestock so close to them all made not one sound.

Until a voice called out that almost made the frightened Annie Homes stab herself with her papa's knife.

"Hello the camp. Mind if I come in?"

CHAPTER NINETEEN

A heated debate quickly took place among the men who considered themselves lieutenants to the Reverend Sergeant Major Homer Primrose III, while Annie watched her father as he studied the darkness that surrounded them.

"Papa?" she whispered.

"Quiet," he said sharply but softly. "Let me look over those hills."

She obeyed, even though she could not see two feet in front of her face. She couldn't see her mother, the wagon, the livestock, the Reverend Sergeant Major Homer Primrose III. She couldn't even see her father, and he stood right beside her.

At least, she thought he was. She could feel his presence, even hear his breathing — barely — and thought he must be turning around. But it was hard for her to tell. The other men were shouting, cursing, and their voices bounced off the rocks in the darkness.

Her father, on the other hand, remained quiet — deadly quiet — and focused on whatever he was trying to do. He probably would have kept right on with his diligence if Winfield Baker's father, Atticus, hadn't called out, "Walter! Walter! Walter Homes, man, will you get over here! We need your input."

"Son of a —" Walter Homes bit off his curse, sighed, and Annie heard him whisper, "Stay with your mother, Annie. Let me see what these imbeciles want."

Footsteps sounded faintly in the darkness, and Annie turned and saw the glow of cigars and cigarettes from what must have been the assembly of the wagon train's leaders. She took a few steps and bumped into someone.

"Annie?" Her mother sounded petrified.

"It's all right, Mother."

"Who do you think those men are? The ones who have surrounded us?"

At that moment, as though on cue, the voice from the darkness called out, "How long does it take you gents to make up your —"

His profanity made Annie blush.

". . . minds?"

"Wait here, Mother," she whispered. "I'll be right back."

She fumbled her way in the darkness, trying to stay as quiet as a mouse so her father wouldn't know she had disobeyed his orders. At least she had the small orange beacons that told her where the men had gathered, as well as their sharp debates, and the potent smell of tobacco smoke.

She stopped about ten yards from the gathering, barely making out a few faces. Someone pulled hard on a cigarette, and she heard her father say softly, "I don't see anything."

"What are you?" said a voice she couldn't identify, "Some sort of nighthawk?"

"Shut up," Mr. Baker said.

"You shut up."

"All of you shut up!" barked the Reverend Sergeant Major Homer Primrose III.

In the darkness, somewhere outside of the circle of wagons, laughter echoed.

"You dumb greenhorns. I can hear you like I was hiding underneath one of your wagons."

The laughter resumed while the men scurried about, causing Annie to back up ten or fifteen more feet, in case someone accidentally discovered her presence.

"He sounds white," Mr. Baker whispered.

"I am white!" the voice barked in the inky night.

"Glory be to God, it's the Devil himself!" said some whiny-voiced Arkansan.

"Shut up." That was her father, and Annie heard him shout, "Who are you?"

Once Walter Homes' echoes fell silent, the man in the dark answered casually. "A traveler. Same as you."

"How did you find us?" the preacher asked.

The man chuckled. "You left a trail a blind man could follow in the dark. Now, it's dark. I'll give you that. But I ain't blind."

"Are you alone?" the preacher asked.

"I left my horse in the rocks. Otherwise, I'm alone."

"How can we trust you?" the preacher called out.

"You can't. No more than I can trust you. But, boys, you're in no-man's-land right now. Mexican bandits. Americano bandits. Apaches. Comanches. And if we don't cease with this palavering in the middle of the night, all of those rapin', pillagin', murderin' scum are gonna hear us and swoop down on us and wipe ever' last one of us off the face of this earth."

"We can't see you," Mr. Baker said.

"Then light a damned fire. Boys, I'm

210

hungry. I'm thirsty. And I'm tired of shouting. I'm coming in. But the first one of you who lifts a gun in my direction, I'll be shootin' to kill."

The gunshot roared. Annie thought she saw the muzzle flash, but that could have been her imagination. She did hear the bullet whine off some rocks, but well away from the wagons and horses, though the abrupt noise caused the mules and horses to begin snorting and stamping their hooves on the hard stones.

"Light a fire," Annie's father demanded.

"But he'll be able to see us," Mr. Baker warned.

"And this way we can see him," Walter Homes said.

Annie felt her way against a wagon, then moved to the back of it, so she'd be out of sight.

He wore buckskins, carried a repeating rifle, and had a holstered revolver on his right hip. His black hat was battered and dusty, just like he was, with a hard face the color of leather, and a thick mustache and weeks of beard stubble. The eyes hardly moved, but Annie figured he took everything in.

"I'd appreciate a cup of coffee if it's handy," the man said as he stepped closer to the fire. The male leaders of the Dead Trout wagon train spread out.

"We're running a cold camp," Walter said.

"Why?"

"We saw smoke signals off toward the northwest," the preacher said.

The man laughed. "Yeah, so did I. Utes. Lookin' for hair to lift and ponies to steal."

Annie's father said, "I thought this was too far south for Utes to raid."

She couldn't see the eyes of the bearded, strong man, but she felt them boring through her father.

"Utes go where they damned well please. Wherever they can find something of value. Like me." He motioned to the fire the men were starting. "It's gonna take a spell before that coffee's boilin'. You gents wouldn't happen to have somethin' a mite stronger to warm a feller up, would you?"

"Johnson," the Reverend said. "Fetch the jug from underneath the seat of my wagon. The one for medicinal purposes."

Annie hoped her snort of utter contempt had not been heard.

"You the leader of this outfit?" the stranger asked.

"Yes. I am the Reverend Sergeant Major Homer Primrose the Third," the prima donna answered.

"Where you bound?"

Instead of answering, the stranger said, "Where you bound?"

"Rapture Valley, Territory of Arizona," the preacher said. "We have left the poverty and ruin and disgrace that has befallen our settlement in Arkansas."

"Boy." The buckskin-clad man turned to Mr. Johnson. "You don't hear too good or somethin'? Didn't your capt'n say for you to fetch that jug?"

Johnson scurried off, and Annie had to slip farther behind the reverend's wagon.

"What about the Utes?" Annie's father asked. "If they are around and are looking to raid someone, should not we be on guard? Isn't this fire unwise?"

The man laughed, but stopped when Mr. Johnson returned with the reverend's jug of Arkansas corn liquor. No, the preacher had finished the corn brew before they ever set foot in the Indian Nations. This would likely be the last of the rotgut he had bought at Five Scalps back in the Texas Panhandle.

After uncorking the jug and drinking greedily, the man pointed the jug at Walter Homes. "What's your name?"

"Homes. Walter Homes."

"Well, Mr. Homes." He took another long swallow, corked the jug, and tossed it to the preacher. "You'd be right exceptin' one fact I ain't shared with you greenhorns." Laughing, he reached for the strap that hung around his shoulder, and pulled it around till a beaded, fringed pouch appeared that had been hanging on his back. He fumbled to unfasten the button, flipped up the flap, and reached inside.

What he pulled out made Annie gasp. Even from this distance, even in the darkness, and with the fire partially blinding her, she knew what the man tossed to Mr. Stanton.

He caught it, gasped, and dropped it. The stranger laughed.

"My God," said Mr. Johnson. "Is that a scalp?"

"Yeah." The stranger pulled out a handful more. "There were five of them. But one was an old medicine man. Silver hair. It'll take all my skills to convince some alcalde that his wiry old hair didn't belong to some Mexican."

"You're" — Walter paused — "a . . . scalp hunter?"

"I am what I am, boys," the scalp hunter said. "But I'm also what you gents need."

"What's that?" asked the Reverend Sergeant Major Homer Primrose III asked.

"A guide. Someone to get you greenhorns

214

to Rapture Valley. As yellow-livered and ignorant you folks is, you'll never get there in this lifetime."

A long silence filled the night. Only the crackling of the fire made sounds. The man in buckskins picked up the scalp that had dropped, shoved it and the others into his bag, and readjusted the pouch and strap so that it was now — mercifully to Annie's roiling stomach — out of sight.

"Do you know where Rapture Valley is?" Mr. Johnson asked.

"Johnson!" Walter Homes snapped. "Surely you don't want this . . . this . . . fiend guiding us!"

Ignoring her father, the scalp hunter looked back at the reverend. "Where's this Rapture Valley?"

"In the basin near Precious Metal," the preacher said.

The dark man's head nodded. "Shore. I can get you there. Since I'm bound for Precious Metal myself, I can even give you my family rate. Dollar a day. Payable upon delivery."

A longer silence.

"Why don't you boys talk amongst yerselves," the man said with a laugh. "But consider this. You need a man like me. You gents ain't seen nothin' yet. You been crossin' civilized country. There ain't no semblance of law, order, God, or mercy between here and Precious Metal. And not a whole lot in Precious Metal."

The Reverend Sergeant Major Homer Primrose III cleared his throat. "Let the leaders gather near my wagon and discuss the proposal by this Mister . . . ?"

"Linton," the scalp hunter said. "Just Linton."

"Mr. Linton," the reverend said.

"That's a good idea. Civilized idea. Debate my merits. Now, how is that coffee cookin', boys? And just out of curiosity? Do y'all have any women with you? Other than that fine-looking cookie with hair the color of midnight hidin' at the back of that wagon over yonder?"

Streaks of yellow angled across the sky toward that lone butte as dawn emerged. Annie helped her mother with their breakfast, and she watched with trepidation as the duly elected leaders of the train still huddled. Other families cooked, and that man, that evil, wretched scalp hunter, just squatted by the fire, drinking coffee, sipping some of the Reverend Sergeant Major Homer Primrose III's liquor, and chewing on beef jerky. She did that until Linton

216

caught her staring at him, and raised the preacher's jug as in toast. The beast even had the audacity to wink at her.

She almost dropped a fork into the hot coals.

By the time the sun had emerged, and the younger men were feeding and watering the livestock, Annie and her mother had eaten breakfast without Walter, though they left him a plate. As they washed dishes, they saw him coming, head down, and Mr. Stanton, Mr. Johnson, and the Reverend Sergeant Major Homer Primrose III walking toward the leathery, evil man, who slowly stood and corked the preacher's "medicinal" jug of rotgut.

"They voted to let that awful person guide us?" Annie said, perhaps too loud, but she couldn't control herself. Her father did not answer, but the look of contempt on his face told the story.

"Wonderful." Annie laughed with sarcasm that bordered on hatred. "Him. Escorting us. To Rapture Valley!"

"Annie," her mother said, "that is enough."

Walter Homes picked up the cup of coffee, lukewarm, and sipped. "If it means anything, the vote wasn't unanimous."

"Your vote?" That surprised Annie, and

she looked at her mother, who had asked the question laced with harsh sarcasm.

"I wasn't alone. Far from it. But we agreed back in Dead Trout that we will abide by the will of the majority. Five to three. In favor of Mr. Linton."

"Now what?" Annie asked.

"We leave." Walter pointed his cup toward the road above. "Back on the trail. See what our guide has to say."

As though he had heard, Linton began barking orders. "All right, folks. Get your teams hitched and prepare to ride. You damned fools wasted enough time yesterday with yer palaverin' and hidin' in this death-trap like a bunch of yellow-livered cowards. Prepare to ride hard all day today, 'cause we won't be takin' no noon break. If you can't keep up with the pace I set, too bad. You'll be alone, and that's your own damned fault."

He laughed, and began kicking out the fire in front of him.

"Don't fear me too much, 'specially you, little lady." He winked, and Betsy Stanton turned around sharply and marched to the back of her folks' wagon. Linton laughed even harder. "We won't push hard like this ever' day, but you lost time cowerin' here, and all of you know that's the damned

218

truth. So we move hard today, part of tomorrow, then we can slow down and you can catch your breath. But not for long. You men hired me to do a job, and that's get you to Rapture Valley in Arizona Territory. That's what I'll do, unless I get kilt doin' it. And unless you get yourselves kilt from your ignorance and cowardice." He nodded with finality.

The Reverend Sergeant Major Homer Primrose III said, "Let us gather around and offer our blessings to the Lord and to Mr. Linton. Come, let us pray. Will you hold hands with us, Mr. Linton?"

"Not by a damned sight. I got to catch up my hoss." Linton stormed away.

Annie heard Winfield say to Hawg, "Reckon he's right. We dawdled here too long. We got to make up that lost time."

"Reckon, so," Hawg said. "Yep. I reckon so."

Annie began kicking out the fire. "Or that repulsive man knows he wants to put a lot of miles between him and any friends of those poor Ute Indians that he . . . scalped!"

CHAPTER TWENTY

When Breen and Keegan came to Purgatory City's largest corral — usually held for beef, now filled with forty ornery, rank, and mean-looking mustangs — Matt McCulloch figured that they had sobered up enough to back out of the deal they had agreed to earlier . . . which is what any reasonable human being would do.

"Matt," Keegan said, and let that sheepish, double-dealing, damn Yankee Irish grin crease his face. "As much as I'd love to work with you, get those hosses up to Fort Wilmont, well . . ." He shrugged.

"What about you?" McCulloch asked the bounty hunter.

"I got two prisoners I'd like to get to Precious Metal," Breen said. "I can wait here, but you know I don't like to wait. I'm with you."

That surprised McCulloch, but he knew what was coming next.

"But . . ."

Yeah, the but. It was the but McCulloch expected from this . . . jackal.

"You, me, and him . . ." Breen nodded at Wooden Arm, about fifteen or twenty yards down the corral, standing on the lower rail of the corral, staring at those wonderful mustangs, unencumbered by that idiotic splint McCulloch had fashioned.

Hell, this morning, McCulloch had tried to talk to the young fool — talking, as always, with his hands and fingers — to get to a doctor. Have a real sawbones patch the boy up, but Wooden Arm adamantly refused. His brother had made this to heal him, and Wooden Arm trusted his brother's medicine. It was second only to Broken Buffalo Horn's power. McCulloch still wondered who the hell this Broken Buffalo Horn was — and just how powerful he might be. But he had to accept the Comanche boy's reasoning. He felt a touch of pride that the teenager considered him a brother.

McCulloch considered another reason he had not pursued that argument. Even armed with a repeating rifle and a fully loaded Colt revolver, what chance did he have at persuading any doctor in Purgatory City, the county, or all of West Texas . . . even all of the Great State of Texas into being willing to treat a Comanche?

Breen shook his head. "You and me and him," he said again and laughed. "We couldn't get those horses to the Pecos River ourselves. I'm not sure we could even get them out of Purgatory City."

Frowning, McCulloch said, "What about your prisoners?"

"Hell, Matt, I was drunk. You know that. You wouldn't hold me to that idiotic idea. Kruger would cut our throats the first chance he got. He's a bank robber, a murderer, a thief in the night. He doesn't know a damned thing about herding mustangs."

McCulloch spit between his teeth. "Not so hard. I learned. Just keep them moving in the general direction. Feed them. Water them. That's all there is to it."

It was Breen's turn to spit. "You left out chasing down the runaways. Keeping them from bolting at night. You also left out all those mean dogs between here and Precious Metal — white, red, copper, blue, pink, purple — who will surely want to take them from us."

"Then take your Kruger and your lady friend on the stage to Precious Metal. Wooden Arm and I can find someone else to do this job with us — for less money than we offered you, too."

222

Breen turned and stared at the Wells Fargo office — the windows shot out, the front door riddled with bullets from that jail-break attempt — and some schoolboys playing hooky who were pointing out the very spot where town Marshal Rafe McMillian had been cut down in a hail of bullets and buckshot.

Suddenly he turned to Sean Keegan. "You Irish lout. Is that what they taught you in Londonderry? How to go back on your word?"

"Londonderry?" Keegan roared. "I never set me bloody toe in Londonderry."

"Well, you sure act like it. You gave your word to Matt McCulloch. Now you're going back on it!"

"Breen, you white-haired little varmint. Let me remind you it was your bloody reasoning not fifteen minutes ago that led me out of my fine little office to tell our fine, addle-minded fool of a friend that we wasn't going through what we said we was going through."

"I was testing you, Sergeant-No-More. And you failed."

"Well, buster, ye is about to fail your next test, because we'll be using what's left of you in ten minutes to grease that broken-armed Comanche's splint."

223

McCulloch stepped between them, but three men had left one of the saloons, and from the look of them, they had been drinking since late last night. They also looked like trouble, for one pointed at the corral and they all started walking straight for the stables. Right toward Wooden Arm. When a cowboy was drunk enough or mad enough to walk, McCulloch knew he meant business.

"Excuse me," McCulloch said, moving toward the street. "Whichever one of you is left standing, he's hired."

The cowboy on the southwestern edge, the bowlegged cuss with the green shirt and brown hat, spotted McCulloch first, and said something to the other two. They kept walking for a few more paces before the man in the middle, whose six-shooter was tucked inside the waistline of his black and tan checked britches, nodded, adjusted his tan hat, and then all three made a slight turn and went directly toward McCulloch. The third man, young, weasel-like looking, with a two-gun rig, grinned with drunken eagerness.

McCulloch stopped and waited, letting his right hand fall beside his Colt.

The threesome spread apart before they halted about twenty-five feet from the former Ranger.

"We don't like injuns in our town, Mc-Culloch," said the middle man, who Mc-Culloch recognized as Zebra Dave, a worthless man who probably earned his drinking money from the cows he rustled from the rancher who was paying him a dollar a day, a place to sleep, and three square meals every day.

"He won't be here for long."

"Oh," said the weasel with a malicious laugh. "He'll be here for a long, long time, Ranger."

The one with the green shirt said, "Like till . . . Judgment Day."

All three laughed, but that stopped when McCulloch saw their eyes move past him. He also felt the presence of a man on either side of him.

The cowboy in the green shirt took a few steps back. Weasel criss-crossed his arms till his hands rested on the butts of the two revolvers that hung low on his hips.

A laugh from McCulloch's left indicated his friend had made the man easily. "I know you," Jed Breen said, though McCulloch couldn't tell who the bounty hunter was talking to. "Saw your likeness on a dodger in Cooter City nine months ago."

McCulloch knew that to be a damned lie.

Cooter City had been wiped out in a flood along the Nueces River ten years ago. Hell, these days there wasn't a place where a wanted dodger could be put. There hadn't been much of a place to hang a wanted poster eleven years ago, either.

"That's a . . . lie," the weasel said, but his face revealed doubt.

"We don't like injun lovers, either," Zebra Dave said.

McCulloch no longer looked at the kid in the green shirt. He figured that boy would be hightailing it for his mama in about thirty seconds. Besides, Sean Keegan hadn't said one damned word, so McCulloch figured the old cavalry trooper had his eyes on the shaking punk.

"Keegan?" McCulloch asked, just to make sure he wasn't mistaken, that it wasn't wishful thinking that he felt a presence on his right. "That undertaker fellow, Percy something . . . ?"

"A. Percival Helton. What about him?"

"He wasn't among those killed during that raid by the Benteens, was he?"

"Nay. The greedy worm is doing a bonanza's worth of business lately."

McCulloch nodded. "I expect his boom will continue. In say . . . ten seconds."

The two-gun punk made the first move,

but McCulloch paid him no mind. The one wearing the green shirt turned and ran, and probably would have made it, but he tripped and fell face-first in the street. By then Jed Breen was cutting lose with his double-action Colt, the bullets popping the kid in both lungs, turning him around so Breen's next two slugs went damned close to the exit wounds the first two bullets had made.

McCulloch took his time, knowing Zebra Dave, like most drunks, like most cowboys, would rush his shot. The bullet blasted dirt onto McCulloch's boots before the Colt was halfway out of McCulloch's holster. The second shot might have done some damage if McCulloch had not taken time to shave that morning. The third shot . . . well that might have hit the bell in the Catholic church's front yard. McCulloch heard the chime, but surely even Zebra Dave couldn't have shot that wild.

One blast from McCulloch put Zebra Dave on his knees. Zebra Dave's last shot went into his own knee. That, McCulloch reasoned, was one damned ugly wound, and would have required amputation of the lower part of his left leg. Knowing the quality of the doctors in Purgatory City, that likely would have killed Zebra Dave anyway, but it didn't matter. Zebra Dave had fallen over to his side on the street and tried to clutch his shattered knee.

"My leg," he choked out, even though it was the bullet that Matt McCulloch had put in the lower part of his chest that killed him.

That should have been the end of it, but the boy in the green shirt sat up, cried out, cursed, and jerked out his pistol.

"Don't be a bloody —" Sean Keegan said, but the kid shot anyway. Glass behind the three jackals shattered.

Keegan put a bullet in the heart, and that was the last fired.

"Idiot," Keegan finished his sentence as the boy flattened onto the street, shuddered once, purged his bladder and bowels, and died with the two other damned fools.

Undertaker A. Percival Helton rounded the corner a moment later, looking as though he hadn't gotten much sleep as of late. His eyes started gleaming when he saw the three corpses, and he sprinted to the center of the melee.

"They're all yours, Worm," Keegan said. "Resisting arrest. Charge it all to the county sheriff's office."

"That's quite a tab you're running," McCulloch said as he holstered his Colt. He looked at Breen. "Was that kid wanted somewhere?"

The bounty hunter was busy chucking out his empties and replacing them with fresh cartridges. "Probably," Breen replied. "But a punk like that, he's hardly worth trying to claim a bounty on."

They turned around and walked back to the corral, ignoring the stares and whispers from people beginning to line the board-walks and streets of Purgatory City. Mc-Culloch saw Wooden Arm. No longer standing on the corral, he had moved to the center, staring with Comanche solemnity at the three approaching men. The mustangs ran wildly in the corral but soon began to stop as the sounds of gunfire quieted and the smell of gun smoke dissipated. The Comanche boy's good hand moved.

"What did he say?" Breen asked.

McCulloch answered Wooden Arm with his own hands first, then looked at the bounty hunter. "He wanted to know what that was all about."

"How'd ye answer the lad?" Keegan asked.

"I told him it was . . . an error in judgment."

"Aye."

McCulloch turned to the Irishman. "Are you with us or are you staying?"

After a stutter, a stammer, and a sneer,

229

Keegan smiled. "Aye. I'll be riding with ye lads." He looked at both boardwalks. "Sheriff Garcia will be coming back at some point, and he might question the charges that have been billed to his office. And I likely have friends at Fort Wilmont who'd buy me some fine Irish whiskey for I hear there are more saloons in that fine, bawdy town than there are in County Cork."

"All right. I think we'd best light out for the Pecos before noon."

"I'll pack me gear," Keegan said.

"Do that. But before you end your account with the county, why don't you charge up some grub? And a wagon with some supplies. But don't splurge."

The former sergeant did an about-face and headed for the nearest store.

"But Sean?"

Stopping on a dime, Keegan spun around on his heel. "Sir!" he barked.

"No whiskey. Not even a dram of beer. I'm serious."

"Ye'll be a hard officer to serve under, sir."

McCulloch smiled. "I'll buy enough to put you under in Precious Metal."

"A bloody fine deal. You'll blow your four hundred and fifty dollars in one night, Matt." Keegan practically danced across the street toward the general store.

McCulloch turned to Breen.

"What changed your mind?"

The bounty hunter chuckled, tilted his head, and nodded at the Wells Fargo office.

"Surely it wasn't the price of three tickets on the stage to Precious Metal," McCulloch said.

"No, not that at all. I just saw those bullet holes and everything, and it reminded me that's from the raid on the jail. The one that led to all that." His head tilted to the county courthouse — the charred part — and the school kids pointing to the black spot where the gallows had been before Sean Keegan had gone into action. "Well, it just suddenly popped into my mind that, after what your pard Mr. Keegan did to Lovely Tom Lovely, the rest of the Benteen boys will be out for blood. Sean's blood. And" — he eased the Colt into his holster — "the Benteens are worth a hell of a lot more than Otto Kruger and Charlotte Platte combined."

Breen's right hand went up and punched McCulloch playfully in the shoulder. "I'll gather my gear. Be back here with two more reluctant hired hands in fifteen minutes."

Spinning on his heel, Breen raced across the street.

McCulloch turned around and saw the mustangs. Wooden Arm stepped into his line

231

of vision and moved his hands.

What did he say?

McCulloch understood and tried his best to make his answer something that the young Indian brave would understand.

He signed, *This is going to be the damnedest thing you ever tried, and you're one crazy maniac to try it.*

Wooden Arm studied McCulloch's hands for a full fifteen seconds, then looked into the white man's face for another ten, looked at the three dead men on the street, then back into McCulloch's hard eyes. The boy grunted, nodded his head in agreement, and walked back to the mustangs in the corral.

CHAPTER TWENTY-ONE

Undertaker A. Percival Helton could not believe the fortune he had been reaping. He laughed at his three former competitors in the business who had either died or moved to what they figured would be a more profitable town where men and women were older, thus more likely to bite the dust. Helton had stayed put, and, by thunder, he felt so happy that he had. Those fools — except the poor soul who had died — overlooked three important factors that no profitable undertaker should have —

Matt McCulloch.

Jed Breen.

Sean Keegan.

The bell above the door to his office caused Helton to mutter a high-pitched curse. By thunder, had not he just sent that fool errand boy off to the general store to pick up more nails and the cheapest wood to be had and charge it to Helton's Undertaker, Coffins, & Funerals? Certainly that kid could not be back yet. He must have forgotten something.

Gosh darn it, Helton thought. He had three coffins to build.

"What is it now?" he squealed.

"You the undertaker?"

He lifted his head. Why, that wasn't that fool boy. That was a man with a hard Texas accent. Maybe he was bringing in yet another customer. The sun always shown on a businessman who knew his business.

"Be right with you, sir. Have a seat. There are tissues handy if you need to cry, and an illustrated catalog of all our services."

That might keep the bereaved busy for a few minutes. Helton laid the pliers on the table, pulled the rag out of his back pocket, and wiped the sweat from his brow. *Confound it, this shouldn't be taking so long.*

He grabbed the tool again, gripping it tighter, and shoved open the corpse's mouth. He found the tooth in the back, a big molar, and squeezed the pliers on that beautiful gold filling. He began tugging, twisting, trying his best to loosen the son of a gun. By thunder, there was just no sense in burying a man shot to hell like he was with gold in his mouth. Helton certainly did not expect any grieving family member to look into this gent's mouth. No one had in all of Helton's thirty-two years as an bona fide undertaker and mortician.

Helton put his left hand on the dead gunman's shoulder, using it as a brace. *Good, good, excellent.* Rigor mortis had set in, so this victim remained stiff as a stone block. Now, if he could just get that danged old beautiful gold tooth to cooperate.

So attuned to his job, Helton failed to hear the tune the spurs with the jingle bobs played as the latest customer walked from the sitting parlor to the workroom, generally off limits to the bereaved family of the deceased. When the man grunted, A. Percival Helton panicked, and the pliers slipped, breaking off the top of an incisor — not that the gent on the table felt a thing.

Helton slipped off his tool, banged into the counter that held all his other accouterments, even knocked over a beacon of his own concoction of embalming fluid. An oath slipped from his mouth. Those ingredients did not come cheap in a remote burg like Purgatory City.

A. Percival Helton gave the big gent with the big mustache and a wicked scar over his left cheek the meanest look he could muster up.

"Beggin' your pardon, Mr. Undertaker,

but I got some boys of mine waitin' outside and just need to ask you a few questions."

Helton tried to remember this man was troubled, grieving, and, well, any man still breathing could be a paying customer. Customers paid a whole lot better than the county, and this stiff and the two others waiting to be ready for burial were county pays.

"Yes, of course." Helton wiped his face. "Let's go into the parlor and I can show you —"

"Here's fine."

The man suddenly didn't look so upset by the loss of a loved one.

"Well . . ." Something about the gent's posture told Helton that argument would be futile. He found a pencil and a pad, and said, "Is the person you wish to be taken care of male or female?"

"Male."

"How old?"

"Twenty-six."

"Oh, how sad. In the prime of life. I'm so sorry. And your relation to the dearly departed."

"Cousin."

"And where are . . . umm . . . your cousin's . . . remains?"

The man straightened. "I figured you had

236

him already."

Helton looked up, then at the corpse who had so fiercely refused to give up a gold tooth, a corpse whose front tooth had been busted by Helton's clumsiness — although he could blame it on this big Texan . . . with . . . a . . . big . . . pistol . . . on . . . his . . . hip.

"Well . . . I have . . . three new . . . um —"

"My cousin's name is Lovely. Tom Lovely. But folks in this part of the state called him Tom Benteen. My name's Hank Benteen. Brother Bob and Uncle Zach is waitin' outside. I'd like to make all the arrangements — burial, tombstone, all that — afore some of your citizens recognize my kinfolk. Cause us to shoot up this dung heap of a town to pieces agin."

Sweat poured down Helton's forehead. His teeth clattered.

"Can I see poor Tom?" the killer asked.

"Well . . . you . . . see . . ."

"I see that you're the undertaker," Hank Benteen said as he stepped forward and pulled the short-barreled Colt from his holster. "The only one in town."

Suddenly, A. Percival Helton prayed that that danged fool of a helper would come back through the front door and cause

Hank Benteen to murder him so that he, unarmed, never-hurt-anyone-because-they-were-already-dead Percival Helton could escape before he was so foully murdered during the biggest undertaking bonanza of his career.

He dropped to his knees, sobbing, wailing, clasping his hands as though in prayer. He begged, screamed, and pleaded for mercy.

"Where's my cousin, you snivelin' pig?"

"He's not here!"

"He's dead. I gotta figure you boys hung him."

"Yes, yes, they hanged him — I didn't — I detest hangings, beheadings, all forms of execution. I detest prisons. No one should be incarcerated. I —"

"Where is he?"

"They . . . he . . . he . . . well . . ."

"Where?"

"Sean Keegan burned him, Mr. Benteen. He said it was a Viking funeral." Helton fell onto the floor, curled in a fetal position, and continued to sob. "He hanged him. Keegan. The . . . Irishman . . . hanged him . . . and then . . . that's why part of the courthouse is in ashes . . . he burned . . . burned the . . . whole gallows . . . with your . . . brother . . . still swinging from . . .

238

the . . . gallows."

"He was my *cousin.* Not my brother. But cousins is as thick as brothers when you're a Benteen. You say . . . Keegan?"

"Sean Keegan. Oh, what a disgrace to the good name of Purgatory City."

"Horse apples. Piss on your damned city."

"Well . . . Keegan . . . you know . . . one of the so-called jackals our late newspaper editor and publisher called him. Sean Keegan. Used to wear the uniform of the United States Army."

"And where might I find Keegan now?"

"He rode out. With Matt McCulloch."

"The Texas Ranger?"

"Used to be. No more. Not in more than a year or so. They're taking horses . . . mustangs . . . somewhere. Keegan joined McCulloch, some Indian and . . . the third jackal. B-b-b-Breen."

"Breen. That miserable bounty-huntin' swine."

"Yes. They left earlier today."

Helton felt relieved when he heard the hammer fall safely on the Colt, and then the revolver slide into the holster.

"All right. So it's Keegan I want. Now . . . where are my brother's remains?"

"Your . . . cousin's . . . you mean —"

"I mean nothing. I tol' you that Benteens

239

are all brothers, cousins or not. He went by the name Tom Benteen, didn't he, damn you?"

"Yes, sir. Yes, Mr. Benteen."

"So where is he?"

"Well . . . he was burned."

"There's ashes then. Ashes that need buryin'."

Percival Helton soiled his britches.

Hank Benteen squatted beside him, jerked the undertaker halfway up, and slammed him against the counter.

"You just left him there, didn't you? You pipsqueak. You left him with the ashes of the gallows and even the damned rope they hung my cousin with."

"Brother. Your bro—"

Hank Benteen slapped the cowardly undertaker savagely.

"You left him outside. All night. All day."

"Yes . . . sir . . . but . . ."

Helton heard the spurs singing as Benteen rose then squatted back down. Opening his eyes, Helton saw the beaker in the killer's right hand.

Benteen's left hand grabbed Helton's shirtfront and slammed him harder.

"Drink your juice, undertaker."

"P-please. That's got —"

Helton tried to remember the ingredients.

240

Mercury. Arsenic. Some wax that would harden. And blue ink. A few other ingredients, but the first two were the ones that would kill him.

"No . . ." He choked, then felt the fluid entering his throat. He tried to spit it out, but Hank Benteen released his hold and slammed a fist into his stomach, causing Helton to spit out some embalming fluid before he had to suck in a deep breath. That caused him to suck down a lot of his own invention, his own concoction. He swallowed. Then without thinking had a second helping.

Over his gagging, convulsing, and spitting out blood, A. Percival Helton heard the spurs chiming as Hank Benteen walked away. He even heard the bell ring as the front door opened and closed.

He tried to spit out the fluid, but just spit out more blood. It just wasn't right, he thought. Not with business so good. But at leas — he started to relax — he could see the silver lining. His teeth were perfect. Whoever worked on him would not have any gold fillings to dig out of his mouth.

CHAPTER TWENTY-TWO

On his fifth attempt at trying to throw a loop around the neck of a colt that had sunk into the muddy bogs of the shallow, ugly, but dangerous Pecos River, Jed Breen cursed to himself for this damned stupid decision to get to Precious Metal, Arizona Territory, driving forty ornery, malicious, vindictive, and headstrong mustangs that were nothing but a nuisance. Hell, he could have been bouncing around in a Concord stagecoach, maybe playing a friendly game of blackjack with a pretty lady gambler. Or gambling with a drummer with a kit of liquor samples.

"You need help?"

Breen gathered up the rope, and snapped at that tough nut Matt McCulloch, always holier than thou when in his element — and this was that damned old Ranger and horse swindler's element. It certainly was not Jed Breen's.

"No!" Breen snapped back without looking at the opposite bank. He might not be doing something he did well, but, by the saints, he had his pride. He wasn't about to become the butt of jokes for the next ungodly number of miles, having to listen to Matt McCulloch and Sean Keegan ridicule his cowboying skills. Hell, that teenage Comanche kid with the badly broken arm would be laughing, too. Not to mention the prisoners Breen was hauling in for a couple of nice rewards.

"Then get to it!" McCulloch fired back. "We're —"

"Burning daylight," Breen finished the rest of McCulloch's sentence, though he whispered it under his breath. Hell, McCulloch had been saying that all morning. Before morning actually, when the night remained pitch black and the only daylight to be found came in the smell of the coffee that McCulloch had started cooking thirty minutes earlier when everyone else — every person who hadn't lost his damned mind — had been trying to sleep just a wee bit more.

The lariat came up, Breen began swinging out a loop, letting his horse carry him a few rods closer in the water but not close enough to get caught in that mud trap. Hell, that would be more than McCulloch — and Jed Breen — could take in one day. He sighed, almost whispered a prayer, and let the rope sail. The head of the bay colt ducked, snorted, twisted this way and that, and Breen swore again. He'd miss again. He ought to just draw the double-action Colt and empty every bullet into that son of a gun's head.

Then the world moved in as though only Jed Breen, the horse he rode, the rope, and the colt remained. It slowed like the minute hands on a clock, barely perceptible. The head of the bay colt turned away from the rope, but the rope just hung in the air. The head lowered, the young horse's nose grazing the reddish-brown water, came up. Breen swore he could see the drops of water falling from the horse's lips and snout, dripping every so slowly and plopping between the waves the frightened, struggling animal kept making. The rope stood still, until the colt's head jerked back up.

Breen barely noticed a damned thing for it all happened so fast. The loop sailed right over the colt's head. Tightened as though the horse Breen rode had pulled back instinctively, which the bounty hunter suddenly realized, it had. He heard the zip as the wet hemp tightened, a snug fit against the muscular neck of the bay.

"Son of a gun!" Breen shouted. "I roped that son of a —"

Hell broke loose.

The colt tried to sit. Breen's horse pulled back. Somehow, the bounty hunter realized to wrap the rope tightly around the horn of his saddle. That almost cost Breen a couple of fingers, which would be a severe hazard for a man who made his living with a gun. Looking back, he saw the bay's eyes bulge and flame with anger, and the horse tried to bite at the rope, tried to pull itself out of the mud that had caught him like a bear trap.

The lariat went taut and Breen's horse lunged away from the furious, screaming colt. For a second, Breen knew he had lost the stirrups, felt his butt lift off the saddle, and he pictured himself being plunged into the Pecos River. Not only that, he could see himself standing up in the shallow water, only to be knocked down by this horse. The rope — one end around the colt's neck, the other wrapped tightly to the horn of Breen's saddle — singing loudly with a zing and the rope breaking, almost slicing Breen's head off. But that would not be the worst of it. The worst would be watching that horse take off with Breen's saddlebags and that

high-powered, straight-shooting Sharps rifle
he carried in the scabbard. Taking off and
loping right into a party of Comanches,
Kiowas, or Apaches. They'd make off with
his horse and long-distance rifle with the
brass telescopic sight, leaving Breen to hear
the jokes all the way to Precious Metal.

Praise the saints, that didn't happen. He
came down hard in the saddle, hard enough
that he thought he might double over in
agony and never entertain a lady friend
again. Hard enough that he knew he would
have to, secretly, check for ruptures or at
least bad bruises, when he had some privacy
in the camp that evening. His knees bent,
his legs kicked away, and his horse bucked
just a little, sending Breen's feet back, and
his boots slid perfectly back into the stirrups.

The horse turned around. Head low, it
began churning, while behind Breen, the
colt lunged and fought against the thickening mud. The rope pulled even tauter, and
Breen leaned forward in the saddle, barely
aware at how he kicked and spurred the
fuming, pounding, driving horse beneath
him.

He felt an amazing burst of freedom, suddenly aware that he was loping across the
Pecos toward the disappearing herd of

horses on the far bank, and the colt ran after him — out of the mud and into the shallows, then surging up onto the wet, sandy banks that quickly gave way to more rocks, more cactus, and more of the rough, harsh Texas land that stretched northwestward into New Mexico Territory.

On the shore, Breen pulled on the reins and let his horse stop. The colt, exhausted, shook off its wetness, shivered, and forgot all of its rage. It just stood there, allowing Breen to ride close to it, reach over, and lift the coiled, wet loop over the tired animal's head. Breen backed his own horse up, gathered the rope, coiling it, and strapping it back underneath the horn of the saddle.

Something splashed behind him, and Breen turned suddenly, reaching for the holstered revolver but stopping when he saw the mawkish, almost obscene splinted arm of the Comanche boy. Wooden Arm stopped his pinto and grinned at Breen.

For the life of him, the bounty hunter couldn't figure exactly why, but he laughed out loud. "Pretty good show, eh?" he heard himself saying. "Folks in St. Louis would pay twelve bits to see that in an opera house." He twisted in the saddle to find McCulloch riding back through the cut in the slopes. His horse slowed, and the old horse trader stood in his stirrups. Breen wished he were closer so he could memorize the expression on McCulloch's face.

A few moments later, McCulloch stopped the horse, studied Breen, the Comanche, and the bay colt. "Hell." He shook his head. "I wasted time riding back here to help you." He stuck his jaw out toward Wooden Arm. "Did he help you?"

"No," Breen said, silently fuming. He had pulled that horse out himself, even made the loop over the wild animal's neck, and he didn't have one witness. It reminded him of all those times he had brought in dead outlaws who had not given him any chance but to use his Colt or his Sharps. And all that time, all that frustration, telling judges and solicitors and coroners and newspaper reporters over and over and over again what had happened, that it was a clear-cut case of self-defense. Well, McCulloch was a former Texas Ranger. He didn't trust anyone.

Wooden Arm began speaking in that harsh Comanche tongue, and using the fingers on his good hand, flashing this and that to Mc-Culloch, who shook his head, whistled, and turned back to Breen.

"The boy says . . . not exactly in these words . . . that you'll make a top hand after

248

all." He spit between his teeth at a yucca plant. "Hell, I wish I'd seen it."

"Well, boss man," Breen said with a smile, "you didn't know you were getting a top hand when you hired me on. You just thought I was a top gun."

McCulloch almost turned into a verifiable human being. "Un-huh," he said, and turned his horse around. "Maybe that cook you made me hire will make you up a special dish. To celebrate. If you got the guts to eat it."

CHAPTER TWENTY-THREE

"Son of a gun," Sean Keegan said, chuckling as he watched Breen push the colt into the herd, then ride to the camp Keegan had been left in charge of.

McCulloch rode in with the young Indian kid, who took the first watch and began circling the herd of ponies and mustangs. Breen slowed his horse to a walk, easily dismounted, and began unsaddling his horse.

"Hell," the Irishman said, spitting into the dirt, and looking back at the outlaw with the scarred face and the buxomly woman who stirred a pot filled with stew. It's a good thing, Keegan thought, that he wasn't betting real money. He had figured Breen would come limping in, dead to the world, hardly able to stand after four days of rough riding since leaving Purgatory City. But the son of a gun looked like he had been riding horses in the United States Cavalry practically as long as Sean Keegan had . . . which annoyed the hell out of him.

McCulloch spurred his horse to the covered wagon, but he left his horse saddled. That was fine. He would ride out to spell the Comanche kid after he ate his supper. Keegan turned around and looked at Otto Kruger as he helped Charlotte Platte fix supper.

He raised his canteen and drank. A moment later, McCulloch's spurs signaled his approach, and the tall, broad-shouldered Texas hard rock with the narrow hips and bowed legs, stood at Keegan's side. He, too, looked at the killer who used guns and the killer who used arsenic and anything else she could get her hands on.

"You kept an eye on them the whole time, didn't you?" McCulloch said.

Keegan gargled with the hot water from the canteen and spit it onto a lonely prickly pear. "Hell, Matt, we've been out with them four days and we have yet to be taken with sickness and die a ghastly death."

"I'd like to keep it that way."

"We'll do like we've been doing, me laddie," Keegan said as he corked the canteen. "Make them eat first."

"The poison could be something she rubbed on the bowls."

251

"We can shuffle the bowls so no one knows what's what."

"Charlotte Platte might be mean enough to be willing to die and kill all of us."

"Nay, laddie. She likes the kid."

McCulloch turned. "The kid? What kid?"

"Your adopted Comanch, of course. Wooden Arm."

McCulloch's hard eyes tried to weed out the joke Keegan had to be playing, but the old horse soldier was deadly serious.

"She dotes on the boy. Rubs salve over his bad arm, then laces the splints back together. Bloody hell, Matt, have ye not been looking at them all the time since we rode out for Precious Metal?"

"Well, I told Breen . . . well, there's — Hell, I have enough on my mind, Sergeant."

"It ain't sergeant no more, Matt. Ye ought to remember that."

"I've known you too long to call you anything else."

"Except an ornery old fool and crotchety Irishman. And those are all ye can say in front of polite company. There's also —"

"I'll try to call you Sean."

Keegan laughed. "How'd ye do helping our friend the bounty killer get that colt out of the quicksand?"

McCulloch shook his head. "He did it on

his own."

"Bloody hell."

McCulloch nodded in affirmation. "I got back to the bank, and he had the rope off the colt's neck, and his clothes — as you can see for yourself — are dry enough to know he didn't lose his seat and take an unscheduled bath."

"Bloody hell," Keegan said again. Why, if he had been gambling for real, he'd already be out of chips and heading back to the bank to pay for some more blues, reds, and whites. Good thing he was stuck in the middle of nowhere.

While the prisoners finished cooking, the three men gathered in the shade beside the covered wagon as the sun began to creep behind the distant horizon.

Matt began drawing a line in the dirt, making observations as he went. "We're here. Should cut through the red bluffs tomorrow, be in New Mexico Territory by the time we pitch our next camp." The line weaved through sand. "Here's the tough spot. Seven Rivers. Though there's really no such thing. Hell, I doubt if you could find seven rivers in the entire territory that anyone who lived somewhere other than New Mexico would call a river. But it's trouble."

"Yeah," Breen said. "They call it rustlers paradise. Home to every horse thief and every cattle rustler in this part of the country."

Keegan looked at him. "You ever bring in a rustler?"

"Hardly. Just by accident." At least Breen rubbed the insides of his legs.

That gave Keegan some satisfaction.

"Stock detectives usually work the rustlers. Not enough money in it for a professional like me."

"You might be working rustlers with me," McCulloch said. "But not for any reward. Just to keep the herd moving."

Breen found a flask, drank, pitched it to McCulloch. "My reward is over yonder, cooking supper for us. I'll collect on both in Precious Metal."

Nodding, McCulloch continued his line. "From here to" — he moved the stick and made a long, meandering way about six or seven inches — "here there's a whole lot of nothing. A good spring, but that could mean a lot of Mescalero Apaches. Or bandits from Old Mexico."

"Or it could be dry," Keegan commented.

Breen nodded. "Or it could be dry."

"It damned well better not be dry," Mc-

Culloch said. He drew the line toward the tongue of the covered wagon. "This is what's left of Fort Sumner. Get from there and the country turns tolerable."

"Aye," Keegan said. "North of there is lovely Las Vegas, New Mexico Territory. A paradise for gamblers, Breen. I've wrecked many a saloon. We'll —"

"We're not going that far north." McCulloch drew the line sharply toward a dead scorpion.

"Bloody hell," Keegan said.

"Save your carousing and destruction of private property for Precious Metal, Arizona Territory," McCulloch said. "We move west."

"I don't recall a bloody trail," Keegan said. "Ye follow the Pecos to Vegas, then down to Santa Fe, and over to —"

"We're making our own trail. our way, the established way, is a lot of wasted time."

"But there's water," Keegan argued.

"There's water here, too." McCulloch smiled underneath his dust-caked beard stubble. "If you know where to look."

"Do you know?" Breen asked.

The old Ranger's head rose and tilted toward the grazing mustangs. "He does."

Keegan knew he meant the Comanche with the wrecked arm.

"You mean," Breen spoke softly, "we've got to trust a damned injun, and a pup of one at that, to find us water."

"You mean," McCulloch said even softer, "We've got to trust a murdering devil and a bank robber named Kruger and a woman who poisoned more men than Otto Kruger has probably killed to help us get across this harsh, violent land?"

Sighing, Breen glanced at the Comanche boy with the horses, then at the prisoners he had brought along.

McCulloch drew the line farther. "There's a pass in the Southern Rockies about here. That gets us to the western part of the territory."

"And the territory of more Indians," Keegan said.

"And men who are worse than Indians," Breen said.

The line moved more. "We'll be in the Malpais about here."

"Malpais," Breen said with a soft whisper. "Bad country. Badlands."

"Bad people, too," Keegan said, and drank from the flask that came to him. "Even worse than us jackals." He tossed the flask to Breen, and filled his mouth with a sizeable chaw of tobacco he bit off from a plug.

The line stretched on. "There's a fort

about here. And another a little more north. Make it that far, and we've hit Arizona Territory."

"Where's Precious Metal?" Breen asked.

Lifting the stick, McCulloch glanced again at the chefs they had, then at the boy wrangler with the broken arm and hair the color of Otto Kruger's black heart. He jabbed a point far beyond the dead scorpion.

Keegan laughed without much thought. "Aye." He spit. "And there's the Painted Desert." *Farther.* "There's where the Apaches wiped out Second Lieutenant Gregg Marion's outfit six years back. Served with ol' Gregg. Lousy officer, nothing but a babe in the woods, wet behind the ears before the warriors cut off his ears, but he took a lot of good men with him."

He wiped his mouth, laughed, and spit again, closer to the Painted Desert but a long way from where they were right then. "And that's the Dead River."

"What's dead about it?" McCulloch asked.

"Usually, everybody that goes there," Keegan said with a laugh.

"Well," McCulloch said, and drew the line south and curved it underneath the Dead River, the Painted Desert, and the tobacco-

257

soaked ant that crawled away from where Second Lieutenant Gregg Marion got wiped out with his command, and he drew the line all the way to Precious Metal. "This is the way the stagecoach line runs. If we follow that, we miss all those other places."

"Aye," Keegan said. "But we're still here. And that's a long way to go before we end this long, hot, dusty, but damned well bloody interesting journey."

"What else?" Breen asked.

Charlotte Platte banged a metal spoon against the cast iron pot that had been placed over the fire. "Supper's ready, boys," she cried out. "Come and get it."

Breen, McCulloch, and Keegan exchanged nervous looks.

CHAPTER TWENTY-FOUR

Hans Kruger put both hands on the batwing doors at the miserable hovel in the middle of nowhere. Inside what billed itself as a way station but was nothing more than a hog ranch between the Pecos and the Rio Grande, it served the worst women and whiskey only slightly less deadly. The clinking of glasses and the giggling — more like wheezing — of a prostitute fell into complete silence. Slowly, tentatively, he pushed the doors open and stepped out of the night wind and into the dimly lit one-room stone shack that smelled of Taos Lightning, smoke, and filth.

The prostitutes had moved away from one of the two tables in the place. The bartender twirled his mustache.

Uncle Zach Lovely trained both barrels of a sawed-off double-barrel at the door. Bob Benteen, each hand holding a Smith & Wesson .44, grinned and eared back both hammers. Hank Benteen removed the cigar from his mouth with his left hand, his right tucked inside the lever of a sawed-off Winchester repeater, hammer cocked, finger on the trigger. At least that weapon was pointed at what passed for a ceiling.

For now.

"Evening." Hank Benteen nodded at the bartender. "Carlos is still serving. As long as you got coin."

"Obliged." Hans stepped through the doorway and let the doors bang their way shut behind him.

"He say that funny, don't he?" Bob Benteen said.

"Like a Hun," Uncle Zach said.

When Hans Kruger reached the bar, he placed his right hand away from the Colt and onto the bar. He used his left to fish out a dollar, which he flipped to the barman.

"The best you got."

The Mexican shrugged. "Best is worst. Worst is best." He ducked and rose quickly, filled a dirty glass with filthy liquor, and put the jug back where he had stashed it. By then Uncle Zach had risen from his chair, and still holding the shotgun, moved through the batwing doors, which again banged.

Kruger shot down the kerosene the Mexican called liquor, eased the glass back onto the bar, and nodded. "Another."

"For a Hun," Uncle Zach said as he stepped back inside, "he can handle his liquor." The old man looked at Hank. "Nobody's with him."

Kruger made himself turn around to the Benteen Gang, holding the glass at the brutal men and nodding his blessings. Bob had holstered his .44s, Uncle Zach had returned the shotgun, now uncocked, to his lap, and Hank had laid the Winchester on the table, but the barrel pointed in Kruger's general direction, and the fingers on his right hand beat out a horse trot next to the lever.

"Late to be riding," Hank said. "Especially in this country."

"I look for someone." The German accent caused Bob Benteen to snigger.

"Maybe I know him." Hank Benteen smiled.

"Ja, you do," Kruger said. "For it is you, Hank Benteen."

The fingers stopped their trot and inched inside the lever.

Kruger hurriedly explained, "I am Hans Kruger."

261

"Is that 'posed to mean something to me, Hun?"

He felt the wind leave his sails. It was a discouraging fact to learn that despite robberies, murders, and the occasional swindles in Arizona, New Mexico, one town in California, and five places in Texas, Hans and Otto Kruger didn't rank with the Benteens.

"Dere are vanted posters on me and Otto, my brother."

"Congratulations."

He smiled. *"Danke."*

"What the hell does that mean?" Uncle Zach growled.

"It is German. For tank you."

"You ain't in Rome no more, you damned Hun," Uncle Zach said.

Hans Kruger blinked.

Hank Benteen shook his head and spit on the floor. "Rome's in Italy, you idiot." Then he nodded again at Kruger. "So you're Hans Kruger and you're wanted. Why are you looking for me?"

"I need to join you."

The outlaw leader shook his head. "We're full up."

"But Tom is —" Kruger realized his mistake and gulped down the liquor. The guns were trained on him again. He dropped the glass, only after he had emptied it, on the bar, and quickly removed his hat out of respect for the dead. "*Bitte.* Let me explain."

"Make it good, Hun. You got ten seconds."

He'd never been able to do it in such short time, but Hans Kruger tried. "The man you —" He didn't finish, but only because two rifle barrels pointed through the doorway just above the batwing doors.

The twin barrels of a big shotgun came up at the bottom of the doors, and a Texas voice boomed,

"Don't try it, you damned Benteens. If just a-one of ya blinks, you all buy a ticket straight to Hell."

Hank Benteen was halfway out of his seat, knocking over the chair, but he could not get the rifle up in time, and he knew that. He looked with malevolent eyes at Hans Kruger, who was stunned by this turn of events. The leader of the cutthroat killers snarled, "You traitor, you Judas, you miserable son of a —"

The batwing doors opened, and the two men with rifles went in, two graybeards wearing dusters and big Texas hats.

As the shotgun barrel rose, the third, a smaller man, snickered. He had more wrinkles in his face than on the prostitute who had moved away from the Benteens.

"Gotch ye boys." He slapped his side with his left hand, keeping the right on the scattergun. "Gotch ye good."

"Shut up," said the taller of the graybeards. Then back to the Benteens, "Reach."

Slowly, Hank Benteen's right hand left the table and joined the left hand high over his head. Uncle Zach pitched the shotgun on the table and followed his nephew's movements. Bob Benteen wet his lips, but leaped up, trying for his holstered .44s.

It was the wrinkled man who cut Bob Benteen down, blasting his chest open with both barrels of the shotgun and riddling the prostitute behind him. The impact of the buckshot drove him back, knocking over the prostitute as she screamed and died. He slammed into the wall and sat on the floor, both eyes seemed fixed on the trail of blood he left as he slid across the hellhole. The woman lay facedown in a lake of crimson.

"I gotch him," the wrinkled man said. "I —"

The bartender turned around and cried out, "You murdered my wife."

The thinner of the graybeards shot the Mexican between the eyes, and he crashed beside wherever he kept the jugs of his awful brew.

For a moment, Hans Kruger wondered if

these men would kill him, but once the ringing died down and the smoke drifted
through the opening above the batwing
doors, or holes in the ceiling, the taller of
the graybeards looked at Kruger and said,
"Who the hell are you?"

"Ich bin —" Quickly he stopped, thought,
decided these men were bounty hunters,
and said, "John Smith."

The thinner graybeard laughed, and to
Hans Kruger's surprise, so did Hank Benteen, which did not seem logical considering that of the three people cut down so
violently and so unexpectedly in this place
in the middle of nowhere, one happened to
be Hank Benteen's brother.

"All right, John Smith," the tall graybeard
said, "if you want to live, this is how you'll
play this hand. You'll sign a statement that
the bartender was killed by Tom Benteen
and —"

"That's Bob," Uncle Zach corrected.

"All right. The bartender was shot dead
by Bob Benteen. That's what started the
row. Zach killed the woman. Claude, Zeb,
and me each killed the Benteens."

Hank laughed. "You're not taking us in?"

"Corpses are less trouble. And dead men
don't talk."

They were looking at the Benteens, the

265

tall man, the thin man, and the cackling man with whiskers, so Hans Kruger drew the Colt from his holster and cracked three shots, downing the thin man with a ball through the temple, the cackling idiot with one that shattered his spine, and would have hit the tall graybeard in the heart but that man was fast and moving around. The slug just spun him around and dropped him to his knees, his left hand clutching his right shoulder.

He was still game, though, trying to raise the rifle, but Hank Benteen kicked it out of his hands and drew a .45 from his holster. When the tall man said, "Please," Hank shoved the barrel into the man's mouth, breaking off a couple of teeth.

"Unh-unh," Hank Benteen told the wild-eyed man. "Corpses aren't no trouble. Dead men don't talk." He pulled the trigger.

Hank Benteen stepped around the dead Mexican, found the jug, and filled glasses for himself, Uncle Zach, and Hans Kruger. He raised his own toward his dead brother.

"You were a good brother, Bob."

"For a damned simpleton," Uncle Zach said.

All drank — Kruger, too — and then Hank Benteen pointed the Colt at Hans's head. "Now talk," he said, and thumbed back the hammer. "But because you saved our hides, I'll give you thirty seconds. Starting now."

It was quite simple, Hans Kruger managed to say. Hank and Uncle Zach had to be chasing the man who had killed Tom Benteen, hanging him in Purgatory City, then burning the body with the gallows. Kruger could not remember the name of this evil person, but he did know that he rode with the man who had taken his own brother prisoner. Some nefarious scoundrel named Jed Breen.

"Breen?" Uncle Zach said. "The bounty hunter?"

"*Ja.*"

That had taken longer than thirty seconds, but Hank Benteen lowered the Colt's hammer, then dropped the revolver into his holster.

"Go on," he ordered.

"Otto Kruger is being taken to Precious Metal," Hans said. From what he had managed to hear, the man who had murdered Tom Benteen and the bounty hunter who was taking in his brother for blood money were — this confused him until his head ached — driving ponies to sell in Arizona.

"With some other . . . what is the word . . . ? Jackal?"

Hank Benteen killed his liquor. "McCulloch." He nodded at his uncle. "The Ranger."

"The trifecta," Uncle Zach said. "Always wanted to kill McCulloch. And Breen, too. Now we got to add this Sean Keegan to our list." But he looked at the dead nephew still staring at nothing and still sitting against the stone wall. "But we is getting short on Benteens and Lovelies now."

"Yeah, but this Hun's faster than greased lightning with a six-gun." Hank nodded at Hans, held out his hand. "You just become a Benteen, Otto."

"I am Hans," Kruger corrected.

CHAPTER TWENTY-FIVE

"Let me get this straight," Sean Keegan said after dropping his saddle and bedroll beside the covered wagon in their camp for the night. "Texas wanted this chunk of land some time back?"

Matt McCulloch handed the cup of coffee to Charlotte Platte, who cursed him, took the cup, and drank it about halfway down.

"Satisfied?" she said.

He handed the cup to the ugly-scarred Kruger.

"I have one," the German said bitterly.

"I know," McCulloch said. "We're swapping."

The man's wrinkled, ugly lips turned into a menacing frown, but he took McCulloch's cup in his left hand, and shoved the cup in his right toward McCulloch. The old Ranger nodded, and handed the cup to Platte, who again, took a healthy swallow before shoving the cup to McCulloch.

He drank and turned to face the old Irish soldier. "You were saying?"

"I was saying that you Texans got the best deal of your lives when you didn't get this piece of desert. Texas already had enough of that. The bloody United States of America got swindled when it took this country after the war with Mexico." Keegan spit and reached over to take the coffee cup from Otto Kruger's hand. "New Mexico. Ain't a damned thing new about this. It's bloody hell."

Jed Breen trotted up to the camp, reining up a few feet from McCulloch and Keegan.

The old soldier lifted his cup, "Coffee?"

Breen unloosened the canteen from the horn and drank. "I'll stick to water. Till Precious Metal." He stoppered the canteen and nodded at McCulloch. "You were right."

McCulloch emptied the dregs from his cup and tossed it to the murderess. "How many?"

"Ten."

"Know where they're camped?"

"There's a cave in the hills to the south of here. Hard to find. But your Comanche friend got me there."

"Can you find it without him?"

Breen nodded.

"Would somebody bloody well tell me what the hell's going on?" Keegan said. "I thought you said Breen and the scalp lifter rode out to find water."

McCulloch said, "I said rustlers. Not water." He pointed. "The Pecos River is a hundred yards over there. Why the hell would we need to look for water?"

"Because the Pecos water tastes like piss." Keegan straightened. "Rustlers, did ye say?"

"This is a rustler's paradise," McCulloch said. "Ten men."

"But they're in a cave," Breen reminded him.

"Cave it in," McCulloch said.

Breen's head shook. "That would take a wagonload of nitroglycerine."

"Are you two talking about ambushing those sons of dogs before they even try to take our herd?"

"If they take the herd," McCulloch said, "We lose time. That's the first problem. Besides, if these mustangs scatter, we'll never round them all up." He pointed past the fire. "Breen's cargo is our other problem."

"But what if those ten laddies are just grand wayfarers in this lovely country? Out on a vacation or leave from their dull,

271

routine jobs? What if you cave them in, trap them forever, and they had no intention of stealing your horses?"

"That's their problem," McCulloch said. "Anybody in this country, hiding out in a cave, is up to no good."

"They could be hiding out from Indians," Keegan argued.

"Even Indians avoid this section of hell," McCulloch said.

Keegan laughed and finished his coffee. "Good. I needed convincing, and bloody good have I been convinced. We want to get rid of those rustlers, then Sean Keegan's the man to help see you do it."

"How?" Breen asked.

"That's me department."

"You can't find the place," McCulloch told him. "And I'm not letting you risk Wooden Arm's life, getting him into those rocks. You, a kid with a badly busted arm, against ten vermin who prey on those forced to travel this trail? That's not happening."

"Matt, ye know me better than that." Keegan shook his head and chuckled. "I wouldn't be caught dead alone with a Comanch, even if both his arms, both his legs, and his bloody neck had been broken. The black-hearted crazy man would lift my hair and cut my throat. He'll stay here." He winked and hooked his thumb behind him. "To protect ye from that ugly man and that beautiful redhead with poison in her soul."

McCulloch stood there, the rock, the knot on the log, the silent, tall Texan. He did not blink. He did not speak.

Breen cleared his throat. Still in the saddle, he asked, "How do you find the cave?"

Keegan laughed. "That's your department." He turned back to his saddle. "How many rounds have ye for that Sharps?"

"How many do I need?" Breen asked.

"Depends on how well they bounce."

When the mustangs had settled down for the night, having slaked their thirst from the Pecos River, McCulloch waved Wooden Arm into the camp. He looked off to the northwest, wondering where Breen and Keegan would be by this time, and for about the umpteenth time, he began to doubt his wisdom, mostly his sanity, for thinking this plan of his — getting mustangs to Fort Wilmont might work with a bounty hunter and a soldier for partners, and carrying two murderers with them, not to mention a Comanche boy.

"Hair-brained," he said, picturing his long-dead wife, how she would say it,

273

especially how she would smile when she said it.

Wooden Arm dismounted his pinto and grinned.

McCulloch signed him to eat, and then he walked to the edge of the wagon and stared into the desert as the sun sank. Keegan was wrong, of course. When you looked at this part of New Mexico Territory at this time of day, soft, gentle, beautiful light and a desert that seemed serene, not savage, he could see why Mexicans and Indians fought so hard for it. On the other hand, well, it wasn't Texas. Wasn't home.

He found a cup by the pot and poured it. "Take chances," he said with a smile, and looked at the two prisoners as they sat a few yards away, eating with their fingers, their hands in manacles, drinking the same coffee McCulloch consumed.

The Indian boy ate beans with his hands, hungrily, then mopped it up with the sourdough biscuits the woman had cooked up that morning.

He didn't look sick, McCulloch thought.

The boy frowned suddenly, pushed away his plate and the cup with his good hand, and struggled to his feet.

Quickly, McCulloch poured out his coffee, looking with fury at the woman, oblivious to Wooden Arm. The kid crossed the few yards separating him and slid to a stop, dropping to his knees.

"You sick?" McCulloch asked, realized the stupidity of speaking English, and signed the question to the boy.

Wooden Arm's head shook. He wet his lips, and jutted his jaw away to the big empty that stretched toward the Pecos River.

He pointed with his good hand and signed, *There are white men in the rocks on this side of the river.*

McCulloch looked, but saw nothing but shadows, sand, and cactus. *How do you know they are white men?* he asked the Comanche with his hands.

Their horses make noise.

He shook his head in awe and wonder. Make noise. With their iron shoes, of course. And McCulloch had not heard one damned thing.

McCulloch looked at the mustang herd. On a quiet night like this, one shot would be all it took to send the horses into a stampede. They were tired horses, of course, but they were also mustangs, and the leader remained just half-broke.

The boy understood, and he signed, *We must do this without noise.*

"We?" McCulloch whispered, and he was about to protest, tell the kid that he would have to stay behind, that McCulloch would do the killing by himself, that he needed someone to watch after Otto Kruger and Charlotte Platte. But there was another question he had to ask first.

He made the signs to ask, *How many white men are there?*

Four miles northwest, Jed Breen slipped through junipers and eased his way to where Keegan stayed close to their horses, keeping them quiet.

"Those rustlers still have their horses out of the cave," Breen whispered. "Drinking their fill from a stream."

"Good," Keegan beamed. "They won't be hurt by the ricochets."

"Not altogether good," Breen said. "There are only six horses." He softly swore. "There were ten when I was here this afternoon."

In the camp, at that moment, a hundred yards from the Pecos River, Wooden Arm answered McCulloch.

And at that same time, Sean Keegan and Matt McCulloch whispered the same profane oath.

CHAPTER TWENTY-SIX

"Well," Breen said, "what do we do?"

Sean Keegan busied himself breaking open a box of shells for his Springfield. "You figure four of them rustlers are paying a visit to Matt and our mustangs?" He opened the breech and slid a shell inside. Without waiting for Breen to reply, Keegan shouldered the heavy carbine, leaned against a rock, and drew a bead on the entrance to the cave. "Four puny arse rustlers, against Matt McCulloch? I know who I'd be betting on."

Breen drew the hammer back on his Sharps, and a few feet away from Keegan, he lined up the sights in the telescope with the cave. "There is the matter of that herd of mustangs being scattered nine ways from Sunday."

"If anybody can round up a herd of mustangs, I'd say Matt McCulloch's the one to do it." Keegan drew a breath, held it, then exhaled. "And me figures that young

Comanche buck ain't no slouch in that department, neither."

Keegan aimed. Breen aimed. Neither touched the trigger. They were listening, not for the sound of rustlers or horses, but of distant gunfire in the direction of the camp.

"There's also the fact that Otto Kruger and Poison Platte aren't likely to help out Matt or the Indian in a time of trouble," Breen said.

Keegan did not look away from the gunsights. "That's your problem, Jed. You was the bloody bloke who brung them two killers along." He touched the trigger and the Springfield roared, shoving back his right shoulder as though a mustang had kicked it hard.

The report of Breen's murderous Sharps echoed the thunder from Keegan's cavalry carbine.

Even as they turned around, opening the breeches, ejecting the smoking brass cartridges, and shoving fresh loads into their respective guns, the deadly pinging of ricocheting bullets rose out of the cave, accompanied by the curses and screams of men inside.

Breen turned back around first, cocked the Sharps, and aimed. Keegan was just a second behind. Their long guns roared, and they reloaded again, hearing the deadly *ping-ping-zing-ping-zing-ping* of heavy lead bouncing around the insides of the cave.

"Why don't you use a Winchester or Henry repeater?" Breen asked.

"Hit a body with them toys, that body might not know he's been hit," Keegan said, snapping the breech shut. "Hit one with this baby, he's down for the count."

They came up quickly, and Keegan swore. "Damn. One of them monkeys made it out. He's heading for the horses."

"I see him," Breen said as he swung the rifle to his left. "You keep the others in the cave." He waited, finding the running man in the scope, then led the barrel ahead of the rustler.

"It's dark," Keegan snapped. "You can't —"

"He's got a white hat and a white shirt," Breen reminded him, then barked furiously, "Keep them others in that damned cave. I'll take care of —"

Keegan's Springfield roared, and a moment later, so did the Sharps. Breen kept his right eye on the edge of the telescope, searching briefly, then smiling. "That one's down for the count, too," he said, and began reloading.

"I'll say he is," Keegan said. "You blowed his bloody head off. Or at least his hat. I saw it flying."

"My bad," Breen said. "I was aiming for his body. Bigger target, you understand."

They were already reloaded, and had aimed into the entrance. The long guns spoke again.

The glow of the cigarette told Matt Mc-Culloch two things. First, the location of one of the men. Second, that these rustlers — or at least this one — was a damned fool.

McCulloch had removed his boots and spurs and pulled out the Apache moccasins from his saddlebags, lacing them up over the legs of his thick trousers before leaving his camp. He had greased his face from the keg hanging beneath the covered wagon, although his dark beard stubble would hide most of his skin, which was more bronze than white anyway. He moved silently in the darkness, looking back every now and then at the campfire where Otto Kruger, under orders of obey or face a grisly death when McCulloch returned, walked around the fire and smoked one of Jed Breen's cigars. Mc-Culloch figured Breen wouldn't mind. It was for a worthy cause. Survival.

In the darkness, he had moved low but

quickly across the flats and making a wide circle before coming up behind the men, or at least one man. The horse snorted and pulled back — reined tightly to a flat rock. The rustler with the cigarette turned around quickly. McCulloch flattened himself silently onto the ground.

The tip of the cigarette grew red, then vanished, and a moment latter it moved down, glowing from the air as the rustler took the smoke out of his mouth and brought it down to the side.

"Quiet, boy," he whispered.

The horse snorted again, making the rustler grow suspicious. When a second horse snorted and stamped its front hooves, the burning tip of the cigarette dropped to the ground. McCulloch heard the boot grinding it out. Next he heard the sound of iron and leather, followed by the clicks of revolver hammers being eared back.

McCulloch turned his head away from the man he had spotted. Two horses. Two men. He'd already seen one, but the other had to be around nearby. The other two horses were gone, and McCulloch knew he'd find them with the herd of mustangs.

He could not see the man, but knew the rustler was coming, searching, investigating, and wasn't quite the idiot McCulloch had taken him for. He made no sound, and in this dark, moonless night, McCulloch could not see him. But it didn't matter. The man had made a mistake that would prove fatal. He had smoked a cigarette, and the smell of tobacco hung over him like the bull's eye of a target at a fancy sharpshooting contest.

McCulloch rose without making a sound, drawn by the smell of cigarette smoke on the rustler's clothing and hands. He stepped forward like a ghost, grabbed the man's right arm with his left, gripping him like a vise — the only gamble here was if the rustler was a lefthander. He wasn't. McCulloch could tell by the weight of the fool's arm. He clutched a revolver, but before he could squeeze the trigger, the knife blade had cut deep into the man's throat. Blood sprayed in the darkness, and the man tried to scream but McCulloch had cut too deeply. Hell, if it hadn't been for that spinal column that connected head to body, he would have decapitated him.

Keeping a tight grip on the right arm, McCulloch shoved the blade deep into the man's back, piercing the heart, just to make sure. Then he wrapped his right arm around the man's waist, feeling the stickiness and the warmth of the blood pouring from the severed throat, and laid the corpse on the ground. He pried the fingers from the man's revolver. A short-barreled Colt from the weight and feel, and lowered the hammer, then shoved the weapon into his waistband. He might have need of that gun in a minute or two. He might have to risk firing, scattering the mustangs, to save his own life — and the life of Wooden Arm.

That second man had to be around somewhere. McCulloch listened. But for the time being, all he heard were the muffled shots in the distance. And that told him Jed Breen and Sean Keegan were doing their jobs. McCulloch had to finish his.

The horses outside the cave bucked and squealed over the fury of gunshots, screams of men, and ricochets.

"Winchesters or a Henry would come in handy about now," Breen said as he stuck the barrel of the Sharps in a bucket of water he had lugged up to their shooting perches. Steam hissed and rose from the water. "Keep a steady fire."

"Them puny bullets would shatter into pieces the moment they hit that granite." Keegan fired. "Fellows in that cave would never know they'd been hit. The lead we're throwing down there, it don't break apart so easily."

Grinning, Breen began wiping the water off the Sharps with a bandana.

Keegan had already reloaded. "That water don't ruin the barrel?"

"No." Breen draped the wet bandana over his shoulder and found another cartridge to ram into the Sharps. "That's a trick I learned from a buffalo hunter some years back." He fired, listened for the ricochets, and started reloading.

"Maybe I should try it," Keegan said, and Breen tossed him the bandana. "Help yourself. I'll keep those boys inside for six more shots."

Frightened by the scent rising from the river of blood that trailed from the corpse of the rustler, those two horses still stamped their hooves in the darkness, snorting, trying to pull free from their tethers. That was all McCulloch heard from around him. It might have been drowning out the sound of the other rustler left in camp, and McCulloch knew he couldn't wait there forever. He had to get to the mustang herd, stop those two rustlers from easing the animals away or stampeding them.

He came up to his knees, looked left and right, then stared off into the darkness where he saw the fire from his campsite.

"Hell's fire," he whispered. "That sneaky little toad."

He came up, and sprinted through the darkness, drawing the dead rustler's revolver from his waistband, hoping his feet didn't land on some night-hunting rattlesnake. A cowboy boot might protect one's calves from those deadly fangs, but an Apache moccasin wasn't that thick.

The rustler's plan was simple and conceived well. McCulloch had to give the gang credit for that. One man stays with their horses, keeping the scent and sound away from the mustangs or the camp. Two men rode out, ever so quietly, to the herd of mustangs, where they would begin to ease the ponies out to their hideout. The rest of the men would stay in their camp — too many men make too much noise — but keep their horses ready in case they heard gunshots and knew their plan had been foiled. If all went well, if everything went according to plan, the fourth man would sneak into McCulloch's camp, and kill everyone as quietly as possible.

A gamble. But rustling always was a gamble.

McCulloch slowed as he moved closer to the camp. With the campfire between them, the rustler with the gun was nothing but a shadow. He had his gun trained on Otto Kruger and Poison Platte, but McCulloch couldn't see Wooden Arm anywhere. Blood rushed to the old Ranger's head. That sniveling little cutthroat of a coward. He had sneaked up behind the Comanche boy and slit his throat — much as McCulloch had done to the rustler's pard.

Worse, the gunfire remained steady from the hills to the west. That told the rustler in McCulloch's camp that surprise had been thwarted, and that no help would be riding from that cave. Of course, that also meant that the money they might get from selling those mustangs would be more. Less of a split four ways — make that three — than ten.

"Where the hell are the others?" the rustler demanded, waving his gun at Kruger. "What the hell is going on here?"

McCulloch listened as he crept closer to the fire. The German killer and the pretty redhead who'd poisoned scores of men to death kept their hands raised. No stampeding hooves. The mustangs remained calm, but McCulloch knew one shot might send them running like hell. He looked down at the guns in both hands, holstered his Colt, put the other back behind his waistband, and drew the knife.

It was risky. He'd never be able to rush the man. Too much distance. And throwing a knife was hard to do . . . to make that perfect throw that would kill a man.

"Hell," the rustler said. "I'm getting the hell out of here. Elliott's plan has gone to bust." He turned away.

McCulloch lowered himself, hoping the fool hadn't caught a glimpse of him. He didn't think he had. The flames from the campfire would have blinded him.

McCulloch waited. He heard the man's footsteps, and quietly unsheathed the knife.

"What do you think?" Keegan asked as he swabbed down the Springfield's barrel for the second time.

Breen listened, shook his head. "No sound."

"Could be playing possum," Keegan said.

"Yeah." Breen turned his head. "Nothing from back at our camp, either."

Keegan rose. "I think I'd be betting that our barrage cut them bloody dogs to pieces." He drew a deep breath, checked the Remington in his holster, and said softly, "I'll go down there. You get back to Matt and those damned mustangs. If any of them rustlers are still alive in the cave, they shall feel an Irishman's coup de grâce."

"Good luck." Breen turned, took a few steps, and looked back after he stopped. "Don't forget to bring those horses with you."

"Aye. Instead of forty to sell in Precious Metal, we shall have fifty if the good Lord's willing."

Breen grinned, even though Keegan couldn't see him, and hurried back to find his own horse.

McCulloch could let the rustler go. Let him run away. In fact, he had almost talked himself into doing that. No risk of shot and stampede. Nothing along those lines.

Suddenly the rustler straightened, turned, gagged, and began coughing as he staggered back toward the fire.

"You . . ." he gasped. "You . . . you . . . dirty . . . little —"

McCulloch popped up, moving quickly to the rustler's back. He had staggered past the campfire, and fallen to his knees, pointing with his right hand at . . . who else? Poison Platte. Clutching his left hand around his larynx, blood spilled from his mouth. He dropped onto his chest, rolled over, and brought both hands to his throat as he convulsed and gagged and bled profusely from his open mouth.

His pistol was nowhere to be seen. He had probably dropped it when the poison began taking effect.

McCulloch didn't know what Charlotte Platte had come up with, but he saw the coffee cup by the fire, and saw the rustler kick, jerk, gasp, and breathe out one hoarse death rattle before his body relaxed, and the blood slowly stopped leaving his mouth.

He kicked the tin cup over, but it was empty, so he kicked it into the fire, glanced once at the dead man, and walked toward Jed Breen's two prisoners.

"Do I thank you?" he asked the widowmaker.

After pushing back her hat, she shrugged. "Probably not. That was for you when you got back. The damned fool just got thirsty."

McCulloch felt revulsion. But he aimed his own Colt at Platte and Kruger. "Where's the Comanche kid?"

After prisoners shook their heads, McCulloch looked past the wagon and toward the flats where the horses grazed — or were being pushed slowly away. "If either of you move from where you stand right now, I'll shoot both of you dead."

He started toward the flats, but stopped, and raised his gun at the back of the wagon. A voice called out in a language McCulloch had heard but never come close to mastering. It was Comanche, but it came from a young voice. The wooden-splinted arm came into view, waving awkwardly, even painfully, and then the teenage Comanche stepped into view.

Wooden Arm smiled.

"Stay here," McCulloch said, not bothering to use sign language, but hoping the tone was one the boy would understand. "Watch them. I've got to take care of the last two —"

His voice stopped. His mouth hung open. For Wooden Arm's right hand held something, one dark, one silver, and McCulloch knew — providing Breen and Keegan had done their jobs — the danger had passed. From the lack of sound from the hills, McCulloch figured they were safe now. For the time being. He had heard only muffled shots from what appeared to be heavy caliber rifles. That likely meant the other six were dead or at least out of commission.

And Wooden Arm had finished the job.

"Mein Gott!" Otto Kruger gasped.

For what the Comanche kid held in his good hand were two scalps.

CHAPTER TWENTY-SEVEN

Lost His Thumb continued to scout the area where the takers of Broken Buffalo Horn's only son had rested mustangs overnight, *and where the three Comanches had discovered the first two dead men. Now,* Killed A Skunk looked at another dead white-eye, who most likely had been guarding the horses — which any Comanche could easily have stolen — before a silent man came up and knifed him.

"The killer of this man wore moccasins," Killed A Skunk told Broken Buffalo Horn, "But he is not of our blood, not of any Indian blood. Too big. The moccasins were worn by a man who is used to riding and walking in white-eye boots."

"It is the same one who took my son," Broken Buffalo Horn said while sitting in the Comanche saddle of his horse.

Killed A Skunk mounted his horse, and he and the medicine man rode to the remnants of a giant campfire and another dead white-eye.

"This white-eye leader," Killed A Skunk said, "the one who has taken your fine son, this is the first mistake he made. A foolish mistake. A mistake no Comanche would ever do. He build his fire big. Very big. He has not done that before. I think this white-eye, this terrible Texan, he gets careless. We should be able to kill him soon, if he make one more mistake such as this one." The warrior grinned. "Kill him . . . easily."

"He made no mistake," Broken Buffalo Horn said. "He was smart. Too smart for those fools. He built the fire big on purpose. That is why he and his friends and my son have continued north, while these travel to their happy hunting ground." He pointed the top of his bow at the man whose face and the blood and gore that came out of his mouth fed hundreds of starving ants. "And how did that one die?"

Killed A Skunk walked to the bloated, vile-looking corpse. He had never seen anyone who had suffered so greatly, even those Mexicans that the Apaches had taken once and tortured to death. But no one had made a slit in this white-eye's stomach and began pulling out his insides so this man could see what they, his killers, were doing

292

ever so slowly. They had not used the fire to heat up one the barrels of the white-eye's long guns and then shove it up the man's rectum, taunting him as he screamed and begged to be killed, to have his misery shortened. The man bled out through his mouth, as well as his anus, as though he had eaten something that did not agree with him. Or perhaps it was something he had drunk, for when Killed A Skunk looked at the charred remnants of cactus spine and ash, he found the blackened cup of tin that white-eyes usually used to drink.

It wasn't water. Even the most repugnant water in the worst places would not do this to a human. But then, whoever said a white-eye, especially a Texan, was human.

He rose and hurried away from the ugly carcass. "What killed this fool white-eye," Killed A Skunk told Broken Buffalo Horn, "I do not know. Something in his belly had to come out, and it came out with blood and bits of his stomach, his throat. He also bit off his tongue while convulsing. A bad death this one had." He nodded at the man off in the flatlands. "Much worse than that one whose throat was cut deep and who was stabbed through the heart. He died like a mule deer I killed for our supper yesterday, bled out like that mule deer, and did not suffer like that mule deer, for I am a good hunter."

"You are the best hunter," Broken Buffalo Horn said. "I am glad you take this journey with Lost His Thumb and me."

Killed A Skunk felt strong, and happy, for he loved Broken Buffalo Horn like he loved his own brothers, but he really wanted to get away from the dead white-eyes, fearing that whatever had caused him to cough up so much blood and gore would slip into Killed A Skunk's own stomach, or Broken Buffalo Horn's, and even Lost His Thumb. That would be terrible.

"And what of those two?" Broken Buffalo Horn pointed to the land where the Comanche mustangs had been grazing, and where more turkey buzzards circled, waiting for the Comanches to ride away so that they could have their breakfast.

So they rode back to the first dead man they had found but had not checked until they had made sure all of these white men were dead. Again Broken Buffalo Horn remained on the back of his horse while Killed A Skunk dismounted and studied the ground. The signs were much harder to interpret, because Lost His Thumb had ridden past this man, and by the direction of the horse prints, had gone to the other dead white-eye, too. And many horses had been here. But Broken Buffalo Horn did not rush, even though the longer it took Killed A Skunk to figure out the story of what had happened, the farther the only son of the Comanche medicine man would travel away from his father, his people, and his salvation.

Killed A Skunk read what each print told him, each mark. He listened to the cactus, the stones, the droppings of the horses, and the prints that were not made by a horse, or a white-eye wearing the big, ugly boots on his feet.

At length, Killed A Skunk felt his heart pounding, and his head spinning, and he rose weakly and breathed in deeply before walking a few paces to stand before Broken Buffalo Horn. "The man who killed this white-eye wore moccasins."

"The big Texan?" The medicine man gestured toward the other bodies.

"No," Killed A Skunk said. "This was a Comanche moccasin, and it was worn by a Comanche . . . a young Comanche."

What Killed A Skunk had said registered, and Broken Buffalo Horn straightened. "My son killed this white-eye."

"Yes," the warrior said. "Your son killed this man." He pointed toward the other dead man. "And if the tracks do not change their course, I will say that it was your son who killed the other white-eye, too."

The wind blew. For a long moment, no other sound came until Killed A Skunk's horse decided to relieve its bladder. When that sound ceased, Killed A Skunk decided to help his friend, make him think better of his son. It was not the fault of the son of Broken Buffalo Horn that he had killed two white-eyes.

"It could be that the big Texan who has captured your son, the man who makes your only son wear that strange thing on his arm, that he controls your son through that evil thing of wood. He threatens to turn your son into a tree, as I have long believed, and he showed how he can kill a man like he did at that camp, making a man cough up all the blood he has in his body."

The medicine man smiled but slowly began shaking his head, and Killed A Skunk fell silent.

"That is a wonderful theory you have, my friend, but my son did this for other reasons. These dead white-eyes, they must have been enemies of the big Texan and his friends who also like to steal Comanche horses. All horses in this land are Comanche horses. We have been in this land forever, or as long as our people can remember forever. These dead men would have killed my son as easily as they would have killed the big Texan or his friends."

Killed A Skunk nodded and told the medicine man how wise he was.

"You overlook one other fact, my fine friend," Broken Buffalo Horn said from the back of his horse.

"What is that?" Killed A Skunk asked.

"My son" — Broken Buffalo Horn could not contain his grin — "has counted coup. And has taken his first scalp."

"Your son has two scalps," Killed A Skunk said several minutes later when they had looked at the last of the dead white-eyes.

"Perhaps he will take the name Two Scalps."

"It is to be seen." Broken Buffalo Horn looked up at the circling buzzards, back at the old camp, and then where the trail of horses led.

Off in the distance, Lost His Thumb waved his lance high over his head.

Turning back to Killed A Skunk, the medicine man said, "Lost His Thumb signals us. We must ride. And give these" — he pointed the top of his bow at the circling carrion — "a chance to have their morning meal."

The trail of the stolen Comanche ponies, the wagon, and the other horses led northwest, into the rugged country of foothills and caves, where the temperature was often cooler.

They discovered the tracks that had carried four men to their deaths. Four foolish white-eyes, two of whom had been killed by a brave Comanche, one by a white-eyed Texan that intrigued Broken Buffalo Horn, and the last who had died the most horrible of deaths.

Maybe, the men they found in the cave had died even worse.

Broken Buffalo Horn let Lost His Thumb read the sign. That did not take quite as long.

When they let their horses drink from the pool near the dark cave's entrance, Lost His Thumb pointed at a position in the rocks above.

"The white-eyed friends of the big Texan remained up there. They fired their big guns into there." He pointed at the cave. "And their bullets did magic, becoming more than one bullet, more than one shot. Inside I found the bodies of six more white-eyes.

Their bodies had been riddled. And afterward, wolves came and ate part of them."

"Wolves must eat, like Comanches. Like all creatures," Broken Buffalo Horn sagely observed.

"It is so," Lost His Thumb said. Again, he pointed at the high rocks. "I found none of the shiny holders of bullets that the white-eyes use."

"They are smart," Broken Buffalo Horn said. "They take those with them so they can shoot again."

"Yes." The warrior nodded again at the cave. "One of the Texans came down from the rocks. The other returned to the big Texan with the wagon and all the horses and" — he paused before softly adding — "your son, Broken Buffalo Horn. First, the taller of the white men entered the cave. I believe three of the white-eyes inside, though likely dying or at least gravely injured, had not crossed to the happy hunting ground. That man shot each of those men in their heads. Then they joined their dead brothers." He shrugged. "But such is hard to tell. The wolves were hungry early this morning."

"Then they shall not bother us," Killed A Skunk said and laughed. "I do not like wolves."

Ignoring the interruption, Lost His Thumb turned and pointed just past the pool of water. "After making sure his enemies would not come after him in this world, that white-eye took the horses that belonged to these foolish and now dead white-eyes, and he rode toward the camp of the big Texan and your son."

"He did not get that far," Broken Buffalo Horn said. He had seen the signs on the trail that cut through the hills same as Killed A Skunk and Lost His Thumb had. "He met up with our ponies, the wagon, the other white-eyes and my son."

"Yes," agreed Killed A Skunk and Lost His Thumb.

"They go north and west," Broken Buffalo Horn said.

"To the land of the Navajos and other Apaches," Lost His Thumb said.

"And other white-eyes, dark-skinned Mexicans, the long knives of the Great White Father, and other miserable white-eyes," Killed A Skunk added.

"We will continue to follow them," Broken Buffalo Horn said, "but we will not rush the big Texan and his comrades. We know they possess much power. I do not wish them to make my son die like that bloody man we found by the ashes. We must be

300

careful. In time, in good time, in time that favors us, we will free my son from the powerful Texans and kill the big one and all the other white-eyes with him."

"Yes," Killed A Skunk said. "You are right."

"And you are wise," Lost His Thumb added. He grinned. "And soon you will have your son back."

"I will have my son back." Broken Buffalo Horn tilted his head back and laughed. He was still laughing when he straightened and pointed the tip of his bow at his two friends. "And we will have fifty horses. Instead of just forty. Those white-eyes keep making us richer."

"More than fifty horses," Lost His Thumb said. "Because they ride three themselves."

"And," Killed A Skunk added, "two pull that clumsy white-eye wagon with the sheet for a roof."

They laughed with merriment, let their horses drink, then rode away so that the wolves they had interrupted and scared off could return for their breakfast.

CHAPTER TWENTY-EIGHT

As they had been doing since the morning after they had wiped out that gang of rustlers to the last man, Jed Breen kept his double-action Colt pressed against the back of Charlotte Platte's head and Sean Keegan kept his Springfield carbine pointed in the general direction of Otto Kruger, while Matt McCulloch unlocked the manacles from the widowmaker's wrists and ankles. Wooden Arm just stared at the proceedings, wondering what these strange white men were doing . . . again.

After gathering the iron bracelets, McCulloch and Breen backed away from the woman.

"Now," McCulloch ordered, "strip." He drew his Colt and waved the barrel.

"You're pigs," she said that morning. Sometimes she used a tongue significantly more virile than pigs, or hogs, or brutes, or even stronger than "Dirty rotten scoundrels."

She tossed her hat into the dirt. The shirt went over her head, and she pitched it with more profanity in front of the former Texas Ranger's boots. Still standing, she managed to pull down the men's pants they had given her, and kicked them close to the shirt. She wore no socks. Jed Breen had reminded them of the days when he had a partner, Mikey Maxwell, and they had captured Garry Cartwright. Garry had taken off his boots, removed his socks, knotted them together and strangled Maxwell to death, stolen the horse, and rode out for Mexico. He made across the border, too, but bounty hunters don't have to follow certain rules like extradition and international boundaries, and Breen eventually found the killer in Nogales and brought him back, strapped over a pack mule with a bullet through his heart.

"All the way," McCulloch told her.

"You're sick. All three of you. And so is the red savage." But she pulled down her bottoms, then took off her muslin chemise, and stood before the three men, the salivating Otto Kruger, and even the Indian teen who stared with wide eyes at the sight of her. Breen moved over to her undergarments and began shaking them out.

"Remember," Keegan said as he positioned himself so he could blow Otto Kruger to hell if he burped too loudly but still get an eyeful of the beautiful murderess. "Tomorrow, it's ol' Sean Keegan's turn to pull that duty with her unmentionables."

"Filthy, dirty, miserable, disgusting, perverted pigs," Charlotte Platte said.

When Breen had finished his search, he looked at McCulloch, shook his head, and back toward the widowmaker. He tossed the undergarments to the prisoner, and aimed his Colt at her while Matt McCulloch holstered his pistol and went through her shirt and pants. Finding nothing, he threw them into the pile at the naked woman's feet.

"The boots," Breen reminded her, waving the barrel.

Those contained nothing but sand, but Breen dumped the grains out, pitched the battered old cavalry style boots back to her, and stood, then kicked at the sand, just in case.

"Do I have permission to get dressed, you stinking — ?" She stopped when McCulloch walked to her, keeping the cocked revolver trained on her chest.

The others watched intently, but made no sound. McCulloch stopped, the gun barrel resting just below her perfect bosoms, and then he reached forward and jerked off the necklace, snapping the small silver chain.

"Hey." Her eyes flashed with bitter hatred, but the Colt stopped her from coming any closer to him.

"We checked that yesterday, Matt," Breen said. "And the day before."

"Yeah," he said, turning the medallion around, looking for some secret opening, but the damned thing was solid, heavy like a piece of gold.

"We also haven't been poisoned lately," Keegan said.

"Yeah." Matt McCulloch held the spinning circle about the size of a double eagle coin, in front of the killer. "What is this to you?"

She stared into his suspicious eyes. "Just a gift."

"From anyone special?"

"Not particularly."

"Then you won't miss it." He jerked his arm back and threw it to the desert floor.

She turned, gasped, then swore, and looked at him with even more hatred, but McCulloch was walking back.

"I'm not taking any chances," he said. "She killed that rustler somehow, and I'm not giving her any opportunity to do one or all of us in the same way."

"Hell, Matt," Keegan said. "Maybe she's just a witch."

"Wrong consonant," McCulloch said.

Keegan frowned. Breen chuckled. "I'll explain it to you over supper, Sergeant."

"Put your duds on," McCulloch said, and slowly slid his revolver into the holster. "We're burning daylight."

They watched the woman dress, and when she had finished and pulled on her hat, Wooden Arm led the horse to her. Before she mounted, Charlotte Poison Platte knew what to do. She held out her arms, clenched her fists, and waited for Matt McCulloch to lock the cuffs back over her wrists. When he didn't, she mounted the smallest of the horses they had confiscated from the dead rustlers and waited. The leg irons would wait until the day was finished.

McCulloch was already in the saddle. "You know what to do," he told her after shoving her ankle chains into his saddlebag. "Same as the past week. Let's get these ponies moving."

Breen had already mounted his horse, and Wooden Arm was gathering the hackamore to his pony. Sean Keegan stayed afoot for a moment, making sure Otto Kruger got into the driver's box on the covered wagon. The scar-faced murderer looked at the old horse soldier after he had settled into his seat.

"Vie do voman go vitout chains?" he asked, like he did every morning. "I drive vagon good. I help."

"You're a big help. I'll be sure to mention that to the hangman in Precious Metal."

The chains rattled, but not loud enough to hide his curse, and Keegan laughed as the ugly man grabbed the leather and whipped out at the animals that pulled the wagon. By that time, Keegan had found the reins to his horse, and he swung into the McClellan saddle.

"I don't see how you sit in one of those things," Breen said, waiting for the soldier before they rode to the herd. "You bounce all over that little thing."

"Aye." The Irishman grinned. "I wish we had an extra saddle so we could watch that Miss Platte bounce around."

"Careful," Breen said with a grin.

"Aye, lad, I know, I know. But for a mad-dog killer, she sure is a woman to look at. Handsome. Downright beautiful for a woman not blessed to have been born in Ireland."

"Yeah." Breen pulled the reins to turn the horse around. "But that rustler might have been handsome, too, before he drank what-

307

ever Poison Platte offered him. You best remember that. For that fellow sure didn't look like much after he drank her brew."

"Which is why we search her every day." They started at a trot toward the mustangs. "I wonder if that dead man knows what a blessing he gave us. Maybe he saved our lives. And let us peer at a goddess as the rays of dawn bathed her in all her morning glory."

"Hell, Sean," Breen said. "I never knew you were a poet."

"But now you know it." He laughed at his rhyme, and nudged his horse to the rear of the herd.

So the days went, morning after morning — even the occasional surprise search during a noon stop. The widowmaker called them paranoids, and Breen explained that word to Keegan, too. When Keegan pointed out that they had found nothing on her person in two weeks, McCulloch ordered that the German start stripping, too.

"Matt," Keegan pleaded. "I don't think there's any need for that."

"She killed that rustler somehow," McCulloch roared. "She can do us the same way, and I'm not dying like that."

"But do we have to search that Kruger's

clothes?"

"Yes, damn it. Do you want to cough out all the blood in your body?"

"There's no blood, left, me boy. It's nothing but whiskey and a pint or thirty of good stout porter beer."

"Kruger strips. All the way."

Keegan sighed. "And I suppose we have to search his clothes the same way."

Breen laughed. "Don't worry, Sergeant. I'll make sure you get the murdering Hun's underdrawers."

When they turned west, they slowed the animals. The wind blew thick clouds of dust, and riding into the sinking sun in the afternoons practically blinded them. This was tough country for anyone, even those like Keegan, Breen, and McCulloch who lived in tough country.

Breen developed a theory that Poison Platte found her killer herbs or powders in the desert, but that maybe they had passed where such poisonous plants no longer grew.

"Don't give Matt any ideas," Keegan chimed in. "There's not a bloody thing to see in this whole country, so please don't deny me — or any of us — our one look at pure beauty."

McCulloch did not. He would not. He

knew she had poison somewhere, but damned if he could find it.

"You could search her cavities," Breen suggested.

"Her teeth are perfect," Keegan said.

"That's not what I meant," Breen said.

Understanding, Keegan chuckled and looked at the former Ranger.

"I don't want to touch her anywhere," McCulloch said, "just in case her damned skin is covered with poison. But I'll be damned if I'm sticking my fingers anywhere indecent."

"What do you know about decency, you lout?" the murderess said.

Matt McCulloch's eyes ripped through her like a .45 slug. "What do *you* know about decency? You murdered that rustler."

"And you're damned glad I did. For he would have killed you, too."

"Maybe. I doubt it. He wasn't very good at rustling. But you also poisoned fifteen miners in Arizona. That's why there's a five thousand dollar reward on you. Imagine it would have been even higher if seven of those lucky fools hadn't survived.

"I shoot a man when he's facing me. Always. You put something in their food, coffee, or whiskey. You didn't give those poor men a chance at all."

Breen corrected McCullock. "Two were women. Well, one was a woman. The other was a girl."

McCulloch swore with venom.

"I had my reasons," the widowmaker said.

"And I have mine," McCulloch said. He drew his revolver. "Take off your clothes. Again."

The next morning, McCulloch realized the mistake he might have been making. After the search, and after breakfast, and when nobody began bleeding profusely from the mouth, and fell over, gagging, crying, and begging to be put out of his misery, McCulloch made her strip again.

"A grand idea, Matt," Sean Keegan said. "Two peep shows in the morning. Maybe we should do it at night again."

"We might," McCulloch said.

The woman fumed, but she took off her clothes, which once again McCulloch and Breen went through meticulously without finding anything. They tossed the clothes back to her.

"You'll never get to Precious Metal if you keep up with your damned perversions. Like you say" — she shoved on her hat — "we're burning daylight."

"Yeah," McCulloch said. "So in the morning, you take off your clothes the minute you wake up, then you go attend to nature's call, and you get dressed before we leave."

"You're all sick puppies," she said. "Haven't you any decency?"

McCulloch tipped his hat. "Most jackals don't, ma'am," he said, before turning around to climb into his saddle.

CHAPTER TWENTY-NINE

Annie Homes was riding in the wagon with her father. She rarely got to sit up there with him, seeing the wonders of the new country for the first time. Usually, she rocked about in the back of the covered wagon or walked along outside next to her father's wagon. She didn't get quite the view of the wild, new, glorious country when she walked — mainly because she kept her head down looking out for centipedes, scorpions, cactus with long sharp thorns, or whatever they were called, so hard they could poke right through an Arkansas woman's shoe. And snakes. Another mule had been bitten two nights ago, and that evil man Linton had cut its throat. Said he had to, to put the poor thing out of its misery, but Annie figured the scalawag simply liked killing things.

Annie spotted Linton riding his horse too hard, too fast, and using his spurs with the giant rowels too cruelly. It was times like these when she wished the sun and dust and wind had not worn her mother out and sent her to swap places with her daughter so that she could take a nap.

Linton reined in sharply, almost pulling his horse to its knees, and turned around quickly, to ride alongside the Homes family wagon. "Well, now, ain't this a fun surprise." He cut in front of her father's draft animals, and turned around so that he was riding alongside Annie and not her father. "You got enough gumption to talk to me, you dark-haired angel, now that you done crawled out of your cave?"

"I don't recall hearing you ask permission to speak to my daughter, sir."

Annie smiled at the look that flashed across the brutal man's face. Her father slapped the leather against the oxen's hide, and Linton rode away. Not far enough, though. She thought — indeed, she prayed — that the louse would ride back to wherever he thought he had business, but a moment later he began walking his horse alongside Annie's father.

"Well, Mistah Homer," the man said as he shook out the makings to roll a cigarette. "I do —"

"It's Homes, sir. Walter Homes." Her

314

father kept his eyes on his team, the trail, and the wagon in front of him. The eyes of the little Randall girls poked out. Annie gave them her best schoolteacher scowl and waved them back behind the canvas. They were too young, too precious, to listen to anything a man like Linton had to say.

"That's right. Homes. The good daddy leading his family and right handsome daughter to better homes. In Rapture Valley." Laughing, Linton spit the tobacco flakes off his lips and tongue, wet the paper, and slipped the cigarette between his lips. It took a while for him to find a match, but he did, then blew it out and held it up for Annie's father to see. "You gots to make sure the match is put out." He laughed. "Don't want to start a fire. Fires can be downright devastating in this part of the country." He spit at the match, dropped it, laughed and shook his head. "I'm sure sorry, Mistah Homes, if any of my spittle hit you. Just had to make sure that match didn't start no fire."

"Your spit cannot hurt me, sir." Still, her father stared ahead.

"Yeah. Lots of folks like my spit. My tongue. My mouth. And other . . ." He was staring at Annie, who saw his lecherous look out of the corner of her eye.

She felt herself repulsed and shamed.

315

Even felt what she thought might have been . . . hatred.

"Do you have somewhere to go, Mr. Linton?" her father asked.

Linton drew hard on the cigarette, removed it, and exhaled. "Yes, sir. That's why I was ridin' down to spread the word." He nudged the horse up even with the closest oxen. Pointing, he said, "There's a tradin' post a mile up. North side of the trail. Figure it'd be good to stop there, make camp."

Walter Homes glanced at the sun. "There appears to be a lot of daylight left."

"You got a good eye there, Homer," Linton said, looked at his cigarette, and drifted back until he rode just behind Annie's father, so he could keep his eyes on Annie herself. "This is rough country, and once we get into the Arizona Territory, it'll get hotter and dryer and much, much, much meaner. So I thought it'd do the boys, and the animals some good. And especially the ladies, especially the prettiest of the lot, to relax. Enjoy. Hell, for all I know, ol' Homer, it might be the Fourth of July. You folks might want to have a dance or two. Save one for me, will ya?"

He started to turn the horse around, to ride back to tell other people about the unexpected delay, but Annie's father said, "Yes. Perhaps you are right, sir. I am sure many of us could stand to buy some new supplies."

Linton coughed on his spit and the smoke from his cigarette. He coughed, then laughed, and pitched the cigarette — without crushing it out, Annie noticed, and without calling attention to herself that she was studying the man in buckskins.

"Well, ol' Homer, I ain't exactly sure what they sell at that tradin' post is what you'd care to have. Can be risky business in that little place. But, hell, I'm one tough ol' bird. But don't forget. If it is Independence Day, you tell your missus and that baby girl of yours that I'd be most honored to have the opportunity to shake a leg with 'em both. I'd even pay the fiddler to play something long and slow." Laughing again, Linton kicked the horse, turned it around, and loped to the end of the wagons.

"I do not like that man," Annie said tightly. "He gives me the willies."

"I care nary a whit for him, either, my child," her father whispered, "but he has gotten us this far, and that is what he is paid to do."

"How much farther to Rapture Valley?" she asked.

He sighed. "I fear I have no idea. I am like our guide Mister Linton. It could be the fourth of July. It could be May, June, August, or September. Time vanishes on a trail, on a journey such as ours. For all I know, it could very well be the year of nineteen hundred."

She laughed. "I can say, as long as we have been traveling, and as many bruises as have been formed on my feet, thighs, and even my buttocks" — she made herself more comfortable on her mother's cushion — "and no matter how much I have eaten, this is not the year of Our Lord nineteen hundred."

Walter Homes laughed and slapped the leather again. "You are right, daughter, for you are perceptive and observant. I misspoke. This has to be the beginning of the twenty-first century."

They laughed.

Yet no one even smiled when they stopped and saw the so-called trading post that awaited them. Well, Hawg's jaw dropped, and he licked the dust off his thick mustache, but before he could make his joke or say something he might have thought would have gotten men to laugh with him, the hard-hearted Linton spoke with finality.

"That ain't no place for tenderfeet and

greenhorns, folks. And like I told my ol'
pard Mistah Homer over yonder, I've ordered this stop for you folks to rest before
we start crossing tough country." He
pointed toward the bright yellow ball that
slowly tried to hide beyond the country that
they faced. "So you get to eat your vittles
and rest up." Linton had not dismounted.
He grinned, nodding at the Reverend Sergeant Major Homer Primrose III. "Padre,
these are your people, so I'm asking you —
and that fellow you pray to all the time —
to give us some help. You better ask him for
more than blessings on yer supper tonight.
Ask him to guide us through the desert."
He turned his horse and trotted to that . . .
that . . . trading post?

Trading for what? Annie didn't know if
she'd have appetite to eat any supper.

"And while ya be prayin', padre," Linton
called back, "ask him to deliver me a full
house, kings over aces, when everybody else
has got nothing higher than an ace-high
flush."

She had heard of sod houses. This must
be one of those, a miserable, poorly con-
structed hut of dirt and stones, with a roof
of canvas covered with more dirt and stones.
No smoke came out of the chimney, for it
was too hot. Whatever food they served in

such a place would not be fit for human consumption. That would not bother Linton any since he had never shown one ounce of humanity.

Maybe, Annie thought, Linton might be murdered inside.

She tensed at the thought, but there were two other horses tethered to the hitching rail in front of that . . . trading post.

Still, she told herself to ask God for forgiveness when she prayed that night before bed. Linton was an evil man. She knew this. But he would pay for his sins whenever the Good Lord decided it was his time. Still, Annie thought, it would not be so bad to encourage the Lord to make it Linton's time.

"That man is something else." Hawg laughed as he turned back to find his wagon.

"He is evil," Annie heard someone say. She even thought it might have been her, but her lips had been flattened into a frown.

"Why, Mizzus Homes," the Reverend Sergeant Major Homer Primrose III said in a slight rebuke, "that is not the kind of words I expected to be spoken by a good, God-fearing Christian woman like yourself."

"I do not like the man," Harriet said.

Annie decided to side with her mom because it did not look like anyone else would. "Nor do I."

"You don't like anybody," Hawg said, having stopped because he was lazy and hoped someone else would do his chores, most likely.

"That's enough, Hawg,"

Annie might have smiled if not for how sick she was at listening to that evil, evil man for what felt like ten thousand miles — or more than a century. Good for Winfield Baker, coming to Annie's defense.

"Well, I don't know if he's good or evil," Betsy Stanton said with a giggle. "But he sure is interesting."

"Hush," Annie's father said. "Whatever Linton is, he was right about one thing. We should rest. Make sure our animals are tended to, make sure our families are nourished." He pointed to the sinking sun. "Let Linton do his ill will inside that hovel. I do not know what the date is, but we shall call it Independence Day and have merriment this night. Dance — except for you Baptists — and sing songs of devotion and merriment."

"Independence Day!" Hawg barked. "I will never celebrate that damned Yankee holiday."

"Then celebrate Christmas," Walter Homes said. "Or your birthday. Or my birthday. Or September twenty-fifth."

"What in heaven's name of a holiday is September twenty-fifth?" asked the Reverend Sergeant Major Homer Primrose III.

"I have no idea," Walter Homes said, suddenly giddy, as if he had been to that dirt structure first and had consumed far too much Taos Lightning. "But let us celebrate it anyway . . . and every other holiday and special day. For we do not know how many more days, birthdays, Christmases, holidays, or anniversaries any of us might live to see again."

CHAPTER THIRTY

The Mexican behind the bar — if one could call it a bar — looked to be the size of one of those old Conestogas some of these pilgrims from Arkansas had brought along. In fact, he was so big Linton wondered how the hoss had fit through the only door to the dusty old watering hole, but he was not about to mention that. The muscles on his arms and neck told Linton that he probably could pull two of those sodbusters' wagons and not even work up a sweat.

"Whiskey." Linton shook the dust off his hat, and gave the bartender his friendliest grin.

"*Dinero,*" the Mexican said.

"Whiskey." Linton settled the hat back on his head.

"Dinero." The big man held out his hand, palm up and open.

"I pay for my whiskey after I've tasted it," Linton said. "Make sure you don't water it

323

down." He thought *like there is any water in this hellhole to water anything down.*

"Dinero."

"Whiskey."

"Dinero."

"Whiskey."

It might have gone on like that for another hour or week until Linton got tired of the joke and plugged the big Mexican with several slugs. Just one, even in the right spot, might not kill that giant quick enough.

But Bruno just said, "Dinero," one more time, and Linton opened his mouth to speak again.

But someone in the corner of the miserable building filled with dust and cigarette smoke said, "Bruno, give this stranger the tequila you serve me. And put it on my account."

Linton moved one of his eyes to the dude in the corner, but made sure big Bruno stayed in his peripheral vision. Big as the barkeep was, he still might prefer to knife one in the back or put a ball in the back of an American gringo's head. The dude speaking looked like, well, a dude. A Mexican dude by the duds, pale blue coat trimmed in red and yellow, and pale blue pants trimmed along the sides with the same colors, but with silver conchos sewed

324

onto the legs up to his knees. His shirt was white linen, with frilly fabric like the trim on some dance-hall gal's dress. A tightly wrapped red silk neckerchief was around his throat. The boots were polished black, and his spurs were the big kind, with rowels even bigger than Linton's. His face was bronzed and neat with a well-groomed mustache and goatee that matched his even salt and pepper hair. It hung underneath his fine hat of Panama straw with a flat brim and crown, and a fine black band around it, also buttoned with silver conchos.

He sure looked like a Mexican. But he wasn't. Not from that accent. And the man with the dude wore the outfit of an Americano. An Americano who had left the states because the law wanted to hang his hide from the closest tree. That man wore two guns. The one who had asked to pay for Linton's drink, wore none.

Linton nodded at the generous dude, but said, "I'd rather have whiskey. American whiskey."

"The whiskey here will kill you," the dude said. "Please, at least sample my tequila. Well, it is not my tequila, but it is the brand I favor. As you say, one must sample first before paying. Like buying a horse. You see how it runs first." He nodded, not at Linton, but Bruno, the bartender.

"All right." Linton laughed. "But if I spit it out, I ain't paying for it."

The dude grinned, bowed, and Linton heard the splashing of liquor into a clean glass.

The clean glass surprised him. In fact, it took him by such surprise, that he sipped the tequila before thinking that it might have been poison.

But it wasn't. Or if it was, it was a hell of a good way to die. The tequila went down as smooth and as rich as chocolate cake. He always thought that tequila was some sort of kerosene you had to take with salt, but this was —

"Smooth, is it not?" the dude said.

"It ain't what I expected," Linton said. "That's the damned truth." He took another sip, nodded at the dude, then killed the rest of the Mexican brew. Still standing, not coughing, thinking this stuff goes down just like water, he set the glass in front of Bruno, smiled at the dude and the dude's gunman, and said, "I'll take another, Bruno. But don't be so stingy with your pour. I'm a big boy. Fill it to the brim."

"You heard the man, Bruno," the dude said with a smile. Next he gestured at the chair in front of the table.

Once Bruno had obeyed the dude and poured a good-sized drink, Linton crossed the dirt floor and settled into the uncomfortable chair.

He sipped. The dude sipped. The gunman rolled a cigarette. Bruno brought over the bottle of tequila, which was another surprise for Linton. He always thought tequila was like corn liquor. It came in jars or stoneware jugs. The barkeep topped off the glasses in front of the two men, and when Bruno moved back to the bar, the bottle of tequila remained on the table.

This evening might turn out to be fine, Linton decided. He wondered if the dude played poker.

The dude, though, raised his glass as in toast. *"Salud."*

Their glasses clinked.

"My name is Don Marion Wilkes." The dude let his glass rest by his side. "This is my associate, Duncan Regret. *Don,* by the way, is my real name. Short for Donald. Do not mistake me for one of Mexico's landed gentry. I hail from Missouri."

"Well, Don Marion Wilkes, señor, I thank you for your generosity." Linton did not offer his name. For all he knew, this dude, fancy dresser that he was, could be what passed for a lawdog in New Mexico. Or a bounty hunter.

"Your accent says you hail from Texas," Don Wilkes said.

"Don" — Linton drank more tequila — "I hail from wherever I want to hail from."

Don Marion Wilkes smiled and then gestured to the open door.

"Are you with that caravan of wagons and settlers?"

"I ain't with 'em, so to speak. They ain't nothin' but a bunch of spud diggers, iffen you ask me. They hired me to guide them to Rapture Valley." Linton laughed mockingly at the name of their destination.

"Rapture Valley." Don Wilkes sipped his tequila, and without asking, topped off Linton's glass.

Maybe this dude wants to get me drunk, Linton thought and laughed. *Well, he's in for one rude awakening.*

"Ah, so you are merely hired to see them to a new land, a new home. That is wonderful."

Linton just drank.

"Do you often hire out to guide families to new settlements, señor?"

"I do what suits me."

"As I see."

Linton's glass settled on the dust-covered table. "What do you see, Don Wilkes?"

"Your true profession." He reached up and gently fingered one of the scalps that hung on the left sleeve of Linton's buckskin shirt.

Linton's own hand rested on his revolver.

"I could say I won that off a drunk in Santa Fe in a poker game."

Don Wilkes brought his hand back, lifted his glass, and waited until Linton had his. Their glasses clinked, and both men drank while the gunman smoked quietly and minded his own business.

"You could say that, but you did not come from Santa Fe. I don't think you've ever been to that little dump of a town."

"How do you know where I been?" Linton's pistol came halfway out of the holster.

"You came straight across Texas," Duncan Regret said without looking away from the open doorway or removing the cigarette from his lips. "The Panhandle. That's gutsy, what with the Comanches and Cheyennes and every other red-skinned devil except the Navajos raising hell all across the territories and states. At least somewhere south of Adobe Walls and north of Palo Duro. My boys found the trail of the wagons. Where you come along, well, that's not quite known."

"You been followin' us?" Linton kept his

eyes on the gunman, and let his gun slide farther out of his holster until he had the barrel aimed at Duncan Regret's stomach.

"I've been here. With Don Wilkes." The gunman removed the smoke and flicked ash onto the dust that coated the table. "My eyes followed you."

Linton wanted another drink of that fine tequila, but he thought he might have to pull his knife. Three men were possible enemies, and he wanted to have all of his options open in case he had to start killing strangers. He tried to paint a brave, unconcerned front, telling Regret, "I think you got some explainin' to do, amigo."

The older gent laughed, nodded, and drank more of his fine tequila. "Señor, do not be afraid. Holster your revolver before Bruno gets nervous and kills you with that double barrel scattergun he holds underneath the bar. Buckshot is nasty and messy and I fear it might also kill my dear associate, Señor Regret. And it might ruin my fine jacket and hat." He drank, smiled again, and leaned forward.

"You joined this party for reasons of your own, and for reasons that I do not concern myself with." He used his glass to touch one of the scalps. "This is what intrigues me. From your looks, your outfit, and the way that knife rests in its scabbard on your other hip, I have already pegged your true vocation. We have" — he drank again — "similar interests. For different reasons. I want you to use your knife. To lift scalps."

That relaxed Linton as though he had drawn into a straight flush. "Well, we might be comin' to some sort of an understandin'."

"Bueno," the dude said.

"Who do you want me to scalp? Apaches? And how much are you payin'? I know what a scalp fetches in Mexico. Even some white ranches in Arizona Territory."

"Not Apaches," said Don Marion Wilkes.

"Mexicans?" Linton whispered so softly that he did not think Bruno could hear over at the bar.

The dude's head shook.

"The Navajos are at peace, mister," Linton told him.

"That is right. For now. But if you do what I say, they will be at war. You will have a fortune in scalps, and a new market — the Navajo market — and I will have the land that now belongs to those ignorant savages."

Linton shook his head, suddenly wondering if he couldn't hold this smooth tequila like he could Taos Lightning or the rankest hooch in West Texas. "You want me to scalp a bunch of peaceful Navajos so they get riled and start a war?" Well, he had killed peaceful Mexicans and passed their scalps for Indians', but that was different. This was —

The dude shook his head. "Not at all. If you killed Navajos when they are at peace, the army would hunt you down and hang you or have you shot by firing squad."

His glass empty, Linton reached for the bottle and did not bother refilling his glass. He drank straight from the bottle, not even realizing he was doing it at first, and when he did, he saw no look of horror or repulsion in the face of Don Marion Wilkes. "Maybe I ain't used to this Mexican brew, Donnie ol' boy, but I just don't know what you're gettin' at."

"Rapture Valley, by my understanding, is somewhere near Precious Metal in Arizona Territory," Don Wilkes said. "Am I correct?"

"That's what I been tol'," Linton said, nodding.

Duncan Regret laughed. "He doesn't even know where he's taking those fools, Don."

Linton looked at the gunman, then back at the dude, who said, "It doesn't matter. Since they shan't get there."

"Ummmm." Linton set the bottle down.

Maybe what he needed was coffee. Or to be in Montana Territory. Or even Canada. Somewhere where he wouldn't be sweating so much.

"How do you plan to take these travelers to Rapture Valley?" the gunfighter asked.

"Well." That was easy enough. Linton tried to draw a trail on the dust-covered table. "We just head west like we're bound for the Painted Desert. But cut south. You know. You follow the stagecoach road."

"Yes," said the gunman. "The Little Colorado and the crossing at Horsehead. St. Joseph. Pine Springs. All that rough country to Beaver Head and past the army boys at Camp Verde. Move your way in to Precious Metal and, hell, anybody there could direct you to Rapture Valley."

"Well . . ." Linton started.

"What you need to do," Don Marion Wilkes said, "is take them to the Dead River."

"Dead River?" Linton shook his head. "That's —"

"Part of the Navajo country," the dude said, "and a place where no white men will be venturing. So when the Navajos attack, no one will be there to see all of those poor people from Missouri —"

"Arkansas." Linton wasn't that drunk.

"Good," the dude said with a smile. "I was feeling somewhat poorly at the thought of massacring people from the state where I was born."

"Wait." Linton leaned back in his chair. He realized he had holstered his revolver, though he didn't remember doing it. "You want to wipe out them homesteaders."

"Yes," Don Wilkes said.

"Scalp 'em?"

"Exactly, my understanding, erudite companion." Don who wasn't a don reached over and patted Linton's shoulder. "Now you know our intentions."

"Those scalps you don't want to keep," Duncan Regret said. "But you're welcome to any money those folks might be carrying. We'll take the scalps to plant in a few Navajo villages."

Linton got the idea. "I take the scalps."

"You know how."

"But that's a passel of people. Some kids, too."

"You have scalped Indian children," Don said with a grin. "Perhaps even Mexican children," he whispered, shooting a glance toward Bruno at the bar.

Linton swallowed. He wondered if he should take another swing of tequila.

"Duncan Regret, noble servant that he has

been for the past two years and two months, has rounded up a number of men about the size of a Navajo war party back in the day. Before they were rounded up by mighty Kit Carson and forced to surrender. Spent a while at some infernal place in the darkest hell of this territory, then returned — like Moses leaving the desert — to their own land. Land that I wanted for myself. And have wanted for far too long. Now I see an opportunity."

Linton saw it, too. "The Indians . . . Navajos, that is . . . they get blamed for this . . . massacre." He couldn't wait, nor could he hold back. He found the bottle and emptied it into his roiling gut.

"We ride unshod ponies," Duncan Regret said. "We dress like Navajos, black wigs and all. We leave enough sign in the desert that when the cavalry comes to investigate, they follow tracks that lead them straight to the Navajos up north of here."

The dude laughed. "We have even captured a couple of Navajos that will be left at the scene. They shall be killed before the attack begins on the wagon train."

Regret let his head nod. "We want to make any relatives of those dead homesteaders feel something good about them. That they took at least some of those bloodthirsty savages with them."

"Like Crockett at the Alamo," Linton said, trying to put it into perspective.

"Maybe they won't feel that good," the dude said.

"But I got to kill them," Linton said.

"No, my good man." The dude reached over and patted Linton's buckskin arm. "You don't have to fire a shot. But we would like you to watch with us as we wipe out those fools. From within the wagons. You will be fine. No harm will come to you if you do exactly as we say."

"And," Regret said, "if you think about turning us in, we can name you as an accessory."

"And you hang with the rest of us." Don Wilkes laughed heartily. "Terrible way to die."

"We will kill them," Regret said. "Every last one of them."

"There's a pretty girl," Linton said. "Actually, a couple of them."

"Alas, they must part ways with their hair, as well," Don Wilkes said.

The wind blew more dust into the miserable saloon, and with it came the music of a banjo and harp, of women and children, boys and men, young and old singing. The travelers to Rapture Valley were throwing some sort of shindig.

"I would offer you another bottle of the most exceptional tequila," the dude said, "But in matters like this, a certain amount of sobriety is needed, I fear."

"Yeah." Linton wished he were back in Texas.

Don Marion Wilkes snapped his fingers, slapped the table, and pushed back his flat-crowned, flat-brimmed, fancy straw hat. "I fear I have left out the most important part."

He reached into the inside pocket of his fine, trim, well-fitting baby blue coat, and pulled out a pouch that jingled. This he dropped on the table as Linton wet his lips.

"Your advance, amigo. Our partner," the dude said with a wicked gleam in his eye. "Just a mere token payment. I understand the rates for lifted hair south of the border. Two hundred pesos for an Indian brave, a hundred for a woman, fifty for a boy. We won't be quite so . . . economical. Well, I won't be called a miser. Your payment, less your advance, will be two hundred dollars, not pesos, but American *dollars,* for every damned scalp — man, woman, child — that you take."

Linton smiled and held out his hand to seal his bargain with the devil himself.

Bruno brought over another bottle of tequila.

CHAPTER THIRTY-ONE

Wooden Arm dismounted, holding the hackamore by his right foot, which pinned the braided horsehair to the dirt. He knelt down. With his good hand, he pawed the earth with his fingers. The other arm remained entrapped within the splint. It probably would have come off already, had Wooden Arm not taken a few spills — common for cowboys or anyone else who had spent far too much time on the back of a horse, especially a Comanche horse or a damned mustang pony.

McCulloch waved Breen ahead to take over his position. "Keep them headed west," he said, and then spurred his horse ahead of the trotting mustangs and rode to the teenaged Comanche boy. Still in his saddle, McCulloch kicked his feet out of the stirrups and swung one leg over, hooking it on the horn.

Looking up, the boy studied McCulloch

and waited.

McCulloch signed, *The tracks of the wagons still lead west.*

Wooden Arm nodded his head up and down and whispered a guttural, "Yes."

The former Texas Ranger smiled, thinking, *Well, hell's fires.*

McCulloch himself had picked up a few Comanche words over the past few weeks, months, that had turned into an eternity. He could say *puhi tuyaitu* (dead grass), *Kusiokwe* (Pecos River), *isawasu* (poison) and *puku* (horse, pony, mustang . . . something like that). Hell, he could even say *kaawosa* (jackal) — if it ever came up in conversation.

"It's a free country," McCulloch said, knowing that would never come out right no matter how hard he tried to sign it to a Comanche. "Military road, maybe, but it's open for all travelers." He pointed, made some vague signs that loosely translated to *They go their way. We go ours. As long as they don't poison any water holes.* He frowned at that thought, twisted in the saddle, and stared at the woman on the left side of the mustang herd, her handcuffs rattling as she kept hold of the reins.

Wooden Arm stood and used his good arm to point to the mesa that paralleled the road. McCulloch frowned. The Comanche kid had taken off after a mustang that decided it wanted to find those proverbial greener pastures, even if McCulloch doubted if any mustang would find anything other than juniper and a clump of brush here and there.

Speaking in Comanche, Wooden Arm pointed and eventually turned to McCulloch and said through his hands, even using his fingers on the hand of his busted arm.

When the boy was finished, McCulloch looked up at the top of the mesa. "Show me," he said while signing the words.

A moment later, he turned and yelled at Sean Keegan. McCulloch pointed at the mesa, then at the boy and himself, touched the spurs to his horse's hide, and followed Wooden Arm, who had mounted his wiry Comanche pony quickly. Off the trail they rode, into an arroyo, up the side, and climbing the rough, red-stoned rise that flattened out about three hundred feet above the trail.

Letting the Comanche kid hold the reins, McCulloch stepped out of the saddle and studied the tracks of two horses, shod, carrying medium-sized riders. He stood and walked along the trail, noticing that the junipers and cactus would have hidden the two riders from anyone traveling below. He moved to the rim's edge and peered through the brush, saw his mustangs, his party, his wagon, even his — dare he call them — friends?

But those tracks had been left by men who were not following the mustang herd. They were at least a day, possibly two, ahead. They were following the wagon train.

"This is none of our concern," he told Wooden Arm with his English and his hands. But they continued to follow the trail left by the riders. A half mile west, McCulloch dismounted again and picked up the crushed out remnant of one of those slim, stinking small cigars the Mexicans favored. And he found the marking of a spur's rowel on a rock where a rider had dismounted and almost tripped. All right. That meant that the two riders were likely Mexican.

Hell, he told himself, *we're in New Mexico Territory, almost in Arizona Territory, both of which once belonged to Mexico. Of course there would be Mexican riders.*

It was still no concern to McCulloch. What concerned him was down below, raising dust and moving west. When the mesa ended, and the trail led down the northern side of the rise so that none of the travelers below to the south would have seen them, McCulloch signed to the Comanche that he had seen enough.

They rode down the slope to rejoin their companions, and Matt McCulloch busied himself focusing on the job at hand. Keeping the mustangs moving, keeping an eye on that evil woman, Charlotte Platte, keeping a watch for any man or men on the rises north and south of them who might be trailing them, and not some party of families heading west.

Yet when they made camp that afternoon, and after they had degraded Charlotte Platte once more by making her strip and drink from the cook spoon or ladle every ten or fifteen minutes while she cooked supper, McCulloch pointed to the ridge that rose off northwest of the trail.

"There were two riders," he said. "Likely Mexican. Following that wagon train."

Keegan looked at the ridge, while Breen looked at what passed for a trail.

"There are a lot of men in that wagon train," Keegan said. "I don't think two men pose a problem."

"Wooden Arm figured they've been following them for a while," McCulloch said.

"Could be sneak thieves," Breen said. "Waiting for those folks to get careless so they could make off with some horse, oxen, maybe some supplies."

Breen spit, shook his head, and added, "From what we've seen of their camps since we started following their trail, they tend to get careless every time they make camp."

"Yeah," McCulloch said.

"It could very well be, laddies," Keegan said, "that those two hombres are just scouting along, taking notes, making plans. Maybe they have been ordered to keep an eye on the pilgrims, then ride up ahead, join their fellow blackhearts. Ambush those pilgrims."

"Either way," Breen said, "those folks aren't our responsibility. All we have to worry about is getting Matt's horses . . . and more important, my prisoners . . . to Precious Metal."

"Wim-men," Broken Arm said, jabbing his good fist west. "Ride . . . wag-gons . . . all-so." He waited to see if he had been understood.

"Hell," Breen said. "That son of a gun was a whole lot easier to tolerate when he didn't speak anything but grunts and barks."

"Women ride in our train, too," Sean Keegan said, nodding at Charlotte Platte.

"That's no woman," McCulloch said.

"And she's worth five thousand dollars,"

Breen said, "in Precious Metal, Arizona Territory."

"Hell," McCulloch said.

"Hell," said Breen.

"He-ell," grunted the Comanche kid.

"Well," said Keegan, "before we all be forgetting what jackals we be, let me, as an old horse soldier, point out that Camp Singletree is yonder way. We could swing by it in a day, two at the most, and one of us can report to the commanding officer what we have found. He can send a company of cavalry to escort those fine pilgrims to wherever they want to set down roots."

"That's not a bad idea," Breen whispered, and McCulloch confirmed that with a short, quick nod.

"Supper's ready!" Charlotte Platte roared, and banged her spoon against the cast iron pot.

"Now that we've settled that troublesome matter," Keegan said with a grin, "let's eat. This day and all this talk have left me famished." He turned toward the cook pot, saw the cook, frowned, and stepped back behind Breen, McCulloch, and even the Comanche boy. "You boys go first. I must remember that my fine mother raised me to be a gentleman."

They did not have to detour south to Camp Singletree. The next evening, blue-coated soldiers rode into their camp. The gruff-looking sergeant nodded and introduced his commanding officer, a pimply faced second lieutenant named Bright. He was, Keegan later said, badly named.

"We are scouting for hostiles." Lieutenant Bright's eyes locked hard on Wooden Arm.

"Apaches?" Keegan asked.

"Navajos," said the kid in blue.

"Navajos." Keegan almost laughed. "Lieutenant, me lad, we've had no trouble with those Indians since before the rebellion ended."

"That is no longer the case," the lieutenant said. "We have reports from Don Marion Wilkes that Navajos have been raiding his cattle, and others say they have far more nefarious plans in mind. Massacre. Taking over the country —"

"That we stole from them." Breen laughed.

That flummoxed the snot-nosed kid, but then he pointed at Wooden Arm. "And what is that, if I may ask?"

"Can't you tell, laddie? Ol' lieutenant me

346

boy," Keegan said, "that's a scarecrow."

"It's our guide," Breen said.

"A Navajo guide?" the lieutenant asked.

His sergeant grunted and added roughly, "Beggin' the lieutenant's pardon, sir, but that ain't no Navajo."

"That's a fact, Sergeant," McCulloch said. "He's our guide. He's on release from the reservation in the Indian Territory. Bill — I mean General Sherman, that's William Sherman — but, hell, we've known each other so long, he's still Bill to me and I'm still Cody to him."

"Cody?"

Matt McCulloch nodded. "That's right. William F. Cody. Buffalo Bill, my pards call me. Ain't that right, pards?"

"Yeah," Breen said. "That's right, *Buff.*"

"Lieutenant" — Keegan pointed west — "here's one thing that might concern you more than our guide and our boss, the gallant William Cody. There is a party of white settlers riding west. You can see their tracks plain as day. They were about a day or two ahead of us, but they move like a snail."

McCulloch picked up the story. "We spotted tracks of a couple of horses — shod horses, not Indian ponies —"

"Unless the savages stole them," the sergeant growled.

347

McCulloch frowned, but let his head nod up and down. "I'll give you that, Sergeant. They could be Indians who ride shod horses, smoke Mexican cigars, and wear big spurs on their cowboy boots."

"They could be trailing those settlers, planning an ambush up the trail," Keegan concluded.

The sergeant twisted in his saddle and looked west, considering, but then his eyes moved to the mustangs, and he forgot about playing hero and rescuing a party of homesteaders. He got the look in his eyes that Keegan, Breen, and McCulloch had seen far too often.

"Good lookin' mounts." He looked back at McCulloch, who just stared.

When the sergeant moved his hand toward his holster, McCulloch put his hand on the grips of his Colt.

"Lieutenant," the sergeant said, "we do have authority to confiscate horses should we need them during wartime."

Most of the color left the green pup's face.

"Wartime?" Breen asked, rising and letting his hand push back the jacket he wore to fight off the desert chill with the coming night. His hand hovered next to his double-action Colt.

"There's this . . . um . . . trouble . . . with

348

the . . . Navajos," the lieutenant said.

"We've been on this patrol since yesterday," the sergeant added.

"Jesus, Mary and Joseph," Keegan said, and the soldiers noticed that he now held his Springfield in his arms. "Since yesterday? Boys, when I rode, there were months I didn't get out of me saddle until it was time to eat the horse that had carried me to Hell and back."

"Well" — the lieutenant looked around — "there's this war."

"There's a war about to start," McCulloch said, "if you make one move toward those mustangs."

"They have a date with this man's army at Fort Wilmont," Keegan said, "and you might have a date with old Lucifer himself if you get in our way."

"Fort Wilmont." The boy officer straightened in his saddle. The Irishman's statement had given him a way of retreating without shame. "Well, that is different, gentlemen, since you have a contract with our brothers in Arizona Territory for your horses, and since you have a signed release for the savage . . . umm . . . Cherokee," he guessed. "I think we have all we need for now."

"Just try to follow that trail," McCulloch

said. "Let those folks know they might have some unwelcome company."

"Yes, yes, yes," the lieutenant said, head bobbing.

"At least send a galloper to them," Keegan said.

"Right. Galloper. Very good, sir. Now —"

"Supper's done," Charlotte Platte hollered again from the fire. "Come and get it."

Hands moved away from the weapons as the wind picked up, carrying with it the aroma of stew.

McCulloch nodded at the young officer and his surly sergeant.

"Gentlemen, we'd be honored if you and your men would dine with us this evening before you ride on about your duties."

"Aye," Keegan said. "We insist."

CHAPTER THIRTY-TWO

Rolling over on his back, Hank Benteen lowered the binoculars and slid back down the embankment, careful not to raise dust or send a stone rolling down toward the horses. A whinny or any other sound could travel a long way in this country.

"What did ya see?" Uncle Zach asked.

"They're getting ready to pull out." Hank did not bother to tell him that this morning, like every morning since they had caught up with the murderer of Hank's cousin, he had focused on the gorgeous woman who took off every stitch of her clothes at gunpoint. She never looked too shamed about baring her breasts and everything else to three tough, dirty, ignorant fools and a crooked-armed Indian boy.

"Why don't we just ride down there and shoot 'em all down like the dirty dawgs they is?" Hank's uncle asked one more time.

"They vood kill *mein Bruder*," Hans Kru-

351

ger said, almost in a panic.

"They'd be the one who shoots us down like dirty dogs," Hank said. "For the last time, Uncle, the men down there are professionals. They've killed more men, I suspect, than the number of Mexicans the boys of the Alamo shot before they got cut down."

The old coot cussed and snorted, and went back toward his horse, mumbling his normal rant. His kinfolk, like his own boy, like all outlaws their age didn't know what it was like. They wouldn't be a patch on Zach Lovely's overcoat. Why back in his day . . .

"No *soldaten*?" the Hun asked.

"Huh? Speak English, buster," Hank said.

Kruger did some ignorant pantomime trying to find the word, and at length did say *soldiers.*

"No. The soldiers are gone."

"Well," Uncle Zach said, "that was your excuse for not hitting them yesterday. Soldiers was too close by. Might come to investigate. Now them soldiers ain't close by, and you still don't want to hit the lowdown skunk who murdered my boy, your cousin, your right-hand man."

"You've always been my right-hand man, Uncle Zach."

That should have shut up the damned fool

for a few hours, at least, but it didn't. Not that windy morning.

"It just don't make no sense, not to me. Maybe I'm just too danged ol' to know no better than how we'd avenge a death before every outlaw, and all my kin, and even this damned Hun turned dandified, gentrified, and petrified. We'd just ride down there, kill 'em all or get killed. By gawd, we'd make a show and get revenge or die tryin'."

"And what would happen to those mustangs?"

"Mustangs?" The old man spit. Shaking his head and wiping his mouth with the back of his coat sleeve, he swore again. "Ponies. Runts. Not like the big hosses we rode. Them things ain't no better than donkeys. They'd stampede, of course. Scatter like the wind."

The old man was so worked up, he couldn't think straight.

Like the wind? Hank frowned.

"What you mean is that our *fortune in gold* would scatter *with* the wind."

"Huh?"

"Those horses, small that they may be, will bring a fortune if we could sell them at a town."

Uncle Zach wet his lips, considering the possibilities. The German tried to follow the conversation without much success.

"My plan is to hit that murderer and his pals when they are in town or at a trading post when they leave the boy and maybe one man with the Hun's brother and that woman. We kill them all" — by *all,* Hank meant Otto Kruger, the woman, and Hans Kruger after his usefulness had disappeared — "then we take the herd into the town, and sell them." He laughed. "That's almost like we were earning honest wages for once in our lives. *Now* do you understand?"

Hans Kruger scratched his head, but Uncle Zach wet his lips again and smiled. "Well, maybe I was wrong about how ignorant folks is."

"There's a crooked trading post a little ways west of here. I'm not sure we can hit them by then, but shortly after they get past Camp Singletree, they'll be following the stage road. That's when we'll hit them. The horses will be easier to round up in that country, and we won't have far to drive them to some place where they can fetch us a profit. You'll get your revenge then."

If it all worked out, maybe Hank would have that fine-looking woman to himself for a little bit. He wouldn't have to see her from a looking glass, either. He also thought of something funny. Hans Kruger and his brother were wanted. Not many people knew Hank Benteen in the Territory of Arizona. If he turned in two dead Kruger brothers for a reward, that would be one mighty funny joke.

Scouting around, Killed A Skunk watched a raven fly across the mesa, then decided that the white man with the see-far glasses had moved away to join his two foolish comrades instead of watching the white woman put on her white-man clothes or watching those who'd stolen Broken Buffalo Horn's son continue their dumb white-man work before leading the fine Comanche ponies farther from the land of the Comanches.

He hurried to where Broken Buffalo Horn and Lost His Thumb waited with the horses.

"Do the three white men still watch from far away?" the great holy man asked.

"It is so," Killed A Skunk answered and took the hackamore to his horse from Lost His Thumb.

"What of those men who have taken my son and our Comanche ponies?" Broken Buffalo Horn inquired.

"What they always do," the warrior answered. "They make the woman stand naked before them."

"Yet they never touch the woman." Lost

His Thumb shook his head. "All white men are fools, but Texans are the worst of the fools."

"Maybe it is their medicine," Broken Buffalo Horn said.

"It is bad medicine," Lost His Thumb said.

"No." The medicine man nodded. "I see the reason now, though why it has taken so long I do not understand. Perhaps the God of All Comanches made me wait to see, but now I see, and it makes sense. These white-eyes get their power from the woman. She makes them strong."

Lost His Thumb and Killed A Skunk exchanged glances.

The great Comanche medicine man said, "I will explain. When each day begins, as soon as Mother Sun has risen and there is light enough to see, these white-eyes have their woman disrobe before them. This woman, her hair is not black like a crow's feathers. She is too tall and too thin and not as beautiful or desirable as any of my wives, but she is still a woman. Pale perhaps, and hair the color of flames, not like a fine black pony, but still, she is not a bad woman to look at."

He let his friends picture the woman.

"When they make their camp, and before

she cooks their meal that fills their stomachs before they go to sleep, these white-eyes again make their woman disrobe before them again." He shrugged. "Sometimes, they make her disrobe in the daytime."

"At least one of them always aims a weapon at her," Lost His Thumb said.

"Because they fear this strong woman," Broken Buffalo Horn said. "They fear her power. She must have great power. She could smote them like Killed A Skunk when he grinds ants into the sand. That is how strong this white-eye woman's power must be."

"So why does she not smote those white-eyes?" Killed A Skunk asked.

"Because she is not their enemy, nor are they her enemies. It is a test. A test that requires much power."

Again, the two warriors looked at each other.

Broken Buffalo Horn laughed. "You do not see, do you?"

"No," said Killed A Skunk, "but we are not holy men. We do not see beyond the horizon."

The great medicine man nodded. "It is true." He drew a breath, exhaled, and said, "What would you do if a woman, the woman of an enemy — not a woman of the Comanche who is spoken for by another Comanche man, but a woman you found on a raid, a white-eye woman" — he grinned — "What would you do if you were in front of that white-eye woman that the white-eyes have, and she disrobed before you?"

"I would —" Lost His Thumb began, but the medicine man cut off the rest of his sentence.

"Exactly." Broken Buffalo Horn grinned wider. "Now do you see?" He did not wait, but explained the obvious, so obvious, he should have seen it long ago, but did not. The God of All Comanches was testing him, blinding him, but now he knew.

"Every day they look at a fine woman. Every day they do not touch this woman, they do not molest her, they even — white men are strange animals — let her put her clothes back on. They grow stronger. Their will grows stronger. They become more and more powerful every day, every time that woman stands before them naked. They will be more powerful than any Apache they should meet on the trail west."

"And what of us?" Killed A Skunk asked.

"They do not know about us," Broken Buffalo Horn said. "But we have watched this woman, too. We have not ridden down to take coups, or take scalps and gain glory for all Comanches."

"I have been tempted." Lost His Thumb hung his head in shame.

"Yes, but you have not ridden down there. Our strength grows, not as much as those white-eyes, but it grows. Theirs grows more because they are closer. But they are white-eyes. We are *Comanches*. We are more powerful than they are already, and the little power we gain by watching this woman from a distance makes us stronger than they could ever hope to be." Broken Buffalo Horn nodded with finality.

"Your own son watches the woman when she is without clothes," Lost His Thumb said.

"That is so, and thus he sees power. But do not forget that my son is trapped by the tree that has become one of his arms. That reduces the amount of power he can gain by looking at this naked woman."

Killed A Skunk had another question.

"What, great medicine man, about the three other white-eyes?" He nodded toward the grove of juniper on the ridge off to the north. "They watch this woman, too. That means they grow stronger, too."

Broken Buffalo Horn tilted his head back, waiting for the Great Spirit to help him solve that mystery. Yes, those white men did watch. They watched from afar, so the power they got would not be as strong . . . like the power he, Lost His Thumb, and Killed A Skunk got. It would be a slight percentage of the power received by those white-eyes in the camp with the wagon and the Comanche horses and the ugly man whose face was scarred and who always wore chains.

On the other hand, those white-eyes who watched from the hills or the top of an arroyo, and sometimes behind cactus, trees, or shrubs had *see-far* glasses. Broken Buffalo Horn had seen more than a few of such white-eye instruments of power. The glasses would bring the woman closer than could be seen with their naked eyes. Those three white-eyes who watched might grow stronger — not strong enough to wipe out three strong, smart Comanches, but —

"Who are those white-eyes?" Lost His Thumb asked.

"I believe they seek the scalps of Comanches and our other Indian brothers," Broken Buffalo Horn said.

"They are bad, bad men," Killed A Skunk said.

"They are bad, bad men," Broken Buffalo Horn agreed, nodding while still considering what must be done. "Yes, and their power grows, too, from watching the white-eyed woman disrobe. It grows stronger because they look through the see-far glasses."

He knew what he must do.

"We must smoke on this." Broken Buffalo Horn broke out his pipe, tamped the bowl with Comanche tobacco, lighted it, offered it to all directions, and passed it around.

The white-eyes with the powerful woman and his son would be moving away again with the stolen Comanche horses. It also meant the other white-eyes — the three men with the see-far glasses — would be leaving, too. Broken Buffalo Horn and his two good friends had fine Comanche ponies to ride. They would catch up. It was a decision that could not be reached without smoking.

It did not take long for the God of All Comanches to let his wisdom find Broken Buffalo Horn and tell him the truth that he must follow.

Lowering the pipe, he said, "I know what must be done." His face turned grim. "The white-eyes with the see-far glasses grow stronger. We cannot let them continue to grow stronger. So . . . we must kill them."

CHAPTER THIRTY-THREE

"Don't you pigheads get tired of this?" Charlotte Platte said as she shook the dirt off her shirt before pulling it over her chemise.

"We're still alive," Matt McCulloch said. "I aim to keep things that way."

"Bastard."

"I've been called worse." He turned and looked off, trying to find Wooden Arm, but the Comanche teen was not back from his mission yet. "Get us breakfast as soon as you get your pants on." He went to saddle his horse.

"But take your time," Sean Keegan said and laughed.

"Pigs," the poisoner of Arizona miners said.

"I've noticed a change in her," Keegan said as he turned to Jed Breen, who had kicked the prisoner's boots back toward her and moved to add fuel to the fire for another

362

late breakfast.

"What's that?" Breen said.

"She's getting darker," Keegan said. "Keep this up, she might look like a red devil herself by the time we reach Fort Wilmont. Red skin. Red hair."

Breen shook his head, but turned back to see if Poison Platte was tanner than he remembered. Alas, he was too late. She was already pulling on her boots.

"Where's the boy?" Breen said, looking around for the Comanche.

"I sent him off on an errand," McCulloch answered, and threw the blanket on his horse's back. Seeing that Platte had dressed, he barked, "Get breakfast going. We're burning daylight."

"Cook it yourself," the widowmaker said.

"I wish the bloody hell he would," Keegan whispered. "Don't like living so recklessly all the damned time."

"You cook," McCulloch said. "That's your job."

"I'm not a bad hand around a skillet," Breen offered.

"No," McCulloch said. "She cooks."

"She did poison fifteen men," Keegan said.

"That's why we search her. Keep an eye on her. But here's why she cooks. I don't want either of you holding a spoon. If we get attacked, I want you with your guns in your hands."

"What about him?" Keegan pointed to Otto Kruger.

"You don't want him without those bracelets on his wrists," Breen said. "He killed a man by driving a spoon through the eyeball. Into the brain. No, as much as I dread coughing up a river a blood and dying that way, I sure don't want a spoon sticking out of my head."

"*Nein*," the ugly man said. "*Bruder.* Me? *Nein. No löffel.* Hans."

The bounty hunter shrugged and said to the man with the scarred face, "Says you."

"What did he say?" McCulloch had the saddle on.

"Said it was his brother who drove the spoon into a man's brains. Until Poison Platte gave him some coffee, you couldn't tell the Kruger boys apart. I'm with you, Matt. I'll take my chances with our current cook." Grinning, he then shrugged and turned to the woman. "Sorry, Charlotte. I tried."

"Thanks for nothing." She was already rubbing grease into the skillet.

"Don't take your eyes off either of them," McCulloch pointed at the woman. "Especially her. I'm gonna ride around a bit, check our back trail."

She rose then, took off her hat, and flung it at him. "You're the poorest excuse for a man I've ever seen. And believe me, I've seen them all."

"Like those you poisoned . . . not to mention the kids . . . the women, too."

"That's a damned lie," she said.

"Tell it to the judge in Arizona. Or the marshal."

"Right." She let out a dry laugh. "The judge's son was one of those I killed. The marshal's brother was another."

"So you admit you poisoned them." Mc-Culloch started to mount his horse.

"After they raped me," she said.

He missed the stirrup and leaned against the horse, looking over the saddle as this vicious, cruel murderess dropped to her knees, shivering without control. She bent forward, stopped herself from falling into the dirt with her hands, and a moment later pushed herself to her knees.

"Peckerheads," she said, sobbing without control. "Vermin." Her head lifted to the blue sky. "Are you satisfied?" she screamed.

Breen and Keegan backed away from her.

"Fifteen men." She laughed, spit, wiped her eyes. "Fifteen." A moment later, she lay on the ground, curled up into a fetal position, and bawled.

Breen made the coffee that morning. Keegan offered Charlotte Platte his flask. They told Kruger to busy himself collecting dried dung for fires, to not go farther than a hundred yards from camp, but not to come back to camp until Breen waved him in. They also told him to watch out for rattlesnakes, scorpions, tarantulas, Gila monsters, and rabid coyotes.

They listened to Charlotte Platte tell her story. After which, none felt like eating. Breen even emptied his coffee cup onto the fire.

One man, the marshal's brother, had taken her from the café where she worked as a cook and waitress. He said he was taking her to the dance. Instead he took her to the mine. Fourteen others waited for her.

One after the other. Over three days. Then the judge's son took her back to the café, tossed her out of the buckboard, and with a laugh, told her they'd come back some other time for they couldn't remember a better dance.

"Bloody hell," Keegan said. "I've met some vermin in me day, but never, never have I heard anything so . . . Turns me stomach, and I've seen plenty of —" He drank from his flask.

"Did you tell anyone?" McCulloch asked.

"No." She shuddered again, and reached for Keegan's flask. "There was no one to tell. Judge's son. Marshal's brother. Thirteen other miners, including the mine owner, his partner, his foreman. Who'd believe a woman, first of all? Who'd believe a cook and waitress?" She shook without control and sobbed another minute.

"I quit my job," she said after Keegan let her have more whiskey. "I wanted to die. Kill myself. Came close a time or two." She let out another terrible laugh. "Then Marty — that's the judge's son — returned. By that time I was out of the boardinghouse where I'd been staying. I was basically living in the streets, too afraid to go to some madam's brothel, too ashamed to go to a church, find a priest, even go to a doctor. It was . . . I just wanted to die."

They let another wave of dry tears run its course.

"That's what I planned on doing," Charlotte Platte whispered. "Kill myself." She shook her head, pushed the wet bangs out of her eyes, and looked at each of the three men for a moment. Then her head lifted to the sun. "There was a half-breed Apache

367

woman in town. She's the type women go to when . . . you know. Women who . . . well, it's the type of person you go to when you don't want anyone else to know what ails you. Or when you want to kill yourself."

The half-breed showed Charlotte Platte the plants she could use, and how to suck venom from a rattlesnake's fangs.

"Glory be," Sean Keegan cried. "I don't like snakes. Could never hold one of them slivering, bloody —" It was the old horse soldier who began shaking.

"You get used to it," Charlotte said. "The half-breed took me under her wing, I guess. She said she could not make the poison herself, because that would be murder, but she would show me. So for a month, I learned. And I grew stronger. That's when Marty came to call on me one more time."

McCulloch cursed softly under his breath. "You poisoned them, instead of taking it yourself."

Her head went up and down. Her tear-stained eyes looked into McCulloch's hard, unblinking eyes. "I didn't do that good of a job," she whispered. "Some of them just got sick. But Marty died. Just like that rustler at our camp all those nights ago. They knew who did it, of course. Because Marty bragged. So did Marshal Timmerman's brother. The judge knew. Timmerman knew. Half of the town knew. So I ran." She smiled without any joy at Breen. "Almost made it. Thought I might get something close to a life back."

McCulloch and Keegan looked at Breen.

"I'll cook breakfast," the bounty hunter said. "You were a lawman, Matt. That's her story. I'm not saying that because there's five thousand dollars if I bring her in. I'm saying that because they might be singing a different tune in Arizona."

The widowmaker laughed. "I knew I never should have told you anything." She climbed to her feet. "I'll cook."

"No need," Keegan said. "I ain't hungry. And Kruger, well, he can starve till tonight."

Breen waved Kruger in as McCulloch walked away. Breen, Keegan, and Charlotte Platte saw the Indian coming out of the desert, appearing as though by magic. After a long conversation with hands, the Comanche kid and the former Texas Ranger walked back to camp.

"What did the kid see?" Keegan asked.

"Somebody watching us with binoculars. He spotted the reflection of the sun off the lenses." McCulloch frowned. "Don't look, but they were northwest of us, on that little ridge. Three men. White men. Riding horses that are about as tired as ours."

"Following us?" Breen asked.

McCulloch nodded.

"Bandits?" Keegan asked.

"Could be. Or it could be just curious travelers, though Wooden Arm thinks they have been following us for a few days."

"How can he tell?" Breen asked.

"Probably because he's a Comanche," McCulloch said.

"So what do we do?" Keegan asked.

McCulloch looked past them at Charlotte Platte, then at the mustangs, and finally back at the two men standing in front of him.

"I'm feeling generous right now." Actually, he felt repelled by Charlotte Platte's story. No matter what Jed Breen had said, McCulloch knew she had told them the truth. But that damned oath he had taken years ago when he enlisted with the Texas Rangers plagued him. Breen was right, in his own way. Maybe. If she wanted to be free, she would have to go to that town in Arizona, and convince a hostile population of her innocence.

Damned oaths men took.

He drew a breath, exhaled, and said, "We ride west. See if those curious people continue to trail us. Maybe they'll part ways, go about their business, find their place in the world. If so, God be with them."

"And if they keep following us?" Breen asked.

"Most likely, we kill them," McCulloch replied.

CHAPTER THIRTY-FOUR

The hovel looked older than the Earth.

"Likely there be whiskey there," Sean Keegan said with a grin, and wet his chapped lips.

"More likely it would kill you," Breen said.

"Many a bottle and many a keg have tried, Breen, me lad," the Irishman said with a laugh. "But nary a one has been bad enough to finish off Sean Keegan."

Under most circumstances, Matt Mc-Culloch would have avoided the place. It had that feel about it, but the signs all said that the wayfarers had stopped there for a night. The man peering from the open doorway in this post of some sort likely had entertained one or more of the braver souls in the train.

That would not have meant anything to McCulloch either, but Wooden Arm had signed and spoken that whoever had been following the wagon train had ridden up to that miserable hut of mostly dirt, at least a day before the wagon train had arrived.

"Stay here," McCulloch finally said, swung into his saddle, and began riding toward the post.

"Matt," Keegan called. "I think you might need someone to back your —"

"Stay put. Don't forget those men trailing us. I'll be back."

Keegan frowned and turned to Breen. "What the bloody hell has gotten into him? He must think he's the guardian angel of those damned fool pilgrims making their way west."

Breen grinned and shrugged. "Once a lawman . . ."

"Two days ago he said we'd kill those hombres trailing us, yet here we are, and they're still somewhere behind us, waiting to make their play."

"Matt's conservative," Breen said. "Takes him a while to make up his mind when it comes to doing something like that." He started to tighten the cinch on his saddle. "I'd say that among us jackals, he has the least jackal in him."

"And that's his biggest failing," Keegan said.

McCulloch had reached the trading post, so Keegan drew the Springfield from his scabbard, and began moving to where he could have a good view of the open doorway.

"Matt said . . ." Breen started.

"Aye," Keegan said as he found a rock to brace the heavy rifle against, and aimed through the doorway. "But as ye pointed out, laddie, Matt ain't the jackal that you and I be. He needs a guardian angel, even if it's a jackal like me."

The big brute of a man sat at a table, reading a newspaper with a cigarette burning in what passed for an ash tray and a stoneware jug, uncorked, at his right elbow.

"Hola," McCulloch said.

The man's dark eyes looked over the paper, then he turned a page.

"Looking for some information about that wagon train."

Without looking at him this time, the man said, *"No sabe."*

"You're reading an American newspaper. Printed in English. From" — McCulloch tilted his head for a better view — "Arkansas."

"No sabe," the man said again, let the paper drop to the table, and found his jug. Cradling it in the crook of his arm, he drank, burped, and set the jug down to take a few puffs on his cigarette.

McCulloch repeated his statement in Spanish.

That made the big man's eyes harden. "¿*Eres la policía?*"

"I am justice," McCulloch answered in English.

The man laughed and rose, revealing his towering height and muscular body. He was like the biggest strongman at a circus McCulloch had ever seen. Hell, he was bigger than some circuses McCulloch had ever seen.

"Amigo," the man said, switching to English, "there is no law in this part of the territory except the law that Don Marion Wilkes establishes." His heavy accent made it hard to understand, but McCulloch caught the gist of it. If the words were not clear, the big man made his point when he smashed the jug against a column post that helped keep the dirty roof from caving in on them. Then he turned the sharp edges of the busted vessel toward the former Ranger.

"Now you don't want to do that, son," McCulloch said with a smile. His hand rested on the handle of the Colt.

"I will kill you now," the big monster said in broken English. "That will make Don Marion Wilkes very happy."

McCulloch pulled the Colt, aimed it,

cocked it. Less than three feet separated them.

"All I want is information. Like why were those men following that train? And who the hell is Don Marion Wilkes?"

"You will find your answers, amigo." The man turned the table over.

Nothing separated the two men but the centipede that scurried across the floor, trying its best to get out of the way of the brawl that was about to start.

"In Hell," the man lunged toward McCulloch.

The pistol roared, bathing the miserable hut in white smoke and deafening the Ranger's ears. He stepped to his right and back, but to his amazement, the big man still stood. *How the hell could I have missed?* McCulloch thought.

The Mexican brute even grinned and started toward the gringo again. When McCulloch pulled the trigger a second time, he knew with all certainty that he had not missed, and that his weapon had not misfired.

Smoke rose from the man's muslin shirt — that's how close the Colt's barrel was to the giant's body — and McCulloch saw the hole the heavy slug had punched through the coarse shirt. He also saw a hole two inches above where the Colt's first bullet had struck.

The leviathan said something in Spanish, but McCulloch could not hear for his ears rang with thunder and the blood rushing to his head.

"I do not die," the monster said in English, laughed, and lifted the broken jug over his head. His laughter turned into a deep-voiced howl.

When the big man took his first step, Mc-Culloch's left hand fanned back the hammer, and the Colt roared again. Keeping his finger squeezing the trigger, McCulloch fanned the hammer, and kept shooting, while he backed up until he was to the right of the doorway. Three more rounds, and then the hammer fell on an empty chamber, though McCulloch heard nothing but the dull explosions from the Colt.

The brutal man still stood, laughing, and while his right hand kept the busted jug over his head, he used his left to rip away the front of the smoldering, bullet-riddled shirt. McCulloch saw what kept the man on his feet, kept him alive. Beneath the shirt he wore a wooden undershirt, and beneath the wood, McCulloch figured there was a steel plate. On the other side of the heavy plate, more wood, and perhaps some wool or cotton just to make it a tad more comfortable.

Bringing the Colt back over his head, hitting the dirty wall, McCulloch prepared to hurl the revolver at the massive monster's head — like that would save his hide — and then maybe he could dive through the doorway and run like hell.

He saw the brute's mouth open as if to speak or laugh, but no words, no noise came out of his mouth, At that moment something entered the mouth of the Mexican, cut his tongue, and blew out a large portion of the back of the killer's head. Blood and brains splattered the wall and the man fell wordlessly onto the dirt. That jarred the building so much that sand began pouring from the roof, followed by stones, branches, thatch, and the nest of a pack rat.

McCulloch could hear nothing but the ringing, yet he knew the roof was collapsing, and he turned and staggered outside, still clutching the empty revolver. Dust and smoke poured out of the opening as he stumbled toward the rails of the corral near the miserable building.

He was still there when Keegan joined him. McCulloch could hear the Irishman whistling. *Good,* the old Ranger thought, *that means I'm not stone deaf.*

"What happened?" Keegan asked.

Shaking his head, McCulloch said, "You wouldn't believe me if I told you." He saw the Springfield in Keegan's hands. "Reckon I ought to thank you."

"Not me," Keegan said. "Breen. Mine's still loaded. I just came to help you. Left Jed back there with his Colt to make sure our mustangers stay put. I figured I could make that shot, but, hell, Jed's Sharps has that fancy scope."

The north wall caved in.

"There goes the crypt," Keegan said. "Let's get the hell out of here."

"Not yet," McCulloch said. He waved Wooden Arm over to read the signs from the corral.

The desert stretched before them, distant hills — Navajo country — and buttes to the north, red sand and red rocks beyond. The stagecoach road dipped south, yet wagon tracks kept moving west.

Wooden Arm shrugged. Keegan spit tobacco juice. The mustangs snorted.

"Why would they go west?" McCulloch asked. "They're not lost. They'd been following the road all this way since they struck it, same as us."

"Didn't ye say that Mex was reading a

newspaper from Arkansas?" Keegan asked, and when McCulloch nodded, he explained. "Well, have ye ever met any gent from that state that had any lick of sense?"

"My mother came from Arkansas," McCulloch said.

Keegan wiped his mouth. "Like ye ever had a mother, Matt." He sighed and pointed. "They probably bought some land in that godforsaken blight of sand and scorn. Suckered, but they are nay our concern, pardner, and we have mustangs — your mustangs — to get to the army. That means following the stagecoach road."

After kicking a clod of dirt, McCulloch swung into his saddle. "It doesn't make any sense. What's ahead, between here and the crossing of the Colorado River?"

"I dunno, Matt." Keegan stared ahead, then back at the approaching mustangs and covered wagon. "More of the same. Dead River, I believe, is a bit —"

"Dead River?" McCulloch stared intently.

"Aye. Though I don't think in my few scouts in this bad country if ever I saw a spot of water. Even after a whale of a monsoon." Keegan cocked his head. "Is something troubling ye, Matt?"

"Dead River," he whispered. "Just triggered something in the back of my head.

Can't place it right now. But I think it was a dream I had."

"I haven't had a decent dream since the one of Peggy O'Doul, fine blond-headed gal, sweet lass . . ."

McCulloch pulled off his hat and waved it toward Jed Breen, who was riding point.

"Keep them moving west," McCulloch yelled. "Straight ahead. Don't let them turn south. We're riding this way." Spurring his horse, he galloped down the north side of the herd, to reach the drag position with Charlotte Platte, to make sure the herd — and this motley outfit of jackals and a woman — rode toward Dead River.

Keegan glanced at Wooden Arm, who smiled like a fool, and awkwardly made it onto the back of his pinto. The boy rode toward the herd of mustangs, too, where Breen was leading them west, away from the road that was the safest way to travel.

"Bloody hell," Keegan said and even considered crossing himself and saying a prayer.

CHAPTER THIRTY-FIVE

Linton had told them this was a shortcut. Easy traveling. But one day since leaving the stagecoach road, Annie Homes felt sick with dread. The land was flat, unlike some of the mountainous areas they had crossed, but traveling proved slow. Six times they had been delayed because of broken axels, stuck wagons, or busted wheels. Another time they had to stop until the choking dust stopped blowing. When the Reverend Sergeant Major Homer Primrose III asked the brutal guide if perhaps they should turn around and take the wagon road, Linton had laughed.

"Ya made yer bed, pilgrim, and here's where yer gonna have to sleep," he had said. "Hell's fire, preacher, this'll save us time." His arm had shot out toward the sinking sun. "Straight shot west. Turn south when we hit dem Sacramento Mountains, and Rapture Valley awaits ya."

This morning proved the worst, even more draining than that evening they had spent at Five Scalps way back, what seemed forever ago, in the Panhandle of Texas.

Mrs. Stanton was sick. She had left Dead Trout, Arkansas, because of her lung ailments. Everyone said that the desert Southwest was almost a cure for lung troubles, but the dust for the past few days had proved so thick, she began coughing, took a fever, and lay in the back of her wagon, being tended almost constantly by Betsy. This day, Annie's mother had gone over to the Stanton wagon to spell the teenage girl, and take care of Mrs. Stanton herself. Annie's mother was a god-fearing woman, with a kind, caring heart.

At least the dust had finally stopped blowing, except for what the animals, wagons, and those people who trudged along beside the caravan kicked up. Annie sat beside her father as they moved west.

Linton rode up, and Annie wished she had volunteered to help Mrs. Stanton. Then she would be inside the back of a wagon, and the vicious guide would not be able to stare at her with such lecherous eyes. He was speaking to the Randalls in the wagon ahead, pointed somewhere to the south, and spit into the wind before turning his horse around and kicking it into a trot. He grinned widely when he realized Annie was not in the back . . . hiding.

Once he twisted his horse around to ride alongside her father's wagon, he said, "We're gonna camp just up ahead, Walter." He pointed again. "Good campground. It's the Dead River."

"River." Walter Homes wet his severely chapped lips. "You mean there's water?"

Linton chuckled. "Only your sweat." His eyes found Annie. "That's a shame, though. It would be something if some of us could take off all our clothes and dip into some nice, clean, refreshing water. Yes, sir, Walter, it would be something nice to do." The laughter grew louder as he tipped his hat, kicked the horse, and trotted off to the Stanton wagon. He called back, "Make camp in the bed of the stream. You don't have to worry about any flash flood. That river hasn't seen water since Columbus set foot in this country."

It was dead, all right — the river — though Annie knew water had flowed here. Maybe during a flash flood. The bed dipped several feet below the land, and the bed was sand, gravel, hard and not, but not one cactus or the tough scrub that grew in this country had sprouted in the bed. She could see trees in the distances, but not any tall trees, not the pines and the elms and the oaks from back home in Arkansas. Maybe the puniest cottonwoods ever to grow. She didn't know. But if a tree, even one more twig than fir, could find water to live in this country, well . . . there was hope.

Still, the sand and the heat and just the bleakness of the land tried to drain her spirits. But they would be in this spot for just one night. One night, and they'd leave Dead River and make their way west. Linton or not, she knew that they would find their way to Rapture Valley.

Her father made them circle the wagons, just as he always did, even though Linton said there was no need to go to all that trouble, that the high banks of the Dead River would offer enough protection, and that it was too hot and windy to work too hard for just one night. Walter Homes remained firm, and the wagons were brought in and the terrain and width of the riverbed meant the circle became more of a triangle and a larger camp than usual. Still, the livestock was brought inside. Annie knew her father had spread the wagons out to make things easier on the women and the sick, especially Mrs. Stanton. Maybe even for Annie's sake, too. She had grown so weary of smelling the dung and urine of oxen and mules and horses, it would be nice to be able to catch fragrances of the desert.

"What's that dust over yonder, Capt'n Linton?" Hawg asked.

Annie had gotten a fire going, with a pot about to boil water for tea, when she heard Hawg calling out. She rose from the fire, and stepped to the side where she saw him pointing to the north through the slight opening between two wagons. She saw the dust, too, created by a fair-sized crowd moving. She frowned. The dust seemed to have settled for the day.

Linton — Annie would not give him any rank, and especially not captain — raised his hand over his eyes and chuckled. "Just the wind, boy."

She felt a shadow cross her and saw her father looking, too. He stared a full minute, then turned, his eyes studying her intently before he moved to the wagon. Annie breathed in deeply and felt her heart jump a bit, for her father had pulled out his musket, and leaned it against the back of their wagon.

"Maybe that's a herd of antelope," Winfield Baker said. "I could go for some backstrap meat tonight."

"Ain't no antelope in this country," Muldoon said. "Just coyote's."

Winfield chuckled. "I could eat coyote, too."

"So could I," Thad said.

They all laughed. Linton moved away from Hawg and approached the northern tip of the wagons, where the Reverend Sergeant Major Homer Primrose III sat getting his cookfire ready.

"Boys." Annie watched her father approach Winfield Baker and the other young men. He lowered his voice, but Annie could hear him.

"Get your guns. Long guns. Have them handy."

Hawg started to laugh until he saw the deadly seriousness in Walter Homes's face.

"The wind's not blowing," Homes said softly. "And when it was, it was blowing west to east. That dust cloud's moving southwest. And it's moving like a lot of horses."

"Wild mustangs?" Thad's eyes beamed. "I'd love to see a herd of those."

"I hope that's what you do see," Walter Homes said. "But let's have our weapons handy, just in case."

The kettle started to whistle. Annie didn't

387

even notice it till her father took it off the fire. The dust stopped just beyond a small rise.

Horses, Annie thought. But not wild mustangs.

"Annie?" her mother called out. "Is that tea ready?"

"In a minute, Ma."

"But I heard it whistling."

Annie sighed, almost cursed, and found the cup she had prepared with tea leaves for her mother. She filled it with hot water, and brought it to where her mother was coating the skillet with grease for their evening supper. "Here's your tea, Ma."

"Oh." Smiling, her mother rose, wiped her hands on the apron, and took the tea, using the apron to protect her from the heat. "It's not for me, child. I shall take this to poor Gertrude Stanton, bless her heart."

Her mother left with the cup of tea, but she stopped when someone called out, "Riders headin' this way."

Hawg and Thad decided to hurry for their rifles. Winfield Baker already leaned his Enfield against his parents' wagon, and Mr. Baker was fetching the long musket he had carried in the War.

"Oh, there ain't nothin' to worry 'bout, folks," Linton grinned with reassurance.

"Those look like Navajos. Peaceful since Kit Carson bloodied their noses. Likely just want to say howdy and see if we're lost. Not many white folks cross this country. Come on, preacher, we'll go speak to them. They might even give us some Indian tobacco or silver, which they take a shine to. They'll bless us and we'll be on our way. Navajos haven't caused any trouble since the 1860s, when y'all was giving Yankees hell, right?"

A few of the men chuckled with good humor, but Walter Homes remained stone-faced.

The Reverend Sergeant Major Homer Primrose III climbed onto the back of a mule, while Linton tightened the cinch to his horse then mounted it. For some reason, despite camping for the evening, their guide had not bothered to unsaddle his horse.

Annie moved so she could watch clearly as Linton and the preacher rode out to the party of four riders. She used her hand to block out the sun, intense even while it sank, and stared hard. The four riders, on small mustang ponies, eased their horses to a stop. She could make out enough of their features. Clean shaven. Long, black hair. They wore moccasins and woolen or cotton britches. Their skin appeared to be deep copper, and she caught flashes of silver and other jewelry that these men wore as cuffs around their ankles, necklaces dangling from their chests and against vests for shirts, one of which looked to be beaded.

The preacher held out his right hand, and he said something, but they were too far for anyone in the camp to catch the words. Linton backed his horse away, and began moving his hands this way and that. Sign language, Annie figured. She didn't like their guide at all, but it was amazing to see . . . how these two different cultures could communicate without using oral words. Amazing.

She had seen Indians, of course, but mostly those of the Five Civilized Tribes — Seminoles, Cherokees, Creeks, Choctaws, and Chickasaws — but never anything like these. It was exhilarating, seeing Indians this close, even though they had to be two hundred yards away.

The Reverend Sergeant Major Homer Primrose III nodded his head, gestured back toward the wagon train encampment, and Linton moved his hands again. Then the preacher lifted both of his hands skyward, and Annie knew what he was doing. Offering prayer or trying to convert the savages to Christianity.

But those Navajos, those four tall men,

390

had something else in mind.

The nearest one raised a rifle and shot the Reverend Sergeant Major Homer Primrose III out of his saddle. By then, Linton had turned his horse around, and was galloping hard back to the wagon train.

It took forever for the sound of the gunshot to reach Annie's ears. All she saw was a blast of white smoke, saw the mule turning around, kicking up in panic, and saw the preacher flying back and landing in the hard brush.

Linton raced on. Another rifle blew out smoke, aiming toward Linton. Then the first shot reached Annie's ears, and it sounded like it would not stop. The second shot came like a distant echo.

"It's an ambush!" Linton screamed.

Annie did not look at him. None of the Indians chased him. The four drew their bows and filled the preacher's unmoving body with arrows. One jumped off his horse and knelt beside the good reverend. When that Indian stood, he raised something in his hand. He screamed, or so it seemed, but the words never reached Annie's ears.

Because Mrs. Donovan was screaming, "We're all gonna be killed. They've kilt the preacher and they'll do the same to us. We're all gonna be massacred. Massacred!"

Suddenly, thunder roared, and dust thickened.

Annie understood. Her father had been right. That had not been antelope or coyotes or the wind causing the dust. Suddenly, she realized that there had been more than four Indians — four lying, murdering Navajos — behind that gentle rise. She did not know how many Navajos were left after Kit Carson's campaign against them, but it would not have surprised her to learn that the entire Navajo tribe were galloping straight for their stronghold.

Stronghold? Wagons with tired travelers, children, women, holed up in a dried riverbed, miles and miles from the main trail where most white travelers would be. They were alone. Alone. In a strange, desolate wilderness.

Where charged the Indians, whooping, shooting, screaming. A bullet punched through the canvas of her father's covered wagon.

"Annie," she heard him yell. "Get down. Get down."

But she could not move.

"There must be sixty or more!" someone yelled, just as Linton's horse leaped over a wagon tongue. "Dirty, stinkin' no good, lyin' Navahos. They've broke their promise.

Murdered the preacher. And here come what looks like the whole damned tribe."

The breath came out of her as she felt like she had been kicked in the back by a mule. Coughing, she cringed, almost cried, and felt a great weight rise off her back.

"Stay down," the voice whispered. "Just lie here. We'll be all right."

It was Winfield Baker. She caught just a glimpse of him as he ran away, toward the nearest wagon, carrying that long rifle of his.

The air became alive with bullets. That dust — the dust she'd prayed would not return — swept upon them. It was a land of dust, of gun smoke, of screams, of horses. It was a land that must have been worse than Hell.

Annie felt her resolve leave her. She thought *Here is where I die. Here is where we all die. At the Dead River.*

CHAPTER THIRTY-SIX

Leaping off his horse, Linton grabbed his revolver and fell to the ground. "Take cover," he shouted. "There must be two hundred of them red Navajo devils." He scurried under the wagon, rolled behind the rear wheel, and laughed to himself as six of Don Marion Wilkes's gunfighters — dressed like they were Navajos when every one of them was as white as Linton — rode toward the camp. It would be over in a few minutes, and the only thing he had to worry about was if that rancher Wilkes planned to double-cross him. Kill him with these dumb pilgrims.

Not that Linton thought that would happen. The old don needed a witness, someone who could say that Navajos started the attack. He grinned — yeah, Annie Homes, the pretty girl with the attitude — would make a perfect witness. With her ma and pa dead and scalped, well, hell, she just might lose that uppity attitude that made her think she was holier than thou, or at least, holier than Linton.

Which, of course, she was. But she wouldn't be for long. Linton grinned again. If she troubled him, well, her hair was so black, it could pass for an Indian's scalp, too.

They came, riding like hell, ready to do some fine butchering. He laid his revolver on the ground, just so none of those killers mistook Linton for some Arkansas hero.

The lead bunch, six men with repeating rifles, closed in. Others circled to the side. He watched those coming straight ahead. A hundred yards. Eighty. Sixty. Forty . . .

A fierce volley sounded behind him. Four men and two horses slammed hard into the ground, sending clouds of reddish dirt into the sky. One of the horses, a pinto, threw its rider hard, and Linton could tell by the way that dude hit that he wouldn't be getting up again, not the way his head tilted. Poor soul was likely already burning in Hell.

The other man came to his knees, blood gushing from his nose and his split lips, sand and cactus spines covering his face. He weaved to his left, then to his right, then fell hard after a geyser of red exploded from the center of his chest. His horse got up, sniffed, and took off at a gallop toward the Painted Desert.

"What the hell," Linton said, and rolled over. He heard the crash of musketry, then someone saying smartly, "Calmly. Fall back, Second Squad. First Squad, forward. Ready. Let them come. Remember, aim low. Steady men, steady. Fire at will."

Gunfire erupted again, and Linton realized others on his left and his right were shouting. He started to crawl back from underneath the wagon, only to remember his revolver in the sand. He turned, snatched it, and looked again at the dead men lying in the dirt, soon obscured by more clouds of dust.

When Linton popped his head from underneath the wagon, he saw legs, legs of men, and the stocks of muskets of all kinds. Six men stood before him — no, six kids. Six boys with snot running out of their noses. They quickly, expertly reloaded their muzzleloaders or breech-loading rifles.

"Fire at will," a voice barked, and Linton turned as more long guns cracked, leaving white smoke rising above the open space between two wagons.

"Fall back," the voice spoke sharply, "and reload. Come on, boys. Give them hell. Remember you're from Arkansas!"

The man yelling, the commander of these kids, was that uppity all so high-and-mighty Walter Homes.

Linton climbed to his feet, looked around, saw more men, more muskets, more gun smoke. He heard volley after volley, and realized that these dumb hicks from western Arkansas were armed. Shooting like they were in some damned war. Hell, wasn't that the preacher's widow — the wife of the man whom Linton had led out to be murdered — commanding some boys, marching around, raising a spatula rather than a sword?

"Fire!" she commanded, whipping down the hand that held the spatula.

Rifles roared. Smoke rose.

"Fall back, boys," she barked. "And reload!"

"Mistah Linton . . ."

He turned, saw Walter Homes a couple of yards before him. "If you have a long gun, you would do better with it, suh. If not, I suggest you stand ready in case any of those riders breech our lines."

Linton blinked. Heard another crash of muskets and rifles. Heard the strangest, wildest, eeriest yell that ever reached his ears. More coyote than human, more monster than man.

Walter Homes leaned back his head and laughed. "By God, boys," he told the teens. "Did you hear Mr. Stanton? That, children, is what a Rebel yell sounds like."

"What do you think you're doin'?" Linton heard himself asking.

Homes was busy at the moment, having one set of six boys step back to reload, while the others went forward to aim and fire whenever they damned well felt like it. The greenhorn spun around, eyes wild with excitement and fury. "What am I doin', suh?" he yelled as the boys squeezed their triggers. "I'm doin' what I was doin' when I enlisted in the Confederate Army, suh. I am protectin' my family, my home, my country."

At the top of the small rise, Don Marion Wilkes lowered his binoculars, and sighed.

"Linton said they was nothin' but a bunch of spud diggers," said Duncan Regret, who sat in the saddle of his horse.

"Apparently, our friend Señor Linton underestimated them," Wilkes said. "Bring them back in, my loyal friend. Leave about a half dozen to keep circling the wagon train, but for the love of God, tell those idiots to stay out of rifle range. Those spud diggers shoot like sharpshooters."

"Arkansas," Regret said. "Hunters, most of them."

"Indeed."

By the time Regret rode back, leaving six white bandits dressed up like Navajos, riding around the train but keeping a great distance, Don Marion Wilkes was grinning. "Southern gentlemen, I see. Let's see how honorable they are. Indians generally carry off their dead. Send six men, one holding a white scarf tied atop his, ahem, war lance, and let us pick up our dead and wounded, and bring them back."

"I ain't sure the boys will go for that," Regret said.

Wilkes's eyes became narrow and evil. "They will go for it or they will be shot dead by you, my loyal *segundo*. We can't let anyone discover that those Navajos are not Indians. See that my orders are carried out, Regret, or you will be holding the flag of truce yourself."

"Capt'n Homes."

Annie stopped, turned, and saw her father walking across the yard toward Betsy Stanton's pa. She didn't remember that much about the late war, but knew her dad had served in the Confederate Army. She always pictured him as the polite farmer, but now

399

she had seen him as he must have been all those years ago. A hero. A leader of men. And now she knew he had been an officer. A captain.

You just never knew.

She had a job to do, too. She had to deliver water to Winfield Baker and those other teenage boys who had hunted in the hills, along the creek beds, and in the Ouachita Mountains back home. Now they had fired rifles at men. Men — savages — who were bent on killing them all.

They had turned them back, these boys, these old men, these gallant Arkansans. Yet there had been a cost. Bullets had hit some of the livestock. Hawg's left earlobe had been shot off. Mrs. Randall had taken a ball through the meaty part of her arm.

The boys drank, thanked her, and Annie picked up the bucket and hurried across the compound to where her father stared through the opening.

"They carry a flag of truce," she heard her father say. "They must want to carry away their dead, their wounded."

"We could pick 'em off right easy, sir," Hawg said.

"Yes, we could," Captain Walter Homes said, "if we were savages. If we were not men, if we did not believe in God. Let them

400

care for their dead, their injured. Maybe they will realize the fruitlessness of their assault and ride away. Let us continue our journey."

"Do you think," Mr. Preston said, "that they would let us bring in the reverend's body?"

The captain's head shook slightly.

"Even if we flew a white flag?"

"It's too risky. The reverend is in a better place now. He watches over us. He would not want one of his flock to risk his life just to bring in his earthly remains."

Turning, he smiled at his daughter. "They have water here, sweetheart." He nodded to the north. "Take those some. That is where the heaviest assault was . . . this time. I must check on the others." He stepped away, turned, and said, "But keep your head down. And if they attack again, stay with Mrs. Stanton. She is sick, and I fear in the confusion, she might be frightened out of her wits." He winked. "Like the rest of us, especially me."

She took the water to the northern point of camp, and felt revulsion filling her mouth when the first person to grab the ladle and drink was that evil man, that worthless guide, Linton. He was dirty and sweaty, but she smelled just his sweat and stink, not gun smoke. She figured, coward that he was, he had not even fired one shot. He had hidden underneath the wagon, gutless coward that he was.

He was right, of course. Don Marion Wilkes had never made a mistake. Oh, what had happened on this day was a bit of an inconvenience, not a mistake. They would still wipe out the Arkansas spud diggers, in due time.

The dead were loaded into the back of a wagon. Two men were badly wounded, but Wilkes took care of that by ordering their throats cut. That, he figured, would put some backbone into the gunfighters he had hired. No quarter for the enemy, and no quarter for anyone who got too hurt to cut down those homesteaders so that the Dead River flowed again . . . with blood.

"What do you think?" he asked Regret.

"They're dug in pretty good. Being in that riverbed is to their advantage, unfortunately. Offers them more protection when we're riding around."

"I thought armies always wanted to occupy the high ground."

Regret drank from a tequila bottle. "Ground ain't that high, Don, sir." He corked the bottle and pitched it to one of his men, a man wearing a black wig with his face and arms lathered with grease to make him look like a red savage. "Plus, those ol' boys know how to shoot. My guess is every one of them old enough fought in the war. And the boys who were too young to have seen the elephant, they been shooting squirrels to put supper on their plates since they was knee high to a grasshopper."

"So we can't wipe them out playing cowboy and Indians?" Don Marion Wilkes frowned.

"Well, they ain't goin' nowhere. And they ain't got water except for what's in their wagons. But you ain't got time for no siege."

He sighed, shook his head, and looked at two of the white men dressed as Indians. "I guess we shall have to rely on our friend. Go fetch Matilda, boys."

"Boss," Regret said with caution. "That'll be hard to explain to the army, if you use that thing. Navajos — hell, no injuns that I know of — ever used a cannon before."

"We shall fire grapeshot," Wilkes said, "not iron balls or explosives. And when all the wagons are burning, there will be no sign that artillery was used."

"That scalp hunter, Linton, might get cut to pieces, too."

"I know, but he would have been cut to

pieces, anyway, once he had completed his service."

"Then who will scalp the bodies?" Regret asked. "The scalps you need to plant in Navajo villages so you can get their land?"

"I am sure you or one of your men will sell your morals for five hundred dollars a scalp. Just a dozen or so bodies, a few children, more women. The rest of the dead we will burn in the wreckage of wagons. Is that satisfactory?"

"Reckon so," Regret said.

Wilkes looked back at the two white men in Navajo disguise. "Bring back Matilda, boys. And do not tarry."

CHAPTER THIRTY-SEVEN

The mustangs turned skittish, nervous, as though they smelled something in the air, felt something. Matt McCulloch had been around horses long enough to trust most of them.

"Wolves?" Jed Breen called out.

"Maybe," McCulloch answered, but he didn't think so. Nor did he think the animals felt a change in the weather. Hell, this was Arizona Territory. The weather never changed this time of year. "Stay with them. Don't let them run," he yelled to Breen, Keegan, and Charlotte Platte. "Keep them here. I want to ride a ways and see what's over that rise. That seems to be what's spooking them." He turned his black around, and it did a bit of a stutter step. Maybe the mustangs' actions had pricked the gelding's nerves. Maybe it heard or smelled or felt that same thing.

McCulloch got the animal under control

and looked at the Comanche boy.

"Come with me," he told the Indian.

The teenager grinned. "You bet," he said in English.

They trotted off at first, just so the mustangs didn't get eager to run, then rode past Otto Kruger on the wagon. Out of decency, McCulloch told the murderer, "Might be some trouble up ahead."

"Might be, *mein Bruder*," the ugly man said with an even uglier grin.

"Might be you won't live to find out." McCulloch spurred the black, and loped away with Wooden Arm, one arm still confined by that outrageous splint, keeping pace without losing his grip as his pony kept pace with McCulloch's big animal.

Hans Kruger lowered the binoculars and turned toward Uncle Zach and Hank Benteen. "The big one and *dummkopf* red devil leave."

"Yeah," Benteen said.

The leader of the Benteen gang and his crazy old uncle slithered up to the top of the arroyo to look at the mustangs and the outfit. Turning to Uncle Zach, Benteen said, "That'd be the Ranger."

"McCulloch." Uncle Zach spit, wiped his mouth, and grinned. "That means that son-

406

murderin' coward's pushin' 'em fool ponies."

"With the bounty hunter," Benteen said.
"Something's spooked those mustangs.
Bounty hunter won't be able to shoot that
long-killin' buffler gun of his on a skittish
hoss." He frowned. "But if we go chargin'
in there, those horses is like to scatter in
twenty-two-and-a-half directions."

He sighed. "But this trail's been a hard
one, a hot one, a dusty one, and we ain't
likely to get a better chance. Get revenge on
that wanna-be hangman and arsonist."

"Have some fun with that gal they got,
too," Uncle Zach said with a lecherous
chuckle.

Wetting the tip of his right pointer finger,
Benteen raised his hand, then lowered it
with a smile. "Wind's comin' from the west.
We let that Ranger and injun ride a bit,
likely they won't hear our shots. If we hit
'em fast and quick, we can kill 'em before
they have a chance to fight too much."

"And maybe we can find some of 'em
mustangs . . . after we done all that needs
doin' here," Uncle Zach said. "Get our
revenge and see what that gal's like."

"We might have to kill the gal with the
others."

"Or take her with us."

Uncle Zach, Hank Benteen had always known, could be obsessed with one thing if that thing wore petticoats. He turned to the German. "You good with that plan?"

The Hun nodded.

"We ride in fast, kill the two men left behind. You get your brother. We'll see what we have to do with the girl."

"Goot plan," the foreigner said.

"All right." Benteen nodded to where they had tied up their horses. "Let's tighten the cinches and get to revengin'."

McCulloch reined up hard and turned to the Comanche boy. Wooden Arm's face told the one-time Ranger that the kid had heard the same thing.

Gunfire. Like a war.

"Stay here," McCulloch said as his horse twisted and squirmed and refused to obey bit and reins. The black was a good horse — hell, he wore the McCulloch brand, and that meant something — just acting squirrely because of the violence in the air. "Stay here," he told the boy again.

McCulloch was already galloping away, but he heard Wooden Arm's voice. "No."

He looked back once, saw the teenager with a busted arm and a hard-charging pony riding right behind him. McCulloch knew he couldn't do a thing about it. White men didn't often win arguments with Comanches, no matter how young the warrior might be.

Gunfire had quieted by the time McCulloch and Wooden Arm had covered the last mile, slowing their horses to walk, looking in all directions. They found an arroyo that cut south, then turned back northwest, and entered it, moving with caution. Both horses sensed danger. McCulloch stopped his horse and turned to the teen. He considered what he was doing, then chuckled and reached behind him to unstrap one of the saddlebags. Everyone in Purgatory City, everyone in Texas, maybe every son of a gun in the Western United States would give him hell for this.

He found the old cap-and-ball-percussion Navy .36, which he had converted into a .38-caliber centerfire, checked the loads, then lowered the hammer, and extended the pistol to Wooden Arm.

McCulloch imagined Sean Keegan's face and what he'd have to say about it. "Giving a red devil a revolver? Have ye lost ye blithering mind?"

The boy smiled, dropped the hackamore over his horse's neck, felt the balance of the revolver, nodded with approval, and shoved the gun inside the top of his breechcloth. "We fight?" he asked in English.

"Let's see who we'd have to fight first," McCulloch said, and they rode through the dry wash until it started to spread out into the desert. Go farther, and someone might see them.

"What do you think?" Killed A Skunk asked.

Lost in thought, Broken Buffalo Horn sat quietly in the Comanche saddle on his horse as the wind blew his braids. His horse stood still as though asleep. Killed A Skunk's pinto, on the other hand, seemed nervous or suspicious. Or maybe it just wanted to feel the wind, pound its hooves, and run like Comanche ponies were born to run.

"Should we smoke?" Lost His Thumb asked. His horse also felt something or smelled something in this strange, barren desert country of the Navajos. He knew they could not smoke. They were too close, and there was no time to fill a pipe with tobacco and make the correct offerings.

"We do not smoke," the medicine man said. "We do not talk. We do not think. It is time to act. To be . . . Comanches."

McCullough and Wooden Arm tied their horses to a clump of creosote, and crawled up the arroyo's edge.

"What the hell?" McCulloch whispered then cursed himself for saying anything out loud. Whispers could be heard the same as gunshots. He studied the scene. A fair-sized wagon train had decided to fort up in the riverbed.

Dead River. He knew where he was. The hair on the back of his neck suddenly bristled. A few Indians — Navajos by the looks of them — rode in a circle around the besieged train. Off to the north, he saw what appeared to be more Indians on both sides of a slight knoll.

He pieced it all together. The Indians had attacked, but whoever had been leading that train — the very same wagon train that had stupidly left the stagecoach road — had some brains about him or had been incredibly lucky.

On the other hand, when was the last time Navajos had gone on the warpath?

No, that didn't make a lick of sense.

McCulloch had to figure something else out. Like what the hell he was supposed to do. Save some damned fool greenhorns. Him, with a herd of wild mustangs — and some saddle-broke animals that some rustlers had bequeathed them — and two prisoners, even if he did think kindly for the

411

woman. Against a bunch of Indians.

He caught Wooden Arm's gesture. The boy was too smart to say anything, so once McCulloch looked at him, he pointed to the nearest Navajo circling the wagons, and signed, *He no Indian.*

McCulloch looked back, followed the rider, then looked at the one a few hundred yards behind that one.

That made sense. White men, traitorous white renegades, had painted themselves up like Navajos and ambushed this train. McCulloch felt his blood rising, practically boiling. He pointed below and dropped down without making a sound. Wooden Arm made it to the wash's bottom, his face confused.

When McCulloch grabbed the reins to his black, the boy stepped up, and whispered in English, "We no fight?"

"Oh, we fight all right," McCulloch said. "But we fight my way." He swung into the saddle, waited for Wooden Arm to climb onto the pinto's back, and then they eased their horses back in an easterly direction. Back to Breen, Keegan, Otto Kruger, Charlotte Platte, and some cantankerous horses bound for Fort Wilmont.

They had loaded their guns. Tightened their

412

cinches. Emptied the flask of Uncle Zach's. Hank Benteen grabbed the reins, put his left foot in the stirrup, and climbed into the saddle. He swung his other boot into the stirrup, then drew his revolver.

"You know what you're doin', right?" he asked the Hun.

"*Ja,*" the Kruger outlaw said. "I ride to vagon. Get *mein Bruder,* vait for you. Kill anyone trying to escape."

"You got it." Benteen spit and whispered urgently to the man behind the bush. "Damn it, Uncle Zach. Will you finish your business so we can get on with this before that Ranger gets back?"

The old contrarian stepped into the wash, buttoning his britches and spitting out tobacco juice. He looked up. "You wait till you ain't no young whippersnapper no mo', nephew." He started wiping his hands on the fronts of his trouser legs. "You'll learn that —"

He stopped talking, suddenly in shock, and looked down at the obsidian point sticking out of his shirt, just below the last rib.

He put his hands beneath the point as though trying to catch the blood spilling out of his body and staining his shirt. Benteen heard the second arrow as it struck

Uncle Zach Lovely in the back and knocked him to his knees, spinning him around a bit so that the third arrow ripped through his throat. His hands flew up to grab the front and back of the arrow, blood coming out of his throat and mouth in torrents.

The first Indian appeared, screaming and waving a hatchet.

"Get the hell out of here!" Hank Benteen screamed, spurring his horse and climbing out of the wash as an arrow ripped so close to his neck he would have sworn he felt the tickle of the feather on the arrow's shaft.

Hans Kruger needed no encouragement. He whipped the reins against his horse like he had been born on horseback, that he had been born a Westerner, that he had ridden for the Pony Express. He rode like hell to save his life. He rode even faster than Hank Benteen.

Both men screamed.

Three Indians followed them, yelling louder.

All of them raced their horses straight for a bunch of wild mustangs being herded by two men and a woman on horseback, following a slow-moving covered wagon driven by a man wearing chains.

CHAPTER THIRTY-EIGHT

He rubbed his gloved hand over the short iron barrel of the twelve-pounder, and grinned. There were few things better, Don Marion Wilkes thought, than an 1841 mountain howitzer. Five hundred pounds of beauty on two wheels, pulled by horse, mule, sometimes even men. Oh, how well mountain howitzers had served him back in the war against Mexico. He wondered if old Zachary Taylor had truly believed him when he'd said that this particular weapon had been lost in the campaign at Burro del Vidaurri.

Wilkes grinned. " 'Shot or projectile,' Captain Dickerson, my commanding officer said. He never thought we could use grapeshot in such a weapon, but I showed him. Just like I showed all those damned greasers . . . even when they came out of that church waving their white shirts and begging for mercy." He nodded at Duncan

Regret. "You, my segundo, will now show those Arkansas dogs the feel of iron." He laughed, mounted his horse, and laughed again. "I shall watch from my perch on that mountain." He pointed to the small knoll that no one, even in the flattest part of the continent, would have called a hill, let alone a mountain. "If you see them waving a white flag, remember, it is nothing but a damned Rebel trick, just like those greasers were trying to pull at Zaragoza."

When Don Marion Wilkes rode away, Duncan Regret nodded at the mustachioed killer dressed as a Navajo, and that one grabbed the first canvas sack.

"Ever seen grapeshot?" Regret asked. The man grunted and handed the sack to another white man dressed like an Indian.

"We used whatever we could," the mustached man said. "Glass. Horseshoes. Nails. Chunks of tin from a Southern roof. It did the job."

"Maybe," Regret said, and watched the other fake Indian shove the sack into the barrel. A third man took the plunger and shoved it down the angled, smooth barrel. "But nothing does the job of pure, lovely grapeshot. Three little iron balls held together by iron rings. All put together in bunches of three. Touch the powder off, hear that explosion, smell the beautiful smoke, and the balls separate from the rings and scatter like birdshot on the way to greet a quail." He chuckled. "What I really loved — and Don Wilkes, he was the same way — were the screams we heard that followed. I could spend all day listening to that beautiful sound, watching all those Johnny Rebs get cut to pieces. Here I am again, years after the rebellion, and I get to butcher a whole lot more."

He grabbed the torch off the small fire. "What makes this better, is it ain't just Rebs from Arkansas I'm killing. Soldiers, I mean. I get to wipe out some women and children, too."

He laughed, watched the man step aside, and asked, "What's the angle and range, Private?"

The gunner stepped back, looking confused. "How the hell would I know, Regret? I deserted from the infantry, not the artillery."

That made Regret laugh even louder. "Let's find out," he said, and touched the fuse with the flame.

The first thought that crossed Sean Keegan's mind when he turned quickly in the saddle was *famine or no, I never should have left Ireland for America.* He saw three Indians chasing two white men and the mustangs thundering west. He figured that wherever you saw three Indians, a bunch of others probably were close.

He spurred his horse, leaned low, and raced out to the right. Damn his luck. That lucky bounty hunter had the left flank — the far side from those Indians. Keegan didn't know who the two white men were, but figured they would have to take care of themselves. He had Matt McCulloch's mustangs to consider, and that hard-rock horse trader would be mad at hell if Keegan and Breen let those horses run like hell.

Running like hell, though, seemed to be a damned fine idea.

He couldn't see the woman. Looked behind, didn't see her. Dust began to blind him, but he did see something ahead. It was the damned wagon, bounding all over the place, trying to outrun the horses. A second later, the horses were going one way, still in the harnesses, and the wagon was moving in another direction.

Keegan couldn't worry about that, either. Still leaning low in the saddle, he wondered if he had tasted his last sip of Irish whiskey. It would have been a damned shame if his last drink had come from his water-filled canteen.

"Hell," Jed Breen said, then squeezed his lips tight, and touched the spurs to his horse's flanks — not that this animal needed any encouragement. As long as he didn't step in a prairie hole, he might have a chance.

Those Indians . . . well . . . they'd likely cut down Sean Keegan first. If they stopped to scalp him, mutilate him, torture him if he were still alive, that also would work in Breen's favor. The damnedest thing was . . . he liked the Irishman.

The woman rode ahead of him. She wasn't the best woman in a saddle Breen had seen, but when you had to either hold on and keep your seat or die, people found a way. Kruger, on the other hand . . .

Seeing the team break free and the wagon bounce over boulders and dead cactus, Keegan remembered the time in that thespian's wagon when he, Breen, McCulloch, and a few others were trying to get away from some rather mean, cruel and vicious Apaches down in West Texas. A similar thing had happened.

But Otto Kruger had no luck. The wagon's front wheel hit a hole, pitching the killer far to the left. He landed hard as the wagon crashed, rolling over and over and over to the right. All that did was force the stamped-ing mustangs away from the wagon — and right toward Otto Kruger. The man's head appeared briefly, then was lost as the hooves of fifty horses rode over the poor man. Well, not quite fifty, not as spread out as the animals were, but certainly enough to pound Kruger's body into a pulpy mess of nothingness. If the coffee Charlotte Platte had flung into his face had not made his identification impossible, the mustangs had certainly done the job.

Jed Breen could kiss that reward money good-bye.

And if he did not ride like hell, he could kiss his own life and hair good-bye, too.

"Maybe they've run off," Annie Homes heard Hawg say.

From inside the Stanton wagon she looked over at poor Mrs. Stanton, who was singing to herself, though death sounded like it whispered in her breathing. Annie lifted her head and decided she would climb out of the wagon to see for herself if the Indians were gone.

"What about it?" Mr. Wilkerson yelled. "Capt'n, do you think those Navajos have

420

left us?"

Someone chuckled. "We sure put a hurt in them."

"Hurrah!" Mrs. Primrose's voice thundered. "Hurrah for the Forty-ninth Arkansas! Hurrah for the boys from Dead Trout!"

Winfield Baker, spying Annie at the front wheel of the Stanton wagon, removed his hat, waved it over his head, and yelled, "Hurrah for the women of Dead Trout!"

"Don't let down your guard, men," her father called out. "Don't leave your posts. There are Indians still on that rise. I can see them plain as day. So do not —"

Thunder roared. At least it sounded like thunder. But Hawg, who had been looking after the livestock, stepped toward the sound and pointed out, "There ain't no clouds nowhere. That —"

The whistling reached Annie's ears, followed by zipping, the tearing of canvas, the splintering of wood. It was instinct that saved her life. The first rip of canvas, and she'd flung herself to the ground, looked up just as Hawg's ugly face vanished in an explosion of red.

Animals screamed. Oxen fell. Mules brayed. Another man spun around and dropped to his knees before he toppled over and shrieked in utter agony.

"Everybody get down!" she heard her father cry out, and even Mrs. Primrose echoed his orders.

Annie flattened her face, tried to bury herself in the Dead River's burning sand as all around her, leaden balls ripped through anything — wagon . . . man . . . canvas . . . animals — with no ounce of mercy.

It passed quickly, the deadly shot, and left behind just the shrieks of men, women, livestock, and the muffled echoes of the cannon shot, like the rumbling of thunder in the distance.

"Grapeshot." That was her father's voice. "Grapeshot."

A moment later, the explosion rang again.

"Everybody on the ground! Cover your heads!"

She hadn't even lifted hers and she ground her face lower into the sand, felt the grains cut into her cheek. She prayed that her father would do what he had just ordered. She prayed for her mother. She prayed for her soul.

The sickening sound began again. Ripping canvas. Metal plowing into wood or bouncing off the iron rims of the wagon wheels. And again, she heard animals screaming, falling into the river bed, kicking, screaming, and dying. She began sobbing.

"Got that double load in it for me this time, gunner?" Duncan Regret asked.

"*Sí, patrón.*"

"Good. Double charge?"

"Sí, patrón."

"Well lower that barrel just a hair boys. Let's give them a taste of Matilda's wonders. And Jésus?"

"Sí, patrón?"

"Cut me a longer fuse for the next round. Another double load, double charge. Just so they'll sweat a wee bit longer. And so I can savor every moment. Fellows, I haven't felt this way since the war down in Mexico."

"You're insane!" said one of the white men dressed like Indians. "You're madder than Don Wilkes."

"Yeah. But if you want to see bedlam up close, ride off to that wagon train in the Dead River. And wait till Matilda speaks again."

Wooden Arm looked over his shoulder as they rode east. McCulloch reined up, turned in the saddle, and looked to the west as the boom echoed faintly.

The Indian teen brought his horse closer

and used his hands and fingers to sign, *Thunder?*

That was one word that hadn't been used much in conversation. Not in this country. Not in this dry year.

"Hell," McCulloch whispered to himself. "A cannon. Those peckerwoods have a cannon." He started to spur his black harder when he heard something else, a rumbling to the east. Then he saw the dust rising, and the black started twisting, wanting to buck, wanting to run away.

He had a pretty good idea what that was, and Wooden Arm must have realized it, too.

"Hell," the Comanche boy said.

The blast of the cannon sounded closer, enormously louder, and it did not take as long for that other sound — that even more horrible noise — to reach Annie's ears.

The Stanton wagon shuddered, sounding like it might fall over and crush her, but at least she would escape this nightmare if she were crushed to death. Bits of wood cut her back, her legs. She cried out in horror, for it felt like no one could survive. Metal rang. Glass shattered. Some of the mules and oxen stampeded, ramming over one of the wagons — at least, that's what it sounded like. A horse leaped over Annie's head, and

424

she didn't know what she should do. Lie there, get trampled to death? Stand up, be shredded to pieces like poor Hawg?

There was no escape. When the ringing left her ears, when she realized she still lived — somehow — and when she heard her father's voice, "Steady men. Keep praying, ladies," she willed herself to raise her head. She could breathe, though her chest felt heavy, and she hurt from the cuts on her legs and her back.

There strode her father, the gallant Captain Walter Homes, weaving through the circling livestock. He had been standing when the grapeshot had ripped its last round. Standing like that Stonewall Jackson she had heard about. Standing, daring the cowards who fired metal balls into an innocent caravan of homesteaders seeking a better life. Daring them to try to kill him.

That's what made Annie sit up. She was a Homes, too. She was no cutthroat. No coward. She —

Annie gasped, for she saw the riddled ruins of the Stanton wagon, perforated by the latest, more intense, more horrific round of grapeshot. The canvas hung by strips, and much of those strips dripped red.

"My God," she whispered. She heard another scream. That one would have come from Betsy. Annie scrambled to her feet and moved to the wagon. She leaped up, looked into the back, and gagged. A rough hand pulled her away. She sobbed, somehow made out the face of Winfield Baker, who pulled her close.

Betsy sobbed. Her father groaned and fell to his knees. Annie's father stopped talking like a soldier and began to pray, and Mrs. Primrose joined in.

"I-I-I —" Annie let young, handsome Winfield Baker lead her away. She made out Betsy, Mrs. Stanton's daughter, sobbing on her knees, her head against her father's. Mr. Stanton trembled, his face appearing whiter than the sands of the Dead River. But maybe that was due to Betsy's tears.

"I should have —" Annie tried. "If I'd been inside —"

"You'd be dead like her," Winfield said. "And if you had been killed, I, too, would have died."

The horses and oxen ran past them, stepping over the carcasses of other animals.

Annie and Winfield had reached the far side of the circle of wagons, but even those wagons bore the scars of grapeshot. Men and women — even a little girl — sat or lay underneath the wagons, sobbing, bleeding, waiting to die. They prayed that this nightmare would end — even if that meant their deaths, for that would end the brutal, merciless assault.

She stopped, pulled away from Winfield as she heard her father begin to pray again.

"Our Father . . ."

Winfield looked at her. "Annie, what . . . ?"

She was about to tell him what she knew. She was about to say, "Winfield, we are all going to die. We are all going to die," but something changed. She heard — no, she *felt* . . . Annie looked at her feet.

Then she looked up into the young man's eyes.

"Winfield," she whispered, "the earth is trembling."

CHAPTER THIRTY-NINE

Seeing the lead mustangs and the rising cloud of dust, Matt McCulloch jerked the big black to a sliding stop. *Well,* he thought, *this is sort of the plan you had in mind. Keegan and Breen — or maybe the horses — oh, hell.*

Yeah, it had to be the horses' idea. They just got a head start . . . which, it suddenly struck him, might work even more to his advantage.

The horses ran hard with that fine pinto, Black Heart, leading the way.

Turning quickly, McCulloch found Wooden Arm just a few yards away from him and spoke slowly in English while using sign language to make sure there was no misunderstanding.

"You take the north flank, my young friend. I'll ride on the south side. We have to keep the horses going . . . straight into those bad white men who are dressed like

Indians."

His horse started dancing, and he needed both hands on the reins. He shouted, "Do you understand what I tell you?" He could not use his hands this time.

"I hear you," Wooden Arm yelled. He had trouble with his pinto, and the boy had only one good arm. "I know what you say." He kicked the pinto and rode off to the northern side of the approaching swirl of dust and the thundering hooves of McCulloch's treasure.

"Oh hell. I sure hate to use good animals like this." McCulloch stood in the stirrups, just to get a better view.

One rider on the north side. He could barely make that person out because of the wind and the dust. Two on the south. One of those he could tell was Charlotte Platte, slapping her hat against the side of her horse, and her long hair blowing in the wind. The wind suddenly whipped the hat out of her hands. But, damn, didn't she look good? Like a Texas woman, riding hard, red hair blowing . . . utterly fearless. For a moment, he forgot about all the men she had poisoned.

McCulloch was galloping, thinking while he rode, trying to figure out the best way. The way Keegan, Breen, and the murderess had flanked the herd might work to his advantage. He needed to turn them north, north toward that hill. He heard the cannon behind him.

Remember that sound, McCulloch told himself. *That's where we'll need to take the horses. Remember it. Figure out where it is.* He spurred his horse — as though the black needed any encouragement — and rode southeast. Three riders on the south side, two on the north once Wooden Arm got there. That might work. It was a long shot, but it seemed to be his best chance.

"What is taking him so long?" Don Marion Wilkes asked to no one in particular. That last shot had been a beauty. He just wished he could see better, but he had given his telescope and pair of binoculars to the artillery men who fired wonderful, courageous Matilda. Don Marion Wilkes could see only with his own, aging eyes. But he could smell victory. He could smell death.

One man's horse bolted, and Wilkes turned his wrath on the idiot whose wig came flying off as he waved his hand in the air, his palm already ugly from the rip the reins had caused when the horse jerked away.

"Boy, you ride with me and you cannot

control your horse. Confound it —"

Another horse tossed its Navajo-disguised rider and galloped back toward Wilkes's hacienda to the southeast. The man sat up, his wig askew, and looked at Don Marion Wilkes with fear in his eye. As well he should have, Wilkes thought, because, by thunder, he was about ready to shoot the next man who couldn't control his horse. He was . . .

The man on the ground shivered. "Don Marion. The earth . . . it moves. The earth . . . moves."

Old Matilda, that glorious grand dame from the Mexican-American war, had left Duncan Regret deaf, but the self-styled rapscallion didn't mind not hearing. He could smell the powder, see the smoke, and observe all the destruction he and Old Matilda had wrought. It made a man proud. It made a man terrifying. It made Duncan Regret feel like he was as powerful as God Almighty himself.

"Hell, Jésus, how long a fuse did you cut?" Regret yelled, laughing, even though he couldn't hear his own words or the reply the Mexican gunner told him. Suddenly Regret realized the gunner hadn't finished his answer. His eyes widened, and his mouth hung open, but no words came out. Then he crossed himself, stumbled, and stood up quickly. Another horse tossed its outlaw playing Indian. Jésus climbed out of the embankment.

Regret drew his revolver.

"Stop, you damned deserter!" he yelled, or at least his mind told him those were the words he issued. But a moment later, he was on the ground, shaken by some unholy force that made the ground quake. *Earthquake?* He had heard of those, but had never been in one. Rolling over, he spit and saw dust, a cloud of Arizona dust rising higher in the sky than the smoke from Matilda. A moment later, he felt himself bouncing on the ground, and he grabbed a spoke on the north-facing wheel of the cannon.

The sense of hearing returned. He heard the thunder, the roar. But he didn't hear himself scream when the horses appeared. Their hooves drowned out everything else around him.

He lunged underneath the mountain howitzer, reached out, and grabbed the spokes to the far wheel, trying to pull himself under the cannon. Hooves tore into his calves, his ankles, and he felt the bones in his feet smashing and breaking. He knew blood had to be pouring from the rips the hooves caused, knew he had just become a cripple, and he knew this damned cannon would soon be detonating a double-charged, double load of grapeshot. The recoil would send Matilda over his body, perhaps breaking his neck, shattering his spine, or both.

He choked on the thick never-ending dust.

When Sean Keegan realized what Matt McCulloch planned on doing, he slowed down his horse, which wasn't an easy thing to do. The animal was as scared as all those running mustangs, and maybe even as petrified as Sean Keegan. As he drifted back, he could barely make out anything through the thick, choking, blinding dust. He was a horse soldier, nailed to the seat of his McClellan saddle. He had ridden into battle against men in gray, men in buckskin, men in breechcloths, and had tasted battle and seen the elephant more times than he could count. And he hadn't been scared until now.

He turned his horse more north than west, and eventually rode out of the dust to find horses scattering, men riding, and men running — red-skinned Navajos, by the look of one. He saw one afoot, and Keegan put both reins in his teeth, clamping down hard. His right hand held the Springfield as his left reached down and grabbed one of the running Indians.

The plan was simple. Grab the Indian's head, jerk him up, slam him into the back of his horse, breaking his neck or back, and dropping him into the sand and cactus.

Bloody hell! Keegan thought as he stared at the hair he had ripped off the running Navajo. Scalped him alive. Without even opening a blade on his Barlow knife. Only . . .

He dropped the scalp and grabbed the reins as he spit the leather out of his mouth. "A wig." He found another Indian ahead, but that one had already lost his wig and his horse. He still held a repeating rifle, though, and he worked the lever while dropping to his knee. Keegan saw the smoke, though he never heard the report of the Winchester. By that time, he had the Springfield butted against his shoulder.

The fake Indian again pulled the repeating rifle's trigger.

Then his Winchester went flying to the south while he was blown fifteen feet into some brush by the force of the Springfield's lead slug that drilled him through his chest.

Keegan reached into his blouse and began to reload while he galloped, reins dragging on the ground. He had no way to control where his horse was going, but he had plenty of men all dolled up like Navajos to fill his gunsights.

The powerful black leaped some twenty yards from the rest of the wild, powering mustangs. McCulloch almost lost his rifle and his seat, and just got a glimpse as all those beautiful, wonderful, wild-eyed mustangs plunged into, over, and all around the cannon and whoever had the stupidity to not abandon his position. What he saw before the black carried him away was horses falling, being trampled by other horses, and the cannon being shoved forward into an embankment. Screams of animals, injured, dying, or still moving like the wind, filled his ears as he kept riding.

A man appeared before him, running south, stopped, and looked up. The black slammed into him, jarring McCulloch again, but he rode on. He did not look back at the man the horse had smashed. He knew the last thing that man had seen on this earth was Matt McCulloch and the wily black horse that had probably broken every bone in his upper body.

He turned away from the stampeding mustangs and looked over his shoulder. Taking reins and carbine in his left hand, he waved at Breen and the others with his right, beckoning them to follow him. He didn't do that for long, though. He had to get his horse under some semblance of control. For the better part of a mile, likely a whole lot longer, McCulloch had realized he had no control over his horse. It was about time to get back that control. Or he might be swimming in the Pacific Ocean before he knew it, all the way to the Sandwich Islands.

Looking over at the companions trailing him, also pulling away from the scattering mustangs, McCulloch waved at them to follow him. A bullet zipped past his ear. Jerking his head around, he saw a white man wearing Navajo silver and a black, battered, open-crowned Navajo hat. He desperately worked to reload his muzzle-loading rifle. McCulloch swore, brought the Winchester up with his left hand, keeping the reins in his right, and touched the trigger.

There was no sound, no smoke, no kick of the rifle, and he knew it was empty. The black powered forward. The man capped the nipple of his rifle. McCulloch had no chance to draw his revolver and fire, so he just rose, and cut loose with a savage Rebel yell.

The shrill scream caused that fraudulent

Indian to jerk his arm and rush his shot. Smoke belched from the barrel, but the leaden ball never came anywhere near McCulloch or his horse. The man rose, cursing, tried to shift the rifle around and use it as a club.

McCulloch already had that idea, and his rifle barrel caught the man in his throat, sending blood gushing from his mouth as his legs flew out in front of him, and he crashed spread-eagled and unmoving on the ground.

McCulloch kept riding, and saw one of the wagons being pushed back, creating a wider opening. Those emigrants who had rolled the old Conestoga quickly slipped under the wagon, while another man waved his black hat before stepping back and out of the way.

It was like family, the former Ranger thought, welcoming a prodigal son home.

CHAPTER FORTY

Duncan Regret could not believe that he was still alive. His legs hurt like hell. So did breathing. Even opening his eyes, pained him, but he could see, and even though each breath caused him to grimace or gasp, he had survived. His hearing had returned. Horses lay around him, legs broken, some screaming, others already dead, and he felt the weight of Matilda's barrel against his left hip. He lay on his side, half buried in the sand, but those horses — and the dirty rats who had driven those crazed beasts — had failed to do something many others had failed to do. They hadn't killed Duncan Regret. And they would pay with their lives.

He was crippled. He hurt all over, but he . . . he . . . he . . . smelled something. He heard something. Beyond him came a shot. Another. But that wasn't what he'd heard. It was something closer. It whispered. No . . . it sizzled. Craning his neck, he looked up at the barrel of Matilda, the mountain howitzer. It was hard to see because of the pain throughout his body and the sand in his eyes, but he thought he saw traces of smoke. And the sound? The sound?

"Oh, hell."

Panic seized him. The fuse. That fuse. All those mustangs, overturning the cannon, killing other animals, wrecking Matilda. And destroying his dreams . . . and those of Don Marion Wilkes. Someone had failed to stamp out the fuse.

His head turned toward the barrel's opening, and he saw it buried deep in the Arizona sand along the Dead River. So deep, he realized what would happen if that fuse burned to the powder. The barrel would rupture, and the charge would split the barrel, sending its contents — two bags of grapeshot — all over the place.

Duncan Regret would be blown to pieces.

"No," he screamed. His hands desperately and furiously began digging at the sand. He gave up, reached out, tried to pull himself from underneath the sand. At that point, he was sobbing without control, choking on his tears, tearing his fingernails out because the ground was so hard. And the sound of the burning fuse almost burst his eardrums.

439

"No. No. No. No. *Nooooo!!!!!!*"

When he paused to catch his breath, he heard an eerie silence. *The fuse,* he thought with great relief, *has burned itself out.*

The explosion would have told Duncan Regret just how wrong he was had he lived to hear the detonation and destruction that ripped his body into pieces the ants and ravens would enjoy for days upon days.

"By the saints, man, we would have shot you off that horse had you not cut loose with that Rebel yell!" The thin old man was walking straight toward Matt McCulloch after he leaped off his horse and started to take a position behind one of the wagons. McCulloch caught a glance at the man holding one hand out, his other gripping an Enfield rifled musket.

The boys from the train were starting to push the wagon back, sealing off the entrance.

"Not yet!" McCulloch's voice boomed. "I got friends out there. They are with me!"

The man who wanted so badly to shake McCulloch's hand stopped. The boys looked at the old gentleman. Another one of the young men, however, who was sitting in the driver's box, raised up his musket, and yelled, "There's a crazy red devil chasing them!! He's almost at them!!"

Shooting a quick glance, McCulloch realized what the boy saw.

"No!" he yelled. "No! That's a fri—" He lunged toward the kid and the wagon.

Reaching out, McCulloch dropped his weapon, oblivious to the galloping horse of Jed Breen's. He had to stop that kid from shooting Wooden Arm out of his Comanche saddle. The entire world — from McCulloch's legs and arms to his voice, to the sounds of the battle all around him, to the beating of his heart — slowed into an eternal crawl. And McCulloch knew he'd never be able to reach the kid in time.

Suddenly, he was lifted off his feet and slammed back hard, with a fury he had never felt in all his years. He crashed hard into the old gent who had so wanted to shake his hand.

Annie Homes lay on her back, metal chimes ringing somewhere deep in her head. Her father had been walking toward a dark-clothed man who had ridden a horse that might have come out of the deepest part of Hades. What then? She tried to clear her thoughts, her mind, but the most likely guess as to what had knocked her into Winfield Baker's body was . . . a volcano had

441

erupted. She saw black smoke rising high over the canvas coverings of most of the wagons, but that was drifting, fading. It could not have been from a volcano.

"Annie?"

She heard that, which meant she was not deaf, maybe not even dead.

Winfield Baker's face appeared before her.

"Are you all right, darling?"

She blinked. She thought. She heard the pounding hooves of horses. Winfield Baker brushed sand and ash off her forehead and slowly lifted her to a seated position.

"Riders are coming in," he told her. "They are shutting the gap."

She was in his arms, but she did not know how that had happened. The faces of men and women she knew, even Mrs. Primrose and Betsy Stanton, passed by. She felt herself being laid onto blankets in the shade and saw his face come closer, and closer, and closer, and felt something cool touch her forehead.

His lips, she thought. *He has kissed me. Just on the head but . . .*

"You rest," Winfield Baker told her. "Just rest. I'll send Mr. Randall over to see you."

That would be the barber from Dead Trout, but he had been known to patch a few cuts and set some busted bones, and he had even tried to cut out Josiah Armagost's appendix two years back, although Mr. Armagost had not survived the surgery.

"Winfield?" she said softly.

His face came back into view.

"Who is that man who rode up?"

"I don't know, Annie."

"He looks like the devil."

He smiled. "That devil might have saved us all."

Winfield Baker walked away, and Annie Homes drifted off into a deep, peaceful, wonderful sleep.

"We have those men surrounded still," Don Marion Wilkes told the men, most of whom no longer looked anything remotely like a Navaho Indian. "We have water, and they are trapped. We have demoralized them."

He looked at the men still with him, those not dead, or not hightailing it for safer climes. Matilda had been blown to Kingdom Come. Clouds of black smoke drifted across the Dead River country. This Indian massacre, so carefully planned, had not gone anywhere near the way it should have gone, but Don Marion Wilkes was not about to quit. "We have killed their leader and several of their men. They have not enough horses to pull their wagons out. And will remain in the Dead River. No one will travel this way. No one will come to their rescue. We shall starve them out. We shall negotiate a truce, and when they accept our truce, we shall smote them all."

That speech did absolutely nothing but waste his breath.

So he added, "And you all shall be paid one thousand dollars in gold for seeing this job finished."

Broken Buffalo Horn's eyes slowly opened, and he stared into the eyes of his horse, which looked down on the Comanche medicine man and snorted. He realized he had held on to the hackamore after being pitched over the side of his horse as it galloped after the fleeing cowardly white-eyes. His hand felt blisters from where the hackamore had pulled tightly, but he still had a horse to ride.

"Can you sit up, my friend?" Killed A Skunk asked.

"Yes," Broken Buffalo Horn said. "Of course, I can sit up. I am Comanche." He waited. When Killed A Skunk just stared at him, he said, "Help me up, my friend."

Lost His Thumb rode up, then waved his bow to the south and west. "The white-eyes we chased have moved into a fort of wagons that have been attacked by a strange group of white-eyes." He held up what appeared to be a scalp, but this black hair did not drip with blood. "They are dressed like Indian peoples."

"Comanche?" Broken Buffalo Horn asked.

"No." Lost His Thumb pointed north. "Those who like silver and black. The ones who many summers ago lived at the edge of Comanche land, at the fort of Long Knifes at Bosque Redondo."

"The Navajo." Broken Buffalo Horn let his head move up and down. It did not fall off, and that was a good sign.

"Yes. That is how they are called. The Navajo."

"And my son?" the medicine man asked.

Lost His Thumb frowned. "He is in the fort with the white eyes. The fort made of the wagons."

For a long while, Broken Buffalo Horn stared at the sand, but had nothing to say. His breathing barely reached the ears of the two other Comanches, but at length, after some great thought, the medicine man looked up. "What of the Comanche ponies?"

It was Killed A Skunk who frowned. "Many are dead, my friend," he whispered. They rode over a wheel gun that kills so many. Some died there. Then the wheel gun that kills so many was swallowed by a monster that breathes fire and rains silver and gray balls. "That killed more ponies, but some of those would have died anyway."

Gunshots began a few hundred yards away.

"They shoot again at the fort made of wagons," Lost His Thumb said.

"Which means they shoot at my son," Broken Buffalo Horn said.

"Yes, it is so." The Comanche warrior shook his head. "And there are three of us. But at least ten times that of them."

"It is not like a Comanche to ask for help," Killed A Skunk said.

"A Comanche would never ask for help," Broken Buffalo Horn said. "But it would not be right to count coup and take scalps in this country without receiving permission from the Navajos. This is their country." He nodded.

"Then perhaps," Lost His Thumb said, "we should see if the Navajos would like to help us take coups and scalps."

Hans Kruger shoved a .45 barrel against the back of Jed Breen's head.

"Vere!" he cried out. "Vere is *mein Bruder*?"

"Easy, pard, easy." A tall man in buckskins decorated with scalp locks walked toward him. "We're in a pickle, ol' boy, and this don't really make me feel so good, but, well, hell, we might need that gent's gun. That's Jed Breen, Hun. A bounty hunter."

"*The* bounty hunter," Breen said.

"*Nein.*" Kruger shook his head. "*Nein.* I vill not do anything until I know vere *mein Bruder* is. Somebody vill tell me or else I vill kill dis bounty hunter. I must see *mein Bruder* —"

Blood and brains exploded from the center of Hans Kruger's forehead before anyone heard the shot. The man in buckskins ran one way, and Hank Benteen went the other way. Kruger lowered the Colt unfired, turned with a look of complete amazement on what was left of his face, and toppled to the ground. He shuddered, messed his britches, and lay still.

Breen rolled over, palming his Colt, and found the homesteaders from the wagon train taking positions. Matt McCulloch crawled to an opening, and Breen took a spot beside him.

Hell's bells, Breen thought. He couldn't find the widowmaker named Charlotte Platte, but the homesteaders began returning fire at those Indians that had them pinned down. "What are our chances?"

McCulloch began feeding cartridges into his Winchester. When he ran out, he frowned, but Charlotte Platte came over holding the gun belt she had just pulled off Hans Kruger's corpse.

"Thanks," McCulloch said as the woman began thumbing cartridges out of the leather loops and placing them into McCulloch's hands.

"What kind of Indians are those?" Breen asked, after not getting an answer to his first question.

"The worst kind," McCulloch answered. "White men."

"Damn." Breen ducked after a bullet whined off the iron wheel of the wagon next to him. "Maybe I should get my Sharps."

"We'd appreciate that," Charlotte said.

McCulloch asked, "You seen Wooden Arm?"

Breen looked north, then west, finally south. He smiled. "Some kids are staring at that splint you made. He's entertaining them, keeping them out of harm's way." Breen pointed. "They're behind a fort within our fort."

"What kind of fort?" McCulloch fired, levered another round into the Winchester, and stared at where he had shot.

"The best kind," Breen said. "Dead horses, dead oxen, dead mules."

"Won't be long before there are dead people," McCulloch said.

"Matt?"

"Yeah."

"Where's Sean?"

McCulloch lowered his rifle. He looked at the still smoldering ruins where that cannon had exploded, at the dead bodies of men and animals all around that spot, and the dead littering the . . . Dead River. *Aptly named.*

"Hell," he said in a dry whisper. "Do you reckon that stinker up and died on us?"

CHAPTER FORTY-ONE

Sean Keegan's head hurt. His eyes opened, and he saw nothing but black. "By the saints, I've drunk meself blind." He saw a light, which slowly came into focus as the moon. That came as a relief, but when he tried to move, to get up and stand on his own feet, his left leg refused to cooperate.

He felt the coldness of the dark, realized it was night, and memories came creeping back.

"Ah, hell." That fine old Matt McCulloch horse had ridden himself to death. Keegan put his right boot just behind the back of that bone-jarring McClellan saddle and began shoving. He remembered riding, remembered shooting, remembered some wilder than sin explosion behind him. *The reins? Right.* He had dropped them after the explosion. By squeezing his legs like a vise, he held on to the galloping horse as it thundered across the desert.

Keegan remembered the poor lad had run until his heart quit pumping. He remembered not having enough time to leap clear of the saddle before the horse fell against the rock that had given Keegan a headache worse than some of the forty-rod whiskey he had tried to lick in Purgatory City or some other blight of the Western community.

Thrown from a horse, stuck under the backside of a runaway, and afoot in the middle of the night in some godforsaken desert in Arizona Territory. The shame of it all.

He gave another shove against the horse's buttocks and Keegan's foot and calf came free, without even pulling off his boot. All he had to do was figure which way he ought to head to figure out if Matt McCulloch and Jed Breen — or anyone else — remained alive.

No campfire. McCulloch had convinced the leader of the wagon train, a nice man named Walter Homes, of that. Campfire would give those tramps targets to shoot at. The full moon already gave them enough. It bathed the interior of the makeshift fort, reflecting off the pale sand and stones that made up the bed of the Dead River. It was just like noon, except for the blackness all around the big white ball in the sky.

Wooden Arm crept up to where Breen, McCulloch, and the widowmaker sat in front of a dead ox. Bloated and already drawing flies, it smelled something awful. The kid pointed his good arm toward the man who smoked a cigarette — despite Mc-Culloch's insistence not to even strike a match — at the northern end of the camp.

"I know," McCulloch said.

"Bad hombre," Wooden Arm said.

Breen cocked his head and looked at the man in buckskins. "Friend of yours?" he asked the former Ranger.

"Scalp hunter," McCulloch said.

"That's a breed of man I have no use for," Breen said as he cleaned his Sharps.

"That's not even a man," Charlotte Platte said.

"Bad hombre," Wooden Arm whispered.

"You know the fellow your scalp-hunting pal is talking to?" Breen asked.

McCulloch's head shook.

"Benteen. Hank Benteen."

McCulloch looked at the man on Linton's left. "You sure?"

"I don't make those kinds of mistakes," Breen said.

"Well," McCulloch said, "we might have

use of his gun before tomorrow's over."

Breen shrugged and opened the breech to his Sharps.

The noise carried, and Benteen and the scalp hunter named Linton turned around, staring, both hands hovering over their side-arms.

Breen chuckled and called out, "Just loading my Sharps for the morning festivities, boys."

Neither of those two men appeared amused.

Wooden Arm suddenly noticed Charlotte for the first time. He pointed his good arm at her and said, "Hat!"

She smiled grimly. "It flew off. My hat. When we were stampeding those mustangs."

"Bad sun," the Comanche kid said.

Breen grinned. "He thinks you'll get sun-burned."

The widowmaker shrugged and sighed. "I do wish I had my hat."

Breen tugged his off and held it toward her. "Ma'am, it would be my pleasure."

She laughed. "I'm not worried about sunburn, boys. The hat. The hatband, rather. That's where I kept my poison."

The bounty hunter started to laugh, then looked at McCulloch, who was looking at Charlotte Platte with his eyes wide open.

He turned to the Comanche boy before shaking his head then asked the woman, "Are you serious?"

"Silver tube," she said. "Hollow. I bend over a pot or filling a cup of whatever. Reach up, press a button hidden behind the feathers. Out comes a drop. Two drops. Four. No more than six. Depends on how much I want them to suffer. It runs down the brim, drops into whatever I'm serving. If anyone saw it, they'd just think it was water from the pot or something. All I had to do was make sure the wind wasn't blowing toward me. Wouldn't want it to blow into my mouth by mistake, but who wants to stand downwind of a cook fire that's blowing smoke?"

"Your hatband." Matt McCulloch shook his head. "How 'bout that? Hatband. I never even thought about it."

Breen eventually looked away from Charlotte Platte and smiled at the old Ranger. "I'm glad neither one of us thought about it." He returned his gaze to the woman and tossed her his hat. "You were a sight to behold, ma'am, and I mean that in my most honorable way. Please, accept my hat as sort of an apology."

"You might need it," she said.

He laughed again. "I don't think so, ma'am. Not after tomorrow."

■ ■ ■ ■

Sean Keegan stopped walking. All around
him he heard snores. A ways off to the
north, he spotted campfires, and he could
see the faint outline of canvas covers of
wagons ahead, but just barely.

A man not two feet in front of him
snorted, coughed, said something about not
wanting anymore to do with those skunks,
and began snoring again.

Keegan realized he had walked into the
middle of a camp of some fellows he didn't
know and didn't want to know. He let out a
silent breath, put one foot in front of the
other, and suddenly felt like he could sleep
for ten weeks.

He might just do that. Might even sleep
that eternal sleep if he stepped on some
horse's ass.

Don Marion Wilkes rode out on a high-
stepping white stallion, his manservant riding with him, and let the thirty-two men
fan out, showing their strength, but keeping
them out of rifle range. He grinned as his
prancing horse stopped fifty yards from the
eastern side of the besieged wagon train.

"Good morning," he called out. "I would

like to speak to your leader."

"Speak," yelled one of the spud diggers.

Looking up, removing his hat, Don Marion Wilkes wiped his forehead. "My fine emigrants, it is going to be a hot day. As you can see, I have more than thirty men. And I have water. I have powder, and I have lead. You have rotting animals that will be bloated and just . . . well . . . stinking even worse than they already are. I have come to offer you generous terms."

"What are they?" the spud digger asked.

Walter Homes listened as the gentleman in the expensive Mexican outfit and riding a fine horse gave his word as a nobleman and landowner that all of the emigrants would be escorted south to the first stagecoach station at Tulia Junction. They would have to walk, of course, and they would have to leave all firearms, even knives behind, but no harm would be done. When they were a mile from the Tulia station, their escorts would ride away.

Homes turned to two of the newcomers, the big Texan with the Winchester and the white-haired but young-looking man who held a big rifle with a fancy telescopic sight. "What do you think?"

"He thinks we're a bunch of fools," McCulloch said. "Ask him what happens if we

456

refuse those generous terms?"

Homes yelled that question across the Dead River sand.

"I have thirty men who will strike you all down. We can starve you out or sweat you out, but if you don't come out under my generous terms, there will be no quarter. It will be like the Alamo in Texas."

McCulloch shook his head. "Bigmouth shouldn't have said that. Not to a Texan."

"Or to an Arkansan," Homes said. "We had relatives down in San Antone."

"Would you like me to shoot him now?" Breen asked.

"Not yet," McCulloch said.

Homes, on his own, offered to Wilkes, "You have seen that we are used to fighting, sir. You mentioned the Alamo. You might recall how many Mexicans died before those gallant defenders were put to the sword."

"But I do not have to charge like Santa Ana. I can wait you out."

"Can you?" McCulloch shouted. "See those buzzards. That'll get a lot of attention on that stagecoach road. Maybe even the Navajos. And the army. It does send out patrols this way."

"Gentlemen, it is already hot," the man said. His horse stopped prancing. "I have offered my men a thousand dollars to kill you all. They are eager to earn such a fine bounty."

"Is that gospel?" Breen yelled out.

"On my word of honor as a gentleman," the man said.

Homes tried to figure out what to do. Could he really trust that man? He looked at McCulloch for help, but it was Breen who had the answer.

"Mister," he said cocking the hammer on that Sharps, "how can you pay them when you're dead?"

Don Marion Wilkes saw his horse trotting away. He didn't feel a damned thing, and couldn't understand why he lay on his back in the middle of the Dead River or what in heaven's name had hit him right in the middle.

Luís, his manservant, knelt over him.

Then the pain hit him, and Don Marion Wilkes gasped. "Luís? Have I been shot?"

"Sí, Don Wilkes." The noble servant pulled up Wilkes's shirt, began loosening his —

"What are you . . . doing?" Don Marion Wilkes had to turn his head, spit out phlegm . . . no that tasted more like . . . blood.

"I take your money belt, Don Marion,"

the noble servant said. "You have no use for it anymore." He held the money belt high over his head and laughed. Then Luís gasped and fell hard onto Wilkes's stomach. An arrow quivered in Luís's back.

War hoops. Hooves. Gunfire. Those sounds came from far away.

Don Marion Wilkes looked at the buzzards circling over his head in the clear, blue sky. He reached up and stroked Luís's slick, dark hair.

"Poor Luís. Poor, poor Luís."

An Indian suddenly leaped before him. It was one of his men dressed like a Navajo. *Good*, Don Marion Wilkes thought. Here was a loyal rider for the great Don Marion Wilkes. He frowned. *Why is that man waving a tomahawk? And why is it coming straight down toward my head?*

"My God!" the kind leader of the wagon train yelled. "That man came under the flag of truce!"

"You cut off the head of a rattlesnake," the bounty hunter said as he reloaded the Sharps, "and the snake dies."

"But that man —"

"That man" — McCulloch stood up, enjoying the confusion among the riders that remained out of rifle range — "would have cut us down, man, woman, child. Now . . . let's see how those boys react to a Rebel charge."

"What?"

One second later, the riders were scattering, and Indians were swooping at them from all directions.

"Hell," McCulloch said. "Those look like —"

"Navajos." Breen laughed. "Riding to our rescue?"

"What the hell?" Linton looked up, saw hundreds of mounted warriors raising dust all over the dry riverbed.

No one in the train seemed to know what to do, but Hank Benteen saw his chance. "Here's where I avenge the deaths of my . . . my . . . gang!" He ran toward the Texan and that sharpshooting bounty man.

Linton saw something better to do. He saw the pretty girl with the raven-dark hair. With all those Indians running around, and none of the spud diggers knowing what to do, he might be able to kill that girl, lift her hair, and make for that prancing horse. He pulled his knife, ran right for her, and felt the taste of wood that split his lips and broke his nose.

Down went Linton. The girl turned,

screamed, and one of those young, tall kids kicked the knife out of Linton's hand.

"You!" the boy yelled, bringing his musket up.

Linton kicked him, knocking the boy down. The scalp hunter sat up, spit out blood, and realized that hayseed from Arkansas hadn't busted his nose and mouth. It was . . . the Indian . . . the damned Comanche kid . . . the one from all that way back in Texas.

That Comanche boy was the one holding a scalping knife.

"No!" Linton screamed, rolled underneath a wagon, and kept rolling until he was clear. Standing up, dust all around him, he ran east. Ran as hard as he could. He looked back once, and saw that Comanche kid who looked like a misshapen scarecrow running after him.

Breen had moved to the front of the wagon, working the Sharps at the fleeing white raiders. McCulloch saw someone race into the dust, and realized the man was that scalp hunter from Texas . . . and Wooden Arm was chasing him.

"Damn." He stepped out to see if he could catch up to the Comanche boy.

"Don't move!" a voice called, and Mc-

461

Culloch turned around.

"I owe you for hanging my cousin," Hank Benteen said.

McCulloch looked at his Winchester, the hammer down. "I didn't hang your brother," he said, which was an honest statement.

"Yeah, but you're here."

"So is the man who hanged Lovely Tom Benteen Lovely," a voice shouted to McCulloch's right.

He couldn't see the man, and he wasn't too certain that he actually heard it, but Benteen turned on his heel, and blood erupted from the front and back of his shirt as he spun to his knees, dropped his pistol, coughed once, and collapsed into the Dead River.

McCulloch turned, tried to go after Wooden Arm, but a bullet splintered the wagon's side, sending wood chips into his face. He fell back, cursed, came up, and tried to roll over.

Charlotte Platte leaped on top of him, yelling, "Stay down, you dumb fool. Stay down."

He realized the uselessness of it and sighed.

Linton saw the dead Mexican with the arrow in his back, scalped, laying atop that dude the bounty hunter had blown off his horse. His plan was to keep running. Then he saw what the dead Mexican held in his hand. It was a money belt.

He slid to a stop, picked up the belt, turned, and slashed out with the heavy leather and canvas belt at the broken-armed Comanche.

The boy went down, and Linton laughed. Maybe he would get that scalp after all. He stepped toward the kid, saw that obscene splint on one arm, then looked at the other that was moving. Something left the hand, and something hit Linton right beneath the ribs.

Linton lay on the ground, clutching at the hilt of the knife that stuck in his chest. He couldn't get the damned thing out, but then that fool Comanche kid with only one good hand straddled him. The good hand jerked the knife out, and the pain made Linton loose all control of bladder and bowels.

He tried to talk, but blood filled his mouth. He saw the kid take the knife, blade dripping with Linton's own blood, and felt the blade begin to carve across his scalp. Something sounded like a loud *pop,* but Linton couldn't feel much of anything by then. He saw that scalp held in the boy's good hand. Then the boy shouted, and shoved Linton's own hair into his mouth.

A shadow suddenly crossed their faces. But the shade was nowhere near as dark or cold as the blackness that swept over Linton.

Broken Buffalo Horn looked down and smiled as his son looked up. Tears ran down the Comanche medicine man's face. The young Comanche had set out on his vision quest a long, long time ago. He had killed his first enemy, counted coup, and taken his first scalp.

The Comanche medicine man shook his head and laughed. He had forgotten. All those suns ago, in the flats near the bad water place, his son had killed two of his enemies there. This dead white-eye was his son's *third*. Yes. Yes. There would be much singing in the camp when they returned home.

Killed A Skunk leaped off his horse, ran to Broken Buffalo Horn's son and hugged him. "Look!" Oblivious to the gunfire and smoke and noise all around him, he shouted, "Look, Lost His Thumb. Look, Broken Buffalo Horn. We have found your son."

Broken Buffalo Horn shook his head. "No, Killed A Skunk. We have found the *man* who is my son."

Chapter Forty-Two

"When did you get here?" Breen asked Keegan.

The Irish horse soldier shrugged. "It was still dark."

"You sneaked through the line those cutthroats had around us?" McCulloch asked.

"Yeah. I can be quiet. Especially when every one of those fools was snoring."

"So you just came here . . . back to camp. Nobody spotted you?"

"Most of your guards was sleeping. I just found a quiet spot and went to bed."

"Without even looking for Breen or me?" McCulloch shook his head. "Without telling someone all of our guards were asleep? What kind of army soldier are you?"

"A retired one," Keegan snapped. "And a tired one. I'd walked I don't know how many miles during the night."

"Walked?" Breen said. "What happened to your horse?"

Keegan snorted, spun around, and bellowed, "Doesn't anyone in this emigrant train cook coffee?"

McCulloch, Breen, Keegan, and Walter Homes met in the center of the dry sands known as the Dead River before six Navajos and three Comanches.

Wooden Arm smiled at the three. "I speak for you." He made movements with his hand, and McCulloch stepped forward.

He pulled out his knife and nodded at the boy. *I think that splint can come off now, son,* McCulloch signed. He shook his head and apologized. *To be honest with you, son, that splint could have come off — should have come off — two, four weeks back. I just left it on because . . . well . . .*

The boy smiled as McCulloch cut off the leather thongs that held the wood in place.

"Because I Comanche."

McCulloch stared at the boy and nodded again. "I reckon so."

"You are friend," Wooden Arm said. "You gave me life, my name. From now on, I called Wooden Arm."

The Navajos, the Comanche leader with the buffalo headdress, and McCulloch did the talking with signs mostly, interpreted in broken English by the teenage boy.

"My friends" — Wooden Arm pointed to Broken Buffalo Horn, Killed A Skunk, and Lost His Thumb — "and Navajos round up horses we find." He looked at McCulloch with sadness in his eyes. "We count fourteen dead ponies."

McCulloch nodded. "Yeah."

The boy smiled. "Black Heart not one of dead ponies. I help Navajos search for ponies."

McCulloch laughed. "I wish you luck."

"I find Black Heart, I return to you."

If you find him — McCulloch signed the words just to make sure the boy understood — *he is yours. He belongs to you. He is too good a horse for a white man. He belongs to a Comanche.*

There was silence, then Wooden Arm changed the subject. "We escort you to camp of long knives."

"Singletree," McCulloch said, nodding.

"We no get close where long knives live."

"I don't blame you," McCulloch said.

One of the Comanches, a wild-looking one with a thumb missing on one hand, pitched a canvas and leather belt at Walter Homes's feet. The Comanche spit, and moved back into line.

"This," Wooden Arm said to Homes, "carry pale-eyes money. You use. Buy horses. Oxen." He pointed to the Navajos. "They let you pass."

Homes laughed. "I think once we are reequipped, we will follow the wagon road to Rapture Valley. I never want to see the Dead River again."

Four days later, Keegan, McCulloch, and Breen watched the party of emigrants roll out westward on the stagecoach road from Camp Singletree.

"Folks from Arkansas," Keegan said, "are not as bad as I thought. I'm thirsty. Meet you gents at the post sutler's. He serves soldier's whiskey. I'll teach you green peas how to drink it, but know this — only a jackal can handle soldier's whiskey." He tipped his hat and strode across the parade ground.

"Well?" Charlotte Platte asked. "I guess I'm still your prisoner."

Breen shrugged. "The commanding officer signed an affidavit that I brought in Hank Benteen and Hans Kruger. That'll be worth some money."

"You didn't shoot either of those two," McCulloch said. "Hell, Sean saved my hide by killing Benteen. He should —"

"Be a bounty hunter?" Breen laughed. "He's got a lot to learn. Possession is

468

ninety-nine percent of the law, and I brought in those two corpses."

"You are a jackal," Charlotte Platte said.

"No doubt about it, ma'am, but I shot that leader of those cutthroats because a man like him didn't deserve to live. Those men back in Precious Metal didn't deserve to live, either. I don't know any Charlotte Platte." He tipped his hat, smiled at Mc-Culloch, and walked toward the post sutler's, too.

"And what about you?" Charlotte asked as she turned to McCulloch.

He shrugged. "There are plenty of mustangs in West Texas. Maybe I'll have better luck next time." His eyes studied the dirt, but eventually found Charlotte Platte. "And you?"

"A stage comes through Tuesday," she said. "Bound for El Paso. I have just enough money — from someone's money belt that some angel put under my pillow — to get me there. It's just a hop and a skip from Mexico."

"I'm glad, ma'am." He looked at the two men entering the sutler's.

"Matt."

McCulloch looked back at the beautiful murderess. "I've heard there are wild mustangs in Mexico."

He nodded. "Heard that myself."

"Maybe . . . one day . . . you might want to see about catching some of those."

"Maybe so."

"Well" — she smiled — "if you happen by a nice restaurant in some out of the way village near Vera Cruz, I'll buy you a cup of coffee."

"I'd like that, Charlotte." He winked. "But you'd have to be stark naked when you fix it for me."

"I'd like that," she said with a gleam in her eye, and added, "Matt."

"Not as much as I would, ma'am."

She laughed. "You are a jackal."

"Yes, ma'am," he said as he removed his hat, leaned forward, and kissed her forehead. After straightening, he pointed his hat toward the post sutler's. "If you'll excuse me, I need to join a couple of other jackals to teach them a thing or two about soldier's whiskey."

Her eyes followed him all the way until the door at the post sutler's closed behind him.

ABOUT THE AUTHORS

William W. Johnstone is the *New York Times* and *USA Today* bestselling author of over 300 books, including the series The Mountain Man; Preacher, the First Mountain Man; MacCallister; Luke Jensen, Bounty Hunter; Flintlock; Those Jensen Boys; The Frontiersman; Savage Texas; The Kerrigans; and Will Tanner: Deputy U.S. Marshal. His thrillers include *Black Friday, Tyranny, Stand Your Ground,* and *The Doomsday Bunker.* Visit his website at www .williamjohnstone.net or email him at dogcia2006@aol.com.

J. A. Johnstone learned to write from the master himself, Uncle William W. Johnstone, with whom J. A. has cowritten numerous bestselling series including The Mountain Man; Those Jensen Boys; and Preacher, the First Mountain Man.

The employees of Thorndike Press hope you have enjoyed this Large Print book. All our Thorndike, Wheeler, and Kennebec Large Print titles are designed for easy reading, and all our books are made to last. Other Thorndike Press Large Print books are available at your library, through selected bookstores, or directly from us.

For information about titles, please call:
    (800) 223-1244

or visit our website at:
    gale.com/thorndike

To share your comments, please write:
    Publisher
    Thorndike Press
    10 Water St., Suite 310
    Waterville, ME 04901